GOD OF TOIL

By Alex McKinnon

GOD OF TOIL

Copyright © 2021 by Alex McKinnon
Cover Illustrations by Sebastian Kesiak
Graphic Design by Christina Whitfield

First Edition

All rights reserved.

This is a work of fiction. All characters, locations, and incidents are products of the author's imagination. Any similarity to actual persons, places, events, or organizations, historical or current, was purely coincidental.

For Christina, my jetpack.

CONTENTS

Chapter 1: Dark Days — 1
Chapter 2: The Debt — 11
Chapter 3: The Ballad of Old Fat — 27
Chapter 4: The Bed of Beds — 49
Chapter 5: Father's Daughters — 55
Chapter 6: Penance — 61
Chapter 7: Crag's Error — 69
Chapter 8: Fon The Pony — 77
Chapter 9: The Great Healer — 87
Chapter 10: Bad Men Never Look So Tired — 91
Chapter 11: The First Reckoning — 96
Chapter 12: Reznick's Triumph — 115
Chapter 13: The Artist — 126
Chapter 14: The Unwelcome Child — 132
Chapter 15: Funerals — 143
Chapter 16: The Lost Princess — 149
Chapter 17: The Path of Least Evil — 163
Chapter 18: What No One Sees — 168
Chapter 19: The Second Reckoning — 174
Chapter 20: Going Away — 185

Chapter 21: Hospice	193
Chapter 22: For Nothing	208
Chapter 23: Rabbits	213
Chapter 24: The Pit	228
Chapter 25: The Long Rest	235
Chapter 26: Yours	251
Chapter 27: The Days of Dancing	257
Chapter 28: Defeat	265
Chapter 29: Mendala	276
Chapter 30: The Far-Reaching Heart	281
Epilogue	296

CHAPTER 1: DARK DAYS

Small

Everyone knows the story. Some version of it, anyway. It starts with whispers, disputed details no one dares assert too plainly. Some say he was born of royal blood, that he was sent away for fear his ferociousness would impede a harmonious succession. Some say he rose from the earth, or spewed out from the sea, or fell from the stars, some new or ancient ascendant thing that came to blaze a trail we'd been too feeble to see. No one really knows what made him. No one really doubts what he is.

Rufus. I saw him only once: the night of the First Reckoning. I was only a child, but the call travelled far and wide, and every brother and sister who could make the trek was invited. He was legend already but still somehow becoming something even grander. I watched him all night, mesmerized by his impeccable stillness. He was impossible to miss, yet no one dared approach him. As we revelled in a victory we thought would never come, he sat immovable in the dirt by a fire so immense it was seen for miles. No matter how loud we sang or how much drink we spilled, his eyes never left the crackling flames.

I was taken aback by how unfinished he seemed. He was so unrefined. In the hands of a careful sculptor, he'd be smoother, cleaner. There was no beauty or grace in him. He was a triumph of function, blunt and impassive, carved from something harder than rock, conceived and forged by some cruel master to beat and bludgeon. With his mighty spear Penance, so long and heavy only he could wield it, he humiliated any weapon and exhausted every defence.

His rage was famous. It burned hot and steady, a hearth to which we all gathered. Even sitting there in silence, you could feel the simmer of it. Our masters would always say anger was a beast of burden: sturdy and capable but useless without discipline. He had the beast by the reins. He controlled every speck of his being, maybe of all creation. Nothing would keep him from what he wanted, and nothing happened unless he allowed it.

The night wore on. We stamped our feet and sang our songs. I took in all I could of him, expecting to find precious wisdom in even his smallest gestures. I saw so much I'd never imagined. Sadness. Loneliness. He was weary in some way I knew I was too young to understand. Even on that transcendent night, at the most dizzying heights our movement had yet known, peace eluded him. At first, the thought terrified me. How could even this not be enough? Tonight was a beacon we'd chase the rest of our lives. Yet somehow, that perfect light that beckoned us all disappeared in the vast black pit of his heart.

I learned something about greatness that night. It is the highest sacrifice. It is the death of complacency and satisfaction. It is relentless pursuit. It is pain. Greatness is toil and toil greatness. And for now and always, Rufus is its god. The God of Toil.

❊ ❊ ❊

I think of that night often. My master treats me like I'm so young and know so little, but I've lived generations in my limited years. I've seen rises and falls. I was there the day the wild dream of all Nameless came true, and that peak informs these sombre lows we reside in now. My life has been short, but I have the experience of women twice my age.

Since the written word, or at least since the written word the powerful saw fit to keep, the Royal Family has ruled. Just as long, the Nameless have fought. It's the same war that's always been fought, that will always be fought: the eternal conflict between those who have and those who have not. The faces and words change, but the sides remain the same.

The Royal Family has plenty. Gods made flesh, they've ruled man and woman with unassailable might. They think the whole human race crude and low. We are their slaves. Their tools. Our place in this world is at their service. To fill their coffers. To mine their mountains. To build their glimmering temples, sprawling palaces, and the lie.

The lie. The perfect lie. They are high, and we are low. They are divine, and we must submit to their careful moulding. They are unknowable and ineffable, absolute and immaculate. So much as they try, they can't make the untrue true. No matter how much finery they drape themselves in, no matter how furtively they hide behind their masks and robes, we know the truth beyond a doubt. So long as a single one of us draws breath, the word will spread: they bleed. They die. Rufus proved it.

And so, we rebel, we defy. The Nameless reject everything the Royal Family represents. We deny ourselves every comfort, every selfish pretense. Because they clutch greedily at their wealth, we keep nothing we can't carry with us. Because they cloak themselves in beauty and lustre, we shave our heads and wear only black rags. Because they honour names and titles and shared blood, we throw that all away. No family names. No marriages. No heirs. Nothing to distract us from our obligation to one another. They indulge, and we endure. They soften, and we harden. We are the orphans. The mongrels. The forgotten, the unloved, the unmourned. The unwashed, the unwavering, the unyielding. The brutal, the filthy, the ugly. The onerous, the odorous, the anonymous. The Nameless.

It's hard to believe the Nameless grew and spread in the ages before Rufus the way it only lingers and withers in the years since. Maybe that's how all things are. Maybe the Nameless was a flower, and Rufus its bloom, glorious but fleeting.

I catch myself and beat back the thought. Dark days make

the good days shine brighter. Master Terra tells me memory always makes the past rosier and more hopeful than the present. Maybe that's true. All I know is I had a hundred brothers and sisters dancing with me when Rufus killed Prince Darnett. Now I have none. Rufus went away, and the others followed.

Master Terra warns me about dwelling on those sparkling nights. She fears deepening the sorrow of these desolate times by contrast. When I ask her for stories of Rufus as a child, she shakes her head. She hoards his memory, I suppose for fear of the grief it might bring her if she dared share it. I'm told she raised him. I'm told the arm she's missing from the shoulder down was lost fighting for him at First Morning. She is my master, and I wish her no ill. But I hate her for her silence. I want to scold her selfishness. No one, save Rufus himself, knew the path he walked as well as she did. I could walk that path too if she let me.

Maybe there's too much danger in it. Maybe the fires that forged Rufus would burn lesser folk. We are precious few. She has an instinct to protect me, and I understand. I haven't seen a brother or sister in months. For all I know, Master Terra and I might be the last free Nameless. For the time being, anyway.

I have no idea how many of us may be in this heinous prison they call Hospice, Home for the Incurables. The kingdom saves this place for those who affront it most: the rebels, the heathens, the heretics. It is said Hospice is the last cage its inhabitants will ever see, and that's been true so far. It juts out of the earth like a gravestone in the night, a monument to the countless defeated.

Master Terra and I sit patiently in a tree just outside, watching the guards march their circuitous patterns on the high walls. They're easy to track; their golden helmets and ghoulish masks glisten in the moonlight. To serve the kingdom is to make a garish marvel of oneself. Master Terra and I all but disappear into the night in our shrouds.

We wait for a familiar guard to pass by a torch. We know once he does, we'll have a minute to leap from the tree and scale the wall. At the very second we expect him to, he strolls by, the butt of his spear clinking the stone beneath his feet with monotonous rhythm. We slip by behind him, the wind in our wake so slight he might mistake it for a welcome breeze.

We make the long drop down inside the wall, rolling across packed dirt as we land. We quickly scurry beneath a hut for cover and listen for any hints of detection. The night is still. I feel on the precipice of something momentous. There's no telling how many storied Nameless we may rescue tonight. Maybe Swift, whose claws made ribbons of a hundred soldiers. Maybe Cloudparter, whose teachings that shaped warriors for generations.

In the Nameless, only the exceptional win a moniker worthy of any pride. Rufus collected them tirelessly. Zero, the Balance, and God Killer, of course. Only a precious few win the right to choose their own, my master among them. I wonder if they'll let me after tonight. The young learn the way with humility imposed upon us at every turn. I've been Small all my life. I'm eager to be more.

Master Terra stirs me from my idle dreaming with a stern shake of my shoulder. It's time. We have another wall to scale, which should bring us to the courtyard and a step closer to our objective.

We pull ourselves up onto the delicate thatched roof of a hut, and I make myself a ladder for Master Terra to climb at the inner wall. She pauses, her feet digging into my shoulders. I worry for a second she's too old to make the remaining distance to the edge of the wall. I rely on her so much, but I've seldom seen her skills put to real use. What if she's been teaching so long she can no longer do?

Even short an arm, she leaps and pulls herself up without trouble. I am reassured. I raise my hand for her, but something inside the courtyard steals her attention. I wave my fingers, but I'm the furthest thing from her mind.

"Master Terra!" I exclaim.

She looks down on me, frightened, hesitant. What has she

seen?

Reluctantly, she reaches down for me. I walk up the wall with my feet, but she lifts me so easily I hardly need to.

"Calm," she warns me as I reach the top.

I peer down into the courtyard. A legion of Allegia sit, their knees in the dirt, their moulded armour and dragon sigils polished to shimmering perfection. They are a new and fearsome branch of the kingdom's forces. Their emergence has all but wiped out the Nameless. Notorious for both their brutality and zealotry, they fear no injury or death. They fight in perfect concert. We know nothing of their training, background, or upbringing. None have been taken, alive or dead. Only once have I seen one killed. He fought until the last drop of blood left his body. He never made a sound.

They haven't seen us. They are engrossed, transfixed on something at the other end of the yard. I stifle a gasp when I see Princess Reznick emerge atop a stage. The short upturned horns and furious scowl of her golden mask are distinct, but it's the ugly hunch of her posture and the long overhang of her sleeves that make me certain it's her. She strides from one end of her platform to the other, searching the covered faces of the Allegia as if some hint of insolence might slip out from beneath their helmets. With a demeanor between disappointed and appeased, she nods her head to a curtain at the top of the stage.

Out from behind it arrives Prince Mathius himself, a picture of authority. He stands straight and tall, his arms folded neatly behind his back. His whole body is elegant curves, from the strong arch of his back to the subtle rounding of the long, antelope-like horns at the top of his crown, the grandest horns since his father's. His mask's expression is distant and beatific, and for good cause. He is the light of his generation, first in line for the throne, and as beloved as his father is feared. When his siblings Darnett and Ciendy fell, when the Royal Family seemed at its weakest, he made his brother's daughter Reznick his ward and took all the kingdom in his hands. Our utter extermination was his gift to his people, his proof of sublimity.

"It's him," I whisper, awestruck. "Here. Now."

"We have to leave," Master Terra hushes, colour draining from her face.

I linger at the top of the wall while Master Terra retreats the way we came. How can she say that? How can she deny this opportunity? They haven't seen us. They've no chance of defending themselves. One arrow…

"Small!" she calls, quietly but firmly. "Let's go!"

I draw my bow.

"Don't you dare!"

A gaggle of monikers speed through my mind. Liberator? Freeing the Nameless would be the least of my achievements. Peacemaker? Not befitting my stature. Resurrector? After all, I'd be bringing back our movement from the dead, wouldn't I?

I nock an arrow.

"Small!"

From all the way across the courtyard, Prince Mathius fixes the black pits of his eyes on me. A righteous, resolute composure descends upon me. I let loose my arrow, confident it's the truest shot I've ever launched.

It cuts through the air with a whistle and crosses the yard in a blink. It stops short maybe an inch from Mathius's face as though seized by some invisible force. Mathius raises his chin at me, the arrow suspended in the air. With the mildest tilt of his head, the arrow shatters into a million splinters.

The Allegia all rise up and draw their weapons, a cacophony of stomping boots and unsheathing swords. Reznick sets her sights on me and sprints through the mass of limbs and armour like some predatory cat. I drop off the wall and back to Master Terra, and we run like our lives and all lives to come depend on it. They very well may.

Reznick lands on the inner wall with a single soaring vault as the Allegia fumble with a gate. She leaps through the air and reaches the outer wall faster than we possibly could, cutting us off. From beneath her sleeves tumble out long, gnarly tendrils of flesh and tendon, spiked with jagged bone. If there was ever a doubt this was Princess Reznick, it's eradicated now.

She swings one of those abominations, and it whizzes by my face as I step back. I draw my short sword and parry a few more swipes, bone clattering fearlessly across my steel. Master Terra comes to my aid with a sword of her own. We can do little but defend ourselves, the tendrils keeping us out of range. Reznick is too much for the two of us. I lose pace and feel a whip-like snap on my arm. A blaze of white heat surges from the tips of my fingers to my elbow.

I tumble to the ground and hold my arm close against myself, knowing it's broken and useless. In the distance, I hear the heavy shifting of a gate. Soon, the Allegia will be upon us. I make a solemn pact with myself: I won't be taken alive. The question now becomes what can I accomplish in death.

Reznick swings back a tendril for a killing blow, and I brace myself. It never comes. I open my eyes and find the tendril tangled like twisted rope around Master Terra's sword.

"Run!" Master Terra screams at me.

Reznick wrestles the sword free from Master Terra's grip and hurls it aside. Master Terra tosses me her satchel.

"They must not take it!" she exclaims.

I eye the satchel and ponder what could be so important.

"Go!"

I want to stay, but I know that's only arrogance on my part. I obey my master's command, grab the bag with my able hand, and make for the outer wall as fast as my legs will carry me.

Something unseen hurls my master across the yard into the waiting arms of the Allegia. They dutifully pin her face down into the dirt.

"Rufus lives!" she hollers as they bond and gag her. Prince Mathius arrives leisurely, and I can see my master's proclamation intrigues him. Reznick has no patience for it. She merely casts a bitter glance towards her uncle before chasing after me.

With a few careful leaps, I climb up a table to the roof of a hut and then to the outer wall. I strain frantically with my good arm. I can practically feel Reznick's putrid breath on my back. When I make it to my perch, I ready a dagger and hide it against my stomach. I look over my shoulder and see Reznick coming for me. Good. I'm ready.

With another towering bound, she clears the height of the wall. Just as her descent brings her within reach of my swinging blade, the same invisible force that seized my master snatches Reznick out of the air and pulls her screeching back to her uncle's side. She hurls down her arms in a huff and casts a hateful glare his way. He is not shaken.

A party of Allegia set after me, so I leap into the inky darkness of the trees. They'll never get me now. The shadowy places belong to the Nameless for at least one more night.

※ ※ ※

I couldn't have known. I couldn't. No one ever knows what to believe about a god until they see it with their own eyes. You can't trust anything else. The stories about Prince Mathius were ridiculous. Invisible hands with unlimited reach. Command over all things, alive or dead. They call it Divine Will. How could it be so? Loyals exaggerate, and Nameless haven't lived to tell the tale. The shot was excellent and rare. I had to take it. Had to.

This is what I tell myself, sitting alone in a tree someplace far from everywhere. I haven't heard a pair of feet or an inquisitive voice in hours. Somehow, I'm still out of breath. I want to weep. I want to fall from this branch and wallow in the mud until some good soldier comes and slaughters me for town and country. Why shouldn't I? Who would judge or reprimand me? Who's left?

I have to occupy myself. I have to find a way forward. My arm throbs with pain. There. First thing. I need something for it, some rag or cloth for a sling until I can find a sympathetic healer. Ha. Who would dare help me now? Don't do that. One thing at a time.

I reach into Master Terra's satchel. She always packed better than I did. Whatever we needed, she always seemed to have. There. The rope will do. I loop it around my neck and under my wrist, my teeth gnashing at my lip. I am well acquainted with the agony igniting my nerves, as are all Nameless. I don't let it panic me. I grit my teeth and tighten the rope until my arm is pressed against me. It's over. I exhale sweet relief. What next?

I rummage through the satchel. There has to be something else. Among the small arms and bits of food, there must be some contingency, something clever and dangerous reserved for the end times. I find a little scroll, frayed at the edges and bound tight with a bit of string. I unfurl it.

In case of emergency, it says. Then something about…

Rufus. It says I can find him in Paralee.

CHAPTER 2: THE DEBT

Small

Towns like Paralee raise bile in me whenever I visit them. They seem so untouched by what consumes me completely. I resent their detachment. In every civilian, a warrior lies dormant. Denying your fellow means empowering your enemy. Master Terra always found traits to admire. She would say there are flickers of peace and prosperity in places like Paralee, seeds for the harvest to which the Nameless aspire. I never could see what she saw.

I don't know what I'm looking for among the shacks of this market. I take measure of the square from an alleyway and wear my hood high over my head. The Nameless don't have many friends. Markets aren't the place for us. Legitimate people see us as threats to their security, and we don't pay well enough for brigands to entertain. Hardly anyone's left after that.

I'm hunting for someone with something very precious. I don't know if that means looking for the richest person I can find or the most unseemly. Nothing in the world matters like Rufus. His head would fetch a bounty to build a palace, and his fists would bring a revolution to topple one. Master Terra guarded even this puny morsel of information carefully. She'd only have trusted the most commendable with anything of substance. Maybe I should seek out some charity, shelter, or…

There he is. Rufus himself.

He's smaller than I thought he'd be. I suppose I'd feel so even if he were ten feet tall or a thousand. He's there somewhere beneath his beard, robes, and long hair, I'm sure. Every bit of him is an inch slighter and less defined than it ought to be. He has softened his edges, and he moves without sharpness or suddenness. Watching him, he's almost blurry, like some far off image of himself. I suppose that's what he has to be. How else could he hide but to unbecome himself?

I hear him chatter with a shop keeper:

"Whatever happened to first pick, Derry?" Rufus sighs with feigned outrage, picking through some fruit, occasionally honouring a just-right piece with a place in his sack.

"First pick of crap is still crap," the little old man named Derry fires back without a hint of apology or deference. If he only knew.

"You said it," Rufus grunts affably, shaking his head.

Down the way, I hear heavy boots. It only takes me a moment to spot their owners, stomping and strutting about. There are three of them, young and burly by the standards of small towns. They wear their rags with blusterous pride, blind to their meagreness. They sport bleary Royal Sigils on each stretch of fabric large enough to display it. Their leader searches the market for some obscure misdeed with the one good eye not obstructed by his homemade wooden mask. He leers so hungrily I can see the yellowed whites around his pupils from here.

Something about Rufus provokes the leader. Probably his size. Despite the muscle he has layered atop his frame, the leader is still a small man, and no one hates anything as much as small men hate their smallness. That scorn is often redirected every which way, mostly towards women or other things meek enough to be bullied, but men with gentleness to match girth are not immune.

The three men come upon Rufus, make a deliberate and unsophisticated spectacle of ignoring him. Rufus seems content to let them, drawing into himself, keeping his head down. The men shovel through the shop keeper's fruit, indifferently scattering whatever they reject into the mud.

"What's wrong with this market?" bellows the leader,

tossing a tomato over his shoulder. "Don't you people know how to farm?"

"Sorry, Crag…" mutters the shop keeper.

Crag. The leader is perfectly named. I'm always amazed a mother can look upon a baby and suss out its destiny in an instant.

"Don't take it personally," Rufus whispers to the shop keeper. "It's a tough season."

Rufus glances at the crude tattoo etched on Crag's arm: the Royal Dragon. Or at least some layman's attempt at it. It coils its body and it bares its teeth, but it inspires none of the terror it ought to.

Rufus's little look costs him his neutrality, and the leader turns to him as he'd always hoped to.

"Like what you see?" asks Crag, raising his chin and pushing back his shoulders. Rufus does nothing to match the sudden growth spurt of the three men across from him, eyes set on his busy task of sorting fruit.

"Sorry," Rufus answers. "It's a nice tattoo. Really close."

"What did you say?"

Crag smashes a tomato to a pulp with a hammer of his fist.

"Is that necessary?" Rufus groans. "What did the tomato do? That was a good one. You think Derry has good ones to spare?"

"Maybe he should farm better." Crag shrugs, folding his arms.

"He farms fine. I picked him clean."

"That so? This yours?"

Crag gestures at Rufus's sack, and I shiver with anticipation. The kingdom is riddled with pretenders like these: men too weak to serve and too proud to work. They warp their stasis into delusions of heroism. They claim ownership of whatever little corner they were born into, rule little fiefdoms of their own making, and claim bottomless love of community keeps them from some loftier calling. They find nobility in their supposed suffering and use the dream of their denied promise to excuse their petty thefts and abuse. Men so robbed can not be robbers. They are owed too much. These least favourite men of mine have forced a hand, and what comes upon them now will be as frightening and wondrous as a cyclone.

Rufus only frowns a little and hands over his sack. Crag and his lackeys snicker and stare into Rufus as he sets back to curating a new haul from the paltry remains. The brutes lose interest. They continue along to scorch their path of misery and hassle some other greybeard.

At first, I'm alarmed and perplexed. Am I mistaken? Is this not Rufus, the Balance? Have I come all this way for nothing? Is he wounded? Crippled? I didn't see anything but weariness straining his gait.

After a breath, I can begin to make sense of it. There is nothing so disappointing as justice denied. In my disappointment, I lost sight of the higher purpose: anonymity. A great man in hiding must first hide his greatness. For Rufus to settle every score or strike down every insult would cost him the invisibility his exile requires. What better cloak could there be but mediocrity and cowardice?

Yes. That must be it. I'm sure of it.

* * *

Rufus hikes a lonely wooded trail, still stewing. I don't blame him. Who knows better than I the torment of a stayed hand. Because I didn't exercise restraint, my master is captured. Because Rufus did, he's walking home unharmed. Save for a little consternation, I suppose.

I follow him from behind the trees, waiting for my moment. We've been alone some time now. He hasn't spotted me yet. I'll admit that pleases me. Stealth or alertness were never principal portions of his reputation, but I'm sure he's thwarted many ambushes and run down his share of notable assassins. I feel a twinge of girlish pride to count myself their better, but I suppress it.

The rustle of some little creature draws his gaze away from me. I pounce. I get out in front of him, far enough to keep him from swatting at me in surprise. I kneel quickly and bow my head low, hoping I've impressed him.

"Master Rufus," I say, maybe a little too loud in my excitement. "I am Small of the Nameless. I beg your service."

I sneak a look at him through the tops of my eyes. I tuck my chin, trying not to diminish my respectful stance too much. All I can see is a deep, impatient frown on the bottom half of his face. He IS tall.

"You are very confused," he says, striding right past me.

I scramble back to my feet before he gets too far. I hurry to walk alongside him, careful not to crowd him.

"I'd know you anywhere," I tell him. "I saw you on the night of the First Reckoning. I'll never forget it. No Nameless would. The situation is dire."

"It usually is," he sighs. "I'm not interested in taking on any students. I'm no master. Find someone else."

"There is no one else! " I plead. In my urgency, I reach out at him with my able hand and grab his shoulder. He stops in his tracks. I chide myself. I can hardly afford to have both my arms broken.

I cringe in anticipation of a punitive strike. When I open my eyes, I find him paying no mind to the transgressing hand. Instead, he contemplates my injured arm with grudging pity.

"We have to get that looked at."

He nods his head down the path, and I follow him in rapt silence. If Rufus ever took a pupil, word never reached the Nameless. Here I am at his side, a world of possibility ahead of me. I try to calm myself. I know I want too much from this moment. I want to gorge on his knowledge, his stories. Countless questions race through my mind, but I dare not say a word. I know it's not my place. With patience, the answers will come. Still...

"Did you really eat fire to prepare for Darnett?" I blurt out, too fast and too keen.

"Sometimes," he admits unhappily.

"Could you really sleep with it burning all around you?"

"No."

"How did the gods look when you took their masks?"

"Scared."

"Did they have scales and red eyes and forked tongues as Clear Eyes says? Or were they radiant light like the Testaments claim?"

"Neither."

He's in no mood to talk. I still have trust to win.

Before long, we come upon a little cottage, a modest but cozy place. He opens the gate of the surrounding fence, and the sickly sweetness turns my stomach. There's a flower garden too well tended. High on a pole is a birdhouse so elegant and meticulously detailed it must have wasted many precious hours of some silly man's life.

We've trespassed all of a couple of steps when a big, slobbery dog sprints off from the porch with defensive, possessive fury.

"Don't mind him," Rufus tells me, stepping in front of me.

The dog leaps at him, folds of flesh flapping about its whipping, snarling jaws. Rufus fends the beast off patiently with one arm. With the other, he pulls some dry meat from his sack. It does little to dissuade the dog's hateful gnashing and snapping. I follow Rufus as he delicately maneuvers towards the cottage. Just as we reach the door, he shoves the dog firmly aside and tosses the meat into the grass.

The dog makes one last futile surge at us as we slam the door in its face. It barks twice more in frustration then finally turns its attention to the discarded meat out in the garden.

"That's Bandit," Rufus explains, exasperated yet affectionate. "Wife loves animals."

Wife. The word opens a pit in my chest. Maybe she's an ally in need of a false identity. Maybe she's some illustrious warrior in wait. Maybe she's anything but what the word implies.

He hangs up his cloak. He leads me through his little

house, and I know immediately it's a woman's place. There's none of him here, no thought to his dimensions or needs. The hallways and corners are overstuffed, some trinket or precious thing crowding his every turn. He moves with the practiced inoffensiveness of a servant, oh so mindful not to disturb anything.

"You must be hungry," he says jovially, directing me to his kitchen like it's where he belongs. It's workman-like. Whoever his wife is, she must not spend much time here. "You have time to find a tea you like in the Nameless? Probably nothing sweet…"

I sit down at a table, and he stokes a little fire before hanging a kettle right next to a cauldron. He assembles a plate for me, carefully picking through the best of his stock.

"What's she like?" I ask him. "Your *wife*?"

The word falls like sludge from my lips. He frowns, sensing my skepticism. He knows I want convincing. He knows I want the inexcusable excused.

"Brilliant," he says. "Elizabeth is her name. She's a healer. She'll be looking at that wound of yours."

"What do you do here?" I ask.

"Help her, mostly," he says. "Two hands usually aren't enough."

"Are you good at it?"

"Not even a little," he replies.

"Children?"

"No. We've tried, but… no."

He shrinks a little at that last question. The one vow he didn't break, and he regrets it. He sets the plate in front of me with silent supplication, humble as a peasant.

"All this time… I thought you were waiting. Getting ready."

"For what?"

"I don't know. For this. For now."

He turns away from me, shuffles back to his familiar, hollow work of poking at the fire.

"How did you find me?" he finally asks.

"Master Terra," I tell him. "She kept it secret. Right up until they took her."

I see her name bring him to some sad, knowing place. He sensed it was coming. He feels the guilt he ought to, the guilt I want him to.

"You left us," I hush. "Abandoned us? For what?"

He looks at me with such condescension, a knowing parent enduring the blubbering of a child with a broken toy. I could scream at him. I could tear him to pieces. I know I could. I see what's in front of me now. I see I owe this stranger nothing.

"You're an errand boy," I tell him, hoping to get a rise from him. "A handmaiden."

"I do a lot of heavy lifting. Mule's more apt," he jests humorlessly, warning me.

"You were the best of us," I remind him, cutting to the core of his evil. "Better than any of us could ever be.

He shakes his head. I can tell I've hit upon something, some conversation he's turned over in his mind a hundred times.

"I'm not caught up on my lessons, but I believe that's heresy you're spouting," he mutters, turning back to his kitchen counter. "Always the same. Always making up stories to excuse the quit in you. Couldn't just be sweat, blood, could it? Couldn't just be I pushed through when you wore down? And for what? Picking off the stragglers at the back of the pack. Never could have touched the King. Or Mathius. Kids. Rich, spoiled kids. That's what I killed. You'd be proud of that?"

It's a well-honed argument, the self-serving bargaining of a criminal at trial. People will forgive themselves anything.

"You could have done more," I assert. There's no way around this, no matter how much attention he sets to the plate he's preparing. "You didn't. We couldn't. There was no else, and now there's no one left."

That reaches him. I suppose he never expected to outlast us. Those who shirk responsibility always assume there will be someone to pick up the burden. A mother abandoning their baby seldom believes it murder.

"If it makes you feel any better tossing blame around, by all means," he says, quickly raising an apathetic shield again. "You're not getting anything else out of this."

I shoot to my feet, enter his radius. He only exhales curtly, tearing up some bread.

"You'll let the lives of untold fallen mean nothing?" I ask.

"They mean nothing whatever I do."

"The fight is important," I insist. "There are battles to be won. I still believe. Tell me you don't."

"I don't." He looks me square in the eye, defiant. He sets his sights back on his plate. It's coming together. Some tender, torn meat and the best parts of some fruit. I slap it off the counter. It clatters across the floor, leaving juicy debris in puddles and piles.

He looks at me, annoyed. He adjusts just a little to remind me of his size. I'm not impressed.

"The great Rufus," I mutter. "What could turn him into this?"

"What's that?" he asks, stooping his ear towards me, daring me.

"A coward. You sought comfort. Probably in the first harlot's arms who—"

Suddenly, I feel his grip on me. He sits me back down in my chair, smothering my petulance. I swat at the hand gripping my shoulder. Neither of us is budging.

"You have no idea," he says through clenched teeth. "None."

He releases me to my sulking and storms off. In his huff, he tramples the plate I upturned. It finally shatters. He silently admonishes himself for his carelessness and begins cleaning up.

I think about the knife in my belt. I wonder how quickly I could cross the room, whether he'd have time to even raise his head. Could I strike true? How many chances would I get?

I catch myself. I observe the regret and delicacy with which he picks at his mess. He mourns this little slip like a significant, meaningful tragedy. At this moment, he is pathetic. At this moment, my anger fades to numbness.

"There was a time all I wanted was to be you," I tell him, flat and without hesitation.

He stops, takes in the irreparability of the demolished plate. He starts like he has some precious heirloom for me:

"You're in a pit," he offers. "And everything you do digs it deeper. Then someone comes along. Pulls you out."

He gathers as much of the mess as he can in his fingers, tosses it in a bin. He wipes his hands on his thighs.

"I'm not who you think I am," he continues. "Not if I can help it. Fight's over. Was before it started. Let it go. There's peace in this life. You can have it if you want it. Find something. Someone. We've lost enough."

"The Nameless aren't being killed."

He doesn't understand.

"They're being taken," I expand. "We've lost every camp, every master, every student. They take us and bleed us for all we're worth. Everything we know worth knowing, they get. I don't know how. It must be something worse than torture."

I see the questions racing through his head. He searches my face for answers I don't have. I wonder how much Master Terra knew.

"Terra would die before she gave me up," he grunts, assuring himself.

"Is that what you want?" I ask, reaching into my boot for my map. I unfurl it on the table. He inspects it closely enough that I suspect I may have him.

"We gambled everything on this," I say. "They're at Hospice. We found them. Maybe all of them. Death is a gift they've been denied. Your brothers and sisters can be saved. You think there's peace in this life? Give them a chance at it."

He considers all the details of the map and all the possible paths ahead of him. He is trapped on all sides. He frowns and pulls away. He looks out his window.

"Wife's coming," he tells me, sluggish with resignation. "Give me the night."

I oblige, disappearing out of the kitchen. I know I should

make myself scarce. Yet I don't go too far. Curiosity gets the better of me. I press myself against a wall. I watch from around a corner. I want to see her, this Elizabeth. I want to see what's kept him.

There's no power or warrior in the woman I see come through the door, but I suppose men like that often enough. She carries two dead rabbits I imagine are for dinner. I'm thankful she's not too prissy. She's an earthly woman with no pretensions of elegance or glamour. She doesn't achieve much of anything with her figure, but it's hard to tell beneath her draping, mud-strewn clothing. More than anything, I'm struck by her plainness. She has too little of anything to flaunt. Her manner is drowsy, meandering. In a crowd, she'd disappear. Yet standing there, for all the nothing she is, she's everything to him.

She tracks dirt into his kitchen, oblivious to the little mess we left on the floor. He hands her a pretty plate of food. She accepts it gratefully then notices something behind his tired smile.

"Everything all right?" she asks, only half-interested.

"I missed you," he tells her, massaging the back of her neck and kissing her forehead.

"D'Aww," she grins, mocking him.

Rufus

I don't think about my father much. I used to. He haunted all my dreams when I was young. He loomed so large. I suppose most children worship their fathers. Any aptitude at all is a wondrous thing to the small, naive, and incapable.

I was five years old when the Royal Family took him. My memories of him are as vague as they are warm. Geniality, patience, love. Safety in his presence, joy with his playfulness. It's all hazy. I don't even know his name. All I can be sure of is how I felt when they ripped me from his arms. I remember the fear coursing through me, the sadness in his smile, how his clothes hurt my fingers when I grasped at them.

"You'll understand later," he promised. "This is a good

thing. A virtuous thing. You'll be proud."

I never saw him again. The moment came to me again and again, every night of my life before Elizabeth. It never dulled. It always ached and gnawed. I must have loved him. He must have been something. Truly.

He was a healer. That much I'm sure of. He had to be a good one, or the Royal Family would never have come for him. I don't know if he was as good as Elizabeth, but I doubt it. I'm confident he'd have liked her. He was so worried behind that last look he gave me. He'd be happy I'm cared for. He'd be happy I found her.

I don't think about him anymore. Not even in dreams. Not for a long time. Before tonight, anyway.

Where am I? I'm outside. In the yard. The moon is high. It's cool out, yet I'm sweating. How did I get here?

"Love?"

I hear Elizabeth's voice. I turn and find her clutching a blanket to herself in the cold. She affords me plenty of space, her face soft with kindness and concern.

"Was I...?"

"Yes," she tells me. "It was a bad one. What was it this time?"

"My father."

She inhales through her nose, considering.

"Haven't heard from him for a while," she remarks without judgment or worry.

I have fits. I've learned how to avoid them. For the most part. They come from restlessness and worry, from sorrow and apprehension. A troubled mind in the day will follow you into the night. Happiness is the answer. It always is. I'd been doing well until this Small came along...

Elizabeth reaches out her hand to me. "Back to bed," she says.

I shuffle back to her. She tries to cure me of my embarrassment on our way to the porch. She cycles through her tried and true methods. She presses her body against my arm, taps her fingers impishly against my palm. It helps. It always does. She plays me so easily.

She opens the front door. At first, I wonder how it is I missed the storm that tore our home to pieces. Liz's affectionate pat on my sore red knuckles clarifies the matter quickly.

"They're only things," she tells me, steering me through the wreckage of all that's precious to us.

She takes me to our room and sits me down in our bed. She doesn't delay to circle the frame and join me. She's exceedingly accomplished at this dance. Day after day, in a hundred different ways, she bears my baggage with refinement and benevolence. I make a mess of things, and she acts like it's nothing. She protects me from myself, rescues me from my self-loathing.

"Don't worry," she offers lazily behind shut eyes. "You'll be out of hard pointy places soon enough at the rate you're fattening up."

"Love?" I probe timidly.

"What could possibly be more important than sleep right now?" she sighs, only partly joking.

A marriage is a funny thing. In a good one, partners always love each other. But some nights, you love your partner more than others. Sometimes, they're so wonderful and perfect they awaken something even deeper and purer, something too overwhelming to sustain.

Tonight, I love Elizabeth more than I ever have before. I want to tell her, but I know she'll just smile at me like she knows. How could she? That's the trouble. I tell her I love her all the time, and it's always true. I wish I knew words beautiful enough. I wish I stored them away for moments like these. I'm sure if they existed, I'd wear them out like the others.

She shimmies a little. She's given up waiting for me to speak. It occurs to me I've been wrong before about how much I can love her. I've been sure I'd peaked. I was stupid. So, as impossible as it seems, maybe the day will come I love her even more than I do now. What a thought.

I feel her sliding into the beginnings of a happy, peaceful slumber. I've wasted all my time. I have so much to say. I need her to know how grateful I am. What's about to happen... I need her to know it isn't because she wasn't enough. I'm so ashamed. Every day. Sometimes it's hard to even face her.

Elizabeth. You've already forgiven me so much. But I can't just live my life letting you make up for me. I have to do something good. I have to go. If I didn't, I wouldn't. I'll come back. If it's even possible. If you'll even have me.

Small

That wife of his snores very loudly.

Things seem to have calmed down. I was camped out in a tree when it all started. Without knowing, Rufus tore his own house to pieces. I've seen it before in the more seasoned, combat-tested Nameless: men and women losing themselves somewhere in their past and reliving some profound, inescapable horror. I used to think it weakness. So much of perseverance is the graceful endurance of pain. Maybe I overestimated how much I'd endured. Now, I wonder how long until Master Terra's face visits me at night.

Rufus emerges from his home, again himself. Or at least the version of him I've come to know. He's dressed for a long journey and carries a large sack, embroidered with little flowers, dangling by a loose strap over his shoulder. It's not as functional as I'd like, but I suppose it'll do.

He pauses when he comes to his birdhouse in the middle of the yard. Gently, he lifts it off its pole and sets it a couple of paces away. He grabs the pole in both hands, and I'm a little surprised by how much it resists him as he pulls it up like some deep-seated weed. The earth falls away from its base in huge, dense clods, revealing some sort of leather sheath tied tightly around a bulbous bottom.

The hair stands up on the back of my neck as Rufus begins undoing the sheath. Beneath it, I see the briefest flash of what I've been waiting for. The huge stone insignia at the base of the blade is unmistakable. It's the bane of an empire, the hope of a people. Penance.

I'm desperate to hold it, to compare it against other spears, to know its weight. It doesn't look like much in his grip, and that relieves me. He's still who he is. He ties the sheath back in place and makes a walking stick of the fearsome weapon. He sets it out in front of him with every step, like he's some shepherd or holy man out for a stroll.

I descend from my tree to make myself known. He approaches his gate and regards me haggardly.

"That's it." I nod my head to his spear. "Penance."

"I always hated when people called it that," he grumbles, striding right past me.

I start behind him. I haven't taken a second step before he turns to me sternly.

"Where do you think you're going?" he asks.

"With you," I say doltishly.

"Not with that arm." He gestures at my admittedly ratty sling. "You want that thing to fall off?"

"I will not stand aside while my brothers and sisters suffer," I say, straightening, flexing, balling my fists, signalling resolve and obstinance in every way I know. I'll fight him now if he wants it. I'll prove my valour.

"I can see what's coming," he says, belittling me with his patience and docility. "Follow me, you're dead. Stay here. Get better."

He reaches out and sets his hand on my shoulder heavily enough that some primal instinct in me is alerted. Yet I look into his face, and I see a genuine attempt at consoling me. Funny. Even in love, he menaces.

"Right now, you're the last," he explains. "If I fail, it falls to you to carry on the Nameless."

There's little argument against the point, and certainly no convincing him. He pats my shoulder and continues down the path.

"Did you tell her you were going?" I wonder aloud. "Your wife?"

He takes a moment.

"No," he says frankly.

"Why not?"

"She'd have made me stay," he tells me. There's no question of it at all.

He takes a deep, steadying breath. He looks at me for what I shudder to think might be the last time.

"I hope she helps you," he says.

He sets out into the night. I watch him until he's gone.

CHAPTER 3: THE BALLAD OF OLD FAT

Gerald

When Cretia announced with certainty she was pregnant, I was guarded. It was what I wanted, of course. It's what we both strived for. Yet I'd been disappointed before. Twice now, a child I'd envisaged a whole life with died in the womb. The first time was brutal, and the second was worse. There's no pain quite so sharp as being denied once at the gates of what you most desire. But I quickly made myself unwavering in attitude and confidence. I was needed. If the fate I dreaded were to come, I'd be but a bystander compared to my dear wife. My pain, my heartache would be nothing.

I pretended to be happy, and I became happy. Things were different this time. Cretia did everything she could think of to be fit. She walked all she could, breathed deeply and purposefully, ate nothing but the cleanest, greenest things from our garden. Her stomach swelled, and she seemed livelier for it. She was effervescent, glowing from the inside out.

We reached half a year without incident. By then, she was already bigger than she'd ever been. Her energy was waning, but she would not be discouraged. She saw victory around the corner. She continued to grow, distressingly so given her frame. I was a constant comfort to her. I told her everything I could measure informed me the baby was healthy, maybe even the healthiest I'd seen. It was true. Exhausted as she was, she was pleased.

By the end, she was more belly than woman. The pregnancy dragged on much longer than I'd expected, weeks past the norm. The weight of it wore on her terribly, but by that point, nothing would spoil her good humour. She was proud. She could see her strength becoming the baby's. She would feed it with all she could, whatever it cost her.

The birth was difficult, painful. More so than any I'd been party to. She bled and strained arduously. With any other patient, I'd have been terribly troubled. With Cretia, I was petrified. I did my best not to let her see. She needed me so badly. She'd been braver than she'd ever been for the better part of a year now. It was my turn, and I was failing her.

There was nothing I could do to mitigate the hemorrhaging while preserving the baby. My warnings, my pleas fell on deaf ears. She knew the truth better than I did. I shrunk from the task. I could not risk her. If it were my choice, my child or my wife, I would have chosen Cretia. I would have surrendered everything to better protect her. She wouldn't let me. She had come so far, grown so resolute. She'd already sacrificed too much. She pressed through.

After the longest day and night I'd ever known, he came to me. Our boy. Rufus. I'd delivered so many still, frail things that when he came out pink, loud, and twice the size he ought to be, I was blind with happiness. What an ordeal it must have been to carry him. What a gift my wife had given me.

Cretia never even had a chance to hold him.

✻ ✻ ✻

Rufus does not make friends easily. Out of respect for me, some other parents coerce their children into entertaining him. Rufus is too eager to please, and even the young sense it. Every lighthearted delight in youth stems from misbehaving, and in that he is reluctant, timid. He doesn't want to hunt little animals

CHAPTER 3: THE BALLAD OF OLD FAT | 29

or throw stones at birds. He is slow, clumsy, and burdensome on adventures. He takes teasing personally and never returns a barb. He withdraws at all roughness or coarseness. He is much too large for children his age and far too innocent for children his size. They all see something untrustworthy in him. He is so unlike them. They're certain he'll betray them somehow.

He has learned to amuse himself. He babbles to no one and plays with toys, immerses himself in faraway worlds more welcoming than this one. He loves animals, but even they spurn him. Ducks quack and hiss at him when he approaches them with outstretched arms. He stares at every horse, dog, and cat that he comes upon and yearns to touch them. He wisely denies himself for fear of teeth and claws.

I think he will do well with girls when he is older. Kind ones, anyway. He has seldom had an opportunity to prove my theory. When children are very young, the battlelines dividing the sexes are rigid and contentious. Once, after much prodding from some mischievous boys, Rufus pulled on some passing young girl's braid. He never forgave himself. He cried more than she did.

He is sweet, and I love him for it. Yet I worry I've made him too gentle for the world. With his mother gone, his joy has sustained me, bestowed me with purpose. I see so much of Cretia in him. In attempting to honour her, I've chased his happiness greedily. I love his laughter too much. I see other fathers scold their crying sons or work them until they're ready to drop. I don't have the heart for it. Rufus is plump and simple, and he has none of the skills or boldness circumstances have forced upon less fortunate children. He looks to me with every obstacle he encounters. Without hesitation, I clear the way.

These are golden days. I have savvy and wisdom enough for us both. That won't always be the case. Will he ever be a man? Will he ever be the one who is looked to, the one who provides? His smile and spirit won't mean so much to others as it does to me. He isn't tenacious or clever. What will he contribute?

I stop myself. He has virtues, and though they may not be

readily apparent, they are valid. There is a place for kindness. There must be. He will be a doting father and husband to those who have no need for a lion to head the house. He will be studious and fastidious in whatever craft he chooses. He may not find adulation in it, but he will serve some master well.

Maybe he lacks a hide thick enough to bear this brutal world all on his own, but he needn't be alone. People will come to him. Maybe for pity's sake to begin with, but he will repay them with eternal devotion. His happiness will be a fountain from which countless may draw. He will be loved. He is so loved.

* * *

I have overseen many births since Rufus. At first, they filled me with dread. I saw Cretia in every woman that came to me and inevitable tragedy ahead for all involved. Yet time after time, I saw crisis averted. I presented adorable babies to grateful mothers and fathers. I stopped seeing Cretia in women's faces. I saw Rufus in their children and my absolution in their smiles.

Each delivery assured me of my abilities. I had done all I could for Cretia. I was good. I was so good, rich people began recruiting me. Each time they came, their parties were larger, they were from further away, their clothes were more colourful and intricate. I served them well, and they rewarded me. Rufus fattened. Humble people stopped visiting for fear of inconveniencing me. Of course, it was infinitely more inconvenient forcing me to seek them out.

Tonight, a small group of stature and background I do not recognize are in my house. There are three of them. They have come in the black of night. If they are rich, they are not opulent. They are not humble, either. I sit. Despite my offers, they do not. I know they believe it beneath them. They are very serious. They wear high-quality, sturdy leather and masks with angry, twisted faces. They serve the King.

"A concubine is with child," the tallest one tells me, so severely it sounds like the passing of a sentence. "You are chosen."

I look at each of them like I might read something meaningful in their masks. I perceive now how well-chosen they are for the task set before them. A trio like this isn't grand enough to draw attention wherever they may go, but they are more than enough to intimidate a man like me.

I take a deep breath, try to orient myself. Part of me marvels. Word of my skills has reached the Highest. I am recognized. In this work that means so much to me, I am now a confirmed sage. I have brushed with the divine. I will hold a god in my hands.

Yet I sense no cause for celebration. There's something unspoken in the air, something secret and grim. I look around the room and see Rufus watching us from his bedroom door. He understands as little as I do.

The three masked men do not look at him, but I've no doubt they know he's there. In their coldness, they teach me the truth. My anointing comes with a price. Mortal things do not brush so close to gods and live. No man may see the face of a god. Knowing the unknowable will cost me my life. I am leaving now, and I will never return.

"Do what you must," the tall one tells me.

Rufus understands the peril in the air. He's cleverer than I give him credit for. In his sensitivity, he is perceptive, especially for his years. I rise slowly, approach him like he's a frightened animal I must keep tame. He rushes to meet me.

"Don't go with them," he pleads, throwing his arms around my legs and nearly toppling me over.

"I have to," I tell him with my softest voice, pushing away his clutching hands.

"No!"

"You'll understand later," I say. "You'll be proud."

He grabs at me again. It's hard to break away from him. He's determined. Or I am not.

"Please!" he begs. I ache.

One of the masked men opens the front door emphatically. I've only seconds. I hold my son's face in both my hands and lower myself to him. I have so much to tell him. So much trial and tribulation to prepare him for. Yet still, after all this time, I want only to soothe him.

"This is a good thing," I promise him with all the sincerity I can muster. "A virtuous thing."

The tall masked man pulls me away. He's much stronger than Rufus. Much stronger than I am.

Rufus shrieks as the masked men carry me into the night. I look at the other houses in my little village. I know inside them are families that owe me their contentment. The masked men carry me into a carriage and lower a black bag over my head. That's the last I'll see of my boy.

One of those families in one of those houses will come for Rufus. He will have a new father. Maybe siblings. A mother. They will give him what I couldn't. They will explain this critical service I am fulfilling. With time, when his love for them obscures his love for me, he will recall my deeds with reverence and esteem. He will love me more for this. His love is everything.

Terra

I don't walk the roads. What they gain me in expedience, they cost me in stealth. I have to be sure I won't stumble upon anyone before I'll ever get close to a beaten path. Even then, I stick to the woods nearby or seek some other form of cover. But today, I'm spent, in the middle of nowhere, and have many children camped and waiting for me. Today, I walk the road.

Way up ahead of me, I spot something short and round waddling down the center of the lane. I begin towards the trees beside me but then falter, wanting a closer look at this solitary mound. Whatever it is, it doesn't hear me. Not nearly.

It's so slow. I'm on it promptly. It's a child. A boy. Young and plump. His clothes were nice once but are tattered now by mud and the elements. He's been on his pilgrimage for a long time. His short legs are weary. He still hasn't noticed me.

"What are you doing?" I ask.

His head jerks as much as he has energy for. I've startled him. He does not break his pathetic stride. Wherever he's going, it's important.

I come up beside him. He spies me out of the corner of his eye. Up close, he's younger than I thought. Much too young to be out here. For some meat eater, he's a dream of a meal: full, hefty, and unwieldy, the lost babe of some greater beast. There are predators in man and animal out here. Who knows which may find him.

He takes me in curiously. My clothes and bald head are strange to him but not alarming. It's not in him to distrust adults. The sight of me galvanizes him. He's waited a long time to finally find assistance in his quest.

"Where are your parents?" I ask more gently than I ought to.

"Men took my father," he says. If he weren't so drained, he'd have blubbered it.

"Your mother?"

"She's dead."

That's very bad news for me. This is about to become terribly inconvenient.

"Where did they take him? Your father?" I ask.

"This way."

"You sure?" I challenge him. "When was the last time you saw them?"

I can tell he doesn't have an answer for me. Or at least not one he cares to confront.

"Where are you from?" I press, changing my tact.

He clamps up, looks away from me. He won't be going back there if he can help it. I'll have to be more cunning.

"When was the last time you ate?" I ask, hinting at something with my rising voice.

He looks up at me hopefully. If I know when he ate, I'll know how long he's walked. If I know how long he's walked, I might guess where his home is.

"Three days ago," he says, scanning me up and down, dreaming at some treat I'm hiding.

Three days. My heart sinks. Maybe that's one at my speed if I could carry him the whole way. I doubt I could carry him even a mile. Three days at his speed. That's the number that matters. Maybe two days if he's fed and committed. That's assuming I can get the name of the town out of him. Or guess correctly at it. Too long. Much too long.

I hear his stomach groan. I remember he must be famished. I hand him my canteen. He accepts it but keeps his eyes on me, holding out for more.

"Water's more important than food," I explain dryly.

He mopes a little before struggling with the canteen's cork. I open it for him, and he gulps at the water recklessly, spilling it everywhere. Stupid. I snatch the canteen away from him and recork it.

"Conserve this," I say firmly. He doesn't understand. I rephrase: "Don't waste it."

I glance around us. There are a hundred things in this forest to eat if you know what to look for. I doubt he's ever seen a meal that wasn't prepared for him. Maybe I could show him a thing or two that might sustain him for the trek back, but I haven't the time.

"Go straight home," I tell him, widening my eyes and staring directly into his. "The way you came. On the road. If you need to, eat insects."

He looks at me blankly.

"Bugs. But only six legs. Can you count to six?"

He raises six chubby digits at me.

"Good. Nothing hairy, bright, or colourful," I warn, waving the point of the canteen in his face to drive my point home. "Worms and slugs will do. Don't bother with plants. They're too dangerous."

Maybe that was unnecessary. By the look of him, he'd die before eating something green. I've laid it out for him as simply as I can, I think. Worms are plentiful, and many children have practice finding them. If he made it this far, he can make it back. Or at least far enough for someone else to find him.

I grab his shoulder and forcefully reverse his course. I give him a little shove and set back on my way. I was a fool to walk the roads. Never walk the roads.

❊ ❊ ❊

He's been following me for hours, plodding along behind me. He's persistent, I'll give him that. I don't know why I don't run, or hide, or lose him in one of the hundred other ways I'm able. He'd keep looking for me, most likely. Wander and search aimlessly until something horrible happened. I'd rather he give up. I want to see him turn around and head home rather than die. Maybe that's spineless of me.

"Would you go away!" I shout as he struggles over a fallen tree, sniffling. "I told you: you can't come!"

He's holding me up. He navigates these twigs and roots like a ship too big for a channel. His chin is buried in his chest, his face caked in dirt and scratches from snapping branches.

"Too weak!" I yell. "Too old! Too fat! There! You happy? You made me say it."

I don't like being cruel, but we do what we must. He must be accustomed to unkind words. He gives no indication he hears me. He just wipes at his dripping nose and trudges on. I don't think I have it in me to hurt him any worse.

Fine. I run. He pumps his short legs in a panic, sprinting, his belly flying in every direction. I bound over obstacles effortlessly. He gives his blundering best, losing ground quickly.

"I'm sparing you, boy!" I call over my shoulder, not sure he'll hear me over his own wheezing. "This is a kindness!"

I hear him trip and fall into a puddle, and I make the mistake of looking back at the deplorable sight. He scrambles for footing, elbow deep in muck, losing a boot to mud. That compassionate place in me cloys. The fighter in me groans at my defeat.

I slow to a stop.

"Would you at least pick up the pace if you're in such a hurry to die?!" I growl.

He hastens towards me, elated. I motion behind him at his boot, and he circles back, snatching it up and scampering back to me before putting it on.

"I'm Ru—" he begins before I cut him off.

"I don't care," I tell him sharply.

He won't last. I'll take him to camp and put him with the other children. They'll eat him up. We'll leave him in the next town. He'll be grateful to be free of us.

❖ ❖ ❖

Ordinarily, we don't take children so old. The more advanced a person, the more they are themselves, with inclinations and learned behaviour that may impede their becoming who we need them to be. Habit hardens. One must be pliable and open-minded to endure the rigours of our practice. The younger the better.

This new orphan, I'm sure, will prove the rule. I see no potential. He reeks of shelter and privilege. He was loved, maybe even rich. His blood hasn't seen real ugliness for generations.

What to call him? It's a delicate process picking a moniker. We delay it as much as we can. Individuality breeds conceit and elevates the self over the many. Sometimes, if we take on the child as an infant, they'll go years without anything to set them apart. We care for and feed babies the same. Some cry and whine more than others, but it doesn't change their treatment. Mostly, they all become alike. Some pass by sickness or something else, but this is no tragedy. They wouldn't have been fit for what followed.

When the children understand well enough to follow instruction, we give them something to answer to and rage against. Even with identical circumstances and upbringings, defining particularities emerge among the young. They're weak in different ways. True strength begins at comprehending one's own weaknesses, and children must never be sheltered from their failings. If they are little, we might call them Slight. If they are fearful, we call them Coward. They will be known by their vice so long as the vice rules them. Only when they conquer it can they be known by their virtues.

Some never win the battle and are known by what ails them all their life. A select few, myself among them, climb so high no one dares demean them with designation. These elite dub themselves. When I was young, I was Dirt. Low, messy, abundant. I came to love it. Now, I am Terra. It means the same thing, but it carries none of the connotations. And it sounds like Terror.

Given his time out in the world, the new orphan's particularities abound. I see heaps of deficiencies in him, so many that it's difficult to isolate a defining one. Slow? Perhaps. Sloth, Long Breath, Weeper? All true, but they only hint at the whole. It'd be wrong to dwell on this any longer. He deserves no special consideration. Best to keep with the irrefutable and overt.

Old Fat it is.

※ ※ ※

Old Fat towers over his peers, a mountain in a valley. The children resent him immediately. They hate his protruding belly and full head of hair, taking them for the abominations they are. They sense the scandalous inequity of his girth to their lean muscle. With them watching, I right the wrong.

When the time for dinner comes, Old Fat rushes to the stew pot, his stomach grumbling. I spurn him, and he takes his proper place behind the other waiting children. I pour each child their portion as slowly as I can. When Old Fat's turn comes, the pot is all but empty, and his share is the least of all his peers. Commensurate with his rank, of course. He eats it quickly. It's the first food he's seen since he found me. When he finishes, he doesn't set down his bowl. He just holds it out in front of him, too bashful to actually ask for any more but quietly expecting his politeness might earn him something extra. He doesn't get any.

I send the rest of the class to their cots, and they nestle cozily into their meagre blankets beneath the tent. Old Fat notices the lack of a discernible spot for him and looks to me. I gesture at the stark emptiness of the clearing in which he sits. Uncertainly, he sprawls, hopeful he might please me.

"In the Nameless, you earn everything," I tell him bluntly and walk away.

He makes a pillow of the fatty folds around his elbow and watches me go.

* * *

Old Fat can't do presses to save his life. Evidently, he doesn't even know proper form. I'm not sure he knows the shortcuts he's taking, so I make him know. When he doesn't lower enough, I bury my foot into his back and make him push against it. When he leans too much into one hand, I kick it out and let his chin bang into the dirt.

All the other children reach their quota well before him. They wait for him to finish, impatient and fuming. There's nothing children hate more than waiting.

* * *

It's Old Fat's turn in the ring now. Inside this simple circle takes place our most sacred rite, the purest and most essential test of our mettle. Here, the children see the fruits of their labour. In combat, they measure themselves against each other. The toilers see their progress, and the dawdlers see their lagging. The best win a greater share of food and rest, and the worst receive a greater portion of hardship.

"Mud," I call. The other children lower their heads, trying to hide their snickering.

The pride of my class steps across from Old Fat, half his size but twice as imposing. Compact, fast, and muscular, Mud is brutality in miniature, a budding rose promising razor thorns. Old Fat looks to me, expecting instruction. Mud knows better, staring deeply into his opponent, finding a feast without end.

"Begin," I say simply.

Mud juts across the ring before Old Fat can turn back his head. Mud plunges a sharp fist into soft belly and meets Old Fat's gasping mouth with a leaping knee. Old Fat's jaw clacks as his head whips back, his teeth no doubt finding tongue.

Old Fat swats helplessly with open hands, arching his back to further lean away his frightened face and its red grit teeth. Mud charges through, downing Old Fat between a sweeping leg and thrusting palm. Old Fat's breath leaves him as he lands flat on his back with a sharp thump.

Old Fat, swaying, rises to his knees, assuming his defeat total and final. Mud measures his opening carefully, praying I don't interrupt. I indulge him.

As if an artist revealing his most accomplished work, Mud plants his front foot, spins, and hurls his heel across Old Fat's jowls. The sickening snapping and clattering finally win Old Fat a bit of sympathy from his peers. A chorus of involuntary hisses meets the bounce of his head off the packed dirt.

"Enough," I say.

Mud turns to me and bows. I'm a little bit startled when Old Fat pushes himself off the ground. He carefully mimics his batterer's bow before offering him an open, friendly hand. Mud turns away in a huff, annoyed. No doubt he's frustrated his best strikes didn't attain their purpose. He must have been hoping for a knockout. He shouldn't fret. He'll get ample opportunity to test his progress so long as Old Fat's around.

❦ ❦ ❦

Old Fat's watching, fidgeting woefully with his plump fingers. His hair is crusty, matted, and beginning to twist all on its own into filthy little braids. He still wears the same clothes I found him in. He's barely had water enough to drink, let alone clean.

I've set all his peers in a line across from him. I don't look at him for a second. One by one, I give them what I deny him. Smoothly, simply, I shave their heads, gliding a wet blade easily over the supple skin of their knobby skulls. I make sure there's tenderness in every touch, honour and veneration too. The water is warm, and I lather the children's scalps thoroughly. I want to give Old Fat as much to envy as I can.

Distracted looking at Old Fat, I nick a young girl I call Snow's ear. She flinches. I stare at her callously for ruining my performance, and she settles back into firm, stoic dignity. Old Fat still covets plenty. Good.

The next morning, I march down the line. Sticking out above the clean scalps, I find a stubbly, patchy head covered in unwieldy cuts. It takes me a moment to recognize Old Fat. He's hacked off his hair as best he could, which isn't well at all. Red lines crisscross his bald-ish head where he hurt himself, so consistently I don't know where he began or finished. He must not have learned much as he went along. Must not have cared.

I beckon him forward with a waggle of my finger. He looks at me, eyes baggy and bleary but without a hint of apology. I admire and despise his fearlessness in equal measure.

"Mud," I say forebodingly. Old Fat's eyes don't so much as flutter. I gesture for him to make his way to the ring.

Mud tears him to pieces. Old Fat doesn't seem to mind any.

Snow

It's cold where I'm from. That's all they'll tell me about it. They call me Snow. They make fun of me for being pretty, pale, and fragile. In training, once someone gets a hold of me, I melt. I'm not strong. Not yet. Snow can do a lot of incredible things if there's a lot of it, though. Avalanches, blizzards. I can grow. I am growing. Slowly. Slower than I like. But I am.

People were a lot meaner to me before Old Fat came along. Growing isn't his problem. He's huge. I think we all might be a little jealous of him for that. There's a lot about him people don't seem to like. They pull and poke at his blubber, slap it and watch it jiggle. They scream in his ears when he isn't looking and laugh about how his face gets red. They really hate the soft ones here.

Master seems to hate Old Fat most of all. She punishes him for everything, twice as hard as anyone else. The others think she might like them better if they're bad to him too. Seems like it works. She's a lot nicer to all of us. Even me. But I haven't been bad to him. So I guess you don't have to be.

He cried and screamed and thrashed a lot the first few nights. I asked him to stop, but I'm not sure he even knew he was doing it. It was hard to sleep. Mud beat him up pretty bad. Old Fat never even had a chance to get up off the ground. He got a little quieter. Not enough. A few others helped Mud out next time. They kicked Old Fat a bunch.

Tonight, I can barely hear him at all. He's breathing loud, I guess. Maybe it's a little wheezy, but it's not his fault his nose is all busted up. They did that.

It's way louder when everyone gets out of bed. I was almost asleep. I hear them stomping on him. I don't want to look, but I can't help but try and count the different feet. I didn't know we had that many.

The laughing stops after a while. They all go back to bed. Bored, I guess. I listen for Old Fat for a long time. Maybe he's holding his breath. It's really quiet in here. So quiet it keeps me awake.

Once everyone's asleep, I slip out from under my blanket and crawl across the floor. I'm not that good a fighter, but I'm really sneaky. Master tells me it's because I'm so little. I think it's more than that. I'm skilled. If I had more muscles, I think I'd be the best here at just about everything.

I get to Old Fat without any fuss. His nose is bleeding. A lot of him is bleeding. He's as purple and red as I am white. His eyes are half-open, but they're not looking at anything. They're not wet, either. Not one tear. I think he's breathing, but I don't hear anything. I guess he's learning.

"Psst!" I whisper and wave my hand in his face. "You okay?"

He looks at me. That's good. I crawl a little nearer then rest my head on my arms. I try to be as close as possible so he doesn't have to work too hard to hear me or see me.

"You gonna be okay?" I ask.

He doesn't say anything. I don't think he trusts me. I get it. Everything he's done here has caught him a beating. For all he knows, this is some trick I'm playing. I AM pretty tricky. It's how I get by. But I'm nice too.

"Suck it up," I tell him. "You're just new. They'll lose interest in you. In a while, you'll be another one of us, and they'll leave you alone. They'll probably go right back to picking on me."

That doesn't seem to help much.

"They won't kill you," I offer. "Not on purpose, anyway. There's no point. You're good for something. Or you will be."

He looks away from me, probably deciding I don't have anything useful for him. I push him in the shoulder until he gives me back his attention.

"I've got an idea," I say, pretending it just occurred to me. "Why don't I help you with your lessons? I'm really good. I'm just small. Not like you. If I teach you how to fight and sneak, will you teach me how to be big?"

He looks at me dumbly.

"That's a joke," I tell him, thinking he'll giggle or smile. He doesn't. "With my help, you'll get better faster. Maybe I'm an awesome teacher, and you'll even get really good. Then you can help me out when the other kids feel like beating me up. Deal?"

He doesn't budge, but his eyes move back and forth like he's thinking.

"Hey, can you talk?" I finally remember to ask. "Can you move?"

He shrugs. I guess that answers one of my questions.

Maybe he's worried he can't speak quietly enough. He's been crushed for a lot less than talking.

"Okay," I say. "We'll go when it's really late and everyone's asleep. Like now. But not now, obviously. Tomorrow. I'll show you what to do. If you work harder than everyone, you'll catch up, maybe even get ahead. After that, you're my bodyguard forever. Deal? Deal."

I reach my pinky around his and seal it. He doesn't pull away or resist, so I think it counts. I'm excited. I've never had a friend. Or even someone who might appreciate something I could give them. Maybe I'm being silly. Maybe he won't get that good, and we'll both get beat up anyway. Somehow, for some reason, I don't think it will be as bad if we're together.

Terra

I can't be sure Old Fat sleeps. When he first arrived, he'd bleat all night in his little clearing as quietly as he could. When he fell asleep, he'd flail and shriek in a manner impossible to ignore. The children discouraged that straightaway.

Lately, he's begun putting his restlessness to use. Usually, I find him exercising or practicing with Snow. I don't let them see me. Some nights, he does his patterns in the ring. Some nights, he repeats a single move a thousand times. Lately, I've found him pounding the trunk of a tree until his knuckles bloody. He presses himself. Little by little, I see him discover and expand the limits of his body.

He's improving.

* * *

I'm considering dropping the 'Fat' from 'Old Fat.' It doesn't suit him. There's nothing soft in him anymore. I've starved it out. Every day, he comes in last in the rankings, so every day, he gets the smallest share of food. Even at double the size of the other children, he doesn't bicker. He understands.

Maybe I'll call him Withered. Or Empty. Or Last. No. To change my ways would be admitting a transformation of some kind, and he'll look on that as progress. Old Fat he'll remain.

* * *

Old Fat won his first fight today. It was stupid of me to match him with Sick, stupidity born of idleness. I'd already set Mud, Imp, and Pox on Old Fat so many times. Even though I could see him closing the distance, I let my curiosity get the better of me. He pounced so ferociously I was worried his empty belly had made a cannibal of him.

If I were fair, Old Fat would have had one of the better shares and cots that night. I offered him second from last, just over Sick. Old Fat refused both. Not for pride. He felt no entitlement to better. I think he believes he's onto something. He distrusts comfort and loves his lowness.

* * *

Old Fat nearly killed Pox today. I should have known. He's growing too feral. This morning during exercises, he was faster and deeper in his presses than I'd ever seen him. Even my foot in his back couldn't slow him.

How is he getting so big? Is Snow stealing him food? I should check the inventory. Is he hunting? He's better now at slipping away. I still find his clearing empty every night, but I have no idea where he goes or what he does.

I'll have to keep him out of fights for a while.

* * *

Mud feels the ground giving way beneath him. He doesn't believe in his rank. He watches Old Fat very carefully and tries to match him every way he can. He doesn't finish his meals, makes sure his portion doesn't exceed Old Fat's. He does his exercises just as fervently, at least at the beginning of the day. By night, however, he's depleted. He collapses into his cot, sleeps deeply, and Old Fat's true work begins.

* * *

Mud wants a fight. He's worn down. He isn't beating Imp and Pox as easily as he once did. Matching Old Fat in work and regimen is brutal, punishing drudgery, and he's desperate to prove its futility. Victory would excuse his lagging, free him again to rest and eat his top rank's share. In defeating Old Fat, he defeats his methods too.

At first, I truly believe Mud has every chance. Old Fat has years less training, and I haven't let him fight in weeks. Mud is a prodigy and quicker. He detects weaknesses efficiently and punishes panic. He makes the most of his gifts and opportunities. As much as any student I've had, I'm sure he'll one day win a laudable moniker.

For the first few minutes, Mud makes me very proud. He works his openings well and attacks Old Fat from the side and behind. He keeps his distance, peppering and angering his opponent with sharp, stinging blows. That's good. He knows where his advantages lie.

Mud, brimming with confidence, throws his best strike, that whipping, axe-like sideways kick that strikes fear in his fellow students. Not in Old Fat. Old Fat eats it happily, coming forward, proud to make nothing of it. Mud stumbles backwards, never getting his feet back under him. Old Fat brings him down into the dirt and absolutely smothers him. Mud cowers, wincing and turning away when Old Fat raises his fist.

"Enough!" I yell.

Old Fat lowers his fist lackadaisically and climbs off Mud. He takes his place back in line as if nothing happened. Mud trembles on the ground, trying to catch his breath. He'll be mortified soon as his heart slows.

* * *

Old Fat has made a habit of undoing the progress of the other students. He takes their best then does just enough to show them he's better. At first, it was only a matter of strength. He was too big. It isn't just that anymore. He's fast. Deft. He knows all the best ways to his goal and all the wrong roads his lessers will try. I stop him before he does any harm. Real harm, anyway. No one has felt a single of his blows in months, yet the children still come away shaken.

Mud's confidence is shot. I doubt he could handle anyone anywhere near the top of the class presently. I feed him Snow. She's so flimsy. Her pretty strikes bounce off him, and he builds himself back up by throttling her. Maybe I let it go longer than I should. He needed it. Snow has been trounced before. She will be again.

* * *

Mud wasn't in line for morning exercises. Something has happened. The children are frightened. They won't tell me anything. They wouldn't lie. They wouldn't even speak.

Old Fat's knuckles are red.

I go to Mud's bed. Part of me expects to find him beaten half-dead. His things are gone. At high sun, I search the fields for some hint of him. I find a few random bits of his clothing and some blood. Not too much. Maybe Old Fat was generous. Maybe he let Mud run.

* * *

Ever since Mud disappeared, Snow stays away from Old Fat. He looks at her with pride and little smiles now and then when he wins some trial, but she never looks back. It hurts him, but he brushes it off. He trains alone at night now.

* * *

Old Fat occupies all my thoughts. I love and hate him. I love him for his promise. His body is that of a man now. He's rugged and nimble. He has years to go before his peak. Yet he's starved for instruction. He has no belief in natural progress, so he chases improvement tirelessly, checking beneath every stone and around every corner. He's always listening, always watching, searching for meaning and learning everywhere. For this, I love him. Teachers dream of such a student.

I hate him for his defiance. There's nothing deliberate about it. He has no rebellion in him. When I say go, he goes, when I say stop, he stops, and every order I can formulate is followed through automatically. He's as devoted and true as the best of dogs, trusts me as a loving child trusts a parent's word. His defiance is subtler, unconscious, beyond his control. He defies the core of my teachings. The essence of my beliefs. In his very existence, he proves me wrong.

He is my beautiful monster, a phenom born of malice. Because he was different, because he was scarred by the outside world, because he didn't fit my mould, I abused him. I really thought there was kindness in my cruelty, that I could drive away and he'd be happier for it. So I told myself. Looking back, I can see I poured all my evil into him, all my anger and contempt. I saw ugliness in him and punished him for it.

Where all my patience and good intentions failed, my bitterness has triumphed. I've loved every child under my watch save for him, and now he'll cast the shadow of failure over each and every one of them. I will have to choose between two unacceptable paths. One, to stay with my current methods and accept the mediocrity of my crop. Or worse, to repeat my darkest deeds and rain endless torments for hope of more terrible wonders.

I'll put Old Fat with the senior-most students next. Maybe he'll give them something to shoot for.

CHAPTER 4: THE BED OF BEDS

Small

It's late in the morning when I hear Rufus's wife creaking about her house. She overslept, I'm sure, and now she wonders why. She calls his name louder and louder, only curiously at first. "Rufus?" she asks, increasingly impatient, passing from room to room. Funny. I expected him to take a new name.

I watch her from around a thick tree as she emerges onto her porch. She spots the crater in her yard immediately. She stomps barefooted right past the discarded birdhouse, past the dog so happy to see her, and stares into the little pit now defacing her slice of domestic bliss. It can't tell her anything she doesn't already know. An inevitability has finally arrived.

She curses words I'm a little surprised she knows and looks around hungrily for something to set her rage upon. She very nearly kicks the birdhouse with her naked toes. She catches herself. In a huff, she looks to the woods.

"This your doing?" she spits. I dart behind my tree. She couldn't mean me. Addressing fate or the gods, I'm sure. Then I hear the clomping of her little feet closing in on me.

I come out from behind my tree and spare myself the exposure. She stops in place when she finds me. I can tell I'm only partially what she expected. She probably imagined someone older, or fiercer, or in some other way more respectable.

Eventually, she sees past my young face and little frame,

and I'm nothing more than the black shrouds and bald head she's hated for ages. She slaps me crisply across the face. I take it without protest. It was due. But it stings.

She points a quaking finger in my face, cheeks red and puffing as she struggles mightily to put a voice to her fury. She notices something: my arm in its sling. Spitefully, she yanks me nearer by my good shoulder and scans my injury from every perspective available to her.

"Come on!" she bellows, turning her back to me and striding back to her house. I'm stupefied. She turns her head back to me for only a second and commands me forward with an irritated jerk of her arm. I don't dare disobey her.

❉ ❉ ❉

I sit quietly at a table as Elizabeth rummages through a cabinet. She hasn't stopped berating me since we came through the door. I'm obligated to endure this, I suppose. I have many medicines to take.

"What is it you don't understand?" she asks and continues too quickly for me to answer. "He has no part in whatever it is you're up to. He's needed. Needed here."

Finally, she takes a breath, and I seize this rare opportunity to speak up. "It's difficult for civilians to recognize—"

"Excuse me?" she cuts me off, indescribably offended.

"Your husband made an oath," I continue before she bites my head off. "We all did."

"Then what are you doing here?" she asks, bowing nearer to me, pompous. "You hurt that arm by accident? Did your enemy get worse? Or did you run away from something too?"

I bear her disdain. I feel my resolve waning. I suspect in the years at Rufus's side, she's forgotten the cost of insults. In his shadow, how could she ever know reprisal?

"Do you know who he is?" I ask. "Really?"

"A lot better than you do," she says, setting her attention

back on her cabinet and its drawers. I'm grateful for the reprieve, however brief.

"I mean what he's done. What he's achieved."

"A couple of masks on a wall somewhere?"

"He alone can…"

She scoffs like she's caught me. "*He alone…*" she repeats mockingly. "Hypocrites and cowards to the last…"

"To the last, indeed," I mutter through clenched teeth, leaning back in my chair.

She looks at me, making sure she infers what I intend.

"Good," she says frankly.

I breathe deeply, smothering boiling anger with cool air. "He can save lives," I say. "He can end a war."

"Is that what will happen?" she wonders, head bobbing with cynicism. "One man kills for duty, gets killed for vengeance. The vengeful are slaughtered for their insubordination, and the slaughterers butchered for their tyranny. A wicked king is unseated by a wickeder one. The righteous die, the sanctimonious thrive. On and on, round and round…"

I've heard it. A hundred ways, in some form or other. It's such a temptation to admit the futility in things. It tastes like truth and forgives everything. Why honour your commitments? Why pay that price? Why suffer? Why fight? If nothing matters, nothing matters.

She sits down next to me with some oils and ointment, startling me from my seething. She mixes something in a bowl. It looks like a plaster.

"Your *God Killer*…" she begins, adeptly undoing my bandages. "He made me an oath too. No harm. Only good."

She takes in the ugly colours of my naked arm soberly. I lean towards her.

"Justice done is good," I say, proud of my steadiness. "There is no freedom beneath a throne."

She doesn't look at me, applying some salve with total focus.

"Most people who pound the drum for justice or freedom

don't really care for either," she says quietly. She won't be diverted from her task. "All they really want is their turn with the whip."

She leans away from my arm, supremely satisfied with her work and her platitude. I'll confess to my arm feeling a little better already. That is until she flicks it in a delicate spot.

Elizabeth

That Nameless is perched out there in a tree just past my gate. She acts like she's invisible, but Bandit sits just beneath her, looking up and giving it all away. She sleeps there at night, huddled tight on a branch and leaning against the trunk. It's no simple feat getting up with one arm in a cast. It's so pointless, such an ostentatious display of austerity. Rufus was just like this when we first met. He was suspicious and guarded towards anything that might conceal the gloom of the world for even an instant. I'm sure all the Nameless are.

I come to the tree's roots. I scratch Bandit behind the ear, distracting him for only a second.

"What's your name?" I ask grudgingly, calling up to the leaves overhead, doing the Nameless the favour of pretending I don't know exactly where she is.

For a moment, I think she's going to feign she isn't there. It'd be like them. Finally, the response I should have known was coming:

"I am Namel—"

"What do they call you?" I cut her off, saving us both.

"Small," she tells me, her voice a growl.

"There's no sense staying out here all night, Small." I sigh theatrically. "Come in. I'll fix you a spot to sleep."

"The Nameless do not luxuriate," she tells me plainly, eyes fixed on the horizon like it may pounce any moment.

"I know the rules." I nod my head and fold my arms. "I know they're ludicrous."

I wait patiently. I hear some leaves rustle as she digs her

back deeper against the trunk.

"You're going to get rained on," I tell her before turning around and heading home.

There. I've done my part. Let her get sick and run-down. See if that helps her any. I see her look to the sparsely clouded sky with unflappable skepticism. She thinks she knows better than I do.

❈ ❈ ❈

It's pouring. There's no hint of Small yet. Even Bandit had the sense to come and find shelter on the porch. When he shook himself off, enough water to fill a bathtub flew off him in every direction. Small must be twice as wet.

I'm in the guest room. I've never made so nice a bed. Generally, I don't really bother. Work for nothing, as I see it. Don't see the point unless you've someone to impress. I don't want to impress Small. Not in a traditional sense. In some petty way, I want her to miss out. The warmer and cozier the respite I make for her here, the greater a fool she is for sitting in that tree and soaking herself to the bone. In my dreams, I see her face pressed against the window, staring longingly in at this little piece of salvation I've cobbled together. The thought pleases me.

I take a step back and admire my handiwork. I'm sure I've never seen a bed so inviting. An empty bed, at least. There's only so much a bed can do on its own. It can't give you a chest to lie your head on, or a gentle rise and fall to lull you to sleep. It can't wrap you in arms safe and burly enough to beat back all the world. A bed without Rufus can only be so snug.

I drive him from my mind so as not to think too fondly of him. He must answer to perfect, unblemished scorn when I see him again. I make my way to my own bed. Its blankets are frumpy, its sheets wrinkled. I crawl my way into it. I feel engulfed, suffocated in its immensity. I writhe and turn over until the covers tighten and coil around me. I vacillate from cold to hot and back again. I abhor this bed. Rufus is to blame, of course.

There he is, invading my mind again. At least I'm cross with him. I should give myself permission to think of him so long as I'm mad at him. All the better to punish him when he returns.

* * *

After an uneasy night's sleep, I make my way back to the guest room. A new hope tickles me. What if I found Small lying in that perfect bed, in so deep and wonderful a slumber she didn't even hear me coming? I could wake her, and she'd scramble timidly to her feet, dabbing at her bleary eyes, knowing my victory total and complete. Wouldn't that be something? There's nothing so sweet as self-righteousness defeated.

When I come upon the guest bed, I find it unsullied. If anything, it looks fresher and all the more enticing. Suddenly, the waste of it hits me. Two miserable women and two miserable nights, and the bed of beds untouched for stubbornness alone. My game seems so juvenile.

In the midst of my wallowing and self-flagellating, something jumps out at me from the floor by the window. Dampness from the rain. To be expected. But among it… boot prints.

I look again at the bed, crisp, clean, and beautiful. More beautiful than last night. More beautiful than I could make it. Maybe Rufus could. Or someone with his militaristic precision and meticulousness. But not me. Never me.

I swell with joy and pride. Such a victory. A victory for all time.

CHAPTER 5: FATHER'S DAUGHTERS

Reznick

I hate the extravagance of this hall. This room was conceived exclusively for grovelers to gawk at Uncle. I'm sitting on a marble floor, my back against one of a dozen columns dotting the path to a golden throne raised on a little stage. I loathe standing beside chairs like that in rooms like these, dissected interminably by well-dressed nothings we pretend are our guests.

For now, it's just Uncle and his Darling here with me. And the two Allegia he has lugging his latest painting, I suppose. They don't really count. With equal fascinations, Darling plays with her toys and Uncle admires the portrait. I don't know how he keeps falling in love with these pictures that come our way. We have so many, and this one is very typical. He looks regal and irreproachable at its center. His Darling is at his right hand. I'm at his left, standing straighter and taller than I ever have or ever would. Their likenesses are exact, but I see nothing of myself up there in those brushes and strokes.

It amazes me the things that can occupy Uncle. By right of birth and might, the world is his. Yet he has such an eye for detail. He can watch his Darling play for hours. He has boundless patience for her inane, inarticulate little thoughts. He's utterly fixated on the essential process of this painting's hanging. His men endeavour beneath its immensity, trying their best to adjust and angle it on the wall behind the throne.

"Something on your mind?" he asks, not turning to look at me.

He never lets anything go unspoken. Never leaves me to my moods. As I say, an eye for detail.

"I could have caught the Nameless welp," I grumble. "You should have let me."

"We fight on our terms," he states disinterestedly. "Not theirs."

"Then you live in a palace of fear," I'm proud to say. The phrase has lived in me for hours. "Why gild a cage? Our enemy mocks us. Questions our valour."

"Don't trouble yourself with the tittering of little people."

He dismisses me so easily.

"Lend me some riders," I say, shooting to my feet. "Let me find them. Snuff them out. If we let them go free, they'll assemble their forces."

"To what ends?" he counters, ridiculing me with his stillness. "They'll never build strength enough to match ours. But for us to venture out… meet them on their field… why expose ourselves to harm them? We'll gather where it suits us. Strike them down at our leisure."

I feel my blood surging, my sweat dripping. My heart beats so loud and fast I'm sure I'm vibrating. I'm ready to jump out of my skin, and he just stands there, composed, waiting for all the world to come around to him. Like it ought to. As it must.

"They'll spread and fester forever if we let them!" I spit. I try to calm myself. No matter how impeccable my argument, emotion will diminish it. "They'll inspire more to their derangement."

"We who beat back the darkness need not fear the lost," he says.

He always has some immutable, immortal adage in his quiver, like all history's wisdom was accumulated at his service.

"If we find their nest…" I begin.

"Enough," he raises his voice only slightly, expecting this little flash of anger will tame me. "I'll have no more of this. We'll send word to our forces."

His Darling senses rare tension. She pulls her attention away from her toy. She looks upon my humiliation with pity and concern. Her mask is so gentle, so unassuming, without even a single horn to menace me. She takes so much after her father. She's so blind and innocent, so untainted by the bitterness and unpleasantness of the world. She'll probably inherit all his potency and grandeur. Without even dedicating herself, she'll race past me. I could spend every waking second chasing and pressing the outer edges of my potential, and if she fulfills even a fraction of hers, she'll rule me. Without ever lifting a finger. Without ever shedding tears or blood. All because she is her father's daughter, and I am mine.

"You doubt me," I mutter at Uncle "You fear my failure, that I'll tarnish our line. I am not my father! His weakness is not mine!"

"Don't speak against the family," he drones with practiced distance. He turns his back to me and sets his sights back on the hanging of the portrait. "You will stay by my side, under my guard. The day will come when it falls to you to defend our line. Nothing comes before the family."

I've heard this refrain, this well-worn doctrine of expectation and duty. Before I can snap at him, he flicks his wrist. I freeze in anticipation, not knowing what he's decided on. I see the Allegia's armour rattling as Divine Will seizes them, the painting finally hung just so.

"There," he says, admiring the exquisite symmetry. "Perfection."

That cold fear straightening my spine melts with relief when I realize I'm not his target. Then comes red, hot embarrassment. He's so secure, so unassailable in his immaculate correctness. All the world bends to him. His brawn turns back rivers, and his kindness softens hard hearts. He doesn't know the Nameless. He wasn't there. He didn't see…

I storm out of the room. I'm not persuasive enough to change him with thought. I'll prove him wrong with deeds.

* * *

I wait until the dead of night to make my move. Guards watch my door until dawn, so I climb out my window and down my tower, using my tendrils like little picks in the stone. No one sees me. No one thinks to look. No one else in all the world can climb as I do, and I've never tried to escape before.

It's not long before my feet find the ground. I'll need a horse now. Who knows how far I'll go or how long I'll look. A horse will ease my travel, and a good one will buy me the respect of whatever folk I come across. Humans have instinctive awe for the mounted. In those that command robust horses, people see their betters and masters. Humans know themselves beneath beasts so swift and mighty, though they may not know they know.

I peruse the stables quietly, secretly, trying to find the most magnificent and strapping steed. I pass a dozen tall, muscular specimens with fearsome names. Blackbolt. Quake. Highwind. They're so alike. It's hard to pick from them. Their colours differ, but that seems too shallow a reason to settle on one over another. I wish I could hear their stories, what chivalrous deeds earned them their titles.

I see a man. Or rather, he sees me. He's old and squat, poorly shaven, and wears an apron. He holds a broom, but he does not sweep. He is rooted to his spot watching me, dumbstruck. He's not the stablemaster. He's something much lower, less dignified. By the smell of him, he spends his days shovelling dung. He's a small man with a small job who's done precious little with his small life. Despite it all, he knows I shouldn't be here.

"My lady..." he begins, stammering.

"Boy," I say, cutting him off sharply. He's twice or three times my age at least, but there's no word I can conjure more suitably demeaning. "Fetch the guard and open the gate."

He hesitates. He's clever enough to know something's

wrong. Barely. If I leave him time to reason, he could spoil it all.

"But the Prince…" he looks over his shoulder, hoping for some overseer to unburden him of a difficult ruling.

"You defy me?" I ask, my voice dripping with disdain.

He looks back at me. He's right to be suspicious. Uncle hardly ever lets me leave his side and certainly never to converse with stable hands. I can see the gears grinding in his feeble brain. I have to convince him he'd rather risk Uncle's anger than mine.

"Yes, my lady," he says with a swift nod before scurrying off on the task I've set for him.

Good. Uncle is immeasurably more formidable than I am in court and in practice. His power is absolute, his authority total. Yet I am more fearsome.

I come upon a half-forgotten sight. Stocky legs. Well-groomed yellow fur. A clean, cascading white mane. Fon. My pony. I'm surprised she's still alive, though I suppose horses live quite a while when properly cared for. So much time has passed since I last saw her. Lifetimes. She's changed so little compared to me. I was so young when she carried me about. I remember being afraid of falling off her back and being giddy at the thrill of it. How sheltered, how cowardly I must have been. I'm taller than her now.

I grab her by her harness and pull her closer to me. She flares her nostrils and whips back her head, but I'm stronger than she is. I don't think she recognizes me. We didn't spend all that long together. After my father passed, I lost interest in such soft, girlish diversions. She's a ridiculous creature. Winsome and useless. She couldn't carry me halfway round a pen now, I expect.

I cast back my mind. She may have been the very last thing my father gave me. Had to be. I played with her so briefly. I was only the girl that'd adore this silly trifle for a moment. Tonight, Fon is obscene to me. The legacy of a witless man to a frivolous girl.

She pulls her snout away, ineffectually fighting my grip. I let a tendril fall out my sleeve, and I whip it down across her neck. I slice right through. Her head lingers a moment before tumbling down to her hooves. She stands a while before collapsing to the dirt.

I take the first horse I see after that. I don't even see its name. I'll call it what I like.

CHAPTER 6: PENANCE

Swift

I'm in a tent as big as most houses, so this must be quite a to-do. Sitting cross legged in the sand at the far end are some wrinkly, rickety masters. They're old enough that I'm confident their backs ache and knees hurt. They'd be more comfortable with some cushions or chairs, but they're proud of their humility. I suppose there's comfort in that.

I know most of them. They're all higher-ups. Some have more clout than others, but they all sport weathered, serious faces. They whisper and catch up, blabber about very important trivialities. A couple of positively ancient geriatrics I don't recognize sit so still I wonder if they're sleeping with their eyes open. I suspect of everyone here, they matter most.

They insisted I bring my two best men, so Iron and Star are here with me, looking around like they might find something incredibly distinct about this tarp we're under. They're not used to gatherings of this magnitude, and they're taking in as much as they can, maybe even worrying about damage they might do. I wish I could chide them. Act like you've been there.

My steel claws click a little as I tap them against the plate on my forearm. It's my not-so-silent protest, my little show of impudence. Iron and Star know better than to voice any impatience or displeasure. They hold their spears stiff like perfect statues, occasionally swallowing as quietly as they can muster. They're good soldiers. Too good to be here with me. It won't be fair. But orders are orders.

Terra comes in through the back of the tent, and I'm happy to see her. Chances to reconnect with an old sister are rare. She catches my eye, and she shares none of my joy. She says so much with just that look. She warns me. I finally sense the gravity of the situation.

Old Fat ducks his head to enter the tent, anything but. His muscles are long and sinewy, and chiseled lines snake everywhere a vain boy dreams for himself. He's bigger than I let my men get. A blade only needs so much help piercing flesh. After that, quickness is better. Even so, I can tell there's little waste to his bulk. So be it. More to hit.

He walks to the center of this place, reluctantly letting us all take in the spectacle of him. He looks at me through the sides of certain, hungry eyes. He doesn't see anyone in this tent but me. Not Iron or Star with their spears to cut him, or the old masters with their authority to distinguish him. I feel a surge of kinship; Old Fat knows who truly matters here, and so do I.

"Ready," I hear Terra say, portentous and emphatic.

I raise my claws. Iron and Star take their stances. Old Fat doesn't budge. I search his body for a weapon. I can't find any. He stares into me like there's something inside me that belongs to him, and he can't wait to snatch it back.

"Go," Terra says.

We lean forward an inch, and Old Fat explodes from his spot. It's so fast and vicious we're already backpedalling. Stupid. Our line is broken, and he's given himself the space he needs.

An instant of retreat, and Iron is already defeated. Old Fat shatters him with utter indifference. It's a functional, effortless blow that changes Iron for all time. He'll never be so canny or courageous again.

Star plunges his spear. In a blink, somehow Old Fat's hulking frame isn't where it ought to be, and the spear is snapped in half. Star's face disappears behind Old Fat's hand. When Old Fat pulls back his fingers, he takes Star's face with him, marring the nose and lips I know so well with unfamiliar red craters.

Old Fat sets his sights on me. He respects me enough to

let me gather myself. I remind myself that no one is supposed to die here. I've seen war and carnage aplenty in my life. Today, I've seen all of two punches. Old Fat didn't mean them to be excessive. Just decisive.

He comes in my direction, and I know immediately he feels no ill will towards me. He's interested in my opinion of him. He swings his battering ram limbs with precision, yet lets me get around them. He shows me his perfect balance, his command of momentum. He demonstrates the flexibility of his kicks. I don't dare try to block them, but he gives me the dignity of pretending I might. He knows I'm the best he's had so far, and he wants to savour the experience.

I've been in Old Fat's place. I can recall the days of youth and promise. I was never the titan he was, but I had most of his confidence and some of his fleet-footedness. Legend was expected of me, and I wrote it with these claws. You learn quickly that whatever you do, it isn't enough. No matter how much you deliver, you can't live up to the dream of your potential. Your ceiling reveals itself, and no matter how high it is, its finality is devastating.

Your followers lose interest. They turn their backs, move on to the new prodigy who may yet still tease and tantalize with their mysterious, ill-defined peaks. But you remain yourself, with nowhere to go. I'm sure I'll be loved when I'm gone, like all the other hallowed martyrs to the cause. For now, I stand at this gate behind which hides sublimity and beat back many young prospects looking to cross through. Every single one of them had fanfare, a procession of wrinkly masters thirsty for my defeat. It hasn't come yet. I relish thwarting them.

My knuckles find Old Fat's ribs, and I can see he's pleased for me. Another couple landed strikes and he reaches a benevolent hand out at me like a teacher stepping in to pacify a pupil. It misses me, and I introduce my fist to his jaw. I stagger him, not so much with my prowess, but my insolence. He finds me discourteous. Good.

I launch another straight fist, and he slides past it and

hurls his head at me. For my daring to believe it was a weak spot, I suppose. It crashes into me like a meteor, and I am in pieces. In no time at all, he's on top of me, holding my jaw still in one hand. I need out fast. I work every hold I can think of, claw at his joints and pressure points, wriggle and shoot my hips.

An elbow clatters into my chin, and the blurry side of the world comes back to me like an old forgotten friend. A strange, warm peace washes over me. Nothing's ever so bad as you expect it to be.

I think I hear a "stop" somewhere. Another crash comes, followed by black.

I wonder what they'll call him.

Old Fat

I think a lot about forest fires, their majesty and their terror. I was young when I saw my first. I often played in the woods as a child, and I wept in awe when I saw orange, red, and blue eating up my lonesome sanctuary. My father, as he always did, knew what to say. He explained the order in it, that forests must cleanse themselves. To scatter seeds of new life, the old and decayed must be cleared away.

This is what I think of as I climb off Swift. I admired him so much, and I've defiled him. There was so much grace in how he built himself. So much faculty and efficacy. But I've cracked his clean, rigid lines and tenderized his carefully honed points. I've wasted all his mindful labour and methodical tending. He'll be back, I tell myself. He'll be better.

I look into the faces of the High Masters. All their lives, they've waited to be impressed as I've impressed them. They hide their elation behind gruff non-expressions, but I can see their minds reeling, making plans. They whisper little comments among each other, and I think about telling them to speak up. Why should they have their secrets? They serve me now. I am the tip of the sword, and all Nameless exist now only to better direct me.

They tell me to stand. They rise to meet me, straightening so I don't tower too much over them. They look smug and generous with what they have to tell me, as though it might be some delightful surprise. They drone on officiously, appraise me, place me as a star in a constellation, tell me how much I still have to do before I'm anything more. They have to say it this way. We must control our expectations. Aloud, at least.

While they blather, I look for Master Terra's face among their subdued grins and twinkling eyes. I can't find her, and at this moment, she's all that matters to me. I hear a little shifting. Over my shoulder, I find her. She tends to Swift, dabs at his bloody face, checks his bruised and battered places. I swear she tries not to look at me.

The High Masters give me my prize. They ask me for my new moniker. I'm curious if they have any guesses. Something big and hard, probably. They look at me like I'm going to teach them some perfect word they've never heard but always knew ought to exist.

"I am Rufus," I tell them. They strain for deeper comprehension, search the histories inside their heads for some relevant significance.

"I am Rufus," I say again, keeping the rest for myself. It is who I've always been, who I'll always be. My father gave me this name, and it's all I have of him. I will never part with it.

Terra

I'm proud of Rufus. I am. Swift is a veteran. He knows the rules. He'll be back. Maybe he'll be recovered in time for the celebration. Rufus will honour him. One day, after some pivotal conquest Rufus etches into the ages, Swift will be happy to have been part of his story.

Rufus and I are alone, as we so often are. We walk in silence, leaves crunching loudly beneath our feet as we maneuver through trees. We have a simple task before us, and I'm grateful for the respite. We're going into town to gather supplies to feast in tribute of Rufus's moniker. We travel light so we may come back with full arms. Work so modest always leaves Rufus gruff and distant. I'll load him up to excess with rations and tools for the way back. Maybe he'll be happier overburdened.

Rufus is an ideal companion but poor company. He is doting to a fault and incapable of levity. He does not converse with me. He listens and answers. Even now with his moniker, he sees me as a master rather than a sister. He serves me. He might always serve me, for better and worse. There are advantages. With him at my side, I feel no danger. Every victory is assured, every challenge a romp.

There aren't many places that will welcome Nameless happily. Of these precious few, Penance is my favourite. It's a quiet, simple town, so quaint, harmless, and remote that it veils its services to us easily. The sun shines bright there, too bright for us to hide, or so the Royal Family believes. It's too agreeable to be dangerous, too happy to be illicit. We have many allies there who greet us with smiles and who will congratulate Rufus on his extraordinary achievement.

I smell the delectable odour of searing meat and steady fire in the air. The indication of civilization lightens my mood. We might get a meal. We may find old friends and a place to lay our heads. I see the town's signpost high on a hill, and my spirits rise. I know that stone insignia well.

We reach the high ground and look down with awe and horror at a desert of ash. At first, I'm confused. I assume I've strayed somewhere off the path. I see no hints of the Penance I knew. All that's left is flecks of grey in the air, piles on the ground, and a huge red mark painted prominently at the center of it all: the Dragon, its mouth open wide, the brand reserved for the most heinous betrayers.

A wild fury erupts inside me only to be quickly smothered by sorrow. We are culpable. I am culpable. A whole community wiped away for helping the Nameless. People I knew. Lawrence, the blacksmith who fixed my weapons. Lillian, the barkeep who gave me scraps when she closed her doors. Stein, the little thief who shared with me the secret comings and goings about town. All gone.

I finally notice Rufus again. He takes in the town coolly. He didn't know it like I did. He's still young.

"Did Prince Darnett do this?" he asks.

I don't know. How could I? Few have seen the breadth of Darnett's powers and lived to tell the tale. He rules the flame, that much is known. He could likely raze a town like this, but it'd be beneath him. The task is more befitting an army.

"Yes," I say plainly, not knowing why.

Rufus accepts my judgment solemnly. For a moment, I worry I've doomed him, that I've set him on a reckless, vengeful path that can only end in ruin. Yet I see no anger in him, only a careful consideration that chills me to the bone.

He approaches the signpost. He wraps his fingers around it firmly and begins to pull. At first, I search for meaning in the futile gesture. Then the earth at the post's base begins to give way, the futility disappears, and the meaning reveals itself.

Rufus leans the signpost on his shoulder and returns the way we came, purposeful, the stone insignia swaying high behind him.

❧ ❧ ❧

From then on, Rufus was never without the signpost. In a sense, Penance was with us wherever we went. The post was his trophy and talisman. He shortened the base and made a weapon for himself. When enemies saw the stone insignia declaring its name, they cowered. When friends saw it, they crowded. In either case, people knew they were among loftiness. They forgot the town. They remembered the weapon.

For a time, Rufus swung it like a hammer. He bludgeoned and crushed his foes. It was effective though gruesome. Blunt force does not kill cleanly. Rufus would have kept on with it, but the battering chipped and scratched at the stone. There would come a day when the insignia would split, and as inevitable as it was, it'd surely be taken for an omen. So, Rufus affixed a blade to the post's top. His enemies would die quickly by spear. Somehow, they never seemed to appreciate their good fortune.

CHAPTER 7: CRAG'S ERROR

Rufus

I've been walking for hours. I feel like it's been night for days. My thighs ache and my mouth tastes like salt, but all I can think about is the noisy mush my feet have become. This spear is heavy. My clothes are heavy. My bones are heavy. My hair is heavy. I miss my bald head. Rain rolled off it so smoothly.

The ground sticks to me with every step I take. I don't know how it expects me to stay, or what it wants with my boots. My stomach is cross with me. I'm starving, nauseous, or both. Good. I've fat to spare. Eat that, why don't you. You'll have plenty. Gorge on it. Choke.

Loud, rhythmless clacking steals my attention. A sign that reads 'Inn' whips in the wind. The place looks nice. Warm light trickles out from every tiny crack in the wood planks that make up its walls. I don't know how I can hear the crackling fire inside and the soft, friendly murmurs over the rain, but I do.

I can feel my training pulling me away. Don't, it tells me. Indulgence is weakness. Pain is strength. You're wasting time. One foot in front of the other. Never backwards. Never sideways, even. No waste. No joy. No rest.

So juvenile. Adolescent and destructive. The philosophy of the angry and restless, defying the unhappiness that comes so easily to them. Attitudes like that only build weapons, and weapons build nothing at all. I have to sleep, don't I? How much can a warm plate and a soft bed possibly hurt? If anything, it'll restore me. Oh, what untold new vigour it will bring me.

Having sufficiently convinced myself, I push my way through a heavy door. The inn keeper isn't as happy to see me as I'd dreamed. I understand. It's late. Even if I am welcome, the puddles I'm leaving wherever I stand are not.

"Beautiful night," I offer. He doesn't look up from the book he's writing in, only points wearily up at a sign with prices etched.

"Pay now," he says shortly but softly. "There's soup if you want it."

He stays so still I wonder what's stopping me from wandering right past him. I leave the coins I'm pretty sure he wants and a little bit more on top of his desk. I pour myself some soup from his pot. The burn of the bowl on my palms is luxury beyond compare.

I'm feeling better already as I take a seat on a bench at a long table, laying my spear at my feet. I slurp from my bowl, warmth flows down my throat, and I finally take in the place. A blazing fire burns bright in a hearth at the far wall. Stairs lead to a second-floor walkway and several rooms. Leaning over the railing, I spot a figure I know too well: Crag. His lackeys can't be far.

I set my gaze back down on my soup, smoothly and nonchalantly, pretending I don't recognize him. I slurp loudly, but I still hear the steady descent of little feet in heavy boots. I ignore it.

Impossible to ignore is the scrapping of the bench directly across from me. Crag leans low on the table to meet my downturned eyes. His little friends drop down on either side of me. I smile politely and raise my bowl to them before taking another sip.

"Don't see you around these parts much," observes Crag. I'm not sure he remembers me. Doesn't matter. He sees a victim, and that's familiar enough.

"Just passing through," I say with a playful melody in my

voice. "Weak bones couldn't carry me further. Lovely scenery."

"Where are you headed?" he asks.

"Catching up with some family," I tell him. I'm not a very shrewd liar. I can deal in half-truths much more easily.

Crag grunts and nods, accepting my words, unsatisfied. His friend to my right glares a hole through me. I think his name is Rover. I tip my bowl to him.

"There were rumours of a man passing through these parts some time back," Crag remarks, focusing every morsel of his modest intellect on my reactions. "One of the Nameless."

A man. Wrong as they are, I'm sure they mean Small. I resent her for being spotted, even in passing. At half my size or less, she has no excuse.

"What are the Nameless?" I ask, searching their faces, playing dumb. Delicately, subtly, I slide a foot over my spear.

"Rebel rats." Crag spits on the floor with disdain. "Enemy to all proud loyals. Are you pledged to those who beat back the dark?"

"Of course," I say lightly. "Who likes darkness?"

Crag doesn't seem inclined to return my amiability. He leans back on his bench, admires the spear between my feet.

"What's that?" he asks.

"Walking stick," I tell him, keen to move on from something so trivial.

"What's with the sheath?" he insists.

"It's an heirloom." I shrug, indulging the banality. "Keeps it tidy. My wife teases me for being so careful with something so worthless. I'm sentimental."

"Must have something worth protecting at the top of it," presumes Crag, reaching down. "Something worth seeing. Mind if I have a look?"

I kick the spear away, and it slides across the room. I can't let them see the insignia. They'd know it. They'd tell.

Crag's friends shoot to their feet and loom over me with all the menace they can muster. I can tell I've spent their patience. I hope they have some sense in their heads.

"Do you know who I am?" I ask, hinting at an answer not worth grappling with.

"Should I?" Crag asks, undeterred.

"Of course not," I scoff. "That's my point. Why treat strangers like this? What's to gain? In all likelihood, I'm just some poor farmer or peddler with nothing worth stealing."

Beneath the table, I open my purse. I pour some coins into my hand and set them in front of Crag.

"There," I say. "That's what I can part with it. You're richer now, and your generosity spares me starving. We all win. I hope it was worth your time."

Crag doesn't take his eyes off my purse until it disappears back into my pocket. His friends widen their stances, digging their heels into the floor on both sides of the bench.

"And if you're not some poor farmer or peddler?" Crag asks, leering up at me.

I frown and look at him very seriously, promising him something grave.

"It's not worth it," I warn. "You boys aren't soldiers. Don't play at it. Take your winnings. The wise man fights only when he needs to, which is almost never."

"The righteous man fights whenever he ought to," Crag retorts, sickeningly haughty. "Which is almost always."

"Well..." I sigh, putting out my hands, exasperated. "I guess we've found the difference between wise and right. That's enough for a night, isn't it?"

The one I think is called Reaper grabs my shoulder and tries pulling me to my feet. Fine. Who doesn't appreciate help getting up. I lift my feet over the bench, then kick it towards the table, tangling Rover and Reaper's legs. They trip and hit their faces against the floor.

Crag scurries over the top of the table with a roar, drawing his sword as his friends fumble for theirs. Seems extreme. Crag pounces at me, so I duck, and he spills himself across the empty table behind me. Terrible. It'd be a shame if we broke anything. It's a splendid inn.

Rover and Reaper swipe at me clumsily with untended, rusty blades. Their ineptitude amuses me. With every miss, they nearly stumble to the floor, closer to wounding themselves than their target. A thrust from Rover misses me so badly I have to keep it from maiming Reaper. Reaper rewards my courtesy with a kick in the back.

I catch my balance on the stairs. Rover and Reaper chase me up to the overlook, hacking and scratching the nice wood of the walls. I lower my head, and Rover crashes his sword deep into a door, trapping himself. Reaper ducks under his friend's arm. With a shrill, warrior's scream, he misses me so badly he loses his sword and dives headlong over the railing.

I snatch Reaper by the back of his belt before he falls and breaks his neck, bracing myself against the rail. Just as I begin pulling his thrashing, idiot body to safety, I see Rover give up tugging his sword and charge at me. I kick him in the chest, but it costs me my equilibrium, and Reaper's flailing pulls me over the railing with him.

Long drops always end sooner than you expect. I shift in the air just enough to save Rover, but I can't do anything for the table beneath us. We crash through it, and I'm not even done groaning before Rover is on top of me and launching ungrateful fists into my face. Much more concerning is Reaper, leaping off the balcony, hoping, I can only imagine, to impale us both with his sword. I guess he managed to pull it out of the door.

I roll backwards and out of the way, pulling Rover with me. Reaper drives his sword into the floor. Naturally, it's stuck again. Just then, I feel a gust of air. I step sideways before Crag can blindside me, but his blade manages to nick my cheek. If it leaves a mark, I'll have to make up a better story than this one.

Crag and his comrades gather themselves, swelling with arrogance as I backpedal. They're oblivious to my spear on the floor behind me. A couple of paces and I feel it on my heel. I kick it up over my head and into my hands, and before Crag and his crew have even shifted their weight forward, I level the three of them with one swing. They're unconscious when they hit the floor. It's over.

I feel pride course through me as I look upon my defeated foes. The heft of my spear feels right in my hands, my muscles tingle with reignited purpose. Bit by bit, reality seeps in. I notice the sweat streaming down my brow. I feel the pathetic wheeze of my lungs straining for air. I see the pointless impoverishing of an inn keeper's business, home, and life.

I turn my head and find the poor man looking upon the wreckage with terror and bewilderment. I clear my throat, prodding him from his trance.

"Don't think I'll stay tonight," I say, looting Crag and his friends for whatever ill-gotten gains they have between them. I set the little pile on the inn keeper's desk.

"Tell them I took it," I advise him with a wink. It's not all lie. Half-truths are easier, after all.

I pull up my hood and head back into the night.

Inn Keeper

I've seen a lot of fights. It's the business I've chosen. I serve drinks, discipline fades, and men become themselves. Women too, though not as often. People hide their impulses until it makes them sick, and then they come to my inn for the medicine. Sometimes I take a profit, sometimes I take a loss. I'm not sorry. Or proud, really.

I'm right on the edge of a profit now, depending on what this Crag fellow and his friends elect to do from here. They were unconscious through the night. They've been awake a little while, going over their damage, no doubt suffering hangovers much worse than I could give them. I figure odds are they lick their wounds and move on. They might try to recoup their losses by robbing me, but it takes a lot of sand to try that so soon after a pummeling. And that certainly was a pummeling.

I hear my door swing open. I don't bother to look.

"Closed," I say. I don't strain the point. Everyone who's come in for a look has got the idea pretty quickly all on their own.

Suddenly, Crag and his friends scramble to their feet. They straighten their backs and raise their chins like tidy upstanding citizens. Something's worth turning my head, I suppose.

Right at my entrance, I find Princess Reznick herself. I'm stunned. She's small, smaller still with her hunch, but it's that dangerous sort of small, the small Crag fancies himself. Even just standing there, even with that little frame, it feels like there's a restless ocean in her, pushing, pulling.

"What happened here?" she asks, her voice slithery and seething.

No one wants to answer her. No one sane would. Crag speaks up, snapping from a daze.

"A rebel visited here and incited a conflict," he says officiously. How he deduced the man last night was a rebel, I can't imagine. I suppose all of Crag's enemies are rebels.

"Oh?" The Princess tilts her head as she advances, interest piqued.

"My associates and I questioned him," Crag blathers, encouraged. "We attempted to detain him."

She evaluates Crag, rightly dubious.

"A citizen's arrest," he assures her. "He ambushed us."

That's one perspective, I suppose. I'd laugh if I weren't so afraid.

The Princess approaches Crag. He stiffens, averts his eyes. She looks him over, hunting for something particularly annoying to justify her contempt. She settles on his tattoo.

"Wipe that blasphemy off," she utters with venom. Crag's hand shoots to his shoulder like that might do it.

The Princess turns away from Crag, terribly bored and unimpressed. She moves for the door. Evidently, Crag wants more from the encounter.

"He was one of the Nameless," he blurts out.

The Princess whips around and is within an inch of Crag so quickly he very nearly retreats a step.

"You know this how?" she asks.

I wonder about this myself. Our man hardly fit the mould. For one thing, he had hair on his head. For another, fat on his body. The Nameless would sleep in a ditch before an inn, and they'd happily slit the throats of any loyals that crossed them. I don't know who the man last night was, but he did all he could not to harm the lot of us. He wasn't Nameless.

"Was he bald?" The Princess turns her attention my way, surmising I'm more reliable. "Did he wear the shrouds?"

I shake my head quietly.

"He wielded a spear." Crag rises up, defensively. It could be true. We never got a look at what was under the sheath. "He was big and monstrous."

Crag lets his ridiculous suggestion linger in the air. We all know who he means, but I don't know how he could dare think it. I suppose last night would be a little less demeaning. In time, surviving Ruthless might even be something to brag about.

After entertaining the possibility for a moment, Princess Reznick sags. She shakes her head in disgust and makes for the door, sensing her time has been thoroughly wasted.

"We could identify him," Crag offers, dreading the end of his brush with renown. "If you took us with you."

"I'd recognize him," she promises bitterly.

"My lady, please!"

In a life I'm sure is busting at the seams with stupid decisions, Crag tops them all. He reaches for Princess Reznick, and his fingers graze her shoulder. The outrageous offence shoots a bolt of panic through me. Just as quickly, some ugly point drops out from the Princess's dangling sleeve.

She delivers judgement and sentence. She pierces Crag a half-dozen times before he staggers backwards, clutching at his gut like he has some chance at keeping the blood in.

"Peasant filth!" The Princess spits, positively shaking with fury and revulsion.

Crag falls into the arms of his friends. Somehow, as I look into his paling face, I swear he has the gall to feel jilted.

CHAPTER 8: FON THE PONY

Snow

The Nameless are nomadic in practice. We never lodge anywhere long. Consequently, we can be difficult to gather when the situation calls for it. Often, important assignments fall to the most available rather than the most capable. Today, I count myself among the former.

We were camped for training a mile or so away from a distinguished horsemaster's stable. There were ten of us. Things had been quiet a long time when word reached our troop that we might have a chance at the young Princess Reznick. Apparently, she and her father would soon be visiting the stable. She was to have her pick of a litter of ponies.

This was a rare opportunity. Young gods seldom left palaces. They were hardly ever vulnerable. Once gods are grown, they're far too potent for us to dream of killing. If we had any hope of wiping out the line, we had to attack the young. Gods do not proliferate easily. If we could keep a new generation from coming of age, then time would defeat the old for us. We had to take the long view.

We weren't a promising bunch. I'd only just won my moniker, and I was the first to do it. They call me Flurry now. It still sounds slight. I knew I wasn't likely to escape Snow completely, but I'd hoped for something fiercer. Still, it sets me a cut above my fellows. Greatness was never expected of us. It's required now.

They're sending Master Terra to lead the strike. I've heard Old Fat's coming with her. No, that's wrong. He won a moniker. I heard he got to pick it. *Rufus*. I wonder what it means. I haven't seen him since Mud...

I never liked Mud. He was skilled, as skilled as I was, but gifted in all the ways I was lacking. He was strong. Fast. Vicious. For all those reasons that had nothing to do with work or effort, he was top of the class, and I was bottom. I resented him.

I don't really know why he hated me, though. I like to flatter myself by believing he was threatened by me in some way. He saw my technique and envied it. Maybe that's arrogant or naive. The strong always hate the weak. They must. It has nothing to do with jealousy. People love their power for what it wins them. We find virtue in what we love. If power is virtue, weakness must be vice.

I quickly forgave that last beating Mud gave me. It was the way, his right as my better. If I could not abide his wrath, it was on me to raise myself up and push it back. But Old Fat... Old Fat learned a different way in his years before the Nameless. I was precious. To him, I was something so much more than himself, something apart from the laws that ruled baser things. You could have done absolutely anything to him, and it'd have been nothing to a single finger laid on me.

Mud had taken on a debt by busting my lip and blackening my eye, a debt he couldn't balance even with his life. I couldn't sleep that night in my cot. I was waiting. I wondered if Mud was awake too. I wondered if he knew what might be coming, if he felt the same trepidation I did. He must have. But if he did, why not run? Why not hide?

At the very hour we would get up to do all our labour and toil, I heard Old Fat rise from the floor. I watched from my cot, paralyzed. I'd never seen so hard a look on so young a face. In my head, I screamed at him to look at me, as if the dismay in my eyes might beat down the vengeance inside him. He was set.

Despite all my silent pleading, Mud didn't budge all the

time Old Fat crept towards him. When Old Fat reached down at him, something stirred. Mud had been plotting. He stabbed at Old Fat with a long bit of sharpened bone. He wasn't quick enough. He'd never learned to fight off his back.

After the first attempt failed, Mud scrambled and sliced at Old Fat. Old Fat caught his hand, smothered a pillow over his face, and broke his wrist like a twig. I barely heard Mud's muffled scream, but the clatter of the makeshift knife on the floor and the sickening snap of bone were so loud I was sure it'd wake everyone in the tent. If it did, no one dared do anything about it.

Old Fat pulled the pillow away and covered Mud's mouth, nose, nearly all his face in a single hand. Mud kicked and struggled all he could, but Old Fat had a hold of him. Old Fat carried him into the night. Finally, I rose from my cot and hurried after them, more afraid for Mud than I could ever be for myself.

Old Fat dragged Mud so easily I could hardly keep pace. In a dark spot where the trees hid us from the moon and stars, far enough that no one could hear, Old Fat hurled Mud toppling into the dirt. Mud was to his feet quickly, fighting with a desperation so certain it haunted me. We were on the threshold of something I didn't want to put a name to.

The fighting was for nothing. Mud was an infant to Old Fat. An injured one. Old Fat swatted him down with an open hand. It was so mighty I shivered. I realized then I hadn't seen Old Fat strike anyone in ages, maybe never with spite.

Mud clawed at the grass, tried to crawl away. His shirt tore when Old Fat grabbed at it, and that won him a couple seconds of reprieve. I wanted so badly for him to yell for help at the top of his lungs. Maybe he was too proud. Maybe he reasoned it wasn't worth angering Old Fat. Maybe he couldn't speak for all the same reasons I couldn't.

I didn't find my voice until Old Fat grabbed Mud in both hands. "Stop," I said. I'm sure I did. It didn't matter. All the fists my brothers and sisters had been spared rained down on Mud. He was dead before Old Fat was halfway finished with him.

Old Fat knew I was there. He had to. But he never said

anything to me. Never even looked at me. He hurled what once was Mud over his shoulder like a sack and carried him out far enough that only wolves and buzzards would find him. I waited. I wanted Old Fat to look in my face and see the wrong he had done, how completely he had forsaken me. But he walked straight past me to the tent. He went right back to that place on the floor where he slept.

I couldn't understand it. It was like this calamity committed in my honour had nothing to do with me. Old Fat, who would do anything Master Terra commanded, would not have heard a single plea from me, despite all my kindness, all my charity.

It took my meeting other great warriors to see the truth of it. He was grateful, but he was powerful now, so powerful, and he hated weakness in turn. As he saw it, only weakness could have saved Mud. Old Fat would have done any cruel thing I asked. If I wanted him to do even worse to Mud or anyone else who wronged me, he'd have done it in a breath. Yet he wouldn't be kind. He would never be kind again.

Now, I look on those cold days with regret. Turning my back to him served nothing. He loved me in his way. He wanted my approval, only drawing the line at degrading himself. He could only do what he believed was right. We were both committed to goods that were high and pure in our hearts, differing though they may be. Perhaps our dreams for the world weren't so irreconcilable. Maybe, with time, I might have shaped him into something generous and forgiving. Maybe he could have looked on the small and tender things of this life with affection.

Or maybe he'd have changed me. Maybe the irresistible force of his will would have made me a weapon like all the others. When I picture that Snow, I do not miss Old Fat. There is nothing I fear so much as unbecoming myself.

✼ ✼ ✼

It's night when Rufus and Master Terra arrive. We've been standing by eagerly. Soon as we spot Master Terra, we all leap to our feet. My brothers and sisters crane their necks for the best view. Master Terra is well known, much admired, and utterly irrelevant. We all look past her.

There he is. Rufus. I'm struck by how easily I recognize him. He was so young the last time we were together, and he's changed so much. Yet he's still the boy I knew somehow. His height, his frame, his demeanour are all transformed, but something essential prevails. He's nothing like he used to be, but exactly like I expected he'd be.

I try to position myself so that he may see me. I don't know if we'll have much time to talk. I have so much to tell him. I want to say I'm sorry for turning from him all those years ago. I understand the hard parts of the world better now. It was no betrayal, what you did. You served me the only way you knew how.

He sees me. For a moment, I worry he might not notice me, that our diverging paths have led us too far apart. Then his eyes flash. He is still my Old Fat, and I am still his Snow. He knows me right away, and I am delighted.

He is not. It's not with anger that he looks away from me. It's pain. He recalls the sting of my rejection. I've forgiven him. He does not forgive me. He hardens, and that fundamental decency I recognized in him disappears. He becomes Rufus again, that ferocious man I've heard so much about but do not know.

Terra

There was a time when I'd worry for my brothers, my sisters, or even my own neck. Then there was Rufus. In matters of war, he is my chief triumph. I thought he was brutal with his fellows until I set him on his enemies. He kills so easily, maybe even more easily than he intends. In the heat of battle, I don't often have time to carefully watch him do his work. Even so, the sounds of it are unmistakable. Sharp, dry fractures. Brief, petrified screeches. Moist sucking sounds.

His genius has afforded him curiosity. He is investigative,

probing. He presses the limits of his strength against the endurance of metal, bone, and flesh. Whatever he sets himself against, he finds wanting. I've seen him tear limbs off of people as easily as petals from a flower. I've watched him collapse suits of armour and the bodies behind them flat as paper. It'd be perverse if it weren't so callous. He has such control. I've never witnessed acts so bloody performed so bloodlessly.

His fame is spreading. It's becoming clear Rufus isn't moniker enough. Many young, fresh faces greet him with some extra title when they meet him. Rufus the Great. Rufus the Conquerer. Rufus the Brutal. Some dare address him by a different moniker entirely. The Blight is most common among the aggressive and excitable. The Balance is popular among the cloying and idealistic. I suppose Rufus is a different man to different people. In any case, he does not suffer these flatterers lightly. He corrects them quickly and severely, cuts them deep without even raising his voice. They do not misspeak twice.

Even now, his devotees steal glances at him. Rufus is down in the dead leaves below with the other men too big to sit on branches. We're on a wooded hill, looking down on a winding road. The intelligence was correct. Our scout confirmed it. A mile out, he saw them: Darnett and his girl on a little holiday at a rich lord's stable. She liked the animals, had a happy, laughing time running around fields and climbing trees. We're in trees too. We aren't laughing.

I can feel Rufus's readiness even from here. He's made a point of not looking at Flurry. Perched in the tree next to mine, she strains herself keeping one eye on him and one on the road. I wonder if she'd tell me what happened between them. It's always such a temptation to talk in these quiet, waiting places. We never do.

A couple of good-looking men on even better-looking horses come around the bend. They're all four of them so clean and groomed they almost shine. The gods use scouts as well. These men check the road for traps. They're in luck. We haven't laid any. It's good work if you can get it.

Following the scouts are a dozen men, marching in a harmonious rhythm. I imagine them glaring jealously at the scouts, who must be so comfortable in their saddles, but they are soldiers through and through. They carry their spears and colours with equal, unyielding pride.

Behind the soldiers, two lesser men walk on either side of a pony, leading it along by its halter. It's a useless, ridiculous creature, with stubby legs and braided hair. The Nameless don't use horses. Too loud, unreliable, and difficult to maintain. Their aptitudes do not suit us, but at least they present some value. Ponies are another thing entirely. They can not carry, and they hardly run. They're suitable only for the fleeting pleasure of the young, idle, and easily thrilled.

Taking up the rear, finally, is the royal carriage. It's a gilded, glimmering eyesore, coated in stones and metals as durable as they are precious. It takes four rugged horses to drag it, even on this dusty road. It'd be utterly impenetrable, a rock on wheels, if not for the windows on its sides, each guarded by mounted officers, armour on horseback.

I see our target then, hanging halfway out the window, reaching to pet the horse riding next to her. You're a silly, spoiled girl, Reznick. If you stayed in your cart, you'd be safe. Your father permits you too much. If I can tell someone to shoot down that guard, I'll have a clean shot at you. I'll have to be quick.

I turn to signal my plan to Flurry. Both her eyes are on Rufus now. He's sprinting down the hill, berzerk. One scout spots him. It doesn't do him much good. Rufus skewers him with one quick thrust from Penance, lifting him off his horse.

Chaos erupts. The horses rear up, the soldiers ready their arms, the carriage closes its windows. I'm furious. My shot, any shot, disappears. What are you doing, Rufus? There are still more than a dozen trained men between you and Reznick, not to mention Darnett himself. You won't get to her. The glory won't be yours. Are you mad, or selfish, or both?

Our ground forces barrel down to join the melee. Rufus has killed the other scout already. The two riderless horses stomp and kick, inconsolably distressed. Rufus lets loose a primal howl at the closing soldiers, and his brothers and sisters join him without a thought to the danger. They welcome it. They welcome our murder.

They fight. Through the tangle of swinging limbs and weapons, I see light, orange and bright. I see curved, twisting horns framing an odious, gleaming scowl. It's Prince Darnett, walking with intent as though to quash a nuisance. He's fat, nearly spilling out from the robes he probably had made when he was less swollen. In one hand, he holds the little fingers of his daughter Reznick. In the other, he carries a torch.

He stops by the frightened pony and gestures for Reznick to hold it still by the reins. Gently, as though assuring her it's only temporary, he releases his daughter and raises an open palm to the torch. Embers hop off the flame and onto his fingertips like faithful pets. Lovingly, he lowers them down to the leaves and grass at his feet. They feast hungrily and grow rapidly.

Darnett takes back his daughter's hand and marches forward, a new inferno draping him like some immense cape, beautiful and fearsome. With an indifferent flip of his fingers, a wall of fire rushes out like a lake surging out from a broken dam and falls upon Nameless and loyal alike. It gobbles flesh and clothing, ignoring bark and foliage, a rich man hustling to dessert. In their screams, friends and enemies are united.

Arrows from our archers strike out from the trees at Darnett, but an orange curtain passes over him and the Princess, so thick and hot it burns the projectiles to useless dust. The fire explodes out into the air, and the canopy of leaves above us bursts into colour, a sunset in the deep of night. I leap out from my tree in time to see Flurry dissolve in an instant, like she was never there at all.

"Rufus!" I call, searching, warning. I have to reach him before he engages and dies for nothing. He'll retreat if I tell him. The others will follow.

I find him among a pile of collapsed rib cages and shattered skulls, serene and wet with loyal blood. He hasn't been seen. He watches Darnett, transfixed. Without ever averting his gaze, he approaches me, creeping, trying to maintain his invisibility. Good.

"Retreat!" I scream as loud as I can. No one hears me over the crackling and burning. Before I can repeat myself, I feel Rufus's huge paw fall over my mouth. He's never disobeyed me before. Not once.

I fight and struggle as he pulls me down into the mud and shadows off the path. He smothers me, laying over my back. He wants to stay? Why? What is he waiting for? What could be worth enduring this disaster?

He watches Darnett burn the whole forest down. Nothing is safe but Reznick, the pony, and the carriage. The fire dares not harm things so precious. I shut my eyes, bury my face into the crook of Rufus's elbow, and wait for it all to end.

*   *   *

It's morning when Rufus climbs off me, ash falling off his back like dust blown off some ancient relic. The green of life and the red of fire have left this place completely. Grey pollutes the air and ground. What few trees remain are withered and wretched, their vast trunks hollowed, their bare branches reaching into the bleary sky like pleading hands.

Strewn about the ground with me are my brothers and sisters. Some still smoke like burnt meat. Some are scorched black so completely only bones and melted metal possessions remain. My clean, cool flesh offends me. Rufus at least has pink and purple blotches scattered about him.

He reaches down gently to help me up. I shake him off. With all the patience in the world, he gives me space. I sit in the ash for a moment. There's so much of it. It reminds me of a beach.

"Why?" I finally ask, my voice frail. "We could have run. We could have fallen back. We could have saved lives. Not all. But some!"

He doesn't say a word. I shoot to my feet and shove him in the chest, hoping to move him one way or another.

"Or we could have fought!" I bellow, finding my hardness. "Maybe we'd have been lucky! We could have had the girl! Maybe you could have wounded the Prince, or scarred him, or at least harmed him a little. At least we could have died honourably with our brothers and sisters instead of watching them burn!"

My voice quavers. I stop before I humiliate myself further. Rufus waits respectfully until he's sure I'm finished.

"I know how to kill Darnett," he says, bluntly and definitively.

CHAPTER 9: THE GREAT HEALER

Small

I'm beginning to understand why Rufus fled Paralee in the deep of night. Elizabeth is… willful. She's very difficult to say no to. We disagreed on everything when I first arrived: incoming weather, Bandit's behaviour, treatment for ailments. Yet time proved her right again and again. She's difficult to hide anything from. She sees through smoke to true motives so easily. She wears you down.

    I'm at her table now. I've seen her help countless townsfolk with their little scratches and maladies here. Nothing so serious as the wound on my arm. She cuts through the strange plaster cast she installed, and I ready myself for all sorts of abhorrent shapes and colours. I've seen amputations. An arm isn't so important. You can still fight with only one of them. Master Terra fought better than I did. Nameless may still contribute whatever their capabilities. Once, I saw one of my sisters shoot an arrow by laying on her back and holding a bow with her feet. She pulled the string back with her teeth. I could learn that. The Nameless would celebrate my resilience.

    Elizabeth cracks open the cast and exposes my skin. It's fresh, soft, and pale. She purses her lips, too unsurprised to be gratified.

    "You're welcome," she tells me, rising from her seat and heading for the kitchen, leaving me dumbfounded.

I stretch out my fingers then make a fist. I roll my shoulder and turn my elbow, all without pain. I measure my arms against each other to see if one has shrunk or stunted. They're the same save for complexion and cleanliness.

I'm fine. Better than fine. I'm suddenly aware I've never been so well. I could leave right now, refreshed and well rested, and hurl myself into the fray. I could serve better than I ever have. Maybe I could catch up with Rufus. If I didn't stop, if I pressed the whole way, maybe I'd find him. I could run all day and through the night. At this moment, I'm sure I could. He could teach me all his methods and secrets until we reached Hospice, and we could share a victory that would echo through the ages.

Elizabeth returns, gathering up off the table the little tools of her fine work. I look down and find myself on my feet in the middle of the room. She picks up the chair I toppled shooting to my feet. I clear my throat and try to beat down my childish elation. She's polite enough to ignore me.

I realize I haven't thanked her. She has given me my life back, restored all my potential and possibilities. All I could be, I may be.

Guilt floods my senses. It occurs to me that in all my grand plans, there's nothing that would please her. I've never pleased her. All my life, I've only ever been as valuable as I was productive. She's done this uncommon, priceless thing for me, and what have I done for her? If I've protected her at all, it's been the protection the warden provides the prisoner. I trespassed on her world without asking, changed all her plans, forced a toll on her she'd never have paid willingly.

Say I helped Rufus. Say, thanks to me, he freed the Nameless and came home. What would that be to her? How could he help but bring war home with him? Could they stay here? Would they have to pick up and leave, try to make the life they want elsewhere? Would the kingdom permit them? Would the Nameless? So why help me? What could it promise her but defeat?

She could have killed me. She could have poisoned me, or

let my arm fester, or done any of a million things. The kingdom may have praised her for it. That'd have been the end of the Nameless, the death of the grim apprehension lingering in her life. She could have chased Rufus down and made him come home. He said she could do it. I believe him now that I've lived with her.

Instead, here I stand. I finally see her goodness, and it's like dark clouds have parted to reveal a bright sun. There was no thought of self in the gift she gave me. It did nothing for the world she wanted. She has breathed life into her enemy. I am indebted, and I've no idea what I can do that might repay her.

Just then, frantic banging at the door. Elizabeth gestures for me to hide with a tilt of her head, and I oblige. I keep a hand ready on my belt knife's handle as she opens the door. She finds the brutes from the market, faces so sweaty and frightened I hardly recognize them. Crag's arms are slung over the shoulders of his two lackeys. He's barely conscious and positively mangled.

"What happened?" Elizabeth asks, cutting calmly through the urgency in the air.

"He's been wounded," one of them says unhelpfully, huffing.

She waves them in and towards the table. As they enter the house, I slip out. I lose sight of them for a moment on my way to a window I can peer in from outside. Crag's lackeys drop him down roughly on the table.

Elizabeth pulls at Crag's clothes to get a better look at the damage. It's even worse than it initially appeared.

"I need the two of you to listen to me very carefully," she tells his friends, severe but unafraid. "I need water, needle, and thread to start."

The goons scramble. One dashes outside for the well. I adjust my spot. Looking through another window, I see the other fumble about the armoire, pulling out drawers and pouring out their contents.

"Top shelf! In the front!" Elizabeth calls impatiently, trying to pick where to start from a myriad of bleeding holes.

The fool grabs everything he can and dumps it near Elizabeth. The table and floor get most of it, but Crag is not immune. Elizabeth grunts then shoves a rag in her supposed helper's hands while she digs through the mess. The man dabs and wipes at Crag.

"What are you doing?!" Elizabeth groans. "Both hands on the wound. Press. Hard!"

A gurgling gasp wheezes from Crag. Elizabeth finds what she's looking for on the floor, but the forgotten assistant arrives sprinting with the water. He trips and inundates the room. Elizabeth slips a little before finding her feet. She checks on Crag. Panic streaks across her face.

"Hey!" she exclaims, slapping Crag repeatedly on the cheek.

His head falls back. The gurgling stops. One of his friends tries pressing his rag against a different wound. The other uses his boot to try and steer the water on the floor somewhere more out of the way. Elizabeth hardly moves. She grabs Crag's wrist for a customary check of the pulse, expecting nothing, finding nothing. His friends are much slower to comprehend, but they arrive there with time.

CHAPTER 10: BAD MEN NEVER LOOK SO TIRED

Clyde

I swear, Henry, you're slower every day. You call yourself a horse? We have too little time to waste. I'm doing enough getting old for the both of us. If you don't pick up the pace, I'll be heaving bags off this cart into the night.

Who's this? There's a body. Bigger than you, Henry. He'd unload the cart in a minute and probably pull us home faster with you on his back. Wouldn't that be something?

He gives us a wide berth as we come near him. Maybe I gave him too much credit. He looks tired just dragging his bones. Real tired. He's leaning hard on that big stick of his. What's under that sheath? Gods, has he ever slept? Ever seen the inside of a home? Still, look at those legs. Look at those arms. Some food and rest and he'd be a worldbeater.

"You look like you've seen a thing or two," I say. "Long night? Hmm?"

"Many more to go," he says with that kind of politeness that tells me he doesn't really want to talk.

"Don't see many nice folks like yourself coming through these parts," I say, leaning towards him like I got a secret special just for him. "Want to know how I know you're nice?"

"My clean clothes?" he offers half-heartedly, nodding his

head down at the mess of mud with bits of fabric covering him from the neck down. I laugh.

"Bad men never look so tired," I explain, proud of my wisdom. Wisdom is better when it's short and digestible like that. Priests and poets draw everything out so long you lose the thread. I should write a book. A short one. "Nothing wearies a man like kindness punished. Name's Clyde." I wait for a response. "You got one?"

"Nope."

There's no meanness in his voice. I can see him grow a little impatient. He hasn't taken his eyes off the road ahead. Maybe he doesn't like how narrow it's getting.

"How mysterious," I tut playfully. "I don't believe you. Always liked Robert. You look like a Robert. I'll call you Robert."

Robert winces a little as Henry sniffs at him. He have something against horses? Well, he must not be much of a farmer, or soldier, or bandit, or much of anything, really.

"Where ya headed, Robert?" I continue. I don't mind carrying more than my share of a conversation. I don't carry my share in much of anything else anymore.

"Down this road," he says. Ha!

"Well, isn't that something?" I exclaim, playing at astounded. "Me too! Favour an old man with some company?"

I slide down my seat a little and pat the spot next to me enticingly. A bit of rest has to be priceless to him.

"Thank you," he says very graciously. "But no."

"Come on now," I moan. As with all things, persistence is key. "Let Henry here carry you a bit."

"I don't get along with horses," he says.

"What?" I gasp. "What's not to like about horses? Man's real best friend. A dog never carried man across nations! Civilization was built on the backs of horses. We'd never have done a thing without them. We'd have been too beat from walking everywhere."

Suddenly, Henry swings his big dumb head at Robert. Henry lands flush but only knocks Robert sideways a step. I cluck my tongue at Henry and pull on his reins a little. Robert, so very considerate, steps off the road and deeper into the tall grass. The ugly sound of his wet steps fills me with remorse.

"I mostly mean horses don't get along with me," he explains, trying to let me off the hook. That's charitable of him.

"Sorry about that," I say. "He's usually gentle."

It reflects so poorly on a man when his animals misbehave. It lowers the whole species when creatures disrespect us. I'd give Henry a walloping if it didn't tucker me out more than it did him.

"Come on," I say, humbled. "I owe you something now. I'll be straight with you, Robert. I'm getting old, and I'm shaking at the thought of unloading this cart. There it is. I could use a hand. I have a meal and a bed for you if you're interested."

Robert's stomach groans so loud I feel the earth quaking. I have to laugh.

"A man can go without rest or women, but the gods help you if you get between a hungry belly and a full plate!" I yell skyward. Another one for the book.

I slow Henry to a stop. Robert walks ahead a couple of steps, but his stubbornness fades.

"You'd be doing me a service," I tell him.

Robert takes a wide arc around Henry then climbs up my cart. I slide over a bit more. This bench I'm on could fit a family, but Robert's practically hanging off of it to leave me cozy.

I snap my reins, but Henry doesn't budge. He looks over his shoulder at me, reprimanding me for adding to his burden.

"He does not like you…" I mutter to poor Robert, frustrated. I snap the reins again and again.

Only a pinch dejected, Robert climbs off the cart.

"I'll follow behind," he says reassuringly.

Soon as Robert's feet hit the dirt, the cart jerks forward. Henry trots with unbecoming glee, delighted to be free of what is apparently his most hated enemy. Not very hospitable.

❋ ❋ ❋

If ever there was a man born to move heavy things from one place to another, it was Robert. By the time I was done unbuckling Henry and walking him to his stable, the cart was unloaded, and Robert was ready for more.

In my many years, I've generally learned to dread unexpected things. You learn quickly to plan for bad luck. You can't know when it's coming. You have to plan for storms, droughts, fires, sickness. 'Expect the worst, and you'll never be disappointed,' will be the first line in my book. Or maybe 'What might go wrong, will go wrong.' I haven't decided.

So, you can see why Robert was quite a pleasant surprise. Whatever the opposite of a storm is, that's what he was. A breeze. A breeze on a hot day. He came upon the farm and blew into every crevice, making things better wherever he could. He pulled out stumps. He fixed walls. He ploughed fields. He was hungry for ways to help.

After a morning that accomplished the work of a month, I was sure we'd earned a banquet for dinner. I conferred with my wife Myra, and she couldn't wait to get started. We don't entertain much. Opportunities to indulge her hostly fantasies are few and far between.

After a bit of fretting, she established goose would be best, and I pretended I knew enough to confirm the rightness of her conviction. I walked out into the yard and told Robert all about it. He begged us not to strain ourselves. I knew he would. Good men never take on debt without a struggle, no matter how much they're owed.

He fought me all the way to the pen. The trick, it turned out, was to ask his help. We were having goose tonight, and all that was left to discuss was how much I'd be troubled. When I asked him to grab the bird for me, he obliged. It thrashed and honked in his hands, but it didn't stand a chance against those big mitts of his.

We went to the shed, and the goose's throes found new heights of frenzy. I guess it knew what was coming. Before I could even find my cleaver, I heard a little snap behind my back, and silence came to us like a welcome friend.

I turned around to thank Robert, but there was something in him that shut me right up. Something mournful. He must have been city folk, I surmised. Death is a matter of course on a farm, and an end so clean was the best the goose could hope for if it hoped at all. He spared it something worse. That didn't seem to soothe him much.

He set the goose down on my table, and I shooed him away so that I could finish the work. To my surprise, he didn't argue. Left to myself, I couldn't help but laugh. All that muscle, and he had none of the heart to put it to its purpose. There was a day a man like Robert would have done nothing but hunt, fight, and kill. He'd be loved for it. Now, these comfortable times have mellowed even the barbarians. Isn't that the way? Everybody wants meat, no one wants to know where it came from.

CHAPTER 11: THE FIRST RECKONING

Terra

It's odd seeing Rufus in chains. It's hard to believe they'd slow him any, save for the couple seconds it'd take him to break them. They might even serve him some if he resolved to escape. It's easy to picture those iron links around some hapless guard's throat. Yet there's a gesture at politeness in the way Rufus wears them, like a young man sporting nice clothes he hates to please an elder. He means to seem diplomatic, I think. He could overwhelm his captors, maybe even run, but there's something else he wants.

We're beside a towering bluff in the deep of night. Flickering orange light and whispers emanate from a cave we're waiting to enter. A very serious man with a mean face summons us in. Inside, we find three legends so grand they've earned sturdy wooden chairs to sit in. They're perched high to better loom over us.

This small council has come together to judge Rufus. These High Masters will determine our fate. They are Talon, Long Stride, and Clear Eyes. Their names don't suit them much anymore. Talon, once famous for nails sharp and hard enough to cut throats, is yellow and brittle everywhere now. Long Stride has shrunk and hunched. Even Clear Eyes, still so wise and so steady, watches the world from behind heavy lids with milky, foggy irises.

These three can not fight. Instead, they scheme, plot, and set young blood to the task. They haven't the stoutness between them of a student, but they command the swords of a thousand seasoned warriors. The charges they've placed on Rufus are desertion and cowardice. The punishment would be death. I fear it'd take every one of those thousand warriors they rule to carry out the sentence.

"You know why you're here?" asks Clear Eyes, grave and disappointed.

"Yes," Rufus answers flatly.

"What have you to say for yourself?" demands Clear Eyes. "How do you excuse standing by while your brothers and sisters died burning?"

"How do *you*?" Rufus asks plainly.

Suddenly, there's danger in the air. The mean-faced man sets his hand on his sword. It won't help him. Everyone in here is dead if Rufus wants it so.

Clear Eyes shifts a little in his seat. He didn't get where he is by panicking.

"Not easily," he answers. "It is the burden of our station, a station earned with trial and endurance. Sometimes, for a greater good, a price must be paid."

"But not by you," Rufus infers, nodding his head with understanding.

My mind races, searching for Rufus's intentions. Has he put himself in the presence of masters to topple them? Have I unwittingly made myself party to insurrection?

"Know your place!" bellows Long Stride, evidently not understanding his own. He pounds an infirm fist on the arm of his chair.

"Calm," Rufus tells Long Stride with dismissiveness. "There was a price to be paid. I couldn't be the one to do it. It bought us something."

"What's that?" asks Talon, scratching at her chin, intrigued.

Rufus looks to her. There's something almost lecherous in

his eyes, some wrong and evil secret tickling him.

"I saw him," he says, leaning towards Talon conspiratorially. "Darnett. I can kill him."

A hush falls upon the cave. We all scrutinize each other's faces for some cue to proceed. Long Stride crosses his arms with a haughty huff. Talon taps her nails uneasily. Clear Eyes leans forward with skeptical severity.

"I had to see him myself," Rufus continues, unabashed. "Stories weren't enough. I had to see him fight. People show you who they really are when they fight. I can get him."

"How?" Clear Eyes asks. The superiority and snobbishness have left his voice. He's willing to contemplate the notion that Rufus might have something for him.

"He doesn't make fire," Rufus explains with a sort of hushed, confident giddiness. "He only commands it. Fire is like any living thing. For it to be fierce, it needs to eat. In forests, at war, it has plenty. Wood, grass, clothes, flesh. In his home, there's nothing. Only his things. The rich love their things. He won't burn what he loves."

Rufus lets silence hang, but no one comes to the conclusion he intends. Clear Eyes leans back in his chair.

"We hit him where he lives," Rufus says, quietly and simply. "You raid First Morning."

The masters wait for more, the thought so absurd it demands annotation. Rufus says nothing, and their tutting and harrumphing begin.

"First Morning is a stronghold," says Long Stride. "It has stood for centuries. It has beat back armies."

"It's not made for war." Rufus shakes his head. "Not anymore. It's his home. It's like he is. Soft and complacent. It has every luxury. Servants. Sewers."

Rufus pauses for his implication to linger, but the old masters can't fathom it.

"Years ago, all throughout the grounds, they built tunnels," Rufus explains with impatient deliberateness. "To hide their waste. At the river, there's an opening for it all to drain. It's a few feet wide. Has to be at least that all the way. I'll fit on my belly with my spear. I'll follow it in. Past the walls. As deep as it'll take me."

All the masters but Clear Eyes swallow hard, suppressing wretches.

"Do the gods make waste?" asks Long Stride with the curiosity of a child.

"Of course they do," sneers Talon. "They eat, don't they?"

"Do they?"

"It doesn't matter," Rufus says, cutting curtly through the chatter. "The servants do. And the servants can never be too far from their lords."

"That river is an hour by horse," Talon exclaims with a scornful wave of her hand. "Two by foot."

"Probably four by crawl," Rufus shrugs.

"The drain could crowd and clog," Clear Eyes utters sedately, gaze set unwavering on Rufus.

"I'll break through."

"There could be enormous distances where there's no air at all. Only water and filth."

"I'll hold my breath."

"What if the drain narrows? What if there's no way out?"

"I'll die."

No thought they can conjure deters Rufus in the slightest. He's foreseen it all. The masters can't look past the lowness of it. It is low. Unthinkably low. No person with any dignity or love of self would dare. That's exactly why it's possible.

"Send packs at the gates," Rufus continues. "Only those willing to die. Draw the standing forces and hold them off. Attack during the day. They'll have fewer torches lit. If I win, you'll hear. All the world will hear."

Clear Eyes sees it even if the others don't. There's something here. Sinking to such depths to finally scale so high... it'd be right, somehow.

"Clean yourself off before you fight him," Clear Eyes offers. "Waste will burn even if wet."

Rufus's lips tighten a little. He nods his head, grudging but grateful. Finally, a contribution.

Rufus

I hate going before the High Masters. I know their monikers. I've heard their stories. They have little else for me. They are capable of nothing but command everything. Let the qualified criticize me, my brothers and sisters who still know the war for what is rather than what it was. Master Terra and those like her.

I'm much more content here with her where we are now, wherever it is. These between places, the middles of nowhere we make camp, are home. This fire, this dark night, this alone feeling are familiar. There's tranquillity in the familiar.

Master Terra lays in the grass, her eyes on the stars overhead, pondering something or other. There's no pride in her. Nor is there excitement for what's to come. She is sombre, anticipating something inevitable and undesirable, like bad news about a missing friend. So be it. Let her stew. I have plenty to occupy myself. I'll shave my head.

I wet my scalp and ready a razor without so much as a word escaping either of us. I run the blade blindly across the back of my skull. She does nothing. I've seen her help so many of my brothers and sisters with the task. I've seen her snatch razors from clumsy, searching hands and do in an instant what was taking some amateur ages. She's never raised a finger for me. Not once. No matter how many times I cut myself.

I know what she's thinking about: the brothers and sisters I sacrificed to bring us here. I didn't know Snow would be there when Darnett burned us up. It shouldn't matter. I had to see him. I had to watch him. The price had to be paid by someone. It'd have been wrong to alter my plans because I knew these brothers and sisters better than I expected. That'd be weakness. Hypocrisy.

It wouldn't have accomplished anything to talk to Snow. She wouldn't have died any cleaner or happier. Maybe she thought less of me for a second when I barged in and exposed us. Maybe she was killed afraid instead of knowing and proud. It wouldn't have made the fire that consumed her any cooler. Being ready wouldn't have changed anything.

Maybe ignorance was better. Maybe it spared my brothers and sisters the ache of cowardice and doubt. It could be I saved Snow. Saved all of them. They had to die. I had to see. I'll beat Darnett now. If they could have known it with the certainty I do, they'd have volunteered. Lined up just like the forces making their way to First Morning. They couldn't know. They'd have doubted me. If they could see me when I really do it, they'd thank me. Everyone would. Everyone will.

"I didn't want this for you," Master Terra says, disturbing everything. Her words fall like a rock through still water.

My razor splits some skin on the side of my skull. I pretend it didn't happen. I've done it a thousand times, I'll do it a thousand more. I go on.

"I could tell it was doomed," she continues. "Nothing's going to hurt you like you've been hurt. You're always going to remember how things were. You had a home. You had love. You'll always know what's missing. It's too painful."

Pain is strength. The scrape of my blade along my scalp screeches in the silence.

"Everyone else… this is all we know. We never had a taste of any better. Wouldn't know what to do with it."

The same old refrain. She still doesn't see. She looks upon my aberrance as failing. Always has. Because I wasn't like the others, like her, I couldn't succeed. After all these years, she clings to a belief and rejects reality. She denies what's right in front of her. Like a fanatic. Like a loyal.

"I want you to leave."

My fist tightens around my razor as I lower it to rest near my thigh. I finally look at my master. I want her to beg forgiveness for spewing something so brazen. She knows what she's asking. A life's work. Endless hours. A future. A better world for us all. How can she not see what I might do?

"You can spare so many."

The razor drips my blood on the grass.

I wonder how she can be so hateful. I've seen her beam as others in her keep made the climb to prominence. Why does she deny me her regard, why does she refuse me my triumph? She should be the happiest master that ever lived. I am her defining work. All the world will one day know she made me. She wallows when she should rejoice.

I wipe my razor clean against my knee and tuck it away in my pocket.

"There's a fire in you," she says. "Eating its way out. I've fed it. I wish I hadn't. It's grown into something. Something magnificent. Something terrible. If we're not careful… it'll burn this whole world down."

I put my hands down low over the fire. Too low, low enough to grasp its colourful light. I feel the heat roll through my fingers and along my arms as I turn my wrists. I can hear my skin sear. It's nothing to me. I've been doing this since Penance, preparing. You can teach your body to tolerate anything with time. Darnett could open the pits of the earth and spill their molten lakes atop me, and I'd swim right through them on my way to him.

I want Master Terra to cower. I want her to envisage what I could do to her. I want her to know her life's at stake with this blasphemy she spews. But she's beyond afraid looking up at me. There's nothing I can do to shake her certainty in the prophecy she's laid before me.

I give her the simple, obvious truth, the one so many dare not confront:

"Maybe the world needs to burn."

Terra

First Morning, though not as populous or sprawling, is the equal of the Capital in many regards. The rich are similarly opulent and the poor are similarly miserable. In other respects, the cities are as different as the gods that rule them.

The Capital, where the King sits on his throne, was built to be the center of all things. It has roads and rivers, versatility and convenience. Its walls are as tall as mountains, and its gates big enough for ten ships to sail through at once. It can be a bustling market one day, and a fortress the next. It is as mighty and unassailable as the King himself.

First Morning is as much a symbol as it is a city, built on the sight of the battle from which it takes its name. On that holy land, the Royal Family beat back for all time the other dark and ancient races that sought to wipe the meek and humble from this land. So the story goes, anyway. It is a sacred place, which is to say impractical. Though once the seat of power, it has become glimmering and remote. It has forgotten its enemies. Now, it only knows splendour and prosperity by the grace of the Capital. It is where Prince Darnett makes his home.

I didn't know how many would come when we summoned Nameless to lay down their lives. I'd hoped for fewer. I have dozens of brothers and sisters here with me, maybe a hundred. The Nameless do not gather forces like these. We do our work in secrecy and shadow with far smaller numbers. Rufus has transformed us. Every able body for miles answered when he called.

I look around at all my kin so ready to die. In the young, always so eager to leave some mark sizable or terrible, I see delight. In the old, so tired and jaded, I see resignation. None doubt the necessity of their sacrifice. Such is Rufus's influence. He is believed in now. In defying gods, he has become a god. He is king of the kingless. These worshippers' lives are a small price for his glory.

I know now the reasons for our failures, why we could never match the Royal Family and its servants. In these men and women around me, I see insatiable ardour. All these individual hearts and minds have dissolved to nothing for the benefit of an ineffable and indefatigable force beyond their comprehension. In their devotion, they are stronger, stronger than I could ever have made them. As strong as the loyals that slaughter us.

    I want to tell them all to stop. I want to shake them from their fervour and tell them to go home. We serve no kings, we pray to no gods. I know Rufus better than any of them. I beheld who he was. He can fail. He might. Do not waste your lives in tribute to him. You are more than kindling for his pyre.

    I hold my tongue. As I say, I know Rufus better than anyone. I do not doubt that he may win us a substantial victory today. I only doubt its spoils.

    We charge the gates.

✽ ✽ ✽

These men guarding First Morning are no great warriors. With their beautiful armour and bejewelled weapons, they are talismans, not soldiers. But they have many advantages here. They know the terrain. They have numbers. They have the man they call the White Falcon.

    He is famous. He made his name obliterating Nameless in every corner of the kingdom with his greatsword Cleansing Rain. I had heard he'd won a post of some esteem and privilege here at First Morning. I had hoped it had softened him. No such luck. We have lost many good brothers and sisters to the White Falcon. At this rate, we'll lose many more.

    I see him above me, stalking a high wall, swatting incoming arrows aside like flies. He shines in the sunlight, almost blinding. I'm curious how he keeps his robes and the plumes on the mane of his helmet so resplendent given the blood he spills by the gallon. Maybe I'll ask him.

    He strikes down a very ambitious Pox with a single swing of Cleansing Rain, cleaving him nearly in two. He indifferently kicks what once was my student to the melee far below, clearing a path for himself. I scale the wall as he passes by, hoping I might catch him unaware. He senses me. He turns to meet me.

    His first swing misses. I'm better than Pox, at least. I have time to draw my sword. It's lighter and not nearly so well made as his. It won't hold back his blade, but it may still do him harm.

I had hoped I'd be quicker than him. I'm not. He moves his sword as smoothly as I do mine at twice or triple the weight. I've survived longer than most. Even that modest achievement is exhilarating. I feel like I can hear my brothers and sisters cheering me on as I slip around his precision strikes.

I plunge my blade forward. He evades it adeptly, turning and lifting Cleansing Rain high. He slices through my arm so easily I hardly feel it. I stare helplessly as my lifeless hand and everything else from my shoulder down tumble to the floor by my feet. He kicks me in the chest, and I fall off the wall. Darkness consumes me. I never even feel myself hit the ground.

Rufus

There is a way about things, a good and just way that guides objects to product and efficacy. It applies to all things, living or material, found or crafted. It sets one foot in front of the other and allows a man to walk. It's in the rain that falls and feeds the earth. It's in the wheel that turns and the mill that grinds. It is purpose and design.

Violence is visiting wrong upon right. Understand an object's design, see how it achieves its purpose, and you will discover how to harm your enemy. Know which way an arm ought to turn, and twist it the other. A smashed nose can not draw breath. Crushed fingers can not clutch weapons. Deny things their rightful purpose and they will be defeated.

Winning a fight requires meting out these little abominations upon your enemy. Winning a war requires a longer view. How does a river flow. How does a city eat. How does a populace manage its waste.

It's foul here where the drain meets the river, as it must be. First Morning is a place of incredible wealth, with plush halls clambering to best each other in lavishness. When a lord spends one hundred coin on a table, another must spend two. This wretched, poisonous place at which I stand is the real price of extravagance. Coin is only a symbol, an abstraction to ease the mind. The bill for decadence must be paid with stink and ugliness. You can only push it away so far. This river suffers for First Morning as the poor suffer for the rich.

I descend to the mouth of the drain and feel myself sink to my ankles in wet brown. I look into the black maw, listen to the melodic, creek-like trickle of the refuse. I tie off Penance on my back and flatten myself on my belly. I keep my chin high as I can, but I still feel dampness tickle the bottom of my jaw.

It takes me a moment to find the necessary movement. My first attempt catches Penance at the entrance. I sink deeper down, but then my elbows can't pass. Eventually, I tuck myself tightly enough to fit and move maybe an inch at a time.

An hour later, I'm ready to admit someone else may have been better suited to this task. Someone slenderer could have moved twice as quickly. A weapon smaller than Penance would have made a sprint of this crawl. I've no natural talent or aptitude for this. I didn't get where I am by ignoring my weaknesses. Others would have had an easier time if they had my will or endurance. But they don't. So here I am. Happily. I will withstand this. I am built for what comes next. Only I can kill Darnett. Only Penance can strike the blow.

I know I'm nearing my destination when turns and crossways emerge. Down each of them, I see flecks of light promising exits. I never waver. I will go straight as far as I can. The most direct path will always lead to the Royal Family. The world bends and curves to make way for them, not the other way around.

At the top of a steep climb, I reach a dead end and a trough big enough for me to crouch. A little above me, I see a cluster of holes less than a foot wide. Probably a washroom for servants. Only they would be denied privacy so completely.

I listen for unwelcome company. Nothing but distant, hurried steps and far-off commanding voices. The Nameless must be at the gates by now, hopefully occupying the bulk of the standing guard. A firm press above my head opens a latch just wide enough for me to climb my way out.

I'm in the light again, and I really see my own body for what feels like the first time. I'm squalid. I drip all over the brushed marble floor. My hands may never regain their original colour completely. My nails may forever be framed in black. They'll evoke tonight's memory every time I look down. I'll be glad for it.

I raise my eyes and take in the room. It's nice, I assume. Nice enough not to offend a god. At the end of the waste trough, I see a young woman in a crisp gown and headdress, both clean and well cared for. Whether it's love or fear of discipline that keeps them so tidy, I do not know. She's petrified, her eyes wide, her mouth agape and covered by both hands. She heard the combat and came here to hide, I'm sure. She couldn't have known this was where the real horror was.

She scurries past me. Or tries to. I snatch her before she makes the door. I pull her to the back of the room, muffling her screams with my fetid hand. She flails and squirms, claws at my arm, bites at my fingers... all the old stale tricks.

I sit down on the trough and make an anchor of myself. I lean back and hold her close, keep her kicking legs away from me. I'm very patient with her. I put myself in her place, imagine the smell, the shock, the fear. I don't know if she's a servant or a slave, loyal or oppressed. It doesn't matter. Either way, she has to be quiet. She has to heed my hushes.

She doesn't. I snap her neck. It's the merciful thing. Strength affords you mercy. Most would have strangled her or slit her throat. A broken neck is clean. Sudden. Leaves a nice body.

I consider hiding her in the trough. I spare her the indignity. I won't be here long enough for it to matter. Every alarm in the city is already ringing. I set her down gently and clean myself as best I can with the skirt of her dress.

"Margarette?" I hear a satiny voice call from outside. "Are you there? You needn't hide. You'll be safe with us."

Around the corner comes a glimmering mask, twisting

horns, and a bulging robe. It's Darnett. He freezes as if I've found him as good as naked in this billowy, flowing dress he wears. He's so close I see past the black pits of his mask and into the whites of his startled eyes. He has eyes. I know this now. He runs, and I follow.

I am ready. He is not. I am elated. He is afraid. He knows my advantage, but he doesn't know the depth of it. He doesn't know me. He doesn't know my righteousness. No one does. Righteousness untested is no righteousness, and the most righteous are the most tested. I have challenged myself relentlessly. I have held fire in my hands until its burn was nothing to me. I have lived in evil and pain. I have sipped venom so that my bite might poison. I am the villain's villain, fearsome and brutal, and my enemies will know evil more detestable than their own, unyielding and repugnant. I have calloused my hands, blackened my heart, and bloodied my face. I am the wind that carves the mountains and the sea that sculpts the shore. I am decay. If it takes me eons, I will reduce you, Darnett. Bit by bit.

He escapes into a room and slams the door shut. I am on you now. I will open you up. Whether light shoots out or black smoke, I will see you for all you are. Every piece of you. Bone, muscle, tendon, sinew, fat, and whatever else you're made of. You will be made fact. You will be known. And with that knowledge, I will rise to meet your brother, your father, and whatever else in this world carries your blood, name, or dreams.

I barge through the door and find a room worthy of him. Everywhere I look, I see the work of expert craftsmen. Furnishings. Animal hides. Art. On one end of the room, a fire burns bright in a hearth. On the other, Prince Darnett stands by his bed. If I keep him away from the fire, I'll win the day.

He knows it too. He sprints across the room, and he slides beneath the slice of my spear, more agile than I expect. Fine. Give me your best.

With a flourish of his hands, the fire spills out of the hearth like water and juts out at me in a thin straight line. I run right through it and at him. It's no small pleasure to see him scramble. He tries to stay out of my range. He dances nimbly away from me, tosses balls of fire at me like bouquets. I seldom catch alight. When I do, I snuff it out with a quick roll. Most importantly, I keep moving forward, keep him stepping backwards. He'll run out of space. He underestimates his size.

I kick out my foot low at him, and he jumps over it, spinning in the air. Fancy and stupid. His back turns for a split second. I plant that foot he flees and swing my spear like an immense hammer. The insignia crashes across his mask, sending him head over feet. The fire in his hands ebbs and wanes. He looks up at me, that implacable, shining face dented beyond recognition. Its expression is something like terror now. I can see him trembling beneath it, but he isn't afraid. He's seething.

The fire in his hands engulfs his whole body, coating him in a suit of blazing armour. He swings at me with white-hot arms and legs. He misses wide, but I still feel scalding heat pass me by. I grab at him, try to smother his robes with my hands, but he slips my grip. Every inch of him I expose is covered again in a breath. He ignites the objects around us, thoughtlessly. Furniture, walls, paintings. Suddenly, the things in this room mean nothing to him.

I've miscalculated. The plan was to fight him among precious things. I can't win if he burns the whole place down. I finally take in the details of the room thoroughly. The art is idyllic and pleasant, dominated by animals and play. Toys sit on the mantle over the hearth. The bed is a little small for a prince and might seem crowded if shared. I see something beneath it. A child, laying on her stomach, her soft, bundled hands clutched close against the chin of her mask.

This is Reznick's room. Nothing can match her preciousness.

I leap at Darnett and launch both my feet into his chest, sending us tumbling in opposite directions. I'm on my feet and on top of the bed before he can roll his plump frame onto his hands and knees. I raise my spear high, the point set down. If I'm lucky, I can at least skewer Reznick before Darnett cooks me.

"Wait!" he squeaks in delirious panic.

The inferno that seconds ago consumed the room dwindles to little more than candlelight when he reaches out a beseeching hand at me. He raises his arms high over his head, very slowly, as though to placate me. His suit of flaming armour fades to nothing. He's surrendering. The arrogance of it. The entitlement. What does he think he can offer me? There's apology in his eyes, dreams of peaceful resolution. I lift up Penance and hurl it through his chest.

He gasps. I don't know what he's so surprised about. The fire around us expands again, vacillating hysterically. I cross the room and grip my spear. He clutches at the staff as I lift him into the air. His girth pulls him deeper into the blade. I adjust my hands and drive him down onto the bed. His body gives way much more easily than I expect. The spear and its insignia slide right through him, the mattress, all the way to the floor. Behind his mask, I see his eyes strain vainly to see over the edge of the bed.

"Look at me," I spit.

He obeys. I reach out and snatch his mask by the holes in its eyes. A pale, modest face looks up at me. Nothing like I expected. Delicate lips. A big, flat nose. Wide, frightened eyes. I know a thousand faces like this one.

I look for anything new. I've seen softer and harder jaws. Thinner and thicker eyebrows. Bigger and smaller ears. Straighter teeth and more crooked. This is all wrong. Is it a fraud? Some loyal dressed up to draw us into a trap? He wielded the fire. I know he did. Is it a technique that can be learned? A gift that can be bestowed upon lesser beings?

He gurgles and sputters, the red in his body gushing out of him from the old holes he was born with and the new ones I've given him. He tries to push out the spear from his chest, senseless and frantic. I wait for something. All the fires in all the lamps around the kingdom to flicker and fade. An explosion of light to shine down on me. A tremor in the earth to scold me. A crash of thunder. A howling wind. Anything. But his death arrives quietly, no different from anyone else's.

Ages pass while I wait for the rapture, the triumph to come to me. I want to bask in the magnitude of the moment, but I can't escape the banality of it. I've killed more men than I can count. I've seen legions of good soldiers beg for sympathy and just as many fritter away their waning seconds fighting an impossible fight against a spear already through their heart. How can I love anything I know so well? How can I cherish the drawing of a breath or the blinking of an eye?

My heart slows. I finally feel my own seared flesh. I pull my spear out of Darnett, his body cracking but resisting little. I listen to him sink and drip. I hear something else. Faint, wheezing moans.

I hurl myself off the bed and reach beneath it. My hand finds a little ankle. Reznick squeals and claws at the floor as I pull her into the open. I toss her in front of the hearth and ready my spear before I even get a look at her.

She's tiny. The way she clutches herself with her arms shrinks her all the more. Her clothes aren't as nice as the usual royal garb. Her mask is dull, not the shimmering precious metal I've seen before. I suppose this is how they dress when they won't be seen.

She is unharmed. Or at least my spear missed her. She doesn't look at me. She just stares at her father, sobbing. I set the tip of my spear just beneath her chin. That gets her attention. She pushes her gaze even further from me, at some corner of the ceiling.

I lift her mask off with the point of my spear. I set the sharp steel on her far cheek and gently push her face towards me. She shuts her eyes tight. I don't have a good guess at her age. I was always so big for mine. She couldn't be much younger than I was when I lost my father. Still, she's likely too old to forget.

She opens her streaming eyes at me. She seems so ashen, almost sickly. She understands what's happened to her but can't fathom the reason. Parents are gods to children. They shape and control all the world. Their death is unthinkable.

I want to harden. I try to cast my mind forward and picture Reznick as a god, mighty, fierce, and vengeful. I think of the misery and subjugation I can save the world with just a quick little press of my spear. I can't hear past her little sobs. I can't see past her orphan face.

I walk away, half cursing myself for my mercy, half cursing myself for not taking her in my arms. I gather her father's mask and shut the door behind me.

※ ※ ※

The Nameless won't tell me how many of my brothers and sisters died during the assault. When I made it back to camp, no one dared dampen their mood with something so trivial. They uttered some vagaries about acceptable losses and claimed a magnificent victory. When I pressed about Master Terra, no one had any answers. Everyone was too busy preparing to celebrate.

I've never seen so many bald heads and smiling faces. All the brothers and sisters I never knew I had are here, dancing, frolicking, and chanting my name. This day will be a holiday. These festivities will echo through history. Those who lived it will look back with twinkling eyes, tell ever-expanding lies about how many came or how grand the bonfire was. The young will curse the lateness of their birth. Free men and women will wait all year for this date to come back around so that they may again know good will and full bellies.

There will be books, songs, totems, and everything else about me. In a thousand years, acclaimed works and new arts I can't conceive of will sing my praises. Everyone will know what I did. Or will think they do. There were only three people in that room. One of them is dead. Another, I hope, is too young to remember clearly and certainly too young to speak the gospel. I am the witness. I know the truth.

I sit by the fire, fixate on its heat. It's nothing to me. I numbed myself to its wrath, and that cost me its solace. Darnett's mask is stuck high on a pole for all to see. The fire flashes a lifetime's worth of expressions across the priceless gold. Agony, ecstasy, and everything in between, all come and gone in fleeting instants.

I shut myself out from the world, make a grim and solemn spectacle of myself. No one approaches me. Without a word, I make it known I won't tell the tale. What can that help? I'm no poet or bard. There was no beauty in the act, and I've no talent for invention. How did the Prince look, they'll ask? Scared, I'll tell them. But his face? Was it as they say? Beatific and transcendent? Or as we say? Scaly, toothy, and heinous? Neither. Plain and common. Maybe kind if it wasn't so frightened.

How did he bleed? Profusely. What colour was it? Red. Did the earth tremble, did you feel a tempest swirl? No, I felt his breath on my face as I stared into his wide eyes. Did he scoff and underestimate you? No, he was in a panic from the moment he saw me. Did he beg for his life? No, his life was nothing to him. All he wanted was to hide his daughter.

His daughter... so hurt... so confused... understanding nothing...

It was stupid not to kill her. The Royal Family hides away its daughters. Little is known of her aunt Ciendy. She's seldom been seen. If Reznick grows up sad and flimsy, they'll lock her up. I'll never get a chance at her. If she grows up formidable, she'll be cruel, and countless innocent will bear her ire on her long quest back to me. Then I'll kill her anyway just like her father.

Father...

I try not to think too much about all the fathers I've killed. It's the price of revolution. I thought I paid it gladly. I knew vaguely I was leaving orphans in my wake, but I've never looked one in the eye so soon after the deed. Reznick paralyzed me. I felt such a debt to her. I'd have given her all the world if I could.

Stupid. Juvenile. How many worlds do I have to give? Do I have one for every other orphan? Do they deserve less because they are faceless to me, because they were too far away when I butchered their parent? To act with awareness of a consequence and shudder at its arrival is utter cowardice. If wet cheeks and a quivering lip stay my hand, I've no righteousness in me. I curse my weakness.

I spot Master Terra through the crowd. She is seated at the outer edges of the gathering. My spirit soars. I anticipate her nearly bursting with approval when she meets my eyes. Maybe that would rescue me from this despair. She will not look at me. She smiles politely at whoever engages her, but it does not hide her sullenness. Finally, I see what she has lost. Her right arm has been reduced to almost nothing. The healers must have done well for her to survive at all. I want to collapse at her feet and beg her forgiveness. She will tell me there is nothing to forgive, and she will mean it. It will be no comfort.

Laughter shakes me from my gloomy place. All around me, I see joy. Revelry. Gleaming faces finally unburdened of their doubts, their value affirmed and promise fulfilled, their world alight with possibility. I see the immaculate happiness of the poor suddenly made rich, the ugly made beautiful, the weak made strong. Whatever they weren't but longed to be, they are. Through it all, a single thought cloys at me: murder. That's what brings us here. That's what we laud.

I won't say a thing. These dark thoughts are worthless. They've no redemption or salvation to offer. Let the Nameless make tonight what they want it to be. What they need it to be. Let them invent the glory and chase it a thousand years and more. Let it inspire the downtrodden and strike fear in tyrants everywhere. Let my truth be forgotten. Let a better truth reign.

CHAPTER 12: REZNICK'S TRIUMPH

Reznick

I've never killed a man before. I'd hoped for more from my first. Something clean, honourable, meaningful. The first step into some monumental legend that would tower through generations. This was messy and pointless. There was no accomplishment in it. His offence was born of stupidity, not evil. I didn't even know his name. It didn't need to happen at all, and it won't help anything. Such a waste.

I wonder if I'll be held accountable. Will word reach Uncle? I don't think so. It was too insignificant to be much remarked upon. The law exonerates me. I was in the right. He'll be cross I let myself be touched, but that'll be nothing compared to my leaving in the first place. Maybe he'll make some show of condolence for the dead man's sake. Uncle can send the survivors some reparations if he cares so much.

I hate that false benevolence in him. My father was generous with his lessers. He was kind to servants and gracious with common folk. Look what it did for him. Somehow, from the harshest calamity ever visited upon the kingdom, Uncle learned the wrong lesson. He seeks to heal the failures of kindness by doubling the dose. It's self-indulgence. He could go into the land and stamp out all opposition with a flutter of his finger, but he finds it too distasteful. All the realm suffers so that he may indulge his gentility.

I think about my father often. His gentle, doting touch. The way he asked me to explain my lessons to him, playing dumb so that I could learn better through teaching. His eager, incessant laughter. He could will flame to do anything and seldom asked it for anything but a dance. He'd perform for me. He'd hop and twirl, flames flaring and undulating all about him in dizzying, baffling patterns. His little light shows delighted me. I hate him for them now.

My father's raw power dwarfed mine and maybe even Uncle's. My tendrils are nothing to fire. Fire will kill anything with time. He could have been a singular warrior, and now he is the singular disgrace in our family's history.

I bear the burden of my father's defeat. His failures are my legacy. He didn't go out and meet Ruthless in the field. He let himself be ambushed. I was there. My father put me before Ruthless. He spent all his time hiding me instead of meeting his opponent, and it cost him every chance at an advantage. I watched from beneath my bed while they fought, and there was only one result their clash could come to. Ruthless was dogged. Ruthless was angrier. Most importantly, Ruthless held nothing sacred.

Penance came within an inch of my face when it plunged through my father's chest and the top of my bed. I heard the gurgle and rattle of a life filled with regret coming to an end. It took a long time for the grief to fade and sense to return to me. I vowed I wouldn't repeat my father's mistakes.

It was vulgar of that oaf at the inn to allude to Ruthless before me. Unless he was sure. But how could he be? The keeper said the stranger wasn't bald, didn't wear the shrouds. That could be a disguise. Maybe that's how Nameless hide. Maybe they declare their uniform so proudly to make themselves invisible without it. They might be that clever. If so, there could still be hundreds of them out there. Thousands.

I chide myself. I'm dreaming. Like a child. Ruthless would not hide so long only to be exposed by such trifling buffoons. If by some miracle they stumbled on him, why would he let them live to tell the tale? It doesn't make sense. No witnesses. That's the only way for him to do his work.

He let me live too all those years ago. That was different. He wanted all the world to know what he did. He needed a witness.

In any case, the man those brigands spoke of would be worth finding. There aren't many living who can best three armed men. Fewer still that don't serve the Royal Family proudly. If he were one of ours, he'd wear the colours, maybe even sport some mark or other commendation we gave him. There's a chance he's a sympathizer, maybe even a rebel. He may not be Nameless, but he could be close. Close is good enough.

I come upon a modest little house, the first for miles. It doesn't look like the sort of place criminals would make their den. This is a home built for life, peace, and happiness, as best as humble folk can fathom it. Even from this distance, I hear laughter reverberating like music.

I tie my horse at the fence. The front gate squeals when I open it. The laughter stops. I walk through mud towards the front door, light beckoning me through the windows. Animals watch me from their pens, curious, without fear. I am mysterious, but they do not distrust me. Their lives must be good to not recognize a predator when they see one.

I knock at the door. I hear uneasy murmuring. Good. The people inside are afraid. They've something to hide. They've something worth finding.

A decrepit old man answers. He opens the door only a crack so he might sneak a look at his caller. His eyes bulge and his jaw slacks when he sees me. He's so stunned he forgets his manners. He doesn't bow. He doesn't grovel.

Grudgingly, I accept the first words will be mine. I haven't all night.

"Word has spread that an insurgent treads these lands," I say, grave and lofty. The old man shakes as if awakened. "A search must be conducted."

Still stupefied, he forces me to press the door open wide with my hand.

"Y-Yes, of course," he sputters.

Finally, he clears the way for me, bowing his head and shuffling dutifully to a corner of the room. He folds his hands into each other, his thumbs fidgeting obnoxiously.

From a small dining table, his fat, grey-haired wife shoots to her feet. Her hands dart all about her body, trying in vain to flatten the ruffles of her apron, or push back her hair, or sweep away some crumbs. Anything to look more presentable. Eventually, she does something like a curtsey. Maybe they haven't forgotten their manners. Maybe they don't know any better.

I gesture my head to the corner her husband occupies. She lowers her chins and scurries like a rat to join him. She reaches for him reflexively, remembers her place, then copies his acquiescent pose.

I turn away from them, annoyed. These two crones are the definition of irrelevant, and their flailing struggles at propriety do nothing but squander more of my time. Even with my back to them, I can feel their minds racing, wondering what they might do to please me. Wisely, they've settled on keeping silent.

I take a cursory look around their little piece of domestic mediocrity. There's nothing terribly conspicuous or suspect in here. Nothing that presents any value or danger. No weapons. Some knives, forks, and everyday tools come closest.

I'm all but ready to leave and declare this all a loss when I come upon their dining table. Among the meat and mush, something leaps out at me. One too many forks. One too many knives. One too many plates. Someone is missing.

I turn to the couple, suddenly enough to see them dart their eyes off me and set them back to the floor.

"The two of you have some company?" I ask pointedly, crossing the room towards them.

Silence has served them well so far, but that time has passed. They tremble as I advance, more severely with each step I take. I wait patiently for them to babble. I expect every secret they've ever had to come spilling out of them. They say nothing, too brave, too afraid, or too dim.

"Before this goes any further," I begin, looking from one to the other, keeping all compassion or anger from my tone, "understand that it falls to the two of you to present some value."

There's nothing so frightening as control. Uncle taught me this.

They look up at me. They understand their lowness. They understand they're nothing to me. Whatever they have is mine, that much is certain. The only question is how fiercely they'll fight me over it.

I hear steps above me, portentous and reluctant. So that's it, then. I know better than to expect a Nameless. I've learned to protect myself from hope. It has left me raw too many times. The game is over, and the reality of the prize can never match the promise of the hunt.

I look to the stairs, and I wait for disenchantment. Instead, I see him. HIM. Ruthless. Different in a hundred ways, but same in those steel eyes. He carries that spear with him. It's sheathed, but I'm certain anyway. It looks heavy, heavier than anything.

I'm suddenly so awake, so aware. Every detail of this house that once so bored me screams at me, asking to be part of this colossal turning point in all the kingdom's history. I was so ready to forget the ugly colours of the walls, the cracks in the furnishings, the creaking of the floorboards. Now, I know them better than my own name. Lightning rolls through my body. Every emotion I've ever felt reveals its purer, truer self. My future is here, my life begins.

He looks to the old nothings. "Leave," he says.

"Stay," I counter. They don't budge. Already, my authority exceeds his. "History needs its witnesses."

"You sure you want that?" he asks, passing me on the way to the dining table. He doesn't look me in the eye. My victories stack.

He takes a seat with a sigh befitting a fat man. He leans his spear against the wall. He gestures at the spot across from him, mocking me with his aloofness. I sit, returning his volley. I won't be intimidated. He offers me some bread. I refuse it, of course. He shrugs and wolfs it down.

"Is this where you've been?" I ask. "All this time?"

"Just passing through," he answers simply, finally finished chewing.

Incredible. I can't help but laugh, stifling it with my hand. "What fortune!"

"Not how I see it," he says. No, I wouldn't think.

For the first time tonight, he really looks at me. I know the demeanour well. Patient, passive, deferential. It's the attitude of the illustrious and storied conceding their anxious lessers an ear. Good. Let him underestimate me.

"You know... " I begin, lowering my voice so that it may slip by the old nothings. He leans in quite sincerely on an elbow, oh so accommodating. "I wondered why you spared me. It took years for the brilliant spite of it to reveal itself. I understand now. You knew. You knew what my life would be. You knew my very existence would be a testament to failure, a living document of my father's stain on our family. You knew I'd be shunned. You knew I'd suffer."

It's perfect. I've had the words for years, refining them in the dwindling waking moments of sleepless nights. I search his face, and he gives me as little as he can. I lean back in my chair, puff out my chest.

He pushes himself off his elbow and begins pouring himself a cup of tea from a white kettle flecked with flowers. He shows no urgency at all. I can't blame him. He lets the slow dribbling screech through the thick silence.

"My father was no champion. Your name. *God Killer.*" I sneer, with all the disdain and dismissiveness he deserves. "It's a lie."

He sets the cup of tea right in front of me, very firmly. It's the first display of strength he's given me. Finally. Let's go.

"You're right," he says lazily. "Your father wasn't hard like your grandfather. Like me. He was gentle. Sweet. Don't hate him for it."

He makes sure to look right at me. It's so odd, odd enough to shake me. It's love, warmth, and clemency for a deplorable little wretch. It's the look of a man who could never dream of being afraid of me. It's utter, total condescension, an insult I've abided all my life. Uncle looks at me like this. No one else. You least of all. I will punish you.

"Leave," I tell the doddering old nothings, and they scatter out the house. Ruthless watches them out the sides of his eyes, waits for them to be gone.

"There's a lot in my life I'd take back if I could," he says very wearily, lowering his eyes, the picture of supplication. "I hurt you. I wish I hadn't. If it were my life to give, you could have it. It's not. There's too much owing."

He looks back up at me. Once, I saw a dog being reprimanded by its master, having vomited somewhere inconvenient and stupid. It sat on its tail, pushed back its ears, moaned softly, and cast flitting, wide-eyed looks at the omnipotent ruler of its little world. At this moment, the despicable Ruthless looks something like that mutt. I'm sick with disappointment.

"Look at you," I sigh, imitating the distance and superiority of Uncle, "begging and bargaining. I thought… I hoped I'd meet the best of you. All the fury those legends promised. Not like this. There's no glory in this."

He dangles on my hook, hoping for lenience. I savour it. I could live here in this place, and I intend to. I tilt up my mask just enough to sip my drink. The tea is lukewarm, probably meant for daintier constitutions than mine.

"This path you're on… you can change it," he blathers, his voice earnest with the moralizing of an eternal loser. "Look at me. Ragged. Useless. Kill me. What'll it mean?"

"Nothing," I grant, downing the drink suddenly. "But meaning… that comes later, doesn't it? Stories are embellished, the defeated twisted and the winners lionized. An assassin becomes the slayer of a dragon. A room in a house becomes a battlefield doused in blood. Butchering a couple of farmers and some mangy wanderer?"

His face sinks. He sees the gallows now.

"Why can't that be the triumph of a dynasty?" I ask. "Truth fades. Stories linger."

He frowns, dejected but unafraid. I can see him rolling his joints, subtly preparing.

"You'll know," he offers. I let him grab his spear.

"And who else?" I say. That's the end of it.

Rufus

Since Elizabeth came into my world, I haven't found myself in many fights. Save for Crag and his thugs, I haven't raised a hand in years, and few men have raised any against me. I take pride in that. Violence, for the most part, has been a random occurrence in the second act of my life. I've lost my focus and hammered my fingers now and then. I've been kicked by horses more than I care to admit.

Something far, far beyond that is the boot Reznick plants in my chest. It launches me backwards, and once I make it through the window, I'm pretty sure I'll never stop.

I do, thanks to a particularly sturdy tree. I'm not sure where my spear ends up. I find my balance, and then I look for Reznick somewhere in the night. I feel real danger for the first time in ages, and it's like I'm myself again. My senses sharpen, readying for infinite possibility. I hear the scampering of her feet and the shifting of leaves. I look to the treetops and find her. She swings from a branch and catches me beneath my chin with her boots.

I take the blow better than the last, keeping my feet under me, but the wincing of my eyes and turning of my head costs me sight of her. She comes upon me again, from above and behind, but I'm ready. I snatch her out of the air and pull her over my shoulder. I try to pin her in the fallen leaves beneath me, but with the wriggling of her feet and tendrils, she slips my grip.

I eat another high, arcing boot, and her fist lands across my face. That's all fine. The tendrils are my biggest problem.

They're good weapons for her, but she's too young and frenzied to use them intelligently. She could keep me away from her, exploit their reach and attack me from a distance. Luckily, she hates me. She wants to be close to me, to bury the hard points of her body everywhere I'm vulnerable.

I reach for her again. She's faster than I am, fast enough to think she's safe. In close quarters, it's a matter of time. I grasp fistfuls of her clothes, but she slithers out over and over. I know how she feels. Dynamic and dominant. She believes in her momentum. She feels as unstoppable as a coursing river.

I widen my stance and make a rock wall of myself. She bounces off me, staggered by her halted flow. I get a hold of both her wrists and hurl her aside. She careens off the trunk of a tree, spinning like a top.

She scrambles to her hands and knees, and I know her mind is on fire with rage. In the dirt beside her, she finds my spear. Like so many before her, she swells with audacious self-belief. She grabs the spear in both hands and strains against all futility to lift it. She values her dignity too much to give up, and I seize the moment, lifting my knee into her head. She tumbles backwards, and I kick the spear up into my hands.

I'm not worried anymore. An old, exultant peace comes upon me, seductive and dangerous. I castigate myself for the satisfaction I feel, ready myself for the reckless swing of her tendrils sure to come. She launches them both at me, and they snatch at the staff of my spear. I turn my spear end over end, tangling her tendrils, reeling her in closer and closer. She tries to dig in her heels. She pulls away with all her might, refusing to surrender.

I drive the butt of my spear into the dirt to trap her, and I fire a clean, hateless fist straight into her mask, careful to only put enough on it to stop her. Apparently, I underrate her. She's very strong. She tries to kick at my head. I swat her foot away and put just a bit more on a cutting blow across her cheek. I crack her mask clean off her head. Her legs wobble, her head drops, and she falls to her knees. I listen to her breathing. I keep another fist at the ready and hope she's finished. She raises her chin, spits in my face, and I see red.

I swing my leg around and thrust my heel into her chest. I regret it instantly. She shoots backwards. I hear some sickening, brittle snap when my spear steals her tendrils right off her wrists. She wails and writhes, the blood already surging out from beneath her sleeves. For a vanishing moment, I'm the furthest thing from her mind.

She wallows in defeat, lifting up her sleeves to gape at the jagged shards of bone and meat protruding from folds of flesh on the insides of her arms. I'm sure she was once ashamed of those things that used to be her tendrils, hated their bizarreness and ugliness. I see her longing for them.

"It's not fair..." she sniffles. "It's not right..."

She's not talking to me. Not really. I approach her with as much delicacy as I can muster.

"I've prepared for you all my life!" she bellows at me, and I stop in my tracks. "And still you take from me! Like I'm nothing!"

She's right. I know she is. Suddenly, she's so frail. I've maimed her, in and out, and I'm so, so sorry. She looks up at me, eyes dripping with loathing, her soft cheeks quivering. I see her face again. All I see is a child. A child I've ruined.

"What more could I have done?!" she screams. Her voice falls, weakening. "What's left for me now..."

I wish I had something, anything for her. I wish I could give back all the things I robbed from her. But they're gone.

"Kill me," she begs.

My heart plummets deep into my gut. I draw a breath for words and wisdom, but I don't have either. I shake my head.

"How can you be so hateful?" she asks.

No. This is important, Rufus.

"Run," I tell her. "Go anywhere. Find something. You're not your family. You're not what's happened to you. You're not what anyone says you are. You can do anything. You can decide."

It's the best I can do. I see the anger leave her eyes, and the path that will save us both unveils itself to me:

"Come with me—"

Before I can finish, she drives the sharp edge protruding from her forearm into her neck and opens her throat. No. No no no no.

I race to her. I put my hand on top of the wound. What would Elizabeth do? The first thing is to stop the blood. There's so much of it. Pressure. Wrap it. Bandaging. I claw at my rags with my free hand, try to tear free a piece of fabric.

Reznick's looking at me. She sees how afraid I am. She's so proud.

CHAPTER 13: THE ARTIST

Clyde

Robert and the Princess only fought for a few minutes. A few swings, a bit of clattering, some grunts, and then it was over. It's so strange that something so important could come and go so quickly.

I didn't even see it all. I couldn't watch. I don't have the stomach for fighting. When they flew out of my house one after the other, I grabbed Myra and ran inside. All I could think to do was hold her tight. We just shut our eyes and listened.

It was quiet for a long time before I had the sand to get up and have a look. I followed the path of destruction as far as it went. Eventually, the crushed branches and cut trees petered out, and it was like nothing happened at all. That's where I found the Princess's mask all bent and bloodied. She was nowhere to be seen. It was only then I understood how big a mess I'd gotten myself into.

I went back to the house and told Myra my best guess at what happened. I decided I had to go into town and tell the local guards about it. It was our responsibility as citizens. She wanted to push back, but she has as little stomach for fighting as I do. Regrettable as it might be bearing such bad news, it'd be a hundred times worse if we were found to have any part in covering it up.

In the morning, I grabbed the Princess's horse and started to town. I didn't dare ride it. It made Henry look like a gutter rat and was probably worth more than my life. I walked beside the majestic beast the whole way, its reins in one hand, the mask in the other. I hadn't walked so far in years. I was distressed to find myself a much older man than I expected.

When I finally made it to town, my feet could barely carry me. The guards rushed me when they saw the mask, like I came on them by accident and might escape at any second. I may as well have been some criminal they'd caught red-handed. They seized me by my arms, screamed questions at me so loud and fast I never had a chance to answer.

I'd barely gotten a word out when they dropped a black bag over my head. This was too big for any of them. I'd answer to someone higher.

✤ ✤ ✤

The black bag comes off from my head and light floods in, overwhelming me. The men dragging me toss me down on cool stone, and I'm lucky I don't break my fragile bones. I'm in some prestigious hall bigger than a wheat field. Pillars tall as trees hold up a pointed ceiling that leads my eye towards a very grim portrait of Prince Mathius and Princess Reznick. The painting is misty with dark colours, ominous and stormy.

No less imposing is the Prince himself, sitting on a raised throne beneath his likeness. He appraises me, suspicious and haughty, and I wonder if a man so poor has ever been so near him.

"Tell me everything," he commands, his voice filling the room.

I lift my chin off the floor and prostrate myself as quickly as I can, careful not to try his patience or scuff the floor. I have to be on my best behaviour. I need all my fanciest words.

"I found a man on the road," I begin, trembling and pleading. "He was filthy, tired. I had no idea who he was. How could I? Then the Princess came to the door…"

I pause. The Prince grips the arms of his chair in anticipation. I choose my words very carefully.

"She was investigating," I continue with utmost caution. "The man hid."

"You hid him," the Prince declares.

"No!" I exclaim, my stomach a pit. "We didn't know who he was! We opened our hearts!"

The Prince shoots to his feet, and I wince, hoping whatever is coming comes swiftly. I open my eyes and find him waiting. I try to calm myself, try not to aggravate him.

"What could we do?" I ask, my voice low and relinquishing. "They tore our house to pieces. I couldn't have stopped them."

He descends a step from his platform, and I can't beat back my terror.

"The moment I could serve you, I did!" I yelp, entwining my hands, imploring. "I came to your men! I knew it'd bring me here, and I did it all the same!"

He stands over me. I bow my head and shut my eyes. I clench my mouth shut and keep my whimpering to a murmur. I can't do anything about my tremors and convulsions. I swear the whole world is shaking.

A gloved hand comes to rest on my shoulder, tender and magnanimous.

"Did she suffer?" I hear the Prince ask, soft and sad.

I open my eyes and look up at him. I feel a plaintive hope in him, the search for meagre solace in tragic times. I wish I could give it to him.

"I'm sorry," I say simply. "I don't know."

He nods graciously. He pats my shoulder. I feel a gentle wind embrace me, lifting me up and placing me lovingly on my feet as lightly as a mother letting down her child.

"How could you have known?" he repeats, drifting back to his throne. "Reznick could be... forceful. She was troubled. She would intimidate when unnecessary."

His tone is so fair, so accepting. He talks to me like a life-long friend.

"I hoped I'd show her the way," he continues, descending drearily into his chair. "She did not trust in me. You showed virtues she lacked. Mercy. Pity. Thank you."

I feel a wonderful unburdening. I am born anew. I see now, the clouds parting and the sun emerging as if for the first time. I am in that shimmering, resplendent light priests and poets have tried and failed to put to words since First Morning.

"Take him away," he tells his soldiers. They hoist me up by my elbows, as helpful as they were once cruel. "Fix up his house."

I love my prince. I love my kingdom. So long as I live, I will serve them both proudly.

Mathius

When Darnett and Ciendy were slain, Father turned his light away from the world. He locked himself away in the Capital. He saw betrayers in every subject, spies in every lord. He abandoned the poor and needy of the kingdom to their worst impulses. The fate of civilization fell to me. If I hadn't risen to the challenge, men and women would have receded to beasts. I showed the way. I rescued all that was righteous from the maw of anarchy. I became more than myself, and more than myself I remained.

Now, I live two lives. One for my people, one for myself. I hide so much. The kingdom needs me solid and true. So, I bury away my faults, my doubts, my pain. Before the eyes of my people, I am resolute and immaculate. I live the life that is mine alone and behind closed doors. There, I can forgive myself one indulgence. I paint. Every day. No one knows, no one will ever know, because in my art, I am a failure.

In each of my paintings hides a battle I've lost decisively. I refine my technique second to second. Still, I find a curve too round, an edge too sharp, a stroke too long. These imperfections, invisible to most, shine at me. Yet somehow, I cherish these paintings more than any of my works save my Darling and Reznick before her. I feel known when I look upon them, like some ecstatic truth long buried has lovingly been brought to light. In them, I see my weakness shared without apology and made beautiful.

I dream my paintings may live beyond me, studied, admired, and wondered over. On their own merits, they'd forge their own legacy, apart from my name and family, the eminent work of some humble man striving at greatness and maybe, if only fleetingly, clasping it. In that eternal conflict, with those little triumphs, I share the joy and pain of all people. When I strain, I know I am not alone, and it is a comfort to me. A comfort I want for everyone.

A perfect being can not be known to make imperfect things. No one could love these paintings truly if they knew where they came from. My name would poison them and their worship would be tyranny. If people come to love them, it must be without obligation, without expectation. My subjects must see the overcoming, the raging against stasis and decay for themselves. Beauty from beauty is nothing. Beauty from dirt is a miracle.

Art is the only immortality. In their wondrous statues and sculptures, my ancestors are sanctified. I will honour my dearly departed with my masterwork. Reznick will be known as the warrior she dreamed she'd be. Darnett will be as regal as the king he ought to have been. Ciendy…my sweet Ciendy… she will be loved and revered as she deserved.

Of all the tragedies my family has suffered, Ciendy's death still haunts me the worst. I often dreamed of the life I might one day give her. I put it off too long. I failed her. She was denied so much. She never had the opportunities and freedom of a prince, or the father's love that blessed Reznick. She never manifested the gifts Darnett and I did, so Father hid her away. Yet she was still so good, so bright, so curious. She could find scraps of beauty wherever she looked. Every time I visited her, I would find some new critter she'd hidden away. They were always wounded, or lame, or ugly, or unfit for the world in one of a million ways. She would shelter them, love them, nurse them back to health.

I thought I had time. I thought her goodness would win out and melt Father's cold heart. That is not the way of the world. Goodness can not be left alone; it must be pursued and protected, passionately and tirelessly. Ciendy was too gentle. Being shut out from the world made her adore it all the more. I suppose we all share in that hardship. We love most what we can not have.

I will never have my family back. My sister and niece are gone. I will love them all the more for it.

CHAPTER 14: THE UNWELCOME CHILD

The King

My concubine's moans are loud and repellant. I set harsh looks upon her, but I only quiet her in spurts. Perhaps I should command the healer. Maybe he has some potion or tonic to put her to sleep and save us all from this insufferable bleating. Screams are no way to welcome a god into the world.

Darnett's mother was similarly tiresome. I killed her early in the birth and let the healer do his work on a corpse. It seemed sensible at the time. Healers waste so much energy protecting the mother, and it's all for nothing. Later, my advisors proposed it was bad for the child. To see for myself, I was patient during Mathius's delivery. He's been better. Much. For once, my advisors were right.

I don't recall Mathius's mother being so impudent. I suppose she was special, rare in many respects. Beautiful, doting, and fearless in her subservience. So many women need to be frightened into submission. Not her. She trusted. She believed in my righteousness and infallibility. Her sense of self never interfered.

After she gave me Mathius, I promised myself I would never sully myself with any lesser. Yet good concubines are so difficult to find, and I was impatient. It's easy to fool oneself in matters like these. What difference could it make? A mother is but a shell, a chrysalis. The child will never know them. Yet some laws are immutable. Better dirt yields better crops.

This woman's beauty was frivolous, and it blinded me. It's obvious now she was undeserving. Women are so deceptive in their looks. They trick the eye with paints and poses. Looking at her here, caked in sweat and hair matted on her head, she's hideous. With her ploys, she has tainted my line. I'll be glad to be rid of her.

With a booming, guttural bellow, she pushes out my child. She knows well enough to look away, setting her eyes on the far corner of the room. I look down at the healer and see regret in his eyes. He anticipates I'll be displeased with something. What did this horrible woman do? Has she brought me an aberration? Did she smother the child inside her before it ever had a chance?

The healer lifts the baby up to me. It looks pink and wet. It cries. All this is normal. Is the healer so cowardly that he fears his impending sacrifice? Pathetic.

Finally, I see his reprehensible failure. It's a girl he hands me. A girl. The gall. What am I to do with this? Sons carry the line. Sons spread the seed. Sons win the wars. What's a daughter? A nuisance. She can't even bring me grandsons without defiling herself with some brute.

The healer lowers his head, not wanting to face what's coming. I cleave his head from his shoulders. He bleeds all over the floor, staining everything. It doesn't matter. I'll never see anything in this room again.

I bring the baby to its mother. I want her to see her atrocity. Propagation is mysterious. We've no idea what may influence it. Did she wish for a daughter? Did vanity make her will something of herself into the world? Did she think if she disgusted me enough, maybe I'd disown the child? Maybe I'd leave her to raise it?

She has the audacity to reach for it, confirming all my suspicions. I wish I had something worse than death to punish her with, but I don't. I drive a blade in that putrid belly that dishonoured me. She dies slowly, painfully. It isn't enough. Not nearly.

Ciendy

Today's a big day. Today, I take my mark. Today, I join my ancestors and link myself to a chain that has shaped and defined all the world since First Morning. Like all my kin before me, our family's crest will be tattooed onto my back. When I see it, I will know myself a god. I will carry tribute with me wherever I go.

I am terrified.

Father and my brothers are with me. We walk down a long corridor towards some secret chamber buried deep in the earth. We're meeting the man who will do the deed. We will be alone with him. Darnett warns me the man will laugh at my naked body then cut into my back for hours. Mathius assures me the man won't laugh. He doesn't address the more concerning portion of Darnett's teasing. That troubles me.

A stoic, decorated soldier welcomes us in. For a moment, I think opening a door seems like too small a task for a soldier so tall and in armour so grand. Then, I remember. A man will see my flesh, the flesh of a god. Perhaps his skin will even graze mine. That can only end in violence.

Inside, a sturdy, hulking man sits sedately on a stool much too small for him. His beard hangs low over his big belly, and his moustache bristles from the air shooting sporadically from his nostrils. I'm told he's an esteemed master in his field. His art must not be glamorous. He pats the table he's next to with black-rimmed nails then averts his gaze. I disrobe down to my waist. Darnett and Mathius lower their eyes. Father does not.

I climb onto the table and lay my chest down flat atop it, my head dangling over the end. I wait for a moment then consider clearing my throat to win back the bearded man's attention. Fortunately, he begins his slow turn to me, needle and ink in hand.

His hands are even heavier than I expect. They carve into me. I grit my teeth. I want to bite my tongue clean off. I understand now. It's not for love, family, and commitment that I take this mark. I am not accepted or welcomed into my line. This is no blessing or gift. I am tested. Punished.

I feel a burn as the man scratches and snakes his needle along my back. I wonder if he knows he hurts me. I wonder if he's ever considered himself able. He is diligent. Precise. Maybe he doesn't care about my pain. Maybe all that matters is this defining and final piece, a tattoo no one will ever see, a work that will cost him his life.

I'm told this man's master died marking Mathius, and his master before him marking Darnett. It seems such a waste. I wonder why these artists do not run, why they see the burden as such a distinction. They die mutilating children for an audience that could be counted on one hand. Why? Because Father demands it. Because his brand is mighty and I must bear it. Because this mark means I'm his. He will know it. My brothers will know it. I will know it. I hope it pleases him, at least.

I shiver and just barely keep from moaning. The man pulls back his needle. I feel an uneasy stillness in the air.

"Continue," Father commands, annoyed.

The needle plunges back into me. I feel something grip my hand and squeeze. The unseen force gently massages my fingers, composes me. I turn my gaze to Mathius. He's afraid to move an inch, but he tells me so much with just his eyes. I am so very thankful for him.

I find my strength. I don't budge. I hardly even breathe.

※ ※ ※

I think most people would like the Summer Palace if they ever had opportunity to visit. In the high sun, it absolutely dazzles with stone so white and bright it could blind you. The sea beside it is clean, blue, and boundless. Whenever the weather's too hot, you never have far to go before finding shade or a breeze. Even the servants seem happier here. They hold their heads high and proud, emboldened by their station, the beauty and exclusivity of this place an affirmation of their superiority. They are born here, and most are so convinced of its eminence they never leave. They're also forbidden to, of course. The palace's location is closely guarded, and only a precious few are trusted to come and go. It seems too opulent to squander on someone so indifferent as I.

My room is cozy and feminine. I'm sure it was assembled by some famed expert on leisure. There is colour everywhere and pillows in places only the exceptionally creative would think to sit. It's very different from my tower in the Capital. My real room is cold, hard, and grim. It takes me ages to descend the stairs there. Here, I could walk ten feet and feel sand on my toes. Yet for all the warmth and light, I'm as much a prisoner here as I am there. At least at home, I have things that are mine.

Mathius and I sit on the floor at a little table, playing a game of Long Reign. We only ever play what suits me. There are a hundred games he could trounce me at. None of them interest him any. We only play games of cunning and strategy. He thinks that's fair. Really, it favours me. He can't see into me as I see into him. I can bluff and mislead, and he can't hide a thing. He appreciates the challenge, I suspect. Either that, or he believes me so pitiful that I need whatever small victories I can find. In any case, it passes the time.

"How much longer?" I ask.

He scratches at his forehead, a very serious expression on his face. We never wear our masks when we're alone.

"Don't hurry me," he says defensively. "I'm allowed to take as long as I need."

"No, I mean how much longer here?" I clarify, gesturing around at the palace.

"As long as Father pleases," Mathius says, finally moving a piece. He stares at it accusingly, like it may spurn him at any moment.

"Then I better displease him," I say with a shrug, moving one of my pieces with a confident, haphazard slide.

Mathius looks up at me with playful consternation. It's

been this way since I was young. This is one of the many games we play. I make a fuss, and Mathius levels me out. When I was very small, he found me crying in my room. I hated my face. I thought myself ugly, and Father's insistence I never be seen without my mask only convinced me further. It was Mathius that taught me the great lie, that we wear our masks to hide how common we really are. But Mathius isn't common. He showed me his face, and it was beautiful. Just not beautiful enough, I suppose.

"I love it here," he says, hiding the little wound I gave him with a tight pursing of his lips. "It's the only place we're all together."

I pause. I should choose my words more diligently. It's a crime to hurt someone so innocent.

"In my tower, I'm only ignored," I explain. "Here, I am judged."

"I don't judge you," he tells me, moving a piece with stern, foolhardy conviction. "And I don't ignore you, either. I visit you every chance I get, and I can do that more easily here."

"You don't understand." I sigh, playing my turn aloofly. "I can only disappoint Father."

Mathius takes his eyes off the board and stares at me with such incredulity he seems almost scandalized.

"You're amazing," he states like a fact. "Father will see."

I could blush, and I would if I weren't so used to his flattery. It seems such an outrage to cover such a handsome, sincere face all the time. I wonder if anyone else will ever see it. He'll never take a wife, of course. That's for citizens, not gods. He and Darnett aren't terribly close; Darnett sees in him a usurper. They're both so on guard around each other, Mathius especially. His children might get a look. I've never seen Father's face, but Mathius is different. His children will never doubt they are loved. Mathius will make sure of it, and there's nothing so reassuring as his bright-eyed smile.

"You and Darnett are miraculous," I retort, making another move.

"You are a miracle," he insists, an obstinate barrier against my self-loathing.

"No one will cower and awe at what I have to offer. Father won't ever have any use for it."

"Your powers will grow with time," he says, eyes returning to the table.

He thinks that's what I want to hear. Power. That's what boys think matters. They believe the measure of any living thing is its dominion over another. Truthfully, I don't care if the day ever comes when I can level mountains or vanquish armies. There's never been someone as powerful as Father, and I've never seen anyone so unhappy.

Mathius makes his move.

"Father will see," he repeats, folding his arms and nodding his head with certainty. "Once we give him some grandsons, he'll see the good you can do them. Once Leopold passes, there will be no better teacher."

I snort, playing my turn and striking a decisive blow. It's a ridiculous notion Mathius put forth. For one, imagining anything killing Leopold, even time itself, seems absurd. Yet in the shadow of the fanciful suggestion that Father might let me anywhere near his grandsons, I suppose anything is possible. I will never be an aunt, to say nothing of a mother. Father will limit my influence however he can. He won't want me infecting his world.

I gesture my head down at the game board. Mathius finally realizes he's lost.

❈ ❈ ❈

The Summer Palace's training grounds are its least beautiful spot. They are also its most important. Mathius, Darnett, and I stand at the edge of a wide, flat floor in the shadow of a looming pagoda. Tall, thick walls surround us on all sides. It's here that Father assesses our progress. He is perched high on a platform and seated on a throne beneath an awning. If we impress him enough, we win horns for our masks. It is serious, important work, done with none of the flair or pomp typical of the kingdom. Every servant here is blindfolded, and I can't imagine the fate that awaits them should they sneak a look. Only Father may evaluate what happens here. Father and Leopold.

Leopold stands at the opposite end of the grounds, his white beard freshly trimmed and his armour well polished. I don't really know why he is afforded so many more allowances than the other servants. Mathius tells me he used to be someone. A renowned warrior, or general, or something. When I ask Leopold, he won't tell me. He doesn't seem inclined to boast, and I don't like to bother him.

Before Leopold, I had power and anger all mixed up. Father always made them seem interwoven. Leopold is so temperate, so supportive. Father punishes wrong, but Leopold demonstrates right. Maybe his patience and kindness mean he's not as imposing as Father. He's still extraordinary. I'm not sure Mathius, Darnett, and I together could lay a finger on him even on our best day.

I bounce on the balls of my feet anxiously. I'll be the last to go, and my wait will feel like eons. It's best I stay loose. Mathius stands with a straight back and a high chin, arms folded behind him, looking like a statue of himself. Darnett seems like his mind is elsewhere. His head sways. He looks like he's thinking of a song.

Father waves a couple of fingers towards himself. Darnett gruffly lazes forward, taking his stance before Father in the center square, then vibrating with impatience. Father cuts the air with his hand, and Darnett begins his demonstration. Fire leaps off the torches surrounding the square and dashes across the ground towards him. The flames spiral around him, expanding and contracting as he inhales and exhales.

The blaze provides spectacle Darnett does not. He hasn't improved any. He's more inventive with his fire, maybe. It arcs and loops in clean, bright lines, as sensational as Darnett is detached. He summons it back to him with a wave of his hands, and it gathers in a sphere in front of his face. He blows into it, and it bursts into a column of red and orange as tall as the pagoda. That's impressive, at least.

Darnett and Father exchange courteous nods. Darnett leaves the square. He's too old for these shows of compliance, I think. A parent himself, he has little subjugation left in him, particularly ever since Father took Reznick's birth so poorly. That drove a wedge between them. Reznick is very dear to Darnett. It must be easier to love a daughter when she's your only child.

Servants scurry to the center of the square, arms full with weapons of all shapes and sizes. I'm petrified they'll trip and impale themselves because of their blindfolds, but they execute their assignment flawlessly. They set the weapons down, making a nice, tidy ring of sharp steel, then hustle out of sight, eyes planted downwards. They must have practiced for hours.

Mathius steps to the center of the square. He bows deeply to Father, lowering his head nearly to the ground. When he rises back up, he shoots his open hands out at his sides, and the ring of weapons floats up to meet him.

I smile, if only for myself. I do appreciate Mathius's theatricality, and I'm sure I've plenty to look forward to. For his next trick, his ring of weapons splits into three distinct circles. Axes float with axes, swords with swords, and hammers with hammers. They all dance around him with dizzying speed, round and round, up and down. They astonish so completely I nearly lose sight of Mathius himself.

He flows between his strikes and steps like a leaf in the wind. It's beautiful but bloodless. He's so above it all, so untouchable. Mathius only appreciates exertion as a novelty. He has so little cause to move. When he does, it's deliberate, jubilant, and savoured like a good meal. He aspires only to beauty with every flick of his wrist or slide of his foot.

With a coiling of his fingers and a sudden parting of his hands, the weapons shoot away from him in every direction. A pair of blades speed by me by inches, and I curse myself for flinching. Darnett didn't. I tell myself he probably wasn't paying attention.

Mathius bows, graciously accepting Father's sedate nod. Their formality does nothing to hide their elation. Next time I see Mathius, I imagine he'll have horns a few inches longer.

I breathe in, steadying myself. I take my place. Father hardly budges. I begin my pattern. I'm better than Mathius and Darnett. I know it. I've had to be. They're so capable they can't see the use of their own bodies. Fists, feet, and arms can't accomplish anything that fire or Divine Will won't do better.

I know the weight of things. I've held a sword in my hand and understood its utility. My strikes are honed and purposeful. It means nothing to Father. It doesn't matter to him that my punches are cleaner, my kicks higher and tighter. I could be the very best there is. I could be so good I didn't have an equal in the kingdom. Yet the simple truth of the matter will always be that I am limited, and gods must never be limited. Fire will never do my bidding. I won't ever lift things with my mind. No matter how high I climb, nothing but skill will ever elevate me. Someone else could always be better. And that makes me an abomination. I will win no horns.

Father doesn't even wait for me to finish. In the middle of my performance, he lifts himself up and starts towards the exit. I've disappointed him again. I suspect he still clutches to the hope that something incredible will flourish from me someday. Something fearsome and impossible. I've made peace with my lacking even if he hasn't.

I don't stop. I see through my steps until the end. The pattern culminates with a twirling kick that carries me through two complete midair rotations. It's almost like floating but isn't. It's only very, very difficult.

Mathius gasps when I land. He muffles it quickly, catching himself. I hear insistent, forceful applause somewhere over my shoulder. It's so startling Father stops in his tracks and shoots a steely glare past me. I turn my head and find Leopold clapping his hands, his face rigid, proud, insolent. I bow to the empty throne, and then deeply, gratefully to Leopold.

I never saw him again.

CHAPTER 15: FUNERALS

Small

I'm by a river, admiring scenery so splendid I'm tempted to risk my hiding spot for a better view. The sun has fallen behind the trees and painted the sky orange and purple. The water is so still it reflects back the landscape, twice as beautiful. A breeze glides sweet music through the leaves and branches. If it were up to me, I certainly wouldn't spoil all this majesty with a funeral, especially for a brigand like Crag.

His friends carry him on a little raft Elizabeth provided. Apparently, her work means always knowing where to find one. He's light enough, thankfully. Their grief is not too inconvenienced. Elizabeth walks at the head of the pack, dressed very unlike herself. In a clean robe and her hair put up, she's a fair likeness of poise. She carries a bouquet of wildflowers flecked with other specks of natural beauty, and the leg of her skirt sails easily across the grass with her long, elegant gait.

She leads Crag's men to the shore. They set him down gently on white sand. She bends down and sets aside her bouquet. With his friends' help, she undresses Crag with all the gentleness and respect of a nurse serving an elder. She folds his clothes and sets them aside. What will be done with them, I've no idea. They look too small for his friends.

She undoes the bouquet and garnishes Crag with its greens and reds. She covers his wounds and delicate places completely, so effortlessly it seems by accident. He's almost beautiful by the time she's finished, so serene he seems sacrosanct. She holds her hand over his eyes and mutters some words too mild for me to hear. They seem to hearten Crag's friends some.

Elizabeth gestures at the raft and heads to the tip of it. She pulls it into the water, and Crag's friends follow, pushing behind her. She leads the way, wading deeper and deeper, nearly to her waist. With a firm and final press to encourage it along, the raft drifts out, taken by the tide. The three watch soberly until Crag disappears around the bend. I suppose we're to be thankful his inevitable capsizing will happen somewhere out of sight.

The Nameless have no death rituals. We lay where we fall, our bodies picked for whatever tool or weapon may still be of service. Our flesh, we leave to the earth. There's nothing else to be done with it. To pretend otherwise would be maudlin, and worse yet, wasteful. We dare not move our husks for anything but looting. Regard and honour are for the living.

I've never seen a funeral. I've never seen much to be gained from asking about one, either. Of all the indulgences civilians permit themselves, this must be among the most elaborate. So I hope, anyway. To its credit, there are flashes of reason. If you've put down roots in a place and made a home, leaving your dead as they lie might obstruct you. Letting the water take them gets them out of sight and out of the way. There's also a certain logic to send away a dead thing naked. Dead things have no need for clothes. Beyond that, the creatures in the water will digest bare flesh more easily. Perfectly reasonable.

The rest baffles me. Making a dead thing more beautiful than it ever was living. The long speeches, spoken by strangers as if their distance affords them some less biased authority. The docile prayers to faraway, vindictive gods. All so pointless. All so strange.

All strange acts are delusional ones, tricks the mind plays on itself in pursuit of comfort. Death is a fearsome thing, to be sure. There's nothing so frightening as finality, nothing so paralyzing as the inescapable. I do not fear death. I am secure in the knowledge that my life is well spent at service to all my kin. I can see why civilians may need more convincing that their peaceful years weren't without purpose. They hate waste too, I suppose.

Enough time passes that Crag's friends are appeased. They leave tentatively, in case Elizabeth might be offended. She lingers there in the water until they're gone, presumably appreciating her victory in their extended contest of solemnity.

She stays there a while with only me to see. I begin to understand something quite preposterous. It's no act. She grieves. I'd thought her respect was courtesy, some small gesture of pity for the sheep that lost their shepherd. She really does mourn. For Crag! A thief, a bully, and a murderer, I expect, so long as he wasn't too much of a coward. Every shred of faculty he grasped he'd put to evil. He'd have been a scourge if he hadn't been such an insect.

I emerge from my concealment and approach the shore. Elizabeth's eyes don't waver from the bend, in case Crag comes back a new man finally able to contribute something to the world. Maybe then all this might have some worth. I'm shocked to find myself compelled to raise her spirits. I hate her pain. I hate waste.

"You shouldn't grieve," I tell her firmly.

Elizabeth inhales deeply through her nose, I hope relieved to be freed from her self-imposed bereavement.

"Didn't hear you sneak up on me," she notes. "Practicing?"

I feel a twinge of pride. I have been practicing. I've had to train at something. But I shouldn't let her distract me.

"Crag was loyal," I continue. "As much as allowed him to be whatever kind of bastard he pleased. Any loss for our enemy is a victory for us."

"He wasn't my enemy," she claims.

I bristle, folding my arms to keep from balling my fists.

"All this... " I begin. "It's empty superstition. Doesn't mean anything. Pretending he deserved something... it's stupid. He's not worth it."

"We're all worth it," she replies, cool, righteous, and insufferable.

She strides out of the water and right past me without so much as a look.

Rufus

Reznick's so light in my arms. I've never understood how something so small could be so tenacious. Where does the strength come from? She's so unlike me. She has none of my girth or hardness. Yet somehow in this tiny, soft thing, strength abounded.

I think of Elizabeth. She's strong too. Stronger and no bigger, despite what she'd say. I haven't often loved my brawn since we made a home together. But I do when I take Elizabeth in my arms. She'll fall asleep reading in her chair, surrender to her cushy rut rather than face the massive task of walking six paces to our bed. She wouldn't do it if I didn't carry her. Even asleep, I can see her gratitude at not having her slumber spoiled. I'm happy I'm strong then.

Like Elizabeth before her, it's nothing for me to carry Reznick. Yet I see no gratitude in her young face.

I finally come upon some water. It's something between a bog and a marsh, but it's vast enough for me to not see the end of it. It isn't beautiful, but it will have to do.

I set Reznick gently among the stones and pebbles beside the water. I take time and take care. I make a little raft for her from some thin, warped branches and twine. I gather whatever little specks of colour I can find among the dry, cutting shrubs and tall grass. With much trouble and gaze averted, I remove her boots and clothes so she can leave this world as she came in, save for that labyrinthine, snaking tattoo her family gave her. I lay her down on the raft and fold her arms over her chest so she might have some semblance of grace.

I feel foolish. I hate this ugly, inadequate place. I don't know the rituals she deserves, and I never believed in them. I want to know I honoured her as best I could. I don't know why. She'd hate me either way. There's no consolation I could give her, now or ever, especially not with a memorial this shabby. No one will know what I've done here. If they found out, they wouldn't care.

I'm supposed to say something. It's probably supposed to be aloud. The selfishness of this little display gnaws at me. Who does this comfort? Only myself. What's that worth? Yet I want to be comforted. I do.

"I'm sorry," I say, bowing my head like she might see my contrition with her cold dead stare. "If I could take it back…"

I wish I could give you something. Something so much more than this self-serving gesture, something so much bigger than my life.

What can I offer? Something I took from you? A father's love. It's yours. In my heart, you're my child, perfect save for the imperfections I gave you. I love you. Unconditionally. I love all those I've harmed. You most of all. There's nothing you could have done to me I wouldn't have forgiven. I don't know why I can't voice it.

It's not enough. Did you see goodness in yourself? Did your malice serve a higher purpose? Did you fight for a better kingdom? Did you wish for peace? I will deliver it, or I'll desolate and degrade myself until it's here or near. That's it, isn't it? You want me to hurt? I will. I promise you. More than you could dream. You were so young. Too young to know how I suffer. Too new to know love this pure.

"I've thought of you every day," I mutter. "I always will."

I lower her eyelids over her accusing eyes. I push her raft into the inky water. The rocks and weeds trap her, so I follow her in. I pull her through the muck and past the reeds. I'm wet to my elbows. She's floating now, unhindered.

On the tips of my toes and with my chin held high just over the water's surface, I give her one last shove. It takes me off my feet, and I tread until she disappears into the fog. I stay for I don't know how long, waiting for something to happen. I consider all the little indignities that could still befall her. The tide could turn the raft over. Some creature could come along and prey on her.

    I stare at the fog for an age, waiting for anything. It doesn't matter, I tell myself. She's gone.

CHAPTER 16: THE LOST PRINCESS

Mathius

You learn things when you've been around long enough. You see the shapes, the loops, the patterns. You see the same story play out again and again in subtle variations. Each person froths and frets over their turn, their chance at the dance, but in the all-consuming scheme that governs us all, everything has come, and everything shall pass. Things are simpler than they seem.

As a god, I understand that people are basically animals. They share an essential nature with all living things. They pursue it blindly, ignorant of their own tedious predictability. They believe their expanded minds and supremacy over beasts grant them freedom. But they are ruled by their impulses just as all the other low things are.

Fear comes first to every creature with a modicum of intelligence. Fear of death, followed by the fear of what leads to death. Most individuality within the human race flows from this as each sees a different path to the inevitable end. Some fear pain. Some rejection. Some violence. Some exploitation. Some poverty. Some anonymity. It goes on and on. All minds are preoccupied with self-interest, and self-interest is self-preservation.

From there, each person defines power. Power is freedom from what is feared. It is chased relentlessly because all people loathe weakness, especially their own. This, again, leads people in an infinite number of directions. Each flees their fear in their own particular way. Some make themselves completely invisible. They do what they must, cultivate meagre talents and aptitudes as much as is necessary while drawing as little attention to themselves as possible. They risk nothing. For the most part, they do what comes easily to them.

These classic, innumerable mediocrities, ironically, lack for fear. It takes a certain trust in the world to shuffle through life achieving nothing. All substantial people became so by never believing things could get along without them. They feel the ground giving way beneath them and can't be told otherwise.

The more powerful a person in their chosen field, the more profound the fear. A person who made themselves rich did so because they detest poverty. A beautiful person shudders at ugliness. A loving spouse weeps at the thought of a half-empty bed. No one loves so deeply as the lonely. The purest talents flourish in defence against the deepest suffering.

In all of history, there must never have been a man so pained as the Blight. From what, who knows. I never did learn what it was that wounded him so. That's the thing about the truly exceptional. If they were easily explained, there'd be many, many more of them.

He can't be as I'm told he is. He couldn't have been that tall. His spear couldn't have been so heavy. He couldn't have done what he did. No way. Impossible.

But he did. He must have because it's done. I'd like to believe I understand things, that I know where things are going, but how can I? This has never been. This is a new world, only familiar if I squint. A god is dead, and the Blight killed him.

Ciendy

There are some things even Father can't control. When word of what happened at First Morning reached him, he did all he could to smother it. He gathered every servant who saw Darnett's body and silenced them. Reznick hasn't spoken a word that we know of since Mathius took her in. Only a single witness is unaccounted for, but evidently, that's plenty for word to spread. I hear they call him Ruthless. Or the Blight. I suppose it isn't decided.

I don't think Father believes it quite yet. He never trusts any eyes but his own, and all information is only rumour and aspersion until he resolves otherwise. Even when Mathius fetched the body himself and shared the news with sombre certainty, Father was skeptical.

"It's a ruse," he said, gruff and dismissive. "A trick. Black magic or illusion, I'm sure."

Maybe he was holding out hope. He's never handled disappointment well. None can attest to that better than I.

We're at the mausoleum now, among all our distinguished fallen. Here are the ashes of our line, the burnt up vessels of all the gods sent home. Each has a magnificent statue and a little plaque. King Fassil, four hundred and fifty. King Sovaj, Father's father, one thousand and twenty-five. If they're all true, Darnett would be the youngest of them by far.

My eldest brother lies on a cold stone slab in front of us. Even with a sheet covering every piece of him, I'm sure it's him. I see it in the sag of Mathius' shoulders and the uneasy tapping of Father's fingers. The lord of all creation, so indomitable, so fierce, is at truth's door and paralyzed. There will be no denying after this.

With one last thrash of stubborn defiance, Father rips down the sheet. A weak little gasp escapes him, small enough for Mathius and me to think we only dreamed it. He takes in Darnett's pale, peaceful face, and searches for some solution. There isn't any. His son is dead. A father can feel no greater failure.

I've never known Father to blame himself. I've only ever known him to be impeccable and invincible. All the world vexes and dissatisfies him, but before today, it's never touched him. He's never grieved. He's only ever been aggrieved. Before my eyes, he confronts a fact too foul to accept. All his life, he's determined the truth. Yet right here in front of us, heresy stares back unblinking, unmistakable, and definitive.

His hand fidgets and trembles, scratching at his leg. Mathius acts like he doesn't see it. He knows how much Father treasures his loftiness, and there's nothing so undignified as pain. That's the way of fathers and sons. They hide their weakness from each other. A son's excellence is his father's, and the other way around is just as true. The more illustrious they are, the more they honour one another. So, they leave open gaping wounds to make each other proud, as if seeking healing is admitting vulnerability.

I make a grave mistake. I reach out for Father's hand and squeeze it. I think for a second if I don't say a word, if I don't make him admit anything, I can help him. That he'll find some comfort. For only a second, I'm right. I feel his gratitude. He is soothed by being known. Then the shame hits him.

He rips his hand away.

※ ※ ※

We've had trouble organizing a funeral for Darnett. There are no rites for this. Passings of gods are rare, usually tinged with all the jubilance of a return home. The mortal world is a cruel and harsh one. To fulfill one's duty and leave this plane for the next is a joyous occasion. Yet no journey made unwillingly is a glad one.

There would be obscenity in the usual demonstrations. As the story goes, a million flowers and a million songs followed Sovaj's final procession through the Capital. That hardly seems appropriate. Melodies would burn like poison. Flowers would enhance the blackness of the day by contrast.

Death is not our family's domain. I've suggested asking the servants and citizens about it. They know it better. Every one of them has some brother, sister, son, or daughter gone too soon. Whatever wisdom or comfort they found along the way could serve us well. Father berated me for equating our grief with theirs. Mathius was more cordial, but he hardly seemed inclined to pursue the idea.

Father settled on the classic ritual. It would be seen through without adjustment or amendment. "Anything else would mean admitting defeat," he surmised sharply. Mathius and I knew there was no point arguing it any further.

The ceremony was held in the early morning. The order went out to all citizens that attendance would be mandatory. Cautious faces in bright clothing crowded the streets. Confused children eager to dance and yell along to boisterous songs were clutched close against their parents. There's nothing so odd as happy music played unhappily.

We laid Darnett down on a bed so big and wide it took ten men to carry. We covered him in so many flowers he couldn't be seen. The bed barely fit through the castle's front gate, and people pressed nearer each other when they saw it coming down the street. We stood out ahead of it for all to gawk, where anyone might hurl some projectile and harm us if only we were anyone else.

We marched all the way to the sea, our chins held high, a parade of musicians and soldiers trailing behind us. Mathius dragged Reznick by the hand. We were a quarter of the way when it became apparent this was much too far a walk for her. She never complained. Mathius didn't dare pick her up. Neither did I.

When we came to the water, a priest went out knee-deep and said some very nice words in a loud, dulcet voice. He spoke about circles, freedom, peace... everything but death. I was sure I'd seen him before, but I couldn't remember his name. That gnawed at me. It placed two competing, cloying thoughts at the back of my mind. Either this man didn't know my brother well enough to speak on him, or I didn't know my brother well enough to know those who knew him.

The ten men lowered Darnett's bed onto the sand then trudged away. A half-dozen holy men circled about in a hypnotic rhythm, dousing my brother in oil. When they finished, four men in extravagant plate and mail lowered torches into the brush at the edges of the bed. The fire ate hungrily as the men pushed the bed out to sea.

Some new dread came upon me when the flames finally reached Darnett. I choked as if feeling the heat and smoke on him. Part of me expected him to jolt awake and make the flames dance for us as he had countless times before. The fire no longer served him. It ate him just like the flowers.

Reznick cried. Mathius finally took her up in his arms. He guided her head into his shoulder. I fought back tears with shaking breaths. Father didn't budge an inch. He only impatiently watched his child melt to ash. He wanted this day to be over. He wanted to be done with it and never think of it again.

It was clear to me then that any love my Father ever felt for his firstborn was gone. Darnett's slaying was an unforgivable outrage, an embarrassment that cast a shadow so long and dark it smothered all previous fondness. Father hated his own son. He would hate him always, and all his tender recollections would morph into bitter prophecy and ugly portents of doom. It was easier, I suppose. In disowning Darnett, Father absolved himself.

In Father's callousness, I was made callous. I knew all at once I could never win his love. Moreover, I didn't care. I finally saw all his selfishness. We were trophies to him, only as valuable as the glory we brought him. His lessons shaped us not for the world but for his stature. His protection was oppression, a shield against his own diminishment. From then on, he could do nothing for me. He had nothing to offer.

I promised myself I'd never go home again. I would never have a better chance than tonight to escape.

* * *

After the funeral runs its course, a pair of guards escort me to my tower. I think I know them. It's hard to be sure with the masks and armour, and the men themselves tend to be uniform in size and height as well. I think the one on the left is the one I call Squat, and the one on the right is the one I think of as Long.

There's maybe two inches difference between them. I don't know their names. Father doesn't let them talk to me.

We begin the long, narrow, winding climb to my chamber. I feel Squat sink at the thought of the trek ahead of him. Their armour is heavy, much heavier than my robes. They don't walk these steps as often as I do. It's no small feat. It's labour enough to discourage would-be assassins.

As we near the top, I feel Long and Squat fading. They refuse to gasp for air, of course. As much as it'd help them, it's much too base. Their fatigue shows in more understated ways. The dragging of their feet, the lilt of their heads, the weight with which they press the butts of their spears into the steps ahead of them. I'll squeeze every drop of effort I can out of them before I strike.

At the top of the steps, Long straightens with gratification so total and blissful he nearly shines. He pulls the keys from his hip and unlocks the door to my chamber. There. Now.

I kick Long in the back, not knowing what will happen. I've never struck a human with intent. Part of me expects him to explode into bright dust, but he only stumbles and clatters his head against the wall.

I feel Squat panic. His mind reels, searching for some protocol that surely doesn't exist. He reaches for me, and I thrust a sharp palm beneath his chin.

I'm startled by how slow these men are and how little I slow them. They snatch and grab at me, and I dodge their swipes so easily I have time to land two blows for each of their misses. Yet they are unrelenting. Their armour hurts my hands and feet, so I test it against my knees and elbows. That's a little better. But not enough.

Eventually, I accept that the stone of the tower is harder than my bones. I send Squat tumbling down the stairs with a leaping push from both my feet. I sweep out Long's legs and drive his head into the point of a step with my heel over and over. He finally loses consciousness just before Squat is on me again. He leaps at me with both hands, but I slip behind him and jam his head into the wall until he joins Long in an unwelcome sleep.

I sit on the stairs, catching my breath among the tangle of splayed, unmoving limbs. I've won my first real fight. Maybe even easily. It's hard to know without more experience, and I'm not even sure I care to find out for certain. I have so much else I'd rather learn. There's so much I don't know.

I realize that among the many things I don't know is when Long and Squat will wake up. Of that, I haven't any clue. I hurry to my feet and make haste to my room. I've pondered all night what happens next.

First, I need to change out of my best attire and into my worst. Nothing draws the eye like royal robes. I don't have much else to choose from. All my garments but my sleeping clothes are made to be seen. So, my sleeping clothes will have to do. They're loose and comfortable. I'll be able to run fast in them. They'll tear and dirty easily, but it doesn't matter. They only need to last as long as it takes for me to find something else.

What else do I bring with me? As little as possible. Every item is a load on my back. Suddenly, the room I've felt for so long was my prison is full of precious things. My books, my paints, my games. Nothing can come with me. It's all gone, lost from me for all time. It occurs to me now I have Mathius to thank for every beloved possession in here. He lavished thoughtful gifts on me whenever he could, anticipated and supported every fancy I ever had. He'll be gone too.

All at once, the cost of my freedom is real. I've spent all my days dreaming of the future, but my life so far, for all its misery, has not been completely without joy. I've loved Mathius, and he's loved me. Isn't that rare and to be cherished? How can I be sure the world outside my walls will have something to match it? How can I risk the very best thing I've ever had on an unknown?

I think about staying. Maybe it's all a matter of attitude. Maybe I lack perspective and owe reverence to my splendour. Maybe my pain isn't real, the dream of an idle mind. Maybe it's the bleating of a rich and spoiled brat, nothing compared to the despair that haunts the poor, hungry, and lonely of this world.

But I am alone. And I will only be lonelier. All love in Father's heart has died. Worse yet, Mathius will fade out from my life little by little. He's the eldest now. The kingdom is his. His responsibilities are doubled. Young Reznick will be his ward, and he will expend every ounce of energy in him rescuing her from the abyss she has sunk into. He will be expected to sire a child. He will think of me as an obligation. As the days go by, my tower will seem more remote. The climb up my stairs will seem longer. There will always be some reason or excuse not to visit me, and they will always be fair and benign. His goodness will cost me everything, and I will hate him for it.

Bitterness washes over me in an intense wave. I know for certain that staying here is the true risk. Staying here means the death of love. I won't be a burden. I will exit Mathius's life pure and true, and I will match his goodness somewhere out there in a new corner of the world.

I gather up my cloak and run down the stairs. I don't need a last look at my room. Its memory will serve me nothing.

Rufus

I'm weak. I've been weak from the moment I killed Darnett. Something stays my hand. In training, I feel the gap between me and the other Nameless closing. I do not dominate. I merely control. I stop my fists before they find their target. I apply no pressure when I get my holds. The brothers and sisters I'm camped with think it mercy, and they are grateful. They'd find virtue in anything I do at this point.

I am wanted by the kingdom like no other man before me. Since the Reckoning, I've been stationed with a class of young Nameless so that I may hide and they might learn. They look at me with wide eyes and open hearts. They idolize me. I do not care for it. I loathe the thought of disappointing them. I don't like being the elder. My words and movements are watched closely and taken for instruction. I am no teacher. I have no lessons. I miss Master Terra.

We're seated for dinner now around a fire. Ordinarily, I enjoy silence. Even that has been taken from me. Now, silence is stifling, pregnant with anticipation. So much is unspoken. Every one of these half-dozen faces holds back a hundred questions for me. Part of me wishes they would speak up so I might be done with it. I'd love to be done with everything.

You're tired, Rufus. That's all. You've pressed hard and worn thin. Rest. Nourish yourself on your brothers and sisters. Take their love and admiration. It's what we all live, struggle, and die for.

It means nothing to me.

I see a young man called Wind sprinting through the woods. He arrives, hacking and wheezing, trying to catch his breath. I've never seen him so exhausted, or even exhausted at all. I can't imagine how long he must have run.

"The Princess has escaped!" he blurts out as soon as he's able. "She's fled the Capital!"

All my brothers and sisters around the fire turn to me. A whole nation turns to me. There has never been such an opportunity. A god alone and far from home in a world she does not know. She will be exposed. If she were dangerous, we'd have heard. Any one of us might be enough to defeat her.

Trepidation overcomes me. Hope has warped into expectation. I will crush spirits by failing now. I feel rooted to my spot, plagued by doubt. I am so tired. So fragile. But all these young faces look to me.

"Armies of loyals will be after her," I say to enthralled ears. "Armies are slow. We go everywhere. Every town, every camp, as fast as we can. Each of us. Alone."

I nod my head, and my brothers and sisters surge out in every direction. They will scatter and spread as they are taught. I see in their eyes they are fierce, fiercer than I can be. Maybe one of them will make themselves a hero in the coming nights. Maybe they will take this God Killer mantle from me. Maybe one of them will be better suited to it.

I treasure the thought so much I am slow to my feet. I

scold myself. I reach deep into my heart to spark that fire even Master Terra fears, that fire that made me who I am.

I am Rufus. The Balance. God Killer. There will be no other. It brings me no pleasure, but so it must be.

Ciendy

My face chafes. These masks aren't built for running. Sweat makes them insufferable. I can't wait to be rid of mine, but I can still hear Mathius and his party's horses on my heels. I was barely out of the castle when I heard the alarm bells blare. He can still catch me, and I'd rather spare him the devastation in my eyes. That's what I tell myself, beating back an ugly thought: what might he do if his men see my face?

The law is inflexible. I adore Mathius. He loves so deeply. His people, his family, and everything in this world that's worthy or not. I want to believe he wouldn't follow the rules. I want to believe that he'd spare his men. I want to believe he'd hear my plight and let me go. I want it so bad I can't risk the truth disillusioning me. I can't be wrong about him. I won't be.

I listen carefully. I'm sure the steady stampeding of hooves is fading into the distance. I hear real silence for the first time in days. I breathe deeply, take in my surroundings. I'm on a hill, in something I think was once a fort. It's not impressive enough to be called ruins. Even chilled by fresh fallen snow, it gives me all the respite, refreshment, and comfort of home. Or that home ought to, anyway. The home I'm searching for.

Something in the air changes. My mind awakens to endless possibilities, to the dark side of the world my family promised. I'm truly alone now, perhaps for the first time. Anything could happen. The thought had only ever delighted me. Now, those vague, distant threats are real. Who's to say what's around the corner? Anything could be in those shadows. Ruthless himself, for instance.

I regret even thinking of him, worried I might conjure him. I chide myself for the childishness of the tingle in my spine.

I may as well look under my bed or sleep with a light. How far could word of my escape possibly spread? How easily could he drop his matters to chase me? How clever would he have to be to reach me in spite of my brother? What are the chances that of all the places in the world, he'd be here? Then again, where else would he be?

In the darkness, a shape. No. Please. No.

I see his spear first. The blade catches the moonlight for just a moment in its wide, arcing swing. I duck my head a couple of inches, and it misses me by one. I roll across the ground to face him, and he barges out, a behemoth in human flesh. He doesn't give me so much as a second to take him in, but the bald head and black shrouds he shares with hordes of Nameless buy him no anonymity.

The stories always lead with his strength. The spear only he can lift and so on. That he lifts it means nothing to me. The speed and elegance with which he maneuvers captivates me. As Mathius paints with a brush, Ruthless cuts with his spear. Both are artists, and a strange sense of wonder comes upon me with each stroke he speeds by my body.

We move in and out in a nasty, hateful dance. There's something strange in his form. He's conflicted, ambivalent, battling unwillingly but furiously, expertly. He doesn't want to hit me. He swings so wide it'd be my own fault if he connected. He seems content dashing my cloak to ribbons. It'll be no help against the cold now, but I have more pressing concerns.

He invites my strikes. I'm disconcerted by how my fists collapse ineffectually into him. I poke and prod for organs and brittle places, but he must not have any. I'm afraid I'll irritate him, press him so far he changes his mind.

He's giving me every opportunity. Does he want me to get away? No, he obstructs me every time I move to escape. So what else could he want? Not my death, I don't think. So something worse? Am I his toy? I don't see any malice or spite in him. He's a monument to brutal efficacy.

He closes in. He snatches at me, and I feel his fingers graze my hair on the way to my mask. I grab at his wrist. It's nearly too big for me to fit both my hands around. I can't budge him. I drive both my heels into his hips, and I launch myself off him like a spring. He takes my mask and a few strands of hair, but mainly I'm relieved. I know I shouldn't be. He's stolen something very precious, so I've been so often told.

I hope he takes a second to admire his shiny prize, but I'm not so lucky. He tosses my mask aside with utter disregard, and it splits in two against a rock. I roll onto my stomach and try to hide my face in my hand. If he sees me, it's over. I won't ever be safe so long as he lives. I feel my future fading, my pulse racing. I was never afraid of losing the life I had. Now I feel the absence of my life to come. I want to live. I hear his steps coming for me, and I've never been so sure.

I reach for my boot. In a flash, I have my blade at his throat. He stops in his tracks, and I know right away what he wants. For the first time, I look right at him as only I can. I see so much pain, as huge and as inconceivable as the damage he's done. He's so tired, so contrite. He only sees the one road home, that last exit that shows itself to the most lost. He wants me to save him. He wants me to save everyone. All it takes is pressing that little piece of metal just a little bit harder, he tells me without saying a thing. More than anything, I want to tell him I'm sorry. I'm not the one.

He sees I can't, and he hates me for it. His face flushes with humiliation. He swats my blade away, and I'm on the ground before I know anything's even happened. My neck disappears in his hands. I feel his bulk on top of me, and suddenly all my virtues are void. My love, my forgiveness, my patience… all born of cowardice and sloth. The idea of a good and right world seems like the dream of a stupid, lucky rich girl. I renounce everything I made myself, every decision I looked back on with esteem. They're poisoned for all time because they led me here: dead at the hands of a brute, the brute of the world.

His hands shake as he releases me. I suck in as much air as I can. I've never before appreciated air like it deserved. He breaks

me from my sole preoccupation with a firm hand on my chin.
"Run away," he tells me. "Run away and never return."
Who am I to refuse him?

CHAPTER 17: THE PATH OF LEAST EVIL

Rufus

It's not the good I've done that comforts me when I look inward. There's nothing I can put to the scales to balance the harm I've inflicted. There's a place I go to in my mind when I need relief, apart from victory, triumph, failure, or tragedy.

I go to Elizabeth. She looks at me, and in spite of all she knows, she loves me. It's more than acceptance, it's more than forgiveness, it's more than admiration. It makes all my evil seem so insignificant, so fleeting. When I see myself through her eyes, I am redeemed. The best person I know, the best person I could imagine can't be all wrong about me. I can't be so bad.

I'm drawing her now. I took up the habit sometime after we made our home in Paralee. I don't know how good I am. I've never had a teacher, and I've no need to show my work to anyone who could tell me. I take no pride in my artfulness or skill. My drawings don't closely resemble the true look of the world or enhance it in any meaningful way. All I know is when I look at my portraits of Elizabeth, I see her. I recognize the crinkle of her eyes, the subtle shifts in her moods. I'm reminded of the moments we've shared. That's good enough for me.

I etch a new piece as often as I can. It keeps her close, keeps her vivid in the front of my mind. I don't want to forget even a fragment of her. All we are is our memories. Drawing hones and focuses them. I've made legions of portraits on this long road to Hospice. When one wears down from time or the elements, I draw it again, cleaner and better than before.

On my loneliest nights, I spread out as many as I can around me and marvel at the beauty of my life. My favourite is a scene of a summer day. Elizabeth looks over her shoulder at me, her feet in the stream. When I look at it, I remember everything. The feel of the grass on my knees, the way the tree curved just so into my back, the breeze gently stirring the branches and leaves above me. I remember the certainty with which she took the ring I offered her. It's a perfect moment.

I could live in that memory. I could put myself there and leave all the world behind. Maybe I did. Maybe that's what my life with Elizabeth has been. I can't be happy. I can't be comfortable. I can't be this close to all I want. I have so much to do.

I pocket the little scrap of paper and the pencil I was using. I lift my head and finally take in the place my feet have brought me. I feel a sudden, unwelcoming mood, like I've trespassed into somewhere I don't belong. I see a small cloud, dissipating and reappearing steadily. Through wet, tilting trees, I see something watching me: a bear almost as tall as I am, even standing on all fours.

For a moment, I'm paralyzed by its rare grandeur. At first glance, a bear is just a dog. They're much bigger, but they're also much softer per pound. I've loved every dog I've ever seen that wasn't snapping at me, not to mention some that were. Elizabeth said her family kept a bear for a pet for a while. She told me they were playful and silly, that they'd roll about like overgrown toddlers. The image never left me. Even now, it raises the corners of my lips.

The bear does not appear to regard me quite so affectionately. I haven't moved. I won't. I hope it doesn't find me as interesting as I find it. Quickly, I see it has none of my gentle curiosity. I can feel its contempt in the mist of its hungry breath. I plan my next steps very carefully.

First, I make a big show of myself. I raise my arms and bulge my neck. I bellow and grunt. I try to be the giant all the

CHAPTER 17: THE PATH OF LEAST EVIL | 165

Nameless spoke about in stories, but I guess the bear hasn't heard them. My one bold step forward is answered with a slobbering roar that overwhelms senses I didn't know I had.

I know to run. It's immediately evident I won't win a sprint, so I try some swift steps sideways. The wind of a swipe just missing my ear compels me elsewhere. I roll beneath another angry outstretching of the bear's arm and attempt to scurry up a tree. Attempt. I've seen children manage it quicker. Again, I'm cursing my mass.

I'd like to blame the bear hurling its weight into the tree for its collapse, but I know I'm no small contributor. The tree betrays me again, pinning my back into the dirt long enough for the bear to offer reinforcements. It drops its paws onto the tree, shoving bark and sap into my beard.

The bear roars in my face, and I can't help but take offence to the spit falling in my mouth and the ringing in my ears. This is stupid. Animals should know better. If a man picks a fight he can't win, it's one thing. By their nature, men see themselves as the center of things. Between the ears of every man is a boundless kingdom of which he is the master, so vast and ever-expanding that it seems impossible anything could impede it. To men, death is an unthinkable curiosity too strange and exotic to ignore. They flirt and tease with it, blind to its consequences. But animals? A mouse doesn't attack a hawk.

I push into the tree with both hands, raising it and the bear just enough for me to shoot my hips. The lift startles the bear. In the ensuing scramble, I nearly create some distance. The bear pounces before I make it to my feet, and now I'm on my stomach. The bear tries to hold me still with one paw to better bite at me and nearly succeeds. I wriggle free. I feel claws pulling down on my flesh, and I permit myself some anger. I hate this bear. I hate its wet, probing nose. I hate its clumsy, searching paws. I hate its stinking breath and the greedy snaps of its ugly teeth. I hate its coarse hair and overfed belly. I hate it. I hate it.

It chomps at me. I grab it by its ears, pulling it over my shoulder, bringing it into the mud with me. I put it on its back and press my weight into its chest with my elbow. It tries to sink its teeth into my head, but I don't let it. I grab it by its neck to push myself away. It swings its awful, heavy limbs at me. It touches its teeth to my forearm. I pull its jaws off me by its nostrils. I drive the point of my palm as straight and as sharp as I can into its head, again and again.

I think of all the good that can come from this. A belly full of meat. Warm furs for cold nights. Safety for anyone who wanders these woods. I fixate on the little transformations I bring about with each strike. First, smooth skull becomes jagged. Then, dry, cutting fur becomes wet and slick. Sudden, fitful movement becomes very, very still. I don't know how much time passes. When the fog of my fury parts, I find myself screaming my lungs out into some sopping mush that has as much to do with the beast that crossed me as the clouds or the grass. Stupid. Pointless.

I climb out of the mangled mess, diverting my eyes from the beauty I've spoiled, careful not to wipe my dripping hands on my clothes. I scrape the larger chunks speckling my arms on a branch. I try to quiet my panting, hoping the trickling of a stream might find my ears and slow my pounding heart. Instead, I hear a gentle murmur.

I find a young cub poking at what's left of the bear. She squeaks and purrs. She pounces on her mother's paw, butts her head into her shoulder. She's confused, but not afraid yet, too simple to process the sudden ineffectuality of all her tried and true calls for attention. She looks to me like I might have some explanation. Distrust rises up in her, and she calls for her mother's support, backpedalling.

Clear as day, I see all the cub's life in front of me. I see her young fur and flesh tightening against her bony frame. I hear the churn of an empty stomach eating itself. I feel the hot salivation of a predator on the back of her neck and legs too sickly to carry her away from it. I see an innocent thing with nothing to protect it from savagery. There are no good paths ahead of her, but there is one least evil.

I spare her the pain. I only wish I could have spared her the fear.

CHAPTER 18: WHAT NO ONE SEES

Small

It's a grey, tedious day. I'm sitting on the porch, ignoring Bandit's noisy pleas for attention. I'm as bored as he is, but it'll serve me nothing to reward his fussing. His behaviour needs adjustment, not reinforcement.

Finally, I see Elizabeth returning from town. She sulks, lost in thought, but this is not unusual. She's frittered most her days away since Crag's funeral drifting about, sullen and distant. She hardly acknowledges me. I suspect in some way too small and petty to voice she blames me for Crag's passing. I spend my days hovering behind her in wait. I feel silly, a servant doting on a lord. I want to please her. I want to be there for whatever she needs, however she asks.

I rise to meet her as she passes the gate. I expect her to stride right past me as she has a hundred times before, but she slows to a stop as she approaches me. Something is different. She looks up at me, grave and unsettled. She must have news from Paralee.

"Princess Reznick is dead," she tells me.

The words are so impossible to believe I'm slow to react. First, elation swells my whole being. A dream too desperate and audacious to admit has come true. At the brink of extinction, at the final hour of all Nameless, another Reckoning. Rufus, the one and only God Killer, is returned, and all the world is off its axis.

I want to dance and cheer until I see the morose expression on Elizabeth's face. She should burst with pride. Her husband has achieved the unthinkable, triumphed over an evil as heinous and pure as has ever been. It's worthless to her. Nothing I can say will shrink the distance she feels from him.

Just as I work up the courage to press for details, she walks past me. She goes to her room and shuts the door softly, sparing me the rejection of a slam in the face. The door creaks open just a crack. She wants her space and to be alone. I know that. But maybe she needs something. Maybe she'll call on me. I should be close enough to hear.

I cast a fleeting glance through the thin opening between the door and its frame. I see her tiredly sliding an arm out from her robe. I avert my eyes. A rush of bashfulness startles me. The Nameless relinquish any claim to privacy. People only go to private places to hide, and people only hide vices and shortcomings, which are to be defeated, not hidden. If your flesh is soft, harden it. If your techniques are ugly, fix them. Bad habits are as infectious as plague and must be eradicated. Yet still, without thinking, I look away. It's foolish of me. Too deferent. If I want to look, I should. And I do.

She slides out her other arm, and her robe falls enough for me to see her back. My heart jumps, then sinks. She has a tattoo. A dragon. Long, snaking, elegant, and unmistakable. Finer and cleaner than any I've seen. A master's work, saved only for the highest. A loyal. At least. Something even more.

Oh no.

Elizabeth

I hear my door crash open. I pull up my robe and whip around to find sharp steel flying at my head. I duck and find Small at a sword's handle, furious. Was she looking? How could she look? Why would she—

No time for that. I whip my head backwards to save my neck, then follow the momentum pulling me rolling over my bed. A bit of distance. I can get my bearings. Not for long. Small climbs onto the bed obstructing her, and I sweep out her exposed legs. If only my bed were rocks. She lands comfortably in plushness, but at least her sword will do less harm from her back.

I need a weapon. I don't want to kill her. Something dull, heavy. I cross the room, searching. Small rolls to her feet and swings at me in one liquid motion. For the first time, I wish my room were bigger. I spin and weave around her slices then kick her in the chest. It doesn't hurt her, but it pushes her back. She lands in a chair. Plush again. I should have let Rufus decorate. This room would be lousy with solid things.

I reach for a candelabra. It's well built, at least. Sturdy. Small is already on her feet. She raises her sword high and drives it down to cleave me in two. I can only raise the candelabra. It holds, catching the blade between its columns. There. I told Rufus it was worth something.

I twist the candelabra and jerk sideways, disarming Small. I follow my turn all the way around and catch her flush across the chin with the back of my heel. If I were Rufus, I might have knocked her head clean off her shoulders. I do with ten blows what he does with one. But I do it. I can't slice through a tree with one swing, but I can still bring it down.

Small's more surprised than hurt, but that's still something. She hurls all the angry, predictable strikes at me. I slip her punches, push back her rising knees, block her kicks. All her many failures come with a receipt. I try not to injure her. I concentrate on her head. She doesn't use that too much.

She's slowing now, bloodied and staggered. Fatigue defeats everything eventually. We all reach a point where rest is all that matters. She makes one last clumsy effort that guarantees the fight's end one way or another. Her spinning kick misses me badly. I have time enough to put everything I have into a leaping punch that clatters down on the side of her jaw. She lands unconscious on my bed, sweating and bleeding all over my covers.

Finally afforded some peace and respite, I catch my breath. In my safety, all my troubles so far veiled by the immediacy of combat surge to the front of my mind. I groan. I wish I were still fighting.

Small

I wake in a daze, my ears ringing, my eyes bleary and spotty. I'm in my bed. I recognize the feel of it. Less familiar is the scratchy sensation around my wrists and ankles. I'm sluggish, but it comes to me. Rope. I'm tied up. The ropes only afford me a couple of inches, binding my wrists and ankles to the four rugged bedposts.

Elizabeth sits on a wooden chair, calmly surveying me. No. That's wrong. Princess Ciendy basks in her enemy's defeat. I'm in the eye of a storm, the jaws of a beast. What does she want? I won't give her anything. What do I even have to give? Nothing I can think of. My head is throbbing.

"You're going to make too much of this," she tells me, heavy with weary anticipation.

"You're the Princess!" I spit, thrashing against the ropes. My saliva stings the open wounds on my lips.

"Yes, that's part of it—" she begins, but I don't care what she has to say.

"Rufus is a traitor," I set it down bluntly. I can tell she takes exception.

"You don't know what you think you know," she says.

"What was it?!" I demand. "A spell? A kiss? Witch! What has your slave done for you? Has he given us all away? You'll get nothing from me!"

"You have nothing for me," she sighs.

She has no sway over me, I pledge myself. I fear no violence. I won't be misled or seduced. I'm glad I'm not a man. She'll have fewer tools to deceive me.

"I am the Princess," she admits. "You don't know a single other thing about me. You think you hate the Crown? You don't know it. You were never near it. I lived it. I left it."

"You're not loyal?" I ask, barely beating back my disdain.

"I'm not," she says, indulging me.

"Then why take Rufus?" I inquire, cooly now, secure in my righteousness. "If you hated the evil of the world that bore you, you'd have set Rufus on it. If you hated your family, he could have rid you of it!"

She listens to me patiently, assures me with her silence that I can't hurt or deride her. I deny her my anger. She'd see some victory in it.

"What do you think my powers are?" she asks, finding this all very tedious.

We never knew, really. No one did. There was little word on the Princess until Rufus killed her, and none was needed after. It's obvious now what her gift is: influence. I look back on my time here and the fondness I had for her sickens me, forever tainted by her devious manipulation. It must be why her father sent her away. He feared his mind clouded.

"It's not influence," she tells me, shaking her head. "I see. Nothing too specific or detailed, unless I really try. It's more of a feeling. What people hide. What hurts them. That's all. For instance, I know exactly how angry you are. How betrayed you feel. And how ashamed you are of how you felt about me."

I grit my teeth.

"When you know how people think and feel, you see how alike we really are," she explains. "It's hard to hate anyone once you really know them. Everyone is afraid. Everybody aches. From the lowliest peasant all the way to my father."

And Rufus too, I'm sure she's about to say.

"And Rufus too," she concurs, nodding her head. She looks away from me, to somewhere deep in the recesses of her mind. "He was everything they said when he found me. Primal, brutal. And more. He was an ocean of pain. Bottomless, with things so deep and dark I've never seen them since. What you and yours must have done to him..."

She takes a breath, at the threshold of something precious to her, something so rare and bright she strains to put words to it.

"He saw what I saw," she says plainly. "Gods and insects, we're all the same. He could have hated me. Should have. But he didn't."

She floats down from her sweet reminiscence, back into the muck with me. The warmth leaves her face when she finds me unmoved. Nevertheless, she unties my hands. I watch her carefully in anticipation of some trick, but she only sinks back into her chair. I've no chance at striking her with any efficacy until my legs are free. I doubt even then she'd be afraid.

"You don't see it," she says, dejected but unsurprised. "No one does."

She rises from her chair. She turns her back to me and walks away.

CHAPTER 19: THE SECOND RECKONING

Rufus

Another huge celebration. Another big fire. Another great lie.

    This time, there are two masks raised high on stakes. Well, one and a half. Darnett's shimmers, freshly polished. I took one part of Ciendy's and left the other for Mathius. It does nothing to diminish the celebration. Everyone here is just as happy. I imagine the kingdom mourns just as deeply. Never take more than you need.

    The drums pound. Feet stamp. Cries rise high into the air, loud and ecstatic. I've never seen so many Nameless gathered in one place. Everywhere I look, I see people I haven't met, long lost brothers and sisters who love and adore me. They have no idea who I am. They have no idea how I've forsaken them.

    My stomach turns. I breathe deeply. A word gnaws at me, as steady as the beating drums around me. Weak. Weak. Weak.

    Ciendy beat you. How? The least of the Royal Family, the runt of the litter. Smaller maybe than you've ever been. She couldn't have been that good. You wanted it. You must have. You coward. You're tired. Old. Fat. Old Fat. That's who you are. You've let yourself become him again. That snivelling baby is returned, and how many will suffer for it? How many children will be made orphans—

    Orphans. Stop. Don't think of that. There should be a hole in your throat. If not in yours, then hers. Blood that ought to paint the ground still courses through veins. Why? Why? Why?

I know why she lives. It's my weakness, nothing more. Why do I live? She knew who I was, I'm sure of it. She was afraid enough. She was so skilled that she should know anyone else wouldn't challenge her. You don't get that good being afraid of killing. How could you?

She knew who I was. I saw her face. Even with all that fear, she looked right at me and forgot all I might do to her. She saw me. I swear she pitied me. How? Why?

I have to find her. I must undo this wrong. I must serve my brothers and sisters. I should get up and go this very moment. But I don't. I stay right where I am. I'm so tired.

Weak. Weak. Weak...

Terra

Rufus hasn't moved. I don't know if he ever will. The fire has dwindled, the revelry has quieted. Dozens of Nameless enjoy a deep, restful slumber all around him. He wages a quiet war inside his head. He isn't hiding it like he was earlier in the night. The toll shows on his face now. It's all there in his eyes. Sorrow. Defeat.

We've hardly spoken since First Morning. He has avoided me tirelessly. He blames himself for the loss of my arm. I want to absolve him. Other brothers and sisters lost so much more. It'd be crass if I elevated my hardship over theirs. He shouldn't either.

It's not so bad, really. I can still teach, eat, and rest. I'll fight again someday. I must relearn just about everything from dressing to climbing, and that is no small inconvenience. But the more I train with my left hand, the better I get. I haven't seen myself improve so steadily and starkly since childhood. I have fewer years ahead of me than I have behind me. I've been staving off decline for so long. Tomorrow, instead of weary bones aching that much more, I will write a little better, swing my sword a little more neatly. The achievement will please me.

I don't know what Rufus has left to achieve. I don't know that my affirmation or approval have anything to offer. I suppose he could set himself on Mathius or the King. Killing them won't feel any different than killing Darnett and Ciendy did. He confronts something larger now, something even he shrinks from. He confronts his own futility.

All of life is a losing battle against futility. We all have a hole in us. We know our own smallness, and we know time will reduce us to nothing. We dream of victories so glorious they might etch our name in stone and earn us a legacy that might withstand the rot promised us all. Only a handful ever truly accomplish anything. Even among those, some are cursed. Sometimes, a triumph deepens the hole. Sometimes, triumph teaches you the ugly truth: there is no escape. There are no victories. Not really. We all belong to the dirt.

With that truth, I've watched Rufus battle all night. He'll lose. We all do. What that defeat will mean to him, I have no idea. He's less accustomed to it than most.

He comes to something. He knows all his skill and all his mastery mean nothing against what he's preparing to face. Suddenly, I see the boy I spoiled. Rufus is a child again, about to take his first step, on the verge of some world he does not understand. He has so much to learn again. So much to move towards. The thought emboldened me. It withers him. He's so unsure. I'd forgotten how it looked on him.

Everything about him goes heavy, the weight of the world pressing down on him. His shoulders sag. His eyes flutter. He won't stave off sleep much longer. He won't find the answers tonight.

* * *

I've had many bad dreams in my life. I've relived all my worst battles so many times I know them better than my own hand. When they come to me in the night, it usually only takes me a moment to pinpoint the time, the place, the tragedy. As soon as I do, the terror fades, and I can take these visions for the documents they are.

I thought I'd seen so much carnage in my time that I'd never need to invent any. Lately, some war I don't recognize visits me. I see Rufus. He stands in a sea of dead Nameless. All the young children I made into warriors. The faces change every night. I know so many, have so many to choose from. Their expressions are blank, their lips pursed shut. Yet I hear their voices in the distance, screaming and moaning in the midst of crackling and clattering.

I haven't yet numbed to it. I tell myself there's no such thing as prophecy. All dreams can teach you are the feelings and fears you must confront when you wake. Yet try as I might, I've found nothing in the day to protect me in the night. The screams don't stop.

I hear them now. My eyes bolt open. I'm awake. The screams have followed me. It's still dark. Something is wrong. I see old masters fretting and backpedalling. I follow their eyes and find Rufus in the throes of some horrible fit. He isn't himself. He staggers about, swatting and thrashing at invisible opponents, upturning the whole camp. Some gentle soul tries to calm him. Rufus levels him.

I'm not dreaming. This is happening.

Only the young dare approach Rufus. It takes a tender, unseasoned heart to believe good intentions can shield you from the wrath of a tempest. They reach at him with gentle hands, clutching at his arms, shoulders, and waist like hope and patience might suffice. He savages them. He claws their faces, collapses their chests, twists and exposes the bones beneath their skin. The evil I nourished turns against my brothers and sisters. No. These are babes. My children.

"Rufus!" I bellow. He doesn't hear me. He is somewhere far away.

I rush off the ground and into the fray. I pull my way through the frightened and helpless, beg them to clear the way.

"Rufus!" I scream myself hoarse. "Rufus!"

These children refuse to harm their hero. Don't they know? He'll kill them. He'll kill anything.

I leap onto his back and coil my legs beneath his ribs. I wrap the crook of my elbow around his neck and pull my forearm into his throat. That won't stop him. This is much more difficult short an arm. I need leverage. I don't know where to put my hand now.

Snorting and grunting, he pulls me over his shoulder. I'm back in the dirt, looking at the sky. I don't let the bleary stars I see distract me. I start scrambling backwards. A boot crashes into the earth right by me. It'd have decimated me.

I've never felt Rufus's rage set on me. I'm still not sure I have. He looks at me with distant, implacable eyes behind drooped eyelids. He pursues me relentlessly, without doubt or hatred. I'm afraid. More afraid than I've ever been. The White Falcon, Darnett, all my masters were larks. They're nothing to Rufus. He's proven it. I'm in danger. We're all in so much danger.

I reach into my belt and do what no one dared. I pull a knife and slash at his throat.

I'm embarrassed how little I get of him. He pulls back and I barely graze the side of his neck. His fingers fly to the little line of blood and his eyes clear. He's confused. Hurt. Not physically. The wound hardly registers with him. He sees the knife in my hand, and he knows I've betrayed him.

The haze he was lost in parts. The world comes to him. He hears snivelling and moaning. He looks around at the camp. He sees a dozen young faces flushed and damp from wet eyes. Those who don't panic and agonize over their shattered, mangled bodies stare at him with broken hearts, wondering where their fault lies. They're still so young. They can't fight back their tears. They trust him so much. They can only blame themselves.

He wants to tell them what they need to hear, but he can't fathom what the words might be. He looks to me reflexively. I can't show him the way. He's as horrified as any of us. He lifts up his spear and disappears into the night. We don't dare chase him.

We don't even have the courage to call after him.

The eldest gather amongst themselves, oblivious to the injured. Wounds will mend and bones will set. Much more important is what happened to the great champion of the Nameless. What will be the story? Who will be permitted to tell the tale? Can the witnesses be silenced? These old men and women needn't worry. These young souls are devout. They worship Rufus. They will speak no heresy.

Ciendy

Something's chasing me. Whatever it is, it's better than Mathius and his men. I thought I was done with this. Ruthless bought me some quiet hours. He threw the kingdom off my trail. I had a day of peace, and I slept nearly all the way through it. It was night when I woke. Then I heard feet I could not see, approaching from somewhere in the trees. So I ran.

A root catches my foot, and I tumble fast and hard. My elbow and shoulder hurt but not as much as my lungs. I'm grateful for the excuse to catch my breath.

I pull myself up from the wet grass, lamenting my freshly filthy clothes. In the periphery of my eye, I see a mass of shadows so immense I think I'm in the presence of a demon. It's much worse than I feared. From the thicket emerges Ruthless, striding with the purpose and certainty of a hunter coming upon wounded prey.

"Your brother's an awful tracker," he tells me.

He plops down wearily on a stump across from me. He plants the butt of his spear into the earth, and it stands as steadily as a stone tower. I'm frozen. I have absolutely no idea what's coming next.

"Why are you running?" he asks almost idly.

"Same reason you're fighting," I tell him once my stupor passes. I don't need an enemy. Him least of all.

"I'm not fighting," he says with a hard stare.

They're odd words to be uttered so menacingly. I

straighten my back, push back my shoulders, and loom as large as I can.

"I want to be free," I say with confidence.

He feels none of the bond to me I hoped he would. He assesses me with suspicion and incredulity.

"Do you know who I am?" he wonders, narrowing his eyes at me.

"Everyone knows who you are," I tell him. I say it quickly, as though returning a volley. He leans towards me, craning his neck.

"Everyone calls me something different," he says very patiently. "I want to hear it from you. Who am I?"

"Ruthless," I say hesitantly, certain I've walked into a trap. "The Blight."

He sneers. I've amused him.

"And what do they say about me where you're from?"

"They say you were born in blood," I explain, "that you killed with the first breath you took."

He nods his head and leans back on his stump.

"That's true," he says, a little impressed. "My mother died giving birth to me. Is that what you meant? Did you know that?"

I didn't. I suppose I could have guessed. Legends are always simple truths deliberately obscured.

I realize he's waiting for me to answer. I commit to my silence, transforming accidental slackjaw into stubborn defiance.

"My father was a healer," he continues, folding his enormous arms. "He delivered me. Imagine that? So much responsibility. So much at risk. All that life and love in your hands."

He looks up at the moon, dreary. His neck taunts me with vulnerable, pulsing bulges.

"I killed her. I couldn't have meant to, but I did. The way he talked about her, it had to be the worst thing I ever did."

He does not say this lightly, hinting at those grave violations that won him his notoriety. He lowers his head and looks at me with very stern eyes.

"If he ever hated me for it, I never knew," he tells me without a shred of doubt. "He was good. All he did was love. The sick, the needy would come to him. He'd do everything for them. He'd fail some, and the mourners would be cruel. Never shook him. Hate never bothered him. Just another ailment to treat."

He unfolds his arms, rests his clenched fists on the tops of his thighs.

"He thought it was an honour when the soldiers came for him," he says, ice and accusation in his words. "Only I could see the crime. My father did nothing but give. With every breath, at every second. What did your family ever do but take?"

He points a finger at me like the tip of a sword.

"It was an accident I killed my mother," he says. "It was no accident you killed my father. No man may look upon the face of a god. He died so you could live."

He looks at me with all the contempt and certainty of an executioner. It's a show. A flex of muscles, intimidation without intention. If it were anything else, I'd be dead. He's already made up his mind on sparing me. He decided the first night he saw me. The reason eludes him, and he expects me to give it to him. He wants me to beg for the life he permits me. I won't indulge him.

"How old were you when your father died?" I ask simply, without fear.

"Five," he tells me, leaning forward in anticipation of my rebuttal.

"You don't remember him," I say. "You think you do. But it's just a dream. Your mind picking and choosing what suits you, making a story that pleases you."

"I remember him," he says.

He wants to throttle me. No… he wants to *want to* throttle me. So why doesn't he? Why does he need me to force him?

"What did he look like?" I ask. "What were his mannerisms? His tastes? What did his voice sound like? What did he wear? Specifically?"

He shakes his head, annoyed.

"He gave," he repeats. "He saved people."

"Who?"

"Me."

"Who else?"

He turns his head away from me, and I see him scorning himself for not tearing me apart. His heel beats restlessly on the ground. Go on. I'm not afraid. You have nothing to threaten me with.

"You mourn a stranger," I tell him, with all the clarity and intent of last words. "There's nothing of him in you, Orphan Maker. Who have you saved? What have you given? You love that dream of your father? If there's any truth in it, every step you've taken has been away from him."

He looks at me with fire and fury. I do not waver. Then, something impossible: drop by drop, I see tears redden the whites of his eyes. He turns his head away from me, overcome with remorse. I haven't told him anything he didn't already know, yet I've never hurt someone so badly. It's hard to imagine a soul alive has ever hurt anyone so badly. I should be proud. I've wounded my enemy and honoured my family.

He raises a trembling hand to his face and hides behind it. I could grab that spear and skewer him if only I had the strength to lift it. I could take this knife in my boot and drive it into him ten times without him raising a hand against me. Why shouldn't I? What do I owe him? It wasn't pity that spared my life. It was guilt. His self-loathing. He rightly saw in himself a monster, and who am I to deny it?

I could go home. I could take his head with me and be a hero. My name would be written in big bold letters for generations. I could change the future for all the daughters, nieces, and women still to come in our line or any other, imbue them with potential and possibility never before considered. In time, Father would pass, and Mathius and I could rule side by side with no one daring to question my ability. I could be a beloved queen, magnanimous and generous, and my goodness would be deep and true. All the kingdom would know me a warrior choosing kindness over dominance. All because I killed Ruthless and made history.

Yet sitting here, for all his ignominy, I see no evil ahead for the Ruthless before me. He's had his fill. He loved. Deeply. And so he was hurt deeply. He tried to treat the sickness in him with vengeance and found he'd spread and grown the pain he so hated like a pestilence. He'd sooner die than infect again. He can do no harm. Not even to me, the root of all that's wicked in his life.

So die, then. Do your duty. Walk that righteous path you see ahead before you waver, before your mind clouds once more with spite and anger. You'll harm again. It's your nature. Misery will flow as it always does, and whatever levy you raise against it will burst. You were Ruthless, you will be Ruthless. It's only in this vanishing instant you're anything else. I won't be fooled.

My mind's ablaze. He looks at me like he knows I see him. The real him. Everyone I've known has bristled beneath my sight. Powerful and powerless alike protect their inner selves carefully. All fear the truth inside, dread their lies and artifice exposed. Yet Ruthless sits here defenceless, desperate to be seen. These bitter thoughts are not mine alone. He has overwhelmed me.

I know him now. Maybe better than I've known anyone. He's laid down his guard, spread his very being before me and accepted whatever judgment I settle on. I am stunned to find I can't hate him. In this honest place beyond assumption and projection, there is only understanding. There is no hate in understanding. Maybe we can't hate anyone we truly know.

There isn't a soul alive Ruthless doesn't know. He has lived every pain, as victim and inflictor. He has seen the antidotal truth, and it extinguished the anger in him. Ruthless broke past Darnett's mask and found in his enemy a brother. In my niece's face, a daughter, or even his younger self. We gods have spent centuries hiding our faces for fear if people recognized our humanity, they'd deny our divinity. It's so odd that our plainness should save us. If we radiated the ineffable and holy, would I be alive? Would Reznick?

I reach out for Ruthless's hand and squeeze it. I feel his gratitude, bright and pure. So strange that a gesture so small could be the finest deed I ever did.

CHAPTER 20: GOING AWAY

Small

Everything I own is on my back. Good. That's how I like it. I belong in these woods and hills. I was getting soft in that house. Sleeping too long, sweating too little. In hopes of healing, I lapsed in my discipline. No one ever got better getting fat.

The strap of my bag slides across my shoulder for the hundredth time and the weight of my possessions shifts, pulling me sideways a step. I set my bag down, fed up. Was it always this heavy? Did I always have so much? I should throw it all away. I should sleep in the cold and the mud. Uncovered. If I sleep at all. That's how you harden. That's how you become a force to be reckoned with. I need to get better.

I'll kill Elizabeth when I'm better. The Princess. Ciendy. Whoever she is. I'll come back and shoot an arrow through her heart or strangle her with my own hands. If Rufus finds out, if he gives up his quest and comes home, I'll kill the coward myself. If by some miracle he succeeds and brings the Nameless with him, I'll see him tried and beheaded. When I'm better.

I will be better. I have to be. It all falls to me now. Rufus will fail. He's already failed, subjugating himself to her. He'll have nothing for Hospice. I'll need to press myself harder. I'll have to be special. So what if Elizabeth beat me. I wasn't at my best. I can improve. I'm young. There's time.

Not for the Nameless. Not for Master Terra.

She's dead. They all are. It's suicide to chase their freedom. Accept it. Look forward. I'll have to be a leader, inspire hundreds to follow me. Can I train followers? They won't be Nameless unless I get them young. Very young. Can I raise them? Can I find a safe place? No, I'll have to keep moving. We always did. How many can I take with me?

I hear something. A scuffle. I'm grateful to put my mind elsewhere. I put my new skills to the test, treading carefully, imperceptibly. I peer around a tree big enough to hide me. Down a slope, I see some unkempt peasants wrestling with a pair of soldiers. The soldiers are lavishly adorned. They wear their light armour proudly. They shimmer with officiousness and privilege. They're loyal, maybe even noble. One of them is old. An officer, I'm sure. The other is young, just a boy, pretty enough for some estimable future of rank and title. I doubt either has seen much combat. They must have come upon some free folk too steadfast to be robbed.

The old one rips himself free from the grip of some poor, desperate soul and hurls him to the dirt. He unsheathes his sword and raises it high over his head, ready to slaughter his woeful offender. I nock an arrow.

I strike true right through the pink neck just above that glittering, golden collar. The old man gurgles and staggers, dropping his sword, pawing at both sides of the shaft on either side of his throat. He hits the ground in a heap. The peasant, so petrified a moment ago, pats his enemy down and unburdens him of a velvety purse with the Royal Sigil emblazoned across it. He flees the scene.

I may have misconstrued who was the victim and who was the criminal. It doesn't matter. The armour and sigil are unmistakable, and if the soldiers are robbed at the moment, they're robbers in the balance. I should be glad. I don't have many kills in my life. Certainly none so prestigious. Certainly none so cleanly. I've never shot a better arrow. No one has. So where's my joy? Where's my satisfaction?

The young soldier is slow to react. He scans the trees, stupid with panic, never coming close to seeing me. I aim an arrow at him. My hands shake. I know I'm not stable enough to get the neck again, so I aim for his torso. I hit his leg. I feel nothing.

He screams and stumbles like he's never been wounded before. He exposes the back of his head to the two men he's been fighting and takes a wallop for his error. He drops to the ground. After a little more jostling, the thieves are another purse richer.

The thieves follow after their long-gone friend, leaving the young soldier in a daze. That's foolish of them. The young soldier has seen their faces and thinks them murderers. As far as the kingdom will be concerned, the blood of an officer is on their hands. You can't leave witnesses to a crime so reprehensible.

The young soldier climbs dizzily to his feet. I plunge an arrow in his back. A twinge of grief hits me when his anguished cry rings out. He falls to his stomach. I scold myself. He should be dead already.

I pull the knife from my belt and descend the slope, ready to do a vital favour for him and all creation. He jolts when he feels my foot on his back, but he doesn't have any fight left in him. Pathetic. I should reach down, grab that blonde hair, pull back his head, and slit his throat. I should. I don't. I turn him over.

He's younger than I thought. Younger than I am. He's not as handsome as I expected, either. Maybe no one looks handsome when they're dying. His freckled skin is streaked with sweat, and his eyes are damp with fresh terror. I know immediately he's never faced a real battle, never brushed near death. No one is ever so frightened twice. The more you've lived, the less life you have to lose.

So what's the delay? Waiting doesn't serve either of you. Not unless you're going to torture him. Maybe you should. That's not your way. There's nothing to gain. You're not malicious. So do the right thing. Kill your enemy. It doesn't matter how young he is. It doesn't matter he barely knows the weight of a sword. Think of who he might be. Think of who he will be. Do it. Do it. Do it.

Elizabeth

The house is quiet. Truly quiet like it has seldom been. Rufus could go hours without making a noise. Small could go days. But they were always there, always on the edge of something. Silence is different when it's temporary. It's gratifying peace or tense with anticipation. Yet now, with nothing ahead of me I can see, it's terribly, utterly lonely.

That's all right. I was alone for years. I can live that way. I can look inside and find something to sustain me. Easily. When I was young, it was all the strange, exciting adventures I'd have if I were free. There were infinite tastes, smells, and experiences for me to chase. It'll have to be something else now. I'm freer now than I've ever been, yet the possibility of the world has dwindled to nothing. I know what I want, and it's gone.

Maybe I'll go into town. Maybe I'll make some new friend who isn't too busy for me. Who could that be? Some comfortable, bored wife, maybe. She'd whisper to me all the banalities she finds so salacious happening among her neighbours, some precious babe bouncing on her tilted hip. She'd cherish my company. I could help with the child. She could complain about her husband, berate him for his thoughtlessness. I'd roll my eyes about some trivial transgression Rufus committed ages ago. I could pretend I was itching to reprimand him the second he came home. It'd keep him alive somehow.

The thought exhausts me, and relief washes over me when I banish it from my mind. I don't make close friends easily. Never have. I share too little with too few.

It occurs to me then I may never really be known again. Who can I trust? Small learned the truth and ran when she couldn't kill me. Everyone else left alive is loyal, and that means their obligation is to the kingdom, even at my expense.

I trusted Rufus. Shared everything with him. He never judged me. He trusted every decision I ever made except loving him. He never saw the reason in it, no matter how I tried. But he was so grateful. He spent so much of himself repaying me for my love, even though it cost me nothing. And still, he's gone. If the world ever built a man for bearing every burden, it was him. So who's left? Who could there ever be?

A loud knock at my door, less frantic than usual but plenty urgent. I set down my drink, rise from my chair. I pull open the door and find Small. She only half looks at me, her head low and turned away. In her arms, she drags a young, unconscious soldier. It's a boy, really. His armour shines everywhere mud isn't caked.

"He's hurt," she says simply, muscling past me towards the same table Crag died on. She gently sets down the boy atop it then looks at me expectantly.

I wipe my hands off on my pants and then approach. A quick look reveals two arrow wounds. The heads are buried deep, but their shafts are snapped off at an inch. There's still enough for me to recognize them as Nameless. I don't ask about them. Maybe I never will.

Suddenly, forceps, bandages, and salve plop down on the table's corner, close enough to see, far enough to not intrude. I look up at Small, her eyes uneasy but eager.

"Anything else?" she asks.

Small

It's draining work, saving a life. I can see it first hand now. So much happens from moment to moment. In many ways, it's like fighting. The stakes are the same, life and death, yet somehow it seems more important. The strain should be less, but it isn't. Being slow and delicate takes at least as much as being fast and hard. I never knew.

I was drenched in sweat the entire time, yearning to help but sure I would do something wrong. Elizabeth was very patient with me. I did all the simple tasks she told me to do, and she never faltered. When we were done, she told me the boy would be all right. I'd done well. I was a valuable assistant: present, attentive, but never interfering. Better than Rufus, she professed. That mattered a great deal to me.

Colour returned to the boy's face. I wanted to drop him somewhere far from us. Not in the gutter or woods. Somewhere he'd still be safe. She wanted to put him in my bed, where he could wake any moment and see us. So, he stayed where he was. We argued and searched tirelessly for some solution that satisfied us both until the very moment he awoke.

He thought I'd rescued him, or he said he did. He thanked us and asked if he was well enough to leave. I couldn't be sure whether he recognized me or not, but I wasn't worried. He had no vengeance in him, no hunger to punish those who had done him wrong. He was sad, defeated. He needed to be alone. He left his armour with us. He said it was payment. I could tell he wouldn't require it any longer. He was done with fighting. It was time for him to go home.

※ ※ ※

Alone at last, Elizabeth falls tiredly into her chair. This lull we share is comfortable and well earned, but it can't last forever. Sooner or later, we'll have to talk. The war between us is over, but peace will require a difficult negotiation. For now, I'm pleased to be near her again.

"How did the two of you end up together?" I ask before we can talk about what we have to. "You and Rufus?"

A distant, nostalgic smile curls her lips.

"We were in the same spot, really," she tells me, and I can tell she's been waiting years for someone to share the story with. "It was each other or no one. He pretended he was keeping an eye out for me, that he had to teach me the uncivilized world. But honestly? I think he was afraid."

"Rufus? Afraid?"

"He didn't know where he was going any better than I did," she laughs, shaking her head. "He'd been doing one thing his whole life. He couldn't do anything else. ANYTHING else. The food he made..." She gags dramatically. "He worked at it, though. Like he worked at everything. He's a first-rate cook now."

She dips a spoon in her drink and stirs it absently. Her smile fades a little as her mind wanders.

"Do you think he's where he's going yet?" she asks.

I don't know. I don't want to think of it. I shrug.

"All anybody ever talked about was how he killed gods," she says with a little shake of her head. "No one ever mentions how many others paid the price. Officers, soldiers... simple, devoted folk. I wonder what the number could be. Do you know?"

She looks at me hopefully, but there's nothing I could tell her she'd like to hear.

"There were stories," I say. "Couldn't know if they were true."

She nods, accepting my evasion.

"They probably were," she speculates. "I'd believe anything."

She sighs, and a melancholy cloud overtakes her weary satisfaction.

"You never saw what he used to be, did you?" she asks. "Not really. Not from the other side. He was a storm. Black clouds on the horizon, coming for us all."

The happiness in the room is gone, crushed beneath the weight of a certain future.

"If there was ever someone as strong as Rufus, it's my brother. Not strong like how you think of it." She looks at me with severity, making sure I understand the distinction she's about to make. "Strong to the grain. When they meet, they're going to kill themselves killing each other. If anyone's standing at the end of it, they're going to be changed. Different. Pieces missing."

Her expression turns sombre. I thought I saw sorrow when Crag died. I hadn't. She faces the thought of a loss too disastrous for me to ponder. I want to save her from it.

"He'll do it," I offer. "What hasn't he done?"

She takes a breath, beats back her heartache with a smile. She fidgets, tapping her knuckles on the arm of her chair. Anything to not be still. Anything to not dwell in the moment.

"One way or another, my Rufus isn't coming home," she says, trying and failing to mask her disappointment, "and my sweet brother is going away."

CHAPTER 21: HOSPICE

Rufus

I'm close now, assuming this map is worth anything. I might reach Hospice tonight. I don't know whether to hurry or drag. I'm so ready to be finished, but now more than ever, I have to take care. I could find loyals anywhere. I can't be seen. Everything depends on delaying detection as much as possible. In my dreams, I'm in and out of the heinous prison without a single eye falling on me. I break open every cell, take Master Terra's hand in mine, and let the other Nameless fight their way out.

    I was never much of a sneak. Not without Snow or Master Terra to guide me, anyway. Be it fat or muscle, size draws the eye. Only partly meaning to, I've shrunk on this journey. I see the edges and sharp parts of my body again. I'm certainly quicker. I move my spear more effortlessly every day. Yet I feel ragged. Worn. Everything I do takes a bit more from me, and I feel all but empty. I can see the bottom of the pool I draw from, and I am near.

    Thoughts of Elizabeth don't comfort me as they once did. Here at the precipice, she beckons me. "Come to me," I swear I hear her say. "While you can."

    I could turn back now and make my way home. I dream of my wife's open, forgiving face and the warmth of her welcoming embrace. We could pick up our things and move somewhere no one knows us. We could take Small along. She could take a name. We'd call her our sister or even niece. We could make a beautiful life. If I fail, they're doomed. If I fail…

I don't fear death. What else Mathius might do if I were captured is far more distressing. Could he truly pry me open as Small said he would? What could he make me tell him? Master Terra never knew about Elizabeth. What would Mathius find if he had his time with me? I can't imagine surrendering anything. Will I have a choice? Will I even need to choose?

What if I succeed? If I execute every step ahead of me perfectly and achieve all my marvellous hopes, what does that mean? Free Nameless, maybe by the hundreds. Patrols sweeping every town in the kingdom. War and distrust everywhere. Even if no one saw me, with Reznick dead and Hospice emptied, would minds leap to the Balance returned? Would my name be on the lips of every guard and citizen? I might upturn not only my life but all the world.

I could go home. I should go home.

A fly buzzes around my face. I swat it away wearily. Undeterred, it redoubles its efforts, and soon its friends are pestering me. I've intruded on a precious haul. Some carcass or dung heap.

I raise my head and find their bounty. Black shrouds. A bald head. A Nameless, or at least a man meant to look like one, tied to a post in some gruesome spectacle. A placard on a tree reads 'Woe to all Lost Souls.' Hospice must be close.

I don't recognize the man. No one could. Everything that might distinguish him has been taken. His lips, his ears, his nose, his eyes, his teeth... all gone. His flesh is seared or rotting everywhere I can see. I'm meant to be sickened. I'm meant to be haunted by this poor soul all my life, to flee from any path that might lead me back here.

He rattles. My first guess is something is eating him from the inside out. Then his head turns, and a flagging, garbled moan emanates from his tongue-less mouth. He's alive. Barely. I'd be mystified, but it's in keeping. It's nothing to desecrate a corpse. To mangle a man so, to leave him living enough to feel the sun wither him and his stomach starve... that's a hundred times the punishment and sends a thousand times the message. It takes work to create horror like this. Passionate, careful work, craving to be witnessed.

He trembles a little, but he's in too deep a daze to lift his head. I can tell he's afraid still, tired as he is. I wonder what more he thinks could be done to him. He's beyond anything now. Elizabeth or my father might have some obscure method or ointment to ease the pain a little. They'd probably have some soft, gentle words that would make a world of difference. I only have one tender mercy to offer.

I step away from him and unsheath my spear for the first time in years. I dig my heels, steady the blade carefully. I slice through his neck with one clean swoop. His head does a little hop on his shoulders. It lingers a second before toppling down to the grass.

I can hear the tutting of some imaginary onlooker as I wipe my blade clean. People are superstitious about unmaking a body. They want to go to the bugs pristine and beautiful, as if it'll spare them the decay that comes for us all. I suppose that's partly why the torturers did what they did. There's more offence in it.

There's no more sudden, painless death than a beheading done well. That's honour. That's dignity. Going away whole is nothing compared to it. This Nameless won't be buried, anyway.

I sheath my spear and move on. I can't go home. Not yet.

*   *   *

I see it: Hospice, Home for the Incurables. It seems impenetrable, more like a mountain carved down to resemble a fortress than a building made by man. We shall see.

I must prepare.

I find a spot behind a bluff with tree cover on all sides. I won't be seen here. I start a little fire. It provides just enough light for me to ready myself.

I lay out my drawings all around me. I see my wife, as best I can imitate her, in a hundred frozen images. Here in the shadow of Hospice, I know I do this for the last time. By my little fire, I commit all these pictures to memory. There are only two roads ahead of me. If I win, I don't need them. I go home, and I exchange pale imitation for exquisite reality. But what if I lose? What if my enemy takes me? What if they find these drawings, and someone sets them before Mathius? What if he recognizes her? Innocent and slight as they are, isn't that possible?

I burn them up.

* * *

I'm under water in the moat that borders Hospice. Moats are a relic of a time when forces might be gathered by the thousands against the Royal Family. They've served many a Nameless well in the years since. I asked Elizabeth once why they weren't all emptied and filled up with dirt by now. A royal fortress hasn't seen a true siege in centuries. Their utility, or lack thereof, had never interested her. She'd assumed they were decorative.

I've been watching the guards overhead, discerning their patterns. The water refracts them into vague, dancing shapes. I've poked my head up now and then for air. I've been holding my breath for I don't know how long. I may never hold it so long again. The time is now.

A guard I've watched come and go in intervals passes by, and I emerge from the black water to make my ascent. I have a long way to go up this wall. I can only guess how much time it will take me. I know for certain the time I have.

I scale the wall, teetering carefully between quickness and quiet, digging my hands into the thin slits separating stones. I'll make it so long as my slick fingertips don't betray me. I reach the top and never even climb to my feet. I roll across the walkway and down onto a roof just beneath it.

I'm inside. I can catch my breath. No one should come around for a minute or so. I've time to check around for guards. They're different from any I've seen. They must be the Allegia

I've heard so much about. Their masks and armour gleam almost as incandescently as a god's. On the one hand, I'm thankful. My potential captors are easier to spot in the moonlight. On the other, only the truly elite would be so ornate. Whoever these men are, they're not to be trifled with.

I look out ahead of me. I've got an awful long jump if I'm going to make it to the next roof. I don't have a moment to waste. But something catches my eye in the distance: candle light pouring out a window. I adjust myself to get a better look.

I see long, graceful horns. That can only mean one thing. In a chamber stands Prince Mathius, back turned to me. My hand shoots to my bow instinctively. No. He hasn't seen me. I'm safe.

My curiosity gnaws at me. What's he doing? Painting, apparently. I can see him delicately poking and dabbing at a canvas. I angle myself nearer, trying to get a sightline on his work.

Clearer than I could ever envision them, I see Darnett, Ciendy, and Reznick in exquisite, loving detail. He's captured essential characteristics in all of them. Darnett's irreverence, Reznick's simmering rage. But it's Ciendy that captivates me. Even with her mask, even in clothes I've never seen, I recognize her. Her spirit, her sadness. It's the Elizabeth I love, brought to life before me with some strokes of a brush. I see my wife again. Gratitude swells my heart and wets my eyes.

It takes me a beat to recall Mathius is something besides an artist. Finally, I consider what his presence might mean. I should stop right now and retreat. I've heard the stories. I could raise every prisoner in here against him, and he still might wipe us all out. So what are my options? I could wait him out. He must have a home he longs for. He can't want to be here. A jail is still a jail, even to the jailer.

What if he's waiting for me? What if he knew I'd come? It doesn't matter. I have to find Master Terra. I can't leave without her.

I gather myself and just barely make the leap to the next roof. I feel tiles shift and clatter beneath my feet, and for a moment I'm sure I'll fall and be found out. I'm lighter on my toes than I expect, and I scramble well. I lower myself into the courtyard as a pair of men round a corner out of sight. I wait for the murmurs and suspicious whispers of alerted guards. I don't hear a peep. I guess I deserved a bit of luck.

I open a door, and again I find Mathius. Except now, he's staring right at me, only inches from my nose. Not so lucky.

"Found you," he says.

I slam the door in his face. I hear him stumble back a step and grunt. At least I've annoyed him. Before I can escape even a couple of paces, the door blows off its hinges, hurtling at me. I lower my shoulder to absorb it, and after it cracks into pieces, I see Mathius flying through the air at me. *Flying!* As fleetly and weightlessly as a bird swooping down on a meal. Huh. I didn't know he could do that.

I run, for all the good it will do me. I pass by racks of weapons and briefly consider snatching some. My spear is burdensome and keeps me less swift than I'd like. But it's not like I can just drop it wherever I please, and I'm out of practice with anything else.

The swords and knives that enticed me only a moment ago turn against me. They float out from their racks and dart at me in waves. My spear is heavy, but at least it's trustworthy. I swat the incoming blades away like gnats. I turn a corner, and find any chance at an exit blocked by surging Allegia. I look up, thinking I might climb back onto the rooftops. In the sky high above, I see Mathius levitating, rings of swords and knives dancing around him as he watches me. That won't do.

I take shelter beneath awnings, sprinting back the way I came. I hear steel clattering over my head like hail. I need to get inside. I'll stand no chance at defending myself if Mathius can launch projectiles from afar. Close quarters. Cover. Indoors. That's my chance.

I come to the doorway he burst out from and scurry inside. I look for something to block the entrance. I don't find anything. Still not lucky.

A brave Allegia sees me coming down a hall and tries to

cut me off. I club him with a swing of my spear. The insignia collapses his helmet, and he falls in a heap. I pluck a set of keys from him without even breaking stride.

I sprint past empty cell after empty cell. I don't dare consider their significance. At the end of a long corridor, I come upon an expansive room with layers of cells piled so high I can hardly see the ceiling. In each cell, I see bald heads hanging heavily and gaunt bodies chained up. Nameless. For all their misery, I'm happy to see them.

They don't even glance at me as I enter. I scan them quickly, looking for Master Terra among the indistinguishable hoards of starved and desiccated Nameless. I clatter the butt of my spear against the cell bars as I pass by, but my brothers and sisters ignore me.

Finally, I find Master Terra on the second floor. All at once, I'm delighted and devastated. Her thin, wiry arm dangles limply, lifted above her head by chains in the ceiling. I look closely at her scalp and find it scarred, burned. She's been marked. Her and all the Nameless in here. They'll be bald for all time now. They'll never be able to disappear as easily as I did. Clever. Despicable, but clever.

Master Terra is herself, but older, weaker, smaller. All my life, she was so resilient. I realize that some secret part of me thought her capture was only a cunning ploy to summon me back. It never occurred to me she might fade and shrink enough to be conquered. I should have been there for her. I should have taken her away, been some comfort to her. There's still time.

I rush through every key in the set I lifted from the guard.

"Master! Master!" I call, keeping my voice low.

No response.

"Terra!" I try, but it feels wrong leaving my mouth.

I find the right key. I pull the door open so impatiently I nearly tear it from the cell. I grab my Master by the chin in one hand and try to stir her. Her head sways woozily. I set myself on her shackles. My luck turns. The locks accept the same key the door did.

I free her hand and ready myself to catch her drooping body. But once liberated, she jerks awake and launches her foot into my chest like lightning. I stumble backwards out of her cell, startled. She leaps after me, swinging her dangling limbs like whips.

"What are you doing!?" I demand, slipping her strikes.

I get a hold of her and pull up her face to mine. I stare into vacant, foggy eyes. They disquiet me so much she breaks my grip and sends me tumbling over the railing of the walkway. I fall heavily into the center of the room.

Just as I catch my breath, every door in the prison swings open all on its own. The cell bars slam against each other, and a ring fills the room. It sounds like the toll of the biggest bell in the world. The chains holding the prisoners snap open, and the Nameless stagger out, their feet lurching clumsily forward. From every exit, Allegia pour in, surrounding me on all sides.

From somewhere far above, Mathius descends and perches effortlessly on the railing I just toppled over. Master Terra stations herself at his side.

"All men share a single destiny," Mathius announces, addressing the waiting crowd. "To serve."

From my little island in the center of the room, I watch the Allegia all around me lift away their masks and helmets. Bald heads and scars everywhere. So many brothers and sisters I once knew. I look pleadingly into their faces, desperate for some hint of humanity or charity. They look right through me with soulless, callous gazes.

A hundred swords are drawn, and a wave of bodies closes on me. My brothers and sisters walk right into a wide swing of my spear, unafraid. I level the lot of them, but another group descends on me from behind. I need to keep moving. I need to keep my attackers at length. I need out of here.

Just as I part enough of the sea of humanity around me to spot an exit, a heavy iron door flies in like a missile from somewhere above me, just missing my head and shattering the stone floor in front of me. I look up, and I see Mathius, stalking along the second-floor railing. With flourishes of his hands, he rips a torch and some iron bars from the wall behind him. They hover beside him until he shoots his arms down in my direction.

I deflect the bars with my spear and duck behind a lunging Nameless when the torch follows. I try to smother the embers that engulf my brother, but he swings at me. I beat him back with the butt of my spear.

I fight harder, more recklessly. I don't want to hurt anyone. I hear sickening crunches when I crash the blunt of my spear against chests and backs, but my brothers and sisters keep coming. I'll have to take out their legs. If they can't stand, they can't fight. Mathius launches more projectiles at me, but I'm one moving target among many. I suppose he'd harm a thousand of his servants for a chance at wounding me.

Someone manages to pull the sheath from my spear, exposing the blade. No. Punctures will kill, and cuts won't slow. I've too much to consider. I can't beat Nameless back and protect them at the same time. I step away from the hand of some downed sister grasping at my ankle and feel myself kick a helmet. That will do. I drive the point of my spear through the helmet's top, hiding the sharp blade behind rounded steel.

I swing my capped spear again freely, the helmet crumpling a little more with each strike. It's a temporary solution. I dodge another volley of projectiles from Mathius. The only way out is through him. My brothers and sisters are not themselves. They will never yield, no matter how much their bodies are battered or broken. Mathius controls them somehow. He's the one I need to get to. In him is a link I must sever.

The helmet cracks and falls from my blade. My spear is lethal again, which is to say useless. With all my might, I hurl it at Mathius. I just miss, and it embeds itself deeply into the wall behind him like an arrow in a target. It occupies all his attention. It fascinates him. He takes my bait.

Like so many before him, he reaches for it. He tests his mettle. He gestures mildly at it with a single hand, but it barely rattles. He digs in his heels and raises both hands at it. He endeavours mightily.

I double over a Nameless with a knee to the gut. I propel myself off his back and step quickly across the shoulders of my kin like I'm bounding across stones in a pond. Just as I make my way to the second-floor walkway, Mathius rips my spear from the wall with a triumphant roar. He did it. Amazing.

He admires his work, the prized spear bobbing in front of him like a lily floating down a stream. He turns, surprised to find me dashing at him. He sets the point of the spear on me, but I flip it end over end with a nimble kick and steal it out of the air. I hold the blade an inch from his throat, and he freezes. Every one of his servants follows suit, paralyzed.

My heart pounds in my chest, I don't know if from exhaustion or pride. A giddy thrill raises every hair on my body. I've done it. Another feat, another impossible victory. My brothers and sisters are saved.

"Let them go," I command. Small price for the life of a god.

People don't often get this close to gods. I can see hints of him behind his mask. I see his pretty eyes hesitate and consider. There's no fear.

I hear the shifting of steel all around me. I watch every other body in Hospice lift up a sword. Not at me. Not to fight. My brothers and sisters all drop to their knees and turn their blades inwards. A hundred, a thousand sharp points rest readily above just as many chests.

I haven't turned my face one inch from Mathius. I look back at him and find anxious eyes staring back at me. I try to frighten him with my hardness. I try to tell him I know what he knows, that his life is worth all these souls and more. With his mask in my collection, I could be more than a god, raise every downtrodden citizen in this kingdom against his father, erase his line from the world. It's true, in a sense. I wouldn't. But I could.

My fingers tense a little. My spear shudders. He notices. I see his mind race. I try to beat him to every thought he might have. What does he know? He knows he's alive. That means the

Nameless are worth something to me, that I didn't come just for him. What else does he know?

I angle the tip of my spear nearer him. I set my jaw, challenge him, do my best impression of the Ruthless in his nightmares. The Ruthless that killed his brother at First Morning. The Ruthless that snuffed out his niece. The Ruthless that stole away his sister and did who knows what with her. They never found her body, I want to remind him. All you fear is true. And worse.

But he sees. I know he does. A bit of pressure on a thousand swords draws little droplets of blood all around me. Master Terra has no armour. Only rags. She bleeds more easily.

"Don't…" I say, so faintly he might not even hear me.

He says nothing. I lower my spear. That says it all. The thousand swords clatter on the stone floor. I look into Mathius's sneering eyes, boots marching towards me from all directions. As Nameless fight for the chance to pin my arms behind me, I let my spear fall to my feet. I wonder what they'll do with it.

※ ※ ※

My cell is dark, dank, and miserable by design. If it's particularly so, I have no idea. I've never been in a cell, except as a liberator, and that hardly leaves much time to absorb the experience. I don't know if jailers reserve a special place for their most hated enemies. If they do, this is probably it. I'm high up. I'm sure of that. All I hear is wind and dripping. I am very, very alone. That's probably for the best. I expect whatever company I'm allowed won't be very friendly.

I'm standing in the center of the room. Thick chains hold my feet to the floor and my hands over my head. The sturdiness of the shackles is ludicrous in its excess. I couldn't free myself from restraints even half as solid. I wonder if this is my life from here on, or if some special occasion awaits me in the near future.

As if to answer me, I hear steps somewhere beyond the bars of my cell. Boots. They tread purposefully but with little weight behind them. Around the corner arrives Master Terra, or whoever she is now, adorned in that beautiful Allegia armour. She pushes a huge key into my cell's door and forces it open without ever looking at me. She picks up a bowl of some colourful mush off a nearby stool and lifts it towards my lips. She waits for me to reach my head forward to meet her.

I sniff at the bowl. I don't smell anything suspicious. It can't be poison. It might be something else I don't know. I look into my master's face for some indication of what I might be getting into. I should resist the urge to trust her, but my hungry belly convinces me if I was wanted dead, I'd be dead.

I open my mouth, and Master Terra tips the bowl for me. The mush is warm. Some nutritious combination of meat and vegetables assembled with no thought to taste. It's the kind of sludge I used to eat every day in the Nameless. In a strange way, because it tastes like nothing, it tastes like home. This is a good sign in the short term. It means I'm wanted healthy. What that means in the long term troubles me terribly.

More steps. Two pairs, marching heavily in perfect unison, and a third practically gliding at its own pace. Mathius arrives at my door. A pair of Allegia accompany him, staring out from behind masks with dead eyes. Looking at Master Terra's hollowed out, disconcerting expression, I can see why Mathius makes a habit of covering their faces.

The heavy iron door swings open for Mathius as he enters. He comes very near to me, near enough for me to sense the uneasiness in his breath. He's still too far for me to reach if by some miracle I tore an arm free. I'm flattered he entertains the possibility.

"Where have you been?" he asks, straining at calm.

I say nothing. I keep my eyes on Master Terra. She recedes to the wall, so motionless she may as well be furniture.

"Hiding in plain sight?" Mathius continues. "Preserving your mystique? Enjoying retirement? That's it, isn't it?"

He notices me watching Master Terra. She turns her face into the wall, away from me. How petty of you, Mathius.

"I didn't take your kind for the sort to take long rests," he says. "I suppose if anyone earned it..."

He pauses when I look at him. He wants to retreat a step. He doesn't. Instead, he leans a little closer.

"I was always curious:" he begins anew, whispering, confidential, "where are you from? What confluence of cruelty spewed you out? How much agony, suffering, and pain could it possibly take to make someone so wretched? How could it possibly match what you've done to me?"

I feel his hatred on me, deep and true, but only for a moment. He beats it back. He steadies himself with a long inhalation through his nose.

"I know hate to be a poison," he explains, the bitterness in his voice now something gentle, almost mournful. "I've seen it twist and ruin. Your kind and mine. I do not indulge. I walk the righteous path, the way of true strength. I know it. But you... you have brought doubt into my life. Somehow... with your vile, putrid spite... you've wiped away that which I cherish most. My pure and perfect loves. How? It can not be. But it is."

He searches my face with trembling, pleading eyes. I don't know if he's looking for good or evil. I pity him. I really do.

He hardens, ashamed of his lapse in tenacity.

"You're an abomination," he hisses, almost spitting. "I've spent years trying to wrench you from my mind. When you killed my brother, I forgave you. I did. I understood. I saw his defects and accepted your motives, however appalling. But you persist. My niece. A child. Unfinished. My sister..."

He can't put it into words. I couldn't either if something ever happened to her. He points a shaking finger in my face. He blinks his wet eyes and pulls away from me. He paces the room, consumed by the heartbreak I've brought him.

"Generations," he laments. "That is what you've taken from me. At my worst, I'd have given anything just to hurt you. I won't hate you. Or your cult. I promise you this. I offer you peace. I want to save you. All of you. Let me. End the war."

He looks back at me, cooly. Cooly enough to make me

worry.

"There are more of you. Not many. But enough to spread. Remember what you did to my kin and look at yours." He gestures at Master Terra and the Allegia behind him. "I have spared them. They ache for nothing. Before all things, people seek purpose. Your kin have been gifted it. I have cured the incurables. They serve a higher good. Service is selfless. Service is decent."

I stare at Master Terra. Her gaze is still fixed on the wall, rigid and immovable. This isn't service. This is worse than slavery.

"Who do you serve?" I ask him.

He lurches at finally hearing my voice.

"I serve a nation of masters," he insists, collecting himself. "I have a duty to the kingdom. The peace and prosperity of every living creature is my charge. As it should be yours."

There's not a speck of dishonesty in him. He believes. Sincerely.

"The righteous man thinks of others before himself," he continues. "If you love your brothers and sisters, present and future, spare them. They'll torture, butcher, and maim themselves for all time. For what? Some juvenile, self-defeating crusade?"

Mathius is right, of course. There's no winning now. Maybe there never was.

No. There was a moment. I could have killed him. Maybe I should have. Maybe it'd have shaken all my brothers and sisters free. Maybe it'd have meant the end of the kingdom.

Maybe I covet my convictions too much. Maybe I've had too much happiness to ever take the hard road again. Even now, I don't hate Mathius. I see his goodness, his devotion. He rescued his whole nation from ruin after his father withdrew into the Capital. He'd abolish all the pain in the world if he could, without ever a thought of himself. I see Elizabeth in him. I never could have faced her if I hurt him. I'd never risk that.

What about him? What won't he risk? Is his goodness precious enough to him? Can I put the world in his hands? Does he see in me and mine what I see in him? That's what'd it take.

That's how it ends.

"Would you really have hurt them?" I ask, tilting my head towards Master Terra.

He pauses. He knows exactly what I mean.

"I don't know," he says.

It's the intelligent answer. It protects him from a very ugly truth. Sometimes, doubt is our only shield. Some things aren't worth knowing. But it won't win him any trust from me.

I turn my face from him again, even away from Master Terra. I won't hear any more today.

"You're not so special," he says with a little scoff. "The others found the way. You will too. Until then… we'll make use of you."

CHAPTER 22: FOR NOTHING

Small

Months passed. And then a year. We knew the anniversary to the day, but we didn't mark it. Without so much as a word about it, without a single mention of his name, Elizabeth began gathering Rufus's possessions. Once a week, she'd set out a box of what little he had just past the fence at the edge of the yard. Only things without any value: old clothes, rusty tools. As useless as they were, they were always gone by morning.

It started as some symbolic gesture of defiance, I think. Some proof of her own independence and invulnerability. She buried her pain in anger, and the spite pleased her. She wasn't parting with Rufus. Not really. He didn't own much. If she committed herself, she could have been rid of it all in a day. She was only preparing a punishment for his inevitable return.

It wasn't long before she ran out of disposable scraps inside the house. Precious objects were all that remained. She set her sights on his shed. As ordinary as it appeared from the outside, there was no doubting its sacredness. Not once since my arrival had she even thought to enter it. It was his place.

When she turned the lock and pulled open the door, I felt like a graverobber coming upon a rich lord's tomb. I expected the treasures of a storied man. In some way, I anticipated the ghost of the God Killer coming out of that shed. Or at least pieces of him, some evidence or remains of heroism clutched close by a man who couldn't abandon all his glory.

There was nothing of the old Rufus in there. No trophies. No weapons. There were books and a million unfinished little projects. A chair yet to be fixed here, a table with a missing leg there. There were drawings too. Some were animals, some were landscapes, but most featured Elizabeth. She could hardly turn her head without seeing her face staring back at her.

If she faltered, it was only for the bat of an eye. She'd finally ventured into Rufus's secret place, hoping for some fuel to ignite a fire inside her, and found only a temple. She redoubled her outrage. She craved for something to harm him with, and he denied her. How dare he? How dare he? She snatched down a couple of her faces pinned to the wall. She crumpled them up.

She came upon an open book on a table. It was thick, and its cover faced upwards. 'To be a Good Master,' it said. She picked it up and sat down to read it.

I saw her anger defeated then. She quavered and fought valiantly, but there'd be no resisting this. I looked down into the book, curious what might best her after all this time. I saw writing by two hands, in two inks. The first spoke with authority on all the challenges of dog ownership, espousing transformative instruction and dominating the page. The second littered the margins of the first, flooding the open spaces with questions, failures, and uncertainty.

I lost interest in the former when I recognized the latter was Rufus's scrawl. He'd written a whole other book inside that tome. There, in excruciating detail, were all his countless efforts to win Bandit's heart. It was an endless account of the experiments, bribes, and gestures he'd bestowed upon a beast that rejected him utterly and completely.

'Prefers beef.' 'Still chases.' 'Unresponsive.' 'Difficult to distract.' 'Bit again.' On and on with nary a hint of resentment or impatience. Always dated and neatly catalogued. Flipping from page to page, it was obvious it had gone on for years. Elizabeth searched frantically for some hint of breakdown or collapse. She stopped when a particular date stared out at her audaciously:

Rufus's departure, minus one day.

"That bastard mutt!" she shouted, hurling the book aside in disgust and jolting me from my reading.

She buried her mouth in her fist, stifling a frenzy.

"Rufus said it would hate him!" she continued, her fury with new direction for the first time in ages. "It snapped at him the very first time we saw it! I thought he'd win it over. He was gentler than anyone with it, and it never gave him one ounce of kindness back!"

Her voice faded, weary, beaten.

"He could have yelled. He could have hit it. He never did. Not once. He never gave up. Because I loved it."

Her hands fell to her lap, and she sagged in her seat. Her lip shook, and her war against Rufus finally came to an end. There wasn't a piece left of her that raged against him. She admitted her love. She admitted the loss.

"He's gone," she said. It was a confession, a capitulation. "He did everything right, everything he could. For nothing. It didn't matter. It never mattered. He's gone…"

She cried. I'd seen her suffer so much in the time I'd known her. I'd seen her take all the pain of the wounded and frayed for her own. With dry eyes, I watched her lead the dying into their peace. I'd seen her tell mothers their babies never drew breath. In the face of so many horrors, she'd been a well of stability and grace for all the world to draw from.

Here before me, she convulsed with misery. She wept and moaned. A great terror descended upon me. Was she changed forever? Was her vitality sapped? Her hope dead? What would happen to the world if she never forgave it this evil it brought her? What if this shadow descended on her never parted?

I ached at the thought of a world without her goodness. I bent down in front of her, tried to meet her lowered eyes. Without thinking, I squeezed her hands. It occurred to me I'd never touched her with kindness in all our time together. The closest I'd come was trying to kill her. I looked back on the frustration I felt that day. The hate. I'd have given anything to lay my hands on her. Everything was so different.

She fell into my arms. I held her close. Somehow, I was happy for her sadness because it brought her nearer to me. She could cry forever, and I'd stay there on the floor with her, caressing the back of her head. I'd be proud to. It would be what she needed. There could be no higher service.

Elizabeth

It's so much easier to be angry. When the world has wronged you, when enemies surround you on all sides, you can flood your mind with so much vengeance that the thought of what's missing in your life almost disappears. I've spent all these days since you left furious at you, Rufus. I've drained myself to sickness obsessing over your arrogance, thoughtlessness, and selfishness. It did nothing to solve the problem. You're gone, and I miss you.

You love me so much. It blinds you to me. I've seen you draw my face a thousand times, and it's always too thin, always too pretty. You have the gall to tell me I'm wrong, that I don't know my own face. You know it better, you insist, and the next drawing is twice as delicate to tease me.

You think so much of me and so little of yourself. You don't believe me when I tell you I love you. Try as I might, I can't convince you. You don't think I need you. You think your presence only diminishes me. I could never convince you that you were my glue, keeping all my jagged bits together. You're gone, and I'm falling apart just like I knew I would. Why didn't you trust me? How could you not know?

You think the evil in you means there can be no good. I wanted to strike that affliction from you, convince you those transgressing parts of you were gone forever. I couldn't. I failed. In all the time I've known you, the violence I've seen you put out into the world is an instant, a single grain of sand in an hourglass. But it was always there, always just around the corner at every argument or inconvenience. Even when you slept, I would worry about your fits.

You try so hard. Every so often, rarer than anyone, something wears on you, and you move a little too sharply or breathe a little too heavily, and you catch me afraid of you. I can't help it, and I'm sorry. It isn't fair. You're so good. I break your heart, hurt you worse than you'd ever hurt me.

I marvel at the bottomlessness of your patience and forgiveness. They do not serve you. You could dominate. You could take what you please, and nothing could stop you. Laws are meaningless to you. Who would enforce them? All of civilization came to be so that the meek may gather their strength against larger dangers. What dangers are there to you?

I wish I could talk to you. I miss your voice. No one talks me back from the ledge like you do. I wish I could pitch my calls out into the void so loud they'd find you wherever you were, so loud you couldn't ignore them. Come home. Before the angry and bitter of the world make you as ugly and hopeless as they are. Before they convince you for all time you're no good. Before they pull you down with them. I need you.

But you're gone.

CHAPTER 23: RABBITS

Ciendy

It's not even morning yet when a kick at my feet forces me awake. It's Ruthless. Or rather Rufus. So he tells me, anyway. He's standing over me. From here on the ground, he looks as tall as any of the trees around us. I can still see red and purple in the sky behind his looming head.

"We have to move," he tells me.

I'm groggy. I suppose I fell asleep. It'd been such a long day, such a long week, such a long life. I hadn't had a real rest since before Darnett. Even locked in a tower and in the lap of luxury, I didn't feel safe. Yet this morning, I find myself beneath a humongous black cloak, and I don't know if I've ever slept so well.

"Is someone coming?" I ask, pushing myself out from the grass and leaves I made my bed.

"We always move come morning," he says, already striding purposefully away from me.

I lift myself to my feet, brushing off clinging twigs and foliage. I pull the cloak tight around me. It drags past my heels as I chase after Rufus. I don't know how he walks so fast while hardly seeming like he's moving at all.

This is good. He's resolved to help me. He'll know the kingdom better than I do. He'll know all the best secret places to hide.

"Where are we going?" he asks.

Damn.

"Where were you going?" I ask, stumbling.

"There's no place in the Nameless for either of us," he

promises me, his eyes wavering sadly for only a moment. "I'm not going back."

"Do you have any allies who could—"

"No."

That quiets me. He's as lost as I am. Now that I'm really looking at him, he's younger than I'd dreamed. Only years of meticulous, careful direction could warp a boy into this man before me. He's probably never had a free day in his life.

That doesn't matter. I'm still better off than I was yesterday. We can help each other. I hadn't thoroughly invested myself in any particular place when I left the Capital. First and foremost was being anywhere but there. Now, I have a whole kingdom to choose from.

"Oxtra?" I offer. It's a lovely city by the sea, warm and serene, bustling with strangers and trade. Unfamiliar faces aren't regarded with any suspicion; everyone there is from somewhere else.

"People might know me there," he says vaguely. He's sparing me some grizzly details, I'm sure.

"Zalah?" It's a city surrounded by mountains that shine like crystal when the sun hits them from the west.

"Razed it," he says candidly.

"Tunder?" I've never been, but I've heard it's pleasant enough. Leopold was born there, so there must be good people and good stock.

"Sacked it," he says with a twinge of bashfulness.

I frown. Every soul in the kingdom is looking for me, but only Mathius could recognize me. No soul I can imagine wants to see Rufus coming down the road, but he'll be hard to miss. I am a Princess, yet anonymous. He is Nameless, yet famous.

"We're better off keeping away from cities," he decrees.

A faint shadow has grown over his scalp and jaw. I suspect a full head of hair and a beard will go a long way towards obscuring him. I can hardly even picture him anything but himself. I wonder how much like everyone else he might look once he has something to cushion his hard features. I wonder if he might be handsome.

A thought strikes me.

"Paralee," I exclaim.

He searches his memory. "I don't know it," he rules.

"I know someone there," I say, buzzing happily a little.

"Who alive would put you before the Crown?" he asks, already trying to dampen my optimism.

"When I was young, I had a governess," I begin, picturing her plump, matronly face for the first time in years. "Lady Elizabeth Tawndre was her name. It was her job to make a lady of me. No small task, I assure you. I certainly didn't make it any easier on her."

"What's she doing in Paralee?" he asks, and I sense the skepticism growing within him.

"She lives with her family on a little farm in the woods south of the town," I say before lowering my voice. "She was banished."

He nods his head, considering.

"She'll take you in," he mutters, more a realization than a question.

"Yes," I say. I want to say more, but I don't.

Rufus comes to his decision.

"I'll take you to her," he declares.

There's a finality in his tone. He will commit to nothing more. Something in me sinks at the thought of parting ways with him so soon.

❊ ❊ ❊

"We'll make camp here," Rufus says.

I nearly collapse where I stand. I curse my vanity. If I'd been honest, I'd have begged to stop hours ago. I'm new to the road, or at least I'm new to whatever you call these paths people don't walk. The competitor in me insisted I match Rufus stride for stride without complaint.

"I'll gather some food," he says. He must sense my desperation.

Soon as he's out of sight, I splay myself down on a stump, gasping and heaving. I have a whole hour to rub my sore feet and joints before he returns. He carries a sack full of whatever it is he procured. He turns his back to me and pours the sack's contents into a little pot. He mashes it all down into a thick paste. Its loud crunching and cracking haunt me.

He starts a fire easily. I watch closely, hoping I might glean how he does it. I don't absorb as much as I'd like. He drives a little stake into the ground next to the fire, pours a bit of water from his canteen into the pot, then hangs it over the flames. We go the whole time without saying a word to each other. I suspect conversation won't flow easily between us. He does nothing casually.

He hands me a bowl with a portion equal to his own. I look at my dinner, and when I find a colourless mush that could be anything staring back at me, I can't help myself:

"What is this?" I ask hurriedly, hoping I don't come off too unappreciative.

"Meat," he says, more ominously than he intends.

"Meat? What kind of meat?"

"Meat," he tells me again, curtly this time, looking me square in the eye, "and vegetables."

I stare into the slop before me, wondering at its deep, dark secrets.

"It isn't man, is it?"

"No," he tells me humorlessly.

"Or woman?"

That brings a smile to his lips, maybe the first I've seen. He tries to hide it a little, lowering his head.

"It's not people or god or anything else that ought to offend you," he says, trying to ease me in his steady, unpracticed way. "It's good for you."

He sips at his bowl while I watch him suspiciously. I suppose he'd be the last person to poison me, and he's a picture of health. I clear my throat and raise the slop to my mouth. It hits my lips, and I know immediately how severely he has wronged me.

"It's awful," I blurt out after spitting. I hide my mouth in the crook of my elbow to keep from gagging.

"It's good for you," he repeats indifferently then pours the slop straight down his gullet. It passes by his teeth and down his throat so quickly he must not even taste it. That has to be the trick. I mimic him. Bad idea.

"I can't do this," I gasp after hacking.

"Eat. Half the work of good health is eating right," he tells me before taking another gulp. He raises his eyebrows at me as he lets the mysterious evil linger in his mouth a moment. He swallows easily.

"How did you get so big punishing your stomach like this?" I ask, wishing I could scratch my tongue clean. "I've never known a person even half your size who didn't love to eat."

"I do love to eat," he says defensively. "I love what it does for me. That bowl in front of you is the difference between me and a lot of lesser men."

"Tell me sincerely that you like this," I demand, hiding how offended I am behind a laugh and raising the bowl at him so he might see his crime.

"It doesn't matter if I like it," he explains, losing patience.

"Even animals like what they eat!" I yelp.

"I'm a lot more than an animal," he grunts, pouring himself another serving.

"If there's anything that binds all the living things of this planet together, it's a love of food," I say with a bewildered shake of my head. "Somehow, you've spoiled even that for yourself."

"You better get used to it," he says, settling back into his seat. "You fled the life of leisure. This is what existence is far from palace gates. You want away from that crown of yours? You can't get any further than right here."

"You're running too," I remind him. "What are you searching for? Happiness? Like everyone else? I don't know how you can expect to find it without taking pleasure along the way."

I can see my point reach him. I narrow my eyes and lean towards him, deviously.

"What's the best meal you've ever had?" I ask.

He searches his mind, but he doesn't have a ready answer. Before he has a chance to tell me something deeply upsetting about days of starving or the first time he feasted on a defeated foe's heart, I continue.

"It wasn't complicated," I explain, voice hushed like a solemn pledge. "It wasn't some holiday or feast that took hours to prepare. It was rabbit. I chased it all day with my bare hands because my attendant Leopold told me to."

His eyes light up at Leopold's mention.

"Leopold Volun?" He asks.

"Do you know him?" I wonder, a little surprised.

"I'm familiar," he says, dripping with sarcasm.

For a moment, I worry I might give something away that may do a fine man harm. Then, I worry about disappointing Rufus. My story is modest relative to the attention he pays me.

"I caught it," I continue, watching my words. "It took patience. Hours. The key wasn't being quick. Rather, it was being slow, solid. I wore the critter out, and then I approached so gently, so quietly, that it welcomed me. Then we roasted it. Best meat I ever had."

Rufus nods his head soberly. Invoking Leopold's name apparently imbued my story with some wisdom.

"I never hunted rabbit," he finally says.

"They're hard to catch unless you know how," I shrug, folding my arms a little smugly. "You can trap them, of course. But you don't always have the resources on hand."

"I always found it easier to eat ugly things," he explains. "I like rabbits. They never bothered me any."

That may be the first gentle sentiment he's admitted to me. It took admitting to something gruesome. I ponder what ugly creature bore the meat that found its way into the slop before me.

"It's bugs," he tells me grudgingly, tired of the dance. "Crickets and worms, mostly. It's easy to guess which when you bite down."

He slurps the slop. He chews, and I hear a gritty sounding crunch.

"Cricket?" I guess.

"You're a quick learner," he says, almost funny.

"A lot of people might consider eating bugs beneath them," I remark, pretending I perish the thought.

"Haughty folk." He shrugs. "There are two types of people who won't eat bugs: rich people, and people who care more about looking strong than being strong."

"What about people who don't like the taste?" I ask.

"Rich people," he repeats. I suspect his definition of the word 'rich' is somewhat broader than mine.

He stares at me accusingly. I feel him challenging me. I take a deep gulp of the slop. He smirks and shakes his head. I think I've impressed him.

I wipe my chin clean on my sleeve. A little burp escapes me. He laughs, turning his whole head away from me so I might not see. I laugh too.

We settle down. I finish my slop and set down my bowl.

"Seconds?" he offers.

"No, thank you," I shoot back.

He smiles softly and looks into the fire. He adjusts his back against a tree. His eyelids lower, and I feel him drifting away to somewhere lonesome, some melancholy place apart from me.

"You know..." I begin tentatively. "There's a place for you there. In Paralee."

"No, there isn't," he says, dismissing me with certainty.

"There is," I assert, renewing my confidence in defiance. "There's a place for strength everywhere, particularly on a farm. Elizabeth and her family will probably have more use for you than they will for me."

"What makes you so sure she'll take you?" he asks.

"She loved me," I snort.

"She served you," he retorts. "There's a difference."

"No." I shake my head firmly. "She was almost a mother to me."

"Until you cast her out," he says, poking at the fire with a stick.

"Father cast her out. I saved her from worse," I insist, then immediately doubt myself. "Our happiness was real."

Rufus surrenders his argument, cedes with a little raise of his hand. I beam, pleased. My mind wanders back to Elizabeth.

"I was always running, jumping, and climbing when I ought to have been posing demurely," I tell him, my smile fading, my happy retrospection turning bittersweet. "She was helpless to stop me. She had no tools or authority to discipline me. She wasn't allowed to raise her voice to me, let alone lay a finger on me. What could she do? Nonetheless, my misbehaving was looked on as her failure."

"Doesn't sound like she owes you much," he observes.

I bristle. I suspect he won't take my side much in stories about servants. Fair enough.

"She did the best she could," I say with a shrug. "She was very, very kind. That's how she managed me as well as she did. I hated to disappoint her. She played the victim masterfully. Her other genius was to make a game of being good. She helped me understand I could get away with more in private if in public I presented ladylike and harmless. She made us conspirators in a great trick we were performing on all the other people in court."

"Tricked me," he says slyly. I flush with delight for a moment before remembering where my story is taking me.

"She understood the loneliness of my situation. She would let me keep little animals we'd find on our walks. Insects. Hurt mice and birds, abandoned by their parents. She let me take them up to my room and care for them. I needed friends."

Rufus's head bobs a little, I think unconsciously. Maybe he knows the feeling.

"None of them lasted," I admit. "Most were too unfit to live long. Until there was Gossamer. We called him Goss for short.

He was this wispy little bird I could hide in my hands. He had a sharp orange beak and feathers that were green, blue, and everything in between. Even though he was sick when we found him, he was beautiful. And day by day, he grew more beautiful because I tended to him. He was the first creature I'd ever really made any strides with. Everything else died too soon."

I pause to check if I've bored Rufus to sleep. He hangs on my every word.

"I became an addict to progress," I continue. "I always kept Goss near to better serve his health. I would tuck him in my sleeve or down the chest of my robe. He loved me, and he was too weak to move around or make much noise. He was my little secret. One day, I was greedy. Darnett was visiting."

The name makes Rufus uneasy. He keeps impossibly still in the hopes I might not notice.

"He and a dozen lords from I don't know where. I acted out where people could see. It was Darnett's fault. He was such a snake. I had shown him Goss. I was proud. We were up on a stage, and Darnett was pestering me while Father was addressing the assembled. Just these little pinches now and then on my arms and my neck, trying to fluster Goss. Darnett thought it'd be funny. No one could see him. In any case, I doubt they'd have stopped him. So, after ages of it, I took Goss in my hands and I screamed at Darnett. In front of everyone."

The enormity of my misconduct isn't lost on Rufus. Good. I was worried the Nameless had differing attitudes regarding propriety.

"When everyone was silent, Goss chirped." I nearly grin. "He never chirped. For a second, I was ecstatic. It could only mean he was that much better. Then, before anyone could even think or say anything, Father reached out and snatched him."

I clap my right hand shut as suddenly as Father had. Rufus flinches at my demonstration.

"He crushed Goss," I say with a sniff, kicking at the dirt. "I wasn't allowed animals after that. Elizabeth was blamed, of course. That night, away from everyone except for me and my brothers, Father's men lashed her. She was a lady. She wasn't meant for it. She wailed and wailed. I did too."

Rufus is terribly quiet now.

"I threw myself over her. It was stupid, but I was begging, and they wouldn't listen. It only made things worse. People aren't allowed to touch us. It wasn't her fault. Nothing was. But it was a death sentence."

He finally looks at me again. I see pity in his eyes.

"They were going to kill her. Right there in front of me. I pleaded. I didn't have the words. Father didn't even bother to explain himself. I pulled at him, got down on my knees, prostrated myself before him. He wouldn't be shaken. He never cared what I thought. Mathius, on the other hand… his heart went out to me. He talked Father down to exile. Father always respected him, sought to please him. We sent her home to her family, shamed."

Rufus lowers his gaze thoughtfully.

"Father said she'd be safe," I say. "It might have been the only kind thing he ever did for me, and it was only for Mathius's sake. It was for the best. Certainly the best we could hope for. She always talked about home. Her quiet father, stoic but affectionate. Her mother, so like her they could have been sisters. I was happy for her."

"Nothing's so happy as a good family," Rufus says, nustling a little more deeply into his tree, folding his arms over himself.

"I was her child," I say emphatically. "She was taken from me. She will welcome me with open arms."

I set my sights back on Rufus. He breathes steadily and deeply. I always doze off before he does, and he always wakes before me. I can't even picture him sleeping. I swear to myself I'll stay up to see it.

※ ※ ※

I wake more gently this time. I turn and find Rufus, down on a knee, tapping lightly at my shoulder. The sky is brighter than the day before. Rufus must be in less of a hurry.

"Not much further," he tells me.

I cast my mind back, trying to picture him at rest, his eyes shut and peaceful. I'm sure I missed it. Does he snore or toss? I may never know.

He reaches a hand down to help me up. I grab hold, and he launches me up easily before I even get my feet under me. He brushes some debris off my cloak, or rather his cloak. I wonder if I'll get to keep it.

We walk for hours before Paralee appears on the horizon. For a million reasons, I want to ask Rufus to go into town with me. I think about telling him I'm hungry and insisting we share a final meal together. I envisage idly perusing the streets and shops with him, considering everything, settling on nothing. I delay him for ages until we find some rabbits for sale. We laugh, we feast, and we vow to see each other again someday to commemorate the occasion. Elizabeth can wait. She isn't expecting me.

I don't speak up. We circle wide around the edge of the town, never entering, and make our way deep into the southern woods.

Finally, we see it: a little wooden sign reading 'Tawndre.' It hangs from a post by a pair of little steel rings. I scurry up the road past Rufus and slap the sign as I pass it. It swings and creaks. Even though the sound of it is rusty and screeching, it's like music to me.

I can see the trees parting up ahead. I feel tall, untended grass tickle my ankles, and I want to laugh. I come into a clearing and feel the sun unobstructed on me for the first time in what feels like years. It's cooler than I expected.

I search for a house. I picture a little cabin, too small for so big a family, with a porch out front to greet visitors from. I see Elizabeth's face in my mind, startled at first, then smiling wide. Somehow, impossibly, she recognizes me before I even say a word. I leap into her arms, and no one stops me. No one thinks anything of it because it's right. Natural. What loved ones do.

The grass turns grey and dusty by my feet, and I think I've found sand. Then I see the mark etched in the dirt. The dragon, its mouth open wide. The brand reserved only for betrayers and heretics.

My heart sinks when I find what's left of the house. It's a ruin. A charred, black skeleton with all its meat and life picked clean. I swear though nothing but stone pillars and ash remain, I can see pieces of the home I only ever saw in dreams.

As I approach, I see past the house at the true calamity beyond it. Six stakes plunged deep into the earth. On each of them, a cadaver, long dead, bearing witness to the house, rising high enough for the sun to cook. They've withered so much that I can only guess at them by their size. Elizabeth could be one of two. Of the others, one is big enough that it must be her father, and the rest are so small I'm sure they're her siblings.

Rufus is beside me. I don't know for how long he's been there. He is quiet, unsurprised. If he expected this, he should have told me. He should have prepared me.

He waits. He doesn't look at me. He acts like I'm not even there, like I have total privacy to indulge whatever reaction I choose to have. He just surveys Elizabeth and her family sedately. I wonder how many scenes he's seen just like this one. How many brothers and sisters has he seen murdered? Did he ever shed a tear?

"Father said..." I begin, but the words already sound so young and stupid falling quivering from my lips. I stop to keep from embarrassing myself.

I do not cry. I don't know why not. Maybe I'm too shocked. Maybe I've become numb, inured to the depravity of the world. I want to sense my heart breaking, my eyes leaking hot tears all over my cheeks. That'd be the right thing to feel. That'd be what Elizabeth deserved. Yet I feel nothing. It frightens me.

"I could kill him," he tells me, blunt and weary. "Your father. If you ask me to."

I turn to Rufus. He looks deep into my eyes, without judgment or expectation. There's no question of how he might do it, or if he's even capable. All that matters to him is what I want.

The impossibility of the task never occurs to me; I trust his word. Yet I see the price of it in the slight sad sag of his mouth. All he wants is to be finished. He'll delay it indefinitely if I ask him now. He'll admit the ugliness of the world, embrace that essential evil inside him and let it loose on Father. He'll die failing or win bitterly. Either's a tragedy. He'll do it for me.

At this moment, I feel no anger, no hatred. The very face of vengeance stares back at me, but I am not seduced. I see its toll in every speck of Rufus's being.

"No," I tell him flatly.

Father is nothing to me now. I will never think of him. He will hold no influence over me. My only revenge will be a life well lived.

Rufus walks away from me, sifting through the wreckage.

"Good bones," he remarks, knocking at the stone pillars that once supported the house.

We spend the rest of the afternoon taking Elizabeth and her family down from their spikes. There was a reason no one had done it yet. That crest in the dirt was a curse, insuring woe to anyone who tread here and dared show fealty to these betrayers. Superstition alone would leave the Tawndres a monument for all time. The sky might open and strike down who so ever didn't cower before this fearsome sight, after all.

Rufus is not so easily deterred. I watch him lower the father all by himself before I set aside my childish fears and help. He lowers the bodies gently as flowers into my arms now, and I wonder for a moment if he has some magic that only gives them weight when he hands them off to me.

"Don't smell," he warns me on the first. I don't heed him. "Don't worry about sickness. Your people treat the bodies. Harden and dry them. They show better if they don't rot."

I hadn't seen enough dead to know any better. The odour is different than I expect. Stale and crisp, like the bark of a tree.

We lay the bodies down one by one on the grass, saving the two that might be Elizabeth for last. I keep my composure all the way through the first and nearly through the second when the tears rush to my eyes. I lean low to set her down then don't dare stand back up. I weep. I didn't even weep for Darnett. I didn't let myself. Now, here in front of Elizabeth and the God Killer, I can't help it.

Rufus keeps his distance until I finish, patient and placating. When I finally lift myself back up, wiping at my snivelling nose with my sleeve, he timidly reaches his hand out to touch my shoulder. He withdraws it quickly when I turn to him. He never even grazed me.

"What do you want to do with them?" he asks, quick to move forward.

"What would you do?" I wonder aloud before thinking. I should have taken into account who I was speaking to.

"In the Nameless, we'd dig a mass grave, " he says, lying poorly. "If we had time."

He knew that wouldn't serve me even as he said it.

"We have time, " he assures me.

"It's not enough," I tell him.

He frowns a little, out of his element.

"What would they like?" he asks, gesturing at the Tawndres.

I reflect on that for a while. I was a child when I knew Elizabeth, which is to say selfish. I didn't think of her enough. She loved what I hated. She thought so much of the Crown. She loved the kingdom. She found such dignity in all the rituals and was so grateful to be near them. She revelled in the customs and ceremonies I took for granted. She truly believed they might elevate her.

"When Darnett passed, there was a procession. We set him on a raft, a priest said some words, and we sent him out to sea."

"Priests won't touch them," Rufus warns, shaking his head at the crest burnt into the ground.

"We can do it," I suggest.

He considers the bodies a moment. I can see him doing the

math in his head, the math I've already completed. Six rafts, or maybe a single large one. We can use the stakes, but then we'll still need some trees cut down. Then, we'll need to gather some nice things for adorning. Finally, we'll require some way to carry it all to the river. The family's wagon should suffice. It's a lot of work for strangers, a lot of pomp for an unbeliever.

"All right," he says.

* * *

It's deep in the night when we finally take our first rest. I collapse into the grass and lean my back against a sturdy stone pillar. I'm spent from chopping, carving, and carrying. I still have plenty more to look forward to tomorrow. Hiding my exhaustion from Rufus doubles the strain.

I don't even have time to say a word to him before he leaves for the woods. Nearly an hour later, he returns with two rabbits. If I knew what he intended, I'd have insisted on going myself. I'd have caught them much faster. I keep that to myself. I merely thank him.

CHAPTER 24: THE PIT

Rufus

The sun is hot. I'm sitting beneath a tree, cooled by shade and wet grass. My wife dips her feet in the stream, her back to me. She turns…

No. I do not see her. I can not see her.

"Who is she?"

I jolt awake. The ugly world streaks back to me. The lash wounds on my back sting sharply, worse when I move. I'm drenched in sweat from sickness and fever. My stomach aches and panics, no more fat to gorge on. My wrists burn, the weight of my arms dragging them against my shackles.

In the corner of my cell, I see Mathius. He sits on a simple chair much too meagre for him. He rests his chin on his hand, tired but still very curious. He pokes and prods at my brain once a week. Or once a month. I don't know. He walks through my mind, parting veils. I feel fingers where they don't belong. He can't see what I lock away. I put away the stream. I leave my wife behind.

"It's lovely there," he says pleasantly. Like my friend.

He waits for me. I'm not sure I'm even capable of talking.

"Was that her in your master's memory?" he asks.

I look at him, but my face might be too weak to shoot him the warning I intend. He shrugs, unmoved.

"She can't be very beautiful," he ascertains, leaning back in his chair and scrutinizing. "Your master would have remembered her better. She was…. a blur. Memory makes a poor document. Was Paralee where you lived?"

He provokes me, incenses me. Calm, Rufus.

"I suppose you could have kept moving." He entwines his fingers on his lap. "That would have been the soundest strategy. But…"

He pauses dramatically. He quickly looks at me to make sure he still holds my focus.

"I suspect you were past sound strategy then. You looked content. At home. I wager she's still there."

In my distress, I rub my fingertips against my palm. I just barely keep myself from balling a fist. He notices anyway.

"You don't have to worry," he tells me with a belittling shake of his head. "I won't hurt her. You really don't need to bother hiding her from me. It must wear on you, keeping her at arm's length. I could send for her."

I set hard, dark eyes upon him. He isn't discouraged.

"Maybe she'd have better luck talking to you than I do." He indulges in a sigh, then heightens his voice again to a singsong timbre. "I'm glad she means so much to you. I'm happy you were happy. It tethers you. It helps me believe you're not beyond reason. All good things begin with love."

There's no love here. He leans towards me, genuine and kind hearted.

"She could have everything, you know," he continues. "I doubt she was Nameless. She probably doesn't hate me as much as you do. I could be courteous to her. Give her what you'd have liked to. She could be safe. I could promise you that. If you only lit the way."

For a moment, I consider. I've often dreamed of the existence my wife might have if not for me. I'm an anchor dragging at her ankle. There should have been other men, better men for the life that suited her. She could never be completely safe with me at her side. But she loved me. Even though it hurt her, even though it put a ceiling on her happiness.

So, now that I'm ripped from her world, why shouldn't she have everything else there is to have? Who better to give it to her? Who better than—

I stop myself. I can't choose her happiness for her. She can judge it for herself. Mathius can't offer her a single thing she didn't already leave behind.

"Very well," Mathius says, seeing I'm adamant and rising from his seat. "Abandon her if you prefer. I hope she doesn't suffer."

My cell door swings open for him.

"Daddy!" I hear his daughter yelp when he disappears around the corner. If I knew she was near, I'd forgotten. She's never far. I hope she didn't see me like this.

No. I needn't worry. Mathius wouldn't have let her. I relax. Darling has become precious to me. I've been afforded very few unmade minds in my life. Gentle creatures have seldom trusted me. Children have always feared me. Yet Darling looks at me, and I feel her openness even from behind her mask. She's learned nothing from the people who come to gawk at me. For them, I'm a rare, terrible creature from some exotic, shadowy corner.

She is dubious. She's curious about these horrible things that are done to me. It hasn't occurred to her yet to vilify or hate me. I've done nothing to merit her scorn or contempt. I never will.

* * *

I don't count days. There's no end to this sentence. Nothing to wait for. I don't like to think about the things I'm away from unless I have to, and only if Mathius is far, far away.

Happiness is dependent on hope, and hope is dependent on progress. You need things to climb towards in life. A skill. A marriage. A house. A family. In a prison, you control almost nothing. You need to shrink your mind, look inwards for the attainable. One more repetition of an exercise. One more inch on a stretch. One more second of tension. Always forward. Find victories, however small, where you can.

They give me my body here. They break it down and let me put it back together. They want it for something bigger, and they don't trust themselves to do the job with it that I will. They try to trick me, to demean me with hard labour. I plough their fields. I pull their wagons. I turn their gears and lift their gates. I take satisfaction in seeing my muscles returning to me, old friends I thought lost forever. I am a beast of burden and proud of it.

They let me practice my craft. They march me to a little courtyard, seal me up, and take my shackles. In that square no bigger than a bedroom, I'm no longer a prisoner. In my movements and strikes, I am an artist, a teacher, a holy man. I am the highest, I am immaculate. My captors know. They watch. Rapt.

I think they hope to glean something from my patterns and apply it to their forces. I've contemplated lying in my habits. Teach them imperfection so they might defeat themselves. Diminish myself and maybe diminish them. It'd probably be the clever move. I can't bring myself to do it. I tell myself I can't show them anything they don't already know. Work is all that ever separated me. Just because I show the path doesn't mean they can walk it. So what if their soldiers are better a day sooner. Let them take my joy to make their poison.

Mathius

I made sure to limit the spread of word on the Blight's capture. After all, a capture without a conversion is only half a victory, and half a victory is no victory at all for the Royal Family. Still, people can't help themselves. I tell one lord, they tell two more, and so on and so forth. Before long, without a single public proclamation, I had requests from all the great houses for viewings.

Inevitably, every prominent citizen that visited came away disappointed. The Blight is no awesome sight in a cage. He's just a man. Larger than most but also quite docile. He is unconcerned with impressing strangers. I would tell men who thought themselves stalwart that I saw with my own two eyes the Blight fight off a legion of my Allegia. They would nod politely and raise their eyebrows, but I could see: in their minds, they were besting two legions.

Finally, Relek the Builder, an old, dumpy, and very loud man, put it to words:

"When I was young, I'd have shown him a thing or two," he blustered.

I saw the Blight lower his head to mask a small sneer. Relek shook the cell bars.

"Put him in the training pit!" Relek bellowed. "I'll fight him now! No one ever captured me. I have that and more on him!"

The Blight looked at Relek very sternly, humourless and warning. That intrigued me. I pulled Relek aside gently, my mind already racing and plotting. For the kingdom to know the towering achievement of the Blight's capture, people would need to better comprehend the incredible boundlessness of his barbarism. There'd be no shortage of storied warriors eager to prove their mettle.

The first titled man to volunteer himself against the Blight was the Jeweled Sentry, a guard who made his name beating back a raid on the Capital's bank during the last drought. The city's nobles showered him with enough jewels to fashion an extravagant, glistening set of armour. He wore it to the fight, and it shone so bright I wondered whether his patrons would have been better served leaving the bank to the looters.

In front of a dozen or so very affluent entertainment seekers, the Blight dispatched the Jeweled Sentry within a blink of the eye. We gave the Blight a sword, just to be sporting. He never even picked it up out of the dirt. The Sentry charged only to have his head driven into the wall. That was all of it. It was terribly deflating. The Sentry woke up later that day. He begged us to suppress the news for fear he'd be obligated to relinquish his armour in disgrace. We assigned him to a new city.

Some weeks later, the Mover Of Mountains came to test his valour. He was a marvel, huge and lumbering, and he swung a massive hammer with such dexterity it was said he could level all the world if only time permitted. He lasted a few seconds longer than the Sentry. The Blight pulled him down into the sand, coiled around him like a snake, and squeezed the breath from him. It took four of my men to carry the Mover out.

The Dancing Dagger fancied himself a practical man, despite his name. He chided his predecessors for trying to match strength. He thought he could win with agility, dazzle the Blight with swiftness and unpredictability unmatched throughout the kingdom. The Blight wrapped his shackles around Dagger's throat after a single cartwheel.

Matches increased in frequency. Each arrived with more raucous fanfare than the last. Their brevity, at first wretchedly depressing for those who'd travelled far, became a novelty. Bit by bit, the Blight's patience chipped away. Efficacy warped into brutality. At first, he sought out clean, decisive submissions. He soon settled for shattered bones and mangled limbs. Whatever returned him to his cell quickest.

I was turning away lords and good, distinguished servants by the time the White Falcon obliged us with a showing. He'd won his notoriety hunting Nameless with singular success before settling into a more comfortable station as the head of First Morning's standing guard. He was so revered, so irreproachable that my brother's death hardly put a dent in his reputation. I can't imagine how much he'd been pestered before finally agreeing to take up his greatsword, Cleansing Rain.

The White Falcon must have been the first man the Blight recognized. The Blight took more time with him than he had in all his previous matches combined. Yet there was never any doubt.

After humiliating the Falcon for a few minutes by dodging Cleansing Rain's feeble swipes to the jeers of a rabid audience, the Blight grabbed the Falcon's famous plumed helmet in both hands and shot his forehead into the facemask. The Falcon staggered backwards, but couldn't loose himself from the Blight's grip. The Blight swung his own head like a weapon again and again until the Falcon's helmet collapsed.

A hush came upon the onlookers. The pit was so quiet it

may as well have been empty. I'll never forget the image of the Blight standing over his fallen prey, dripping red from his scalp all over the crumpled icon. In a sense, the Falcon was the first man I'd heard of to draw blood from the Blight. Some honour.

The Blight took the Falcon's greatsword. The Falcon hardly had time to concede before the Blight sliced the good man's arm clean off his body, nearly to his shoulder. It was savage, more savage than anything I'd seen in my life. The whole audience stared in silence, mouths agape, hypnotized by the Blight's heavy, callous breaths and the Falcon's beseeching screams. It was only when I heard the cheerful clapping of my dear daughter's tactless hands that we broke from our shared daze. The Blight looked up at her and offered a little bow. She giggled, delighted to be acknowledged by the champion she so admired.

It was then that I elected to put an end to the matches.

CHAPTER 25: THE LONG REST

Ciendy

Once Rufus and I sent Elizabeth and her family to their peace, we had nowhere to go, so we stayed where we were. We determined to build the house back up where it once stood. I went into town to try and find who the grounds belonged to. I took Elizabeth's name. I said I was family, which I like to believe is true. I wanted to pay for the land we were using. With what, I had no idea. It didn't matter. No one would claim it. Cursed land is as worthless as it is feared.

We kept building, never facing a single dispute until a wild dog professed his holding on the territory. Rufus tried to shoo it away, but the beast deduced pretty quickly he was not inclined to do it any harm. It dug in its heels, barked and snapped at him. I gave it some rabbit and set it back on its path. It came back the next day, picked a fight with Rufus, I fed it again, and it left.

It went on like that a week before it stopped bothering to leave us. It was with us morning and night, biting at Rufus when he happened by and plying me for food whenever it could. I was happier for its presence. I liked having something to give affection to. 'It' became 'he', and 'he' became 'Bandit'. I named him for his mercenary ways. He'd do anything for food, save show Rufus kindness.

Bandit watched over us while we did our work, I think imagining himself as our mighty protector. We put up walls together. Hammered, cut, and lifted. Rufus and I made ourselves everything we could. We went into town sparingly, only for essentials. Essentials and books, of course. Rufus bought every tome he could on making, growing, cooking. Medicine was his favourite. As dense and inscrutable as the books were, he grabbed them by the set. I don't think he understood them much. I suspect it made him feel nearer his father somehow.

When we needed money, Rufus found farms to work on while I stayed and built. At first, he was regarded with suspicion. No one trusted his short hair and rags. They denounced where he chose to rest his head at night. So, he'd do a day's work for free. They'd pay whatever he asked for a second.

The whole time, I worried Rufus might leave when we were finished, that he was only lingering until I had a safe and comfortable enough place to live. He always found something new to do, some increasingly trivial thing the house couldn't be complete without. Every day, the project swelled, and a completion date became more remote. My bedroom came first, then a kitchen, then a little lounge, then a porch, then a room for guests. He never mentioned a place for himself.

We spent whole months teaching each other everything we knew. I taught him to sew so we might have clothes and to garden so we might grow grass and flowers over the brand scorched in the yard. It wasn't long before his skill in both far exceeded my own. He taught me all the Nameless methods of hunting and foraging, and I blazed past him there. We'd lived so long in rigidly defined roles, barred from practices that didn't fit the moulds of the seasoned warrior or the elegant lady. I think it pleased us both to find we had talents in unexpected places.

Eventually, we'd built up enough that we had a room to sleep in. When the night finally came for me to put it to use, mystery and anticipation were heavy in the air. We'd never formalized what we were to each other, or where all this time together was bringing us. When the moon was high, and I was fatigued enough to force my courage, I told him I was going to bed. He bid me good night and reposed beneath the same tree he always did.

Or I think he did. I've still never seen him actually get a wink of sleep.

I didn't know to be dejected or relieved when I lowered myself into my new bed, alone. I was too tired to suss it out, yet I turned over all night. I slept better outside beneath the trees with Rufus.

The next night, we again found ourselves sitting by a fire, me on my stump, him against his tree. My head was growing heavy, but I didn't want to go. Nor did I want to admit it.

"Time for bed," he said flatly.

I shot awake, defiance refreshing me.

"I'm not tired," I said, unwavering.

"Sure you're not," he said, unconvinced.

I shook myself in place, widened my eyes, did anything I could to beat back my faintness.

"Do you sleep?" I finally dared to ask.

"Of course I sleep," he snorted, and I could already sense him tightening.

"When?" I pressed.

"When does anyone?" he countered, folding his arms.

I frowned. I plotted a new ploy. I knew I couldn't give him an opportunity to deny.

"We're not running anymore," I said, I hoped gently enough that I wouldn't alert his guard. "I'm not worried. Do you not feel safe?"

He rolled his neck, twisted away from me. I had annoyed him.

"We can trade turns if you like," I tried. "I can watch out."

That didn't help any. I'd overstepped. I should have known. If there's anything men hate, it's admitting weakness. I lifted myself up to go.

"When I was young, the others came for me at night," he said when my back was to him.

I circled back and found his face tilted away from me.

"The other children," he clarified as I retook my seat. "I had to stay up to brace myself. After that, I had to stay up to catch up with them in training. Then, I had to stay up to keep ahead."

"None of that matters now," I told him consolingly.

He set his jaw. He mulled something confidential over in his mind, considering me.

"I have fits," he confessed.

"Fits?" I pushed. I didn't know what he meant.

"I see things when I sleep," he said, lowering his eyes, shifting uneasily in place. "My father. Your brother. His daughter. Battles. Sometimes, I wake up thrashing. Sometimes... I hurt people. Even the last people I'd ever hurt if I could help it."

He lingered for a moment, worried he'd said too much.

"I can help it," he claimed, renewed and resolute. "I'm through putting ugliness into the world. So I don't sleep. If I have to... I go away. Somewhere I won't do harm. Away from people. Where I belong."

I digested what he told me a while in silence. He cultivated such a measured air. I could see why he'd clutch this secret close. I only wished I might do something about it. What, I did not know.

"All right," I accepted with a shrug. "I thought..."

I trailed off. He watched me, waiting. I went to bed. He didn't move.

※ ※ ※

It's funny how quickly change can come given how rare it really is. Rufus and I had hunted and foraged the same path a hundred times without incident, and to our minds, we'd do it a hundred more. Until one day, descending into a deep valley, we found a family of four making camp. They were so unexpected they saw us the moment we saw them. The father was a genial, merry man. He smiled openly and waved his arm wide to greet us.

"Hello, stranger!" he hollered then beckoned us closer.

His wife and children were less forthcoming. They sat huddled together upon a wagon, sizing us up with all the caution of the oversheltered. I fluttered my hand at them to try and assuage them. Rufus returned their sober, suspicious looks as if they were as daunting a danger to him as he might be to them. They couldn't appear more harmless if they tried. Yet our privacy was precious and fragile. Anything might damage it.

"We are the Bagatelles," said the man, daintily pressing his hand against his chest. "I am Nicolas. This dear woman is my wife, Gerta. And our children, Isabel and Vernon."

"Lovely to meet you," I said. "My name is Elizabeth. This big brute is Rufus. Don't be afraid. He's quite gentle. He even speaks."

I looked up at Rufus, who forced a tight smile that did nothing to mollify Isabel and Vernon's skepticism.

"We live up the road," I continued, gesturing behind me.

"Happy to hear it," Nicolas said with a slight but affable nod of his head, appraising Rufus with darting glances. "I suppose we'll be neighbours. We've just purchased this land. It's our intention to build our house in this very spot. Feel free to continue walking whatever paths you please. We are not so reserved."

"Thank you," I said with a modest bow.

"You shouldn't build here," Rufus said gravely.

It was only a polite warning, but it sounded like a threat. So much of what Rufus spoke did, whether he meant it to or not. Nicolas's smile faltered, so I hastily assured him.

"Don't mind him," I said, butting Rufus in the ribs with my elbow.

Rufus looked at me, convinced of his correctness. Yet at my silent urging, he lightened his tone, added a little music to his voice.

"Thank you for all your kindness," Rufus said sincerely before returning to the matter he deemed more pressing. "I don't know who sold you this land, how much you own, how much you paid. But you shouldn't build here."

"Are you making a claim?" asked Nicolas, worried.

"No, no," Rufus said, shaking his head. "Of course not. If

you bought it, it's yours. But return it if you can. Or pick a different spot. I'm trying to help you."

Nicolas raised a discerning eyebrow at Rufus. Gerta drew her children nearer.

"Nicolas, are we in danger?" she demanded.

"You're fine," Rufus said with a tone clumsily imitating soothing. "No bandits, wolves, or anything like that. It's just the land."

They looked at him dumbly, wondering if they were to be victims of some curse or haunting. Rufus stomped down at the earth beneath him a few times before elaborating.

"Feel how soft that is? The ground here is very low. You'll sink. When it rains, you'll have puddles high as your knees. If the river floods? If the trenches break, or the barriers burst? It's all coming here."

Rufus could only see things for their function. He was blind to the beauty of the valley even though we'd enjoyed it ourselves. It was a lovely spot, nestled among blooming hills. The wind glided through the trees with a pleasing melody, and light danced about between undulating leaves and branches. Rufus gave no thought to the trails the children might enjoy exploring, the trees perfect for climbing, or the lovely natural flowers waiting to be plucked. As always, he could only consider susceptibility.

Gerta looked to her husband nervously, but he dismissed her with a little swipe of his hand. His mind was easy, confident.

"Thank you, sir," Nicolas said. "I've been made aware. Paralee has never seen a flood. Rain is rare, and the levees are stout."

"A rain will come," Rufus promised. Pleading did not come easily to him. "Worse than any before."

"Are you a prophet, friend? A rainmaker?" teased Nicolas, little cracks of irritation appearing in his joyful countenance.

"There's always a greater storm," Rufus said firmly. "Something always comes along, fiercer and crueler than before. You have to be ready for it, or you could find yourself at the bottom of a lake in minutes."

I pulled at Rufus's arm.

"It's their choice," I said.

Reluctantly, Rufus nodded his head and shut his mouth.

"Such a worrywart," I said with a laugh I hoped would lighten the mood. "The world is all dark corners and sharp thorns for Rufus. He checks beneath the bed for monsters every night."

Vernon did me the favour of laughing too, and it relaxed us all.

"We'll build it dependable, friend," Nicolas said, outstretching a cordial hand.

"See that you do," Rufus said, smile forced. He gave Nicolas one quick, obligatory shake of the hand.

We were friends after that, or at least we were friendly. They didn't condemn us for the land we chose to live on as the townsfolk did. We changed our walking paths to mostly keep out of their way. Rufus and I helped them build their house. Some people from town helped too.

Within a few months, the Bagatelles had a proper home. There was a nice porch, a barn for some horses, and a fence that somehow made the whole place all the more welcoming. It had come together much more quickly than our house. More hands make less work, I suppose.

For a long time, Rufus was wrong, and The Bagatelles enjoyed as peaceful and idyllic a life as could be. It seemed every time it rained, or even was about to rain, we ran into Nicolas, and he'd tease Rufus about all his needless fretting. Rufus would chuckle and play the fool, admit his worries were childish and cowardly.

No one knew what I knew. Whenever a storm brewed, Rufus stayed up, watching the river for even a hint of danger. Every time he saw dark clouds, he checked the levees and spillways then did what he could to enforce them. Whenever rain fell, the Bagatelles became a little bit safer without ever knowing.

One night, the storm Rufus feared came on Paralee like a swift and deadly strike. Our house leaked from a thousand places. By then, its defences against the elements were nothing to the fortifications we'd raised for the Bagatelles' sake. We could only laugh. We'd worried about our neighbours so long we'd forgotten ourselves. Then we heard a loud crash somewhere in the distance.

The laughing was over. We rushed out of our house and saw the river surging like a charging army into the lowlands. We raced after it, lightning and thunder at our back. There'd be no time to spare.

We came upon the valley where the Bagatelles made their home and instead found the lake Rufus had promised. Only the faintest tip of the house's pointed roof jutted out from the water's surface. It looked like a little stone in a rapid, all but invisible in the torrents of black water and wet foliage.

Rufus dashed in, and I followed. I was up to my chin before we were even close to the door.

"Wait here!" he barked.

He took a deep breath and lowered himself. Over the howling wind, I could still hear him pounding on something. After a moment, the front door of the little house launched up out of the water like a leaping fish. I put my arms over it and propped myself up to breathe more comfortably.

I waded there for minutes that felt like ages. I wanted to hold my breath, to test my endurance. Maybe it wouldn't be so bad. Maybe Rufus was doing it easily.

He burst up without even a single gulp at the air. In his arms were the Bagatelle children, coughing and hacking. He handed them off to me with a trust that startled me then dove back beneath the water. Had he ever seen me swim? How could he know I'd be suitable for the task?

This was always our way. He never doubted me as I doubted myself, and I never dared disappoint him. I rose to his expectations. I earned his confidence, his belief. I kicked my feet and dragged those two children with me to safe harbour on the hillside.

They looked around at their suddenly unfamiliar homestead, eyes wide, teeth shattering.

"Are you all right?" I asked the older sister.

She was healthy enough to nod to me. I checked on her brother, and when I found him well, I ran back into the water.

Rufus emerged to meet me, Nicolas and Gerta with him. They were jostling, scrambling, and encumbering him a hundred ways. I took Gerta in the crook of my arm, and let Nicolas to Rufus. We took them to their children.

Rufus was exhausted when we made the hillside. He let Nicolas fall away from him like clothes discarded after a long day. Nicolas wheezed and coughed so much it seemed dramatic even in these circumstances.

I slapped Nicolas firmly on the back, and he vomited up the water choking him.

"Aria!" he bellowed.

Rufus and I looked at each other. We had the four Bagatelles. What now? Some pet?

"Who?" I asked, steadying Nicolas with a hand on his shoulder.

"Our niece!" exclaimed Gerta, suddenly awake.

"The house was empty," Rufus grunted.

"She sleeps in the barn!" Nicolas said, clutching at Rufus. "She likes the horses better than her cousins!"

With a groan as harsh as a thousand curses, Rufus pushed Nicolas away and charged back into the flood. He reached the barn in an instant, but the horses obstructed him from going any further, thrashing in delirious panic, still tied to their posts at the entrance. There was no way around or through them. Rufus reached for their reins and absorbed a few kicks and snaps for his troubles.

I followed after him. The nearer I got, the more I could sense his frustration. The horses feared him more than the flood. He couldn't bully them to safety. He'd loosened them from their posts by the time I reached him. They rewarded him with whipping heads and attempts to climb over him to fresh air. I think he was ready to kill them when I wrestled the reins from him. Soon as they were away from him, they were as docile and accommodating as beasts could be. Rufus thanked me with a gracious nod of his head, his face red and blue from hooves and bites, then disappeared under the water.

I tied off the horses on safe ground by a tree and waited. Rufus was gone a long while. Too long. His dives into the house were nothing to this. I could only imagine his frenzy scanning every corner of that barn, submerged in inky, dirty water, all but blind. He'd drown to find that girl. I was sure of it.

I began into the water, searching my mind for some miraculous way I might pull his unmoving body to safety. I was halfway to the barn when he breached the new lake's surface with a desperate gasp, a bundle of hair and limbs in his arms. He pulled himself through the water with one arm towards me.

He wouldn't let me take Aria from him. As drained as he was, this was too important. He took her to the hillside as fast as he could, faster than I could, but he was sniffing, sagging. He laid her limp little body down. He parted the hair from her face. She was young. Maybe eight or ten. She wasn't breathing. She was blue. Ghostly.

"Come on," he commanded quietly.

He shook her by her ankle. She didn't respond. He flicked at her ashen cheeks with his fingers.

"Come on," he repeated, this time more like begging.

He pulled at his chin with a trembling hand. She was the object of his scorn now. She had to live. Had to. Otherwise, he would never forgive himself.

"Come on!" he bellowed, shaking her with both hands.

The Bagatelles all flinched and leaned away from the scene, recoiling. An angry Rufus was still a fearsome sight, perhaps more than ever since becoming so rare. I set a hand on his shoulder and pulled him away. He surrendered to reality then. He turned away from the girl, from me, from all of us. I'd never seen him so defeated.

I looked down at Aria. I wanted to chide her for her stupidity, scold her for her selfishness. But she was nothing at all laying there in the mud. Just bones and cold flesh.

No. There had to be something that could be done. What was the problem, the heart of the matter? Water in Aria's lungs instead of air. I had read something about this. I pressed down on her chest again and again. Gerta covered her children's eyes when the limp body jerked, protected them from the ugly sight of my flailing.

Aria needed breath in her lungs. I forced it into her. I shut her nostrils between my fingers and blew into her mouth. Gerta and Nicolas gathered up their children and led them away. Rufus wallowed, flagellating himself at some remote place in his head.

I kept at my work with calmness and clarity, alternating the presses into her chest with the breaths into her mouth. It all made perfect sense to me. Death was an absence of circulation. Aria's life was merely a matter of forcing the water out so air could flow in. Perfectly rational. No question at all.

I wasn't shocked at first when Aria awoke with a hacking cough. I expected it somehow. It wasn't until the Bagatelles pulled her up in their arms and babbled sweetly to her that I knew anything the least bit unusual had occurred. It wasn't until I saw Rufus that I knew the good I'd done.

He looked at me with awe so complete it made me blush. No man living had seen more extraordinary things. He'd tunnelled deep into the darkest abysses, climbed high into the most splendid palaces. He'd waged war, rocked nations. All of it was nothing to this simple act I'd done.

His gratitude was boundless. With only bright eyes, too hushed to speak, he pledged he'd pay this debt all his life. It was ridiculous. Unfair. How could a minute's work buy me so much?

❊ ❊ ❊

The horses died the next morning. Sickness, maybe even infection. The stress and elements had worn them out, left them decrepit, and they never recovered. The news troubled Rufus. He was worn too.

He tried to hide how much the night had battered him. It showed in the coming days. He paled, slowed. No matter how audaciously he raged against weariness, work stopped coming easily to him. He hobbled through chores, brushed me off when I asked him to rest. That was his manner. He would withstand and overcome.

Finally, I found him collapsed in the yard, unconscious. I ran to him, worrying every step until I reached him he'd died. When I came upon him, I could hear his breath fighting him on its way out. It sounded so wrong to hear him labouring with something so trivial. I cast back my mind. In my daze, it was hard to picture him breathing at all. Was he ever winded? No. Not Rufus.

I couldn't carry him inside. I tried and tried, but he was too heavy. I had to leave him to go get help. I don't know that I'd ever been so afraid as in those moments I was away from him. It couldn't have been an hour, but it was long enough for anything to happen. What might I come back to? Hasn't all the world prayed for the invincible Rufus's moment of weakness? How many vengeful predators and grim fates have waited for such an opportunity?

Most people didn't have time for me when I got to town. They turned down their faces and walked right past me. I may as well have been a raving stranger. It wasn't fair. Rufus had done so much for them. He'd built their houses, raised their fences, ploughed their fields. Yet they had no room in their hearts for him.

At the time, I thought it unforgivable the way the town ignored me. It wasn't so much an issue of selfishness on their part. It was incredulity. The storm had taken from all of us, sapped us all of every tangible and intangible resource we had. Rufus had so much strength to spare. He'd be the last to be victimized. No man alive could imagine Rufus's suffering beyond their own.

I was lucky to find Nicolas. Even he hoped to avoid me, but I knew him well enough to grab him by the shoulders and beg. Looking in my eyes, he couldn't deny me. Then I found Joseph, a strapping farmhand, and promised him money I didn't have to come help.

I ran back home. The two men could barely keep up even with me pleading for them to hurry. They were dumbstruck when we reached the yard and saw Bandit sniffing at a comatose Rufus. They hadn't really believed me until just then, I think.

I shooed Bandit away. Rufus was wet with slobber. I vowed I'd tell him when he woke that in his moment of need, the dog had finally shown him some appreciation. But it was just as likely Bandit had been working up the backbone to eat him.

It took the three of us to carry Rufus inside. Nicolas and I each took an arm and a shoulder, and Joseph took the feet. When we dropped Rufus on my bed, I was sure the legs beneath it would snap like twigs. They didn't. We'd built it sturdy.

I'm not sure when Nicolas and Joseph left. I was so busy and frantic I lost track of them completely. I never paid Joseph. I tried to some time later. He wouldn't have it. Nicolas had settled the debt.

Over the next few days, I learned more about medicine than I had in all my previous years combined. I read every book I had and every one I could borrow on the matter. I made a hundred potions, a thousand salves. I fed Rufus, grateful he wasn't well enough to actually taste the mush I prepared him. If it helped, I couldn't see it.

By the morning, he'd sweat through his shirt so completely he left me no alternative but to try and change him out of it. It was a feat to lift him enough to get it off. His chest and back told a long, tragic story of battle and discipline. He looked so unlike me, so unlike anyone. Everywhere my eyes fell was some scar for a wound that should have killed him but didn't. I couldn't see what was actually going to accomplish the deed. It was deep inside him somewhere, lurking.

This was all so wrong. Rufus had survived so much, been

to the edge and back so many times. He'd endured suffering and catastrophe, eaten and breathed more evil than I can imagine. He'd put it all behind him. He was doing good. Real, important good, big and small, wherever and whenever he could. And he was going to die for it.

I hardly left his side except to make things that might help him. It was only then I knew I loved him. It seemed so obvious looking back. How could I have missed it? There was no one else I really trusted. When something happened to me, he was the first person I wanted to tell about it. When I had a question, I asked him. When I was sad or angry, I talked to him until I wasn't.

The impulse kept striking me to call over my shoulder for his help. It was all at once the most ridiculous and sensible thing in the world. How could he be there? But how could he not, now when I needed him and wanted him more than ever before? He'd always been by my side, hadn't he? He always helped steer me through.

"Please, Rufus," I begged. "This one last thing."

He didn't answer. He wasn't behind me, waiting for my call. He was here in front of me, needing me. I couldn't be discouraged. I had to help him. Somewhere within me was the means to heal him. If I didn't have the knowledge, I'd find it. If I didn't have the skill, I'd hone it. He'd been strong so long. I'd carry him now. It was my turn.

* * *

I was nodding off, just about ready to sleep for the first time in days the morning Rufus finally woke. He did it with a start. He sat straight up in bed, confused for only the second it took him to recognize where he was. When he looked at me, it was with embarrassment. He folded his arms over himself, pulled his blanket up, hid those muscles anyone else would have preened with.

"What happened?" he asked without looking at me, hating his vulnerability.

I almost didn't hear him. I wanted to burst from happiness, but I was too tired.

"You fell in the yard," I said. "You were very sick."

I wanted to say more, but the words wouldn't come. It was a delicate subject. I was so proud. I'd never been so proud. I wanted to tell him what I'd done, all I'd accomplished, all I did and learned for his sake. Yet he'd loathe himself for burdening me. Rufus only ever thought of his debts, and I'd only be adding to them.

"Thank you," he said, lowering his face bashfully.

He threw his legs over the side of the bed. Or tried to, at least. It took more than he expected. He braced himself on a corner post, dizzy.

"Stay," I ordered. "Rest. Please."

He obediently settled himself back into bed. It didn't matter if he wanted to or not. He might never defy me again.

I had so much to tell him. I wanted to wipe away every dire feeling in him, every worry of deficit or defect. He owed me nothing. He couldn't. I loved him. He did so much for me just by living, just by being himself, just by loving me.

He did love me, didn't he? He did. It was suddenly so apparent. How else could he be so good? So selfless? I'd wondered at it for so many nights. Finally, I saw. Love. There's such power in it. In loving Rufus, I had accessed an infinite well of courage and stamina. In the short time since his sickness, I'd grown so much, become so much more than I thought I could be. How long had Rufus been drawing from that same well? How could he have felt this invigourating, swelling feeling and kept it to himself? I only understood it just now, and I was so impatient. I couldn't wait any longer, couldn't deny it another second.

"Can I hold you?" I asked feebly.

His eyes shot to me, alert.

"All these days with you lying there... I didn't know what would happen..." I began, starting and stopping. "I just wanted to touch you. But it didn't seem right. It wouldn't be enough without you knowing. So I waited. I put it off until you were better because I wanted you to understand what it meant. How important it was. How important you are."

I tried to compose myself, certain I had just sputtered out gibberish and nonsense. Somehow, he understood anyway. He always understood me.

He shuffled sideways as much as he could, one leg nearly hanging off the edge of the bed. I raised his arm and found my way beneath it. There was a place for my head on his chest, right and natural. He was still until I grabbed his hand in mine. Then he caressed my fingers with little brushes of his thumb.

"I love you," he told me, small, timid.

Did I even need to say it?

"You don't need to say it," he cautioned. "It doesn't have to change anything. I won't ever ask anything of you. All it means is I'm yours."

I smiled, straining and stretching my fingers to entwine our hands. It was such a relief being there, like seizing something that had been just out of reach all my life. Fog had dissolved. Things were so certain, so true.

An incredible, indomitable happiness came upon me. Somehow, implausible as it was, I knew beyond any doubt I'd always be content. All I ever had to do was be kind to Rufus, and he'd repay it a hundred, a thousand fold, as he always had. We'd be so happy making each other happy. It seemed so easy. An unassailable paradise, an unbreakable loop.

"I love you," I declared, as simply and plainly as any fact ever uttered.

I felt his whole body soften. All his life, he'd kept every muscle he had tense, ready to spring at any second. He finally unwound them. He sunk into the bed, so deep and satisfied I thought he might never leave.

I watched him fall asleep then followed him into the dark. As morning broke, I nudged him awake, he smiled groggily at me, and life was everything I wanted it to be.

CHAPTER 26: YOURS

Small

Elizabeth doesn't leave her room anymore. Or if she does, it isn't while I'm around. I spend my days waiting for her door to open, listening in case she calls for me. At first, I didn't dare check on her. Then, when I was sure she wasn't eating, I'd bring her food. I always find her laying on her bed, back turned to the door. She never offers any acknowledgement of my presence, but when I leave a full plate in the morning, it's empty in the evening. So I leave another. For now, that's my life. Switching out plates.

I'm on the porch now, tossing a ball for Bandit to chase. He waits for Elizabeth too, just not so fretfully. I wonder if he senses or cares she's cross with him. I'm compelled to protect him from that. I occupy myself occupying him. He's sweet, playful, and hungry for attention. I understand now why people cherish dogs. It's nice to be needed.

I hurl the ball as near to the edge of the fence as I can, and enjoy the intermission from his panting. I scratch at the short, coarse fuzz growing on my head. I can't help fussing with it. There's nothing so fascinating as your own body becoming unfamiliar. If I grew my hair much longer, then wore different clothes, and maybe lost a bit of muscle, I could look like any other young woman. I don't think I'll do any of that. I like this middle place between Nameless and civilian. I like being different.

Bandit's absence becomes conspicuous. I wonder at first if I threw the ball too far and he lost track of it. I'd be hearing about it if I had. No, something else has his curiosity. I look up and find him fixated on the path beyond the gate. Millen waddles down it, huffing and puffing. I've seen him in town now and then. He's a widower, I think. He's quiet, and he doesn't stare, so I like him fine.

He wrestles a large bundle of I don't know what into one arm then fumbles with the gate's latch. He enters the garden, face red with sweat and urgency. Bandit tries to make friends with him, barking and hopping at him, but Millen won't be distracted. Finally, I notice little feet dangling from the bundle.

"It's my boy," Millen says. He leans his bundle down towards me and shows me a sickly, unconscious face. The boy's quite young. I don't know his name.

I pull him into my arms. He's lighter than I expected, lighter than I think he should be. Millen doubles over and gulps at the air. He'd probably vomit if he thought he had the time. Civilians are never built for running, and Millen maybe least of all.

I kick open the front door, and he follows me in. I find Elizabeth already waiting at the threshold of her bedroom, clutching her coat to her. She's alert, and she cranes her neck for a quick look at the boy. For a moment, all I can be is happy to see her up and about. But then she goes to the cabinet to gather some things, and I remember there are more pressing matters.

I lay the boy down on the table. There are all sorts of things wrong with him. That much is evident. He's soaked with sweat, and his complexion is unlike anything I've seen. The root of his ailment is less easily discerned. He is frigid and unresponsive. He breathes as though in a tumultuous sleep. Whatever it is that tests him, he won't fight it back for long.

"How long since he answered you?" Elizabeth asks.

"Last night," says Millen, casting his mind over his life and scouring for detail. "He went to bed early. He said he hadn't been feeling well. He struggled with the work all day. He said he was sorry."

"Hadn't been feeling well how?" Elizabeth interrupts, certain Millen will yammer on and bury every clue in trivialities.

"I... I don't know," he says. "He doesn't tell me. He tries to be tough in front of me. His mother took care of him. It was his mother he went to when—"

I gently hook Millen by the inside of his arm and lead him outside the room, closing the door behind us. He won't be any use. Without some catastrophic injury to manage, neither will I. The best I can do is to clear a path for Elizabeth to do her work. That means calming Millen as much as I'm able.

After an hour, Elizabeth emerges. She is clean, unsullied. Millen takes that for a good sign, smiling as he rises to meet her. He doesn't know her face as I do.

"I'm sorry," she says almost inaudibly, gazing deep into his eyes.

He looks at her, confused. He searches for meaning, tries to make sense of the chain of events that led him to this impossibility. "What happened?" he finally asks, accepting he can't reason it for himself.

"Your boy was very sick," she says, admission in her voice. "Something inside him was beyond repair. Sometimes... there's just nothing to be done."

Millen's shock doesn't permit him to really hear her. She may as well be speaking a different tongue. He is lost in a world beyond his comprehension. He searches the room, vainly hoping to find something to help explain it all.

I look to Elizabeth, expecting her to communicate a secret to me, something the boy's father needs protection from. Maybe there was some curse on his house. Maybe some evil the father committed had come back around on the son. But I see in her eyes she has spoken only unvarnished truth.

I realize then I didn't think she could fail. Maybe the failures of others could infect her, like when Crag's friends' incompetence cost him his life. But if she weren't distracted or hindered in some other way, her goodness would triumph. Yet right here before me lay a grievous injustice, steadfast and obstinate in the face of her best efforts.

Maybe the father could be blamed. Maybe he waited too

long, neglected his son's cries, ignored a hundred signs. Maybe by growing fat, he couldn't run the boy here quickly enough. I hate him for bringing this ruin into our lives right up until I glance at him. We are bystanders in this tragedy. We are at the edge of a storm, rattled by wind and rain. He is shipwrecked, among forked lightning and waves like mountains, with no port in sight.

I pull him away. Maybe Elizabeth was tired. Maybe her own sorrow depleted her somehow. I banish the thought. I know she did all she could and will do all she can. Even if it won't mean a thing.

※ ※ ※

I wake to crashing glass. I blink my eyes a few times. It's so dark I worry I'm blind. It's only the dead of night. I hear another heavy thud careen off the side of the house. I shoot out of my bed.

I rush out to the front hall and find Elizabeth pressed against the wall by the window. She hides herself while looking out into the garden. She's very calm, if a little sad, holding a cup of water in her lap. I settle myself down, but before I can ask what's happening, a hoarse voice bellows from outside.

"I trusted you!" I hear Millen howl, reeling with drink and grief. "My boy! What now!? What's left!?"

I clench my jaw and ball my fists. How dare he? He has searched for a mark on which to set his rage, and he has chosen the least deserving. We are innocent, and we will not be victims. In his hunger to punish, he mistakes our kindness for weakness.

I'm ready to stomp out into the yard and hurl him back into the woods. Elizabeth deters me with a raised hand. In a huff, I take my spot on the other side of her window, and I see what she sees.

Millen sways about the yard, pursuing a destructive impulse very foreign to him. He hunts for rocks to hurl, unsteady and on the verge of collapse. He kicks at a plant, loses his footing, and falls on his back, defeated.

We listen to him lay there. He gasps for breath but chokes on sobs. Just when I'm sure he's not lifting himself back up, Elizabeth walks right past me towards the door. Before I even have time to protest, she's in the yard, standing over Millen.

I watch them from the window. Elizabeth looms over Millen, so unintimidated she startles him, so fearless she strikes fear. As if to defend himself from a blow he knows he deserves, he tentatively lifts his hand in front of his face. Yet Elizabeth only reaches out her cup of water to him.

He looks at it suspiciously, so she shakes it a little. He accepts it, and when he takes a sip, she sits down next to him in the grass. She waits. She doesn't say a thing. There's nothing to be said. But whatever Millen wants to be heard, she will hear. I'm proud of her. She does not fail.

He drinks thirstily. I should pour him another cup.

* * *

When the sky begins to brighten with the glow of morning, Millen picks himself up off the ground and walks home. He's not happy. He may never be. But he's something better than angry. The fight is gone from him. All that remains is to endure. Maybe we'll see him again. Maybe we'll help him somehow.

Elizabeth rises from the grass, her clothes damp with dew. The light falls from her eyes. She is weary again. She passes by me wordlessly and returns to her bed. She lays down her head and turns her back to me. It feels like we've lived a year in a day. Yet we're back where we started. Nothing has changed.

I watch her through the door she didn't bother to close. I approach it hesitantly. I've changed since I've known her. So much. All my life, I raised arms against misery, sought to defeat it with hardness and hatred. It was easier. But Elizabeth... she dares to love all the world, friend and enemy. It's so brave. So dangerous. Allies will cut you deeper than rivals ever could.

I like to think I share more in common with her now. These are the brightest days of my life. They may be Elizabeth's darkest. What if the unhappiness that used to define me wasn't eradicated like I thought? What if it was merely passed along, transferred, absorbed? What if it belongs to Elizabeth now? I'm petrified to see her more like the Small I left behind.

"I don't know anything," I begin, stammering and inept. "I know what I don't know. I didn't know Rufus. Not really. I can't know what he meant to you. But I know what you mean to me. If he and I had—"

I pause, scolding myself. I'm an amateur in these matters.

"If he and I have anything in common… he's grateful for you. You did right by him. Some things can't be helped. Some things can be. You helped me. All my years, all I did was put more pain, anger, and punishment into the world. I failed every day. Until I met you."

I stop short, afraid maybe of some secret even I didn't know spilling out from me. I watch Elizabeth, hoping for even the most trivial of developments. I want her to move so badly. I want to move her. I want her to be moved.

Nothing. The disappointment stings. I want to recede into a bottomless black hole. For some reason, I'm afraid. I feel as though I'm on the edge of some enormous risk.

"I'll be here when you want me," I say, pulling away. "For as much or as little as you need."

The words come to me just as I turn my back. Suddenly, I don't dare leave them unspoken.

"I'm yours."

I walk away without turning to look at her. I don't need her moved anymore. Not yet. She knows how I feel. That's enough.

CHAPTER 27: THE DAYS OF DANCING

Rufus

If the Nameless taught me anything, it's that people love naming things. It simplifies. I've had a hundred. I heard the Balance whispered in the alleys of poor towns, and Zero bellowed in markets of rich ones. I heard my masters chuckle about the Ancient Prodigy when I started battering my fellow students by the pair. The Blight when I razed Oldport to the ground. My brothers and sisters cheered the God Killer when I butchered Darnett. Every detestable thing I ever did won me some extravagant name or other.

When people started coming around the house asking for Elizabeth's help, I thought about going by some new name. It didn't matter that we lived on cursed land once she started curing wounds and healing ailments. I was surprised how many folks already knew me. We'd laid roots. No one ever questioned me about my past or cast a suspicious eye. 'Rufus' only ever meant to them what I made it mean. It was 'Ruthless' that killed Darnett and Ciendy, 'Ruthless' that upended the kingdom. 'Ruthless' was cruel and barbarous, 'Rufus' decent and generous. The two had as little to do with each other as Elizabeth did with Ciendy.

I've waited a long time for some new name to come along from the good I've done. I've dug holes for foundations. I've chopped wood for houses. I've raised barns for new families. I've returned lost animals, even as they scratched and snapped at me. I've put food in hungry bellies, smiles on unhappy faces. I've done good deeds, humble though they may be. I know I have. And with Elizabeth, I've been near greatness. I've seen screaming mothers hushed and awed with their babies delivered clean and perfect to their arms. I've seen once rotting flesh turned pristine with time and care. I've seen horrified, bloody men brought back from the brink of death or soothed as they were escorted over it. I've been thanked sincerely with wet eyes staring into mine and tender fingers gripping my arm.

All these people I've helped... they only ever call me Rufus. I'm happy to hear it. I doubt it'll catch on.

※ ※ ※

It's been strange passing time beside Elizabeth. My belly has fattened and sagged. I might be shorter, my bones compressing from the weight I've piled on them. Comfort has reduced me and bolstered her. She's more herself since I met her, rounder too, and more beautiful for it. She doesn't work at the spectacle of herself like she used to. There's no glamour or presentation to her beauty. It comes so easily, she's not even aware of it. I don't know how it can float by so unobserved or unattended. It hits me harder every day.

I don't think she ages. Not like I do. I find new grey hairs on my body every day. I wonder what she'll look like old. I wonder if I'll even see her grow in my lifetime. I picture myself beside her, wrinkled, lingering. I wonder how long I'll last. Time will chip away at me as it does all things. My body will fail, and my mind will follow. How many years before she senses the man she loves fading? How long until I'm not myself, until it's a stranger that burdens her? Why should she love a stranger?

I won't waste a second. I will surrender nothing. I will fight and claw to be the man she loves until my dying breath. I will not fail, I will not falter. I will be good, as good as she believes me to be. I will prove her right.

Elizabeth

Love does funny things to the mind. It gives you a terribly inconsistent view of things. Take today, for instance. If I had to, I'd surmise there'd never been a day so perfectly warm and bright. In all the world, there couldn't possibly be a stream so clean and refreshing as the one right here I've dipped my feet in. Rufus, sketching by the tree, his beard rough and his hair mussed, has never been so handsome. Without reason or evidence, I am unshakably certain that there has never been a peace like this or bliss so true.

That's all ridiculous, of course. I'd have said the same of a hundred other days I've spent with Rufus. A more detached eye could distinguish there's nothing particularly exceptional about this afternoon we're spending together. We're not on some terrific or unusual trek; we come to this same spot maybe once or twice a week. Maybe it's a little hotter than usual, maybe there are fewer clouds. There are a thousand streams like this one. All that is true. Yet somehow, I am convinced: a day so exquisite has never been.

You never find happiness quite where you expect it. In my younger days, I'd fantasized of fine adventures, of glory, treasure, and an untethered soul. I never thought of a partner in my life like Rufus, or a community that needed me like Paralee. My dreams of joy were small and greedy. I was alone, and I could not yet see beyond myself. There is no true happiness without love, no true love that is not shared.

I turn and find Rufus down on his knees, holding out both hands to me. He does it so shyly. At first, I think he's showing me a delicate creature, like a wounded bird or peculiar caterpillar. It takes me a moment to see the ring. I'm struck by how small it looks in his hands. He holds it with as many fingers as he can, perhaps worried it might blow away if the slightest gust of wind should catch it. I want to laugh. It seems so pointless. There's no one else. How could there ever be? In our few years together, we've lived a thousand lives. How could anyone know me as he does? How could I trust anyone as I've trusted him?

"I don't need you to wear it," he tells me, pulling the ring away from my reaching hand. "This isn't about claiming you or changing things or anything like that. I'm asking you to marry me now without obligation or expectation. Tell me to starve if you want to. I will. Cast me aside. I'll love you as much as you like, from as far as you like. I thought you should know."

I snatch the ring from him. He scrambles as I reach to place it on my finger, as though it might burn me somehow. I raise his chin and kiss him sweetly. I will share everything with him. Always.

* * *

I don't know that I ever felt powerful until I met Rufus. I had authority over people, I suppose. If I were crossed, and I dared, I could have ruined lives. Rufus assures me there are but a precious few alive who could match me in a duel. I suspect he thinks that flattery, but it hardly means anything to me. Hurting and destroying things never struck me as power. It's so easy to wreck things it's a wonder anything gets built in the first place.

With Rufus, I can change things. I know it because I've changed him in so many significant and little ways. His hard edges have faded. He is less measured and guarded. He speaks too loudly, too happily sometimes. He laughs, boisterous and full.

At our first summer festival, he stood apart from it all like a golem. In a sea of bouncing, merry faces, he was tight, tense, and suspicious. So, I danced by myself. Badly. I asked him to join me, and he declined, of course. He didn't know how to celebrate quite yet. He watched all night expecting something to go wrong.

By the next year, my influence over him had grown so

total that at sunset he joined me for a slow, charming song. We didn't do much but embrace and sway. When the beat picked up again, he tried to amble off, but there was no escaping me. He was deep in my trap. I'd ensnared him.

He was halting at first, his moves too short and too sharp. The smoothness, arc, and confidence that typified his fighting were astonishingly absent in his dancing. I thought for a while it was deliberate, that maybe he feared someone might look upon his unfettered movements and recognize potential awesome and terrible. But he sincerely didn't know any better. He never indulged anything or anyone before me. I giggled at his awkward, laboured efforts. He was pleased to please me.

Now, we dance until my knees wobble and ankles burn. The speed and force that scorched the world instead keep me cackling until the moon is high and the stars are bright. He bends, he leaps, he spins, he lifts. It'd be absurd if it weren't so unabashed. Maybe it's still absurd. Every now and then, I catch sight of some grumps sniggering and muttering to each other. We don't care. They are jealous. They don't have what we have.

Terra

Festivals are priceless chances for assassinations. Nothing hides a person like people. Crowds simplify entry and cover your exit. It's a slower, more patient game. Passing through revellers is like swimming upstream; it costs you expediency. But at a festival, important figures will brush by a hundred faces that could never otherwise get near them. Among such figures is the wicked Captain Lavalay.

I've watched him all night. He's kind with strangers but insufferable with his underlings. I suspect that's to be expected. Strangers ask nothing of him; they feed him and give him drink. His underlings obstruct his happiness with his best interests at every step. "Sir, if they see..." or "Sir, your digestion..." they whisper, discrete, severe, and ignored.

People who've advanced far in their profession seldom tolerate inconvenience. Why else advance, I suppose. At his post, the captain might better appreciate appearances and know better than to abandon his guards. Yet fat after feasting and dizzy with the joy of a bustling crowd, here he is by his lonesome, humming along to a fast tune as he looks for a tree that might afford him privacy enough to relieve himself.

In that very tree, I sit waiting for him. He stumbles about slowly and clumsily. I have time to overlook the festival. It's beautiful from my perch. There are a dozen little huts where merchants sell wares and food, and in the middle is a large clearing where visitors frolic and dance, packed nearly body to body. Many Nameless begrudge peaceful people their mirth. I could never. I worship at the altar of happiness. Why do we fight if not so that others may bask?

I catch my foot bouncing along to the flighty strings of some instrument I don't know the name of. It's then I notice a man jumping, spinning, and whooping in the middle of the crowd. He's athletic. He jumps high. Very high. It's Rufus. It is! But it isn't...

He seems younger than when he left me. He still sticks out, but in a different way. His hair hangs down just past his neck and almost to his shoulders. His beard hides his features, and his cheeks are full and flush. He's still tall, of course. Still mighty, but in a mellower manner. He moves about like he's trying to keep the little things around him amused. It doesn't occur to anyone what he is. It's a sight. A wolf prancing harmlessly among sheep.

He's jubilant. It's unmistakable. Indisputable. He holds the hands of some little woman in his, and they spin, laughing. I want to laugh too.

Dribbling breaks me from my trance. Beneath me, at the roots of the tree, Captain Lavalay. I don't hesitate. I know an opportunity when I see it. I descend from my branch. He doesn't hear me over the stomping feet of the dancers. I slide a blade in and out, and he dies with hardly a gasp. Good, clean work. I'm sure no one detected me.

I'm wrong. Through the space between a couple of huts, Rufus and Rufus alone catches sight of me. I'm proud of him for that. He recognizes me instantly. His dancing stops. That giddy smile morphs into something hard. Somehow, across all the noise, I expect to hear a low, warning growl. He's on guard. He feels something very dear to him come under threat.

The girl he dances with waves her hand in front of his face and follows his gaze into the dark. She can't see me. She looks like a different species than him, puny, unfit, and untouched by the world. She looks so happy. How could she be so happy? How little could she know? She's not so beautiful so as to be so sheltered. She should know the weight and strain of life. But how could she, smiling like that?

I worry he's kept things from her. I worry she doesn't know the real him, that all that beautiful joy dangles delicately by a lie too frail to hold it. Then I look at Rufus again and conclude it doesn't matter. The Rufus I know is gone. He hides nothing from her. He trusts her with everything. How else could she mean what she does to him? He's put all his world in her hands. He will defend her as ferociously as a dog would its master.

That's what his look tells me. He warns me against jeopardizing her contentment without so much as a thought to his own. I want to promise him he's safe, that his happiness is as precious to me as hers is to him, and I'll protect it just as fiercely. Maybe it isn't true. I don't know if I'm capable. But I hope I am.

His face softens as if he's heard me, and I see all the gratitude he's waited all his life to bestow upon me. After all this time, all the suffering, all the years of trying to prove something to me, he finally finds the validation I denied him. He loves me so deeply then. He thanks me for all his happiness. I want to tell him he owes me nothing. In his joy, I am absolved. The great evil of my life is undone, my great shame lifted. He's understood everything I've meant to tell him except this. It's an unthinkable, unknowable thought to him.

I know I have immortality now, an indestructible legacy. I'll live forever in his heart for this nothing I've done for him, perfect, glimmering, and true. What an achievement. What a glory.

CHAPTER 28: DEFEAT

Rufus

Everything becomes mundane with routine. I'm used to lashes. Their stings and snaps mean nothing to me. Their steady rhythm dulls me like a lullaby repeated for the thousandth time.

It takes their sudden stopping for my senses to convene and my mind to focus. I hear Master Terra panting behind me. Her arm and shoulder must be killing her. Mathius really should set younger muscles to the task. Either of these Allegia holding me up by ropes would do the job better. I suppose he thinks it means something to put the whip in her hand. He always keeps her close.

Mathius stands across from me, apprehensive and vexed. He doesn't have the stomach for this sort of thing. He feels the need to prove otherwise to me every now and then. I suppose that's why he's here now.

It occurs to me Darling must be near. I spot her on the other side of my cell's door, pushing herself off the bars and pulling herself back in waves. Children can find play anywhere.

"Let him down," Mathius tells his Allegia. They undo the ropes raising my hands over my head. I lower my arms slowly. I don't rub at my red wrists even though they burn. I don't roll my stiff neck or stretch my tired limbs. My whole life is pretending Mathius can't affect me.

"Step away from him," he says, and his Allegia obey. They're as far from me as I am from him. That's unusual. Two steps and I'd be on him. He's never risked that. He must have something very important to say.

"You must find this all very tedious," he sighs. "Every day, we whip you. Every day, you take it. Why? Never changes anything. I suppose the habit of it has some symbolic value. As the priest honours us, so too must we demean you. There's something in the ritual of it. The Nameless hate rituals, don't they?"

Only the empty ones.

"What gets you through the day?" he ponders aloud. "What do you look forward to? Go on, tell me. You can trust me."

I say nothing. I hear him snort behind his mask, tickled with himself.

"I know what it is." He waggles a finger at me, daring me to snap it off. "The pit. You love meeting my men there. You fulfill your destiny when you batter them. You have prestige there. Of a sort."

He's right, of course. I wish he weren't. I wish I were some gentle, perfect martyr that beguiled my enemies with infinite patience and compassion. I'm not. I'm proud when I strike down the unworthy men he sets upon me. I savour it. I have too few sources of gratification to punish myself for it.

"I don't blame you," he drones. "We follow our successes. We can't help but love whatever most elevates us. If you were a great farmer, you'd be farming. If you were a great father, you'd be doting over a loving son. But you… you're a great killer. Probably always have been. So here you are. It must crush you, leaving those challengers with breath still in them. To have your purpose withheld for fear of reprisal. For fear of what'd I do to you."

If Mathius knew a thing about torture, he'd subject me to this wrongheaded blathering much more frequently. I could have snuffed out every one of those pretenders. I could have taken their heads for trophies on my wall. It would only have cost me lashes and labour.

"What if you were free to do what you wanted? Would you crush those men like ants beneath your feet? Or would you draw it out? Would you eat away at them until you had your fill? How badly would you hurt them?" He pauses, so I know whatever comes next is the heart of the matter. "How badly would you hurt me?"

He has my attention, I'll give him that. He leans toward me, closer than he's been in all the time I've been his prisoner. He raises his chin, tantalizes me with the outstretching of his neck.

"I'm going to meet you in that pit you've made your home," he tells me. "I will undo your legend. In front of everyone who matters, on whatever terms suit you, I will defeat you. If you want to match strength, I'll be stronger. If you want to test skill, I'll surpass you. Whatever it is you cherish, wherever it is you place your conceit, I will prove myself better. There will be no doubt."

He searches my face. I think he wants to see a vengeful spirit come alight in me. He dreams of raising my hopes to better knock me down. He envisions a truer victory, of breaking something elusive inside me.

"No weapons," I tell him simply. They may be the first words I've said to him in months. "No powers."

He looks down at my hands. He pictures those knuckles in his teeth, those fingers around his throat.

"Of course," he answers, almost lighthearted.

He doesn't know a thing about me.

※ ※ ※

It's quite the turnout. Rich people are crammed body to body with no room to sit. They practically fall over each other, less comfortable than they've been in all their lives. I'm flattered they diminish themselves so. They don't even have space to hurl trash at me.

They buzz restlessly, waiting. I feel their anxiety, oppressive in the air. They fret for their leader. Suddenly, however irrationally, they fear what I might do to him. I almost want to comfort them. I want to take their hands in mine like I might a child and tell them they've nothing to worry about. This is a play, a drama, a fiction. The hero always wins, and I don't stand a chance.

The mood changes. The dread shifts into something hopeful and reverent. I set my eyes into the tunnel and see a silhouette take shape. Mathius strides towards me, a blushing bride marching down the aisle to embrace a beautiful future. His robes are lighter than the norm, less intricate, less restricting. I can already see he moves more easily, that he's left me less to grip. When he reaches the center of the pit, he even lifts his crown off his head, his horns along with it. Smart. I definitely would have grabbed at those.

It's no god staring a hole through me right now. There's no finery or embroidery to be seen anywhere on him, no fresh colour or flair. His mask is sturdy and dull, ready to be defaced. He could be a soldier, or even something less. He's erased his majesty to meet me down in the mud.

Someone projecting authority stands between us, chatters about rules of engagement for the benefit of the audience. Mathius won't take his eyes off me. I set mine anywhere but on him, taking in the room. I spot Darling in the front row, crouching to better see me through the bars of a railing. She looks still, attentive. I'm sure she's conflicted. I've made such a fan of her.

The fight starts before I'm ready. There's no hate behind Mathius' blows. They're clean and beautiful, fussed over and cared for, shared with self-satisfaction. I wonder how many hours he's tinkered with them. That punch alone could have taken a lifetime to shape. He's the ideal exquisitely realized, some holy document to fight, train, and live by.

I don't know if I could beat him. If I could, it'd be bittersweet. There'd be a hint of tragedy in it. The triumph of the weeds over the garden, the rot over the crops, the storm over the city. Maybe my ugliness could spoil him like it spoils all things. I don't want to find out. Even if I could win, these guards wouldn't let me. All I can do is keep him from what he wants. All I can do is deny him.

I dance around his strikes, keep him swimming and reaching. He doesn't leave me openings, and I do nothing to create any. The crowd murmurs and grumbles, irked by my fanciful retreating. They're right to be perturbed. There's no method or strategy in anything I do. I'm teasing them, ridiculing their bloodlust.

Mathius disengages from me and stomps over to his corner, frustrated, confounded. He steadies himself, finds new resolve. The dancing is over. I dig in my heels and make myself a wall for his blows. I lean in, cut short his arcing swings, meet his fists and feet before they're ready. I press close to him, keep him stepping sideways and backwards. I make him feel clumsy, inelegant. I get close enough for him to feel my breath on him. I don't lay a hand on him. But he knows I could. Everyone knows.

Something red trickles down from my hair and wets my eyes. Blood. I'm cut. It never dawned on me he might be hurting me with those lovely strikes. I've been so amused flustering him that I didn't notice the heat and tingling smattering my body. I guess that's pain. Not that it matters any. What's my body worth at this point?

My legs teeter. He won't knock me down. I can't let him. I pin him against the wall, lean my shoulder into his chest. Maybe it's more like I've fallen on top of him. He wriggles beneath me, and I can't help but laugh deliriously when I hear his revolted groan, my sweat and blood pouring all over him. I press my face against his mask. It squeaks when I smear him with my damp mess.

With a delicious roar devoid of composure, I feel Mathius set Divine Will on me. He flings me across the arena, and I ricochet against the wall. My ears ring and my vision blurs, but all I can think of while the darkness creeps in is keeping my feet. I wonder why I bother. I've won, haven't I?

I find Darling in the crowd. She looks concerned, I think. I try to steady my swaying just enough to offer her a reassuring look. It's over, I tell her with a coy smile. I'm not hurt, I'm happy.

I feel one last blunt thump on the front of my face before I sleep. Maybe it's Mathius. Maybe it's the floor.

✻ ✻ ✻

Mathius is cross with me. I'm in and out. I hear sharp words in my fleeting lucid moments, but they sound warbly and warped. He didn't take too kindly to my little game, I gather. You can hurt everything a man says he holds dearest, but it's always his pride that sets him off in the end.

A wave of water comes down on me and jolts me awake. At first, I'm pleased, refreshed by its cleansing coolness; I'm seldom afforded such generous portions. Then, I see the emptied, dripping bucket floating all alone in the air, and Mathius behind it. I'm reminded how much I have to answer to.

"Why?" he asks, his voice calm and measured but doing nothing to hide his fury. "Why must you debase us?"

I say nothing. Our conversations are terribly one sided.

"What do you want? Hmm?" He paces about my cell, arms folded. "I gave you your chance at me. Why waste it? You could have killed me. Or at least made me kill you. Now, you're back where you started. What did that serve? HMM!?"

I look away. I always look away. He's in here without Allegia, which is rare. I suppose he thinks this is too personal for even the mindless to witness. Peeking around the corner, at the furthest edge of my bars, I see Darling. She watches us closely, enthralled. She's likely never seen her father so distracted. Mathius doesn't even know she's there.

He grabs the beard beneath my chin and jerks my face towards him.

"You're not going home," he says clearly and slowly. "Not so long as I draw breath."

He knows I can reach him from here. He must. It's only a chain around my ankle that keeps me against the wall. My nails are talons now. I could open his throat in a second. Maybe he thinks he can stop me. Maybe he could. Or maybe I've enraged him so much he'd gamble his life to get his hands on me.

I laugh in his face. He shoves me away and recoils two steps. I've won the game again.

He raises his arm, and I'm lifted off my feet. He straightens his hand, and an icy grip seizes me by the spine. He parts his fingers, and something tugs at my limbs and digits, stretching me, tearing me.

"Is this what you want?" he demands, resenting my lack of struggle. "My dignity? That's worth your life?"

My muscles and bones strain as they lengthen beyond their nature. He winces a little at the cracking noises. I laugh some more at him for that.

He flicks his wrist and hurls me against the wall so hard the ceiling releases dust in geysers. The chain around my ankle rattles. The bolts locking me to the wall quiver. He doesn't notice. He storms out of my cell, slamming the door behind him in disgust. It bounces in and out before lingering open a crack.

I let myself feel the pain once I'm sure he's gone. I huddle myself against the wall, clutch my knees to my chest. I'm careful to hide the chain behind as much of my body as I can. It's looser. Loose enough, I don't know. My muscles ache, burn, and scream at me as if I'm to blame. I don't know if I can put them to work. But I have to. My cell won't be open long.

Before I have even a moment to find some leverage, I hear the creak of my door. I look to it, ready for disappointment. I find Darling. She's all by her lonesome, slowly pressing open the door with one hand and carefully balancing an overfilled bowl of water in the other. She spills a little, so she transfers the weight of the door to her shoulder to better cup the bowl with both hands.

She approaches me as delicately as she can, blind to me, all her awareness set on the terribly important sloshing inside the bowl. When she reaches me, she seems quite taken with herself. She lifts the bowl up to me with her stubby fingers. Behind her mask, I see her bright eyes crinkle with the glee of a good deed done well.

I move my mouth towards the bowl slowly so as not to

frighten her, but she isn't the least bit worried. What a sweet girl.

Mathius

I should kill him. I should kill Ruthless and be done with it. I can let some soldier do it. They can stick him like a pig. No one need know how thwarted I've been. We can make a story of it. We can act like it's some commendation bestowed upon some worthy and singular soul by a benevolent god.

Maybe we could say it was destiny. We could give a devoted patriot some illustrious, gleaming weapon. Give it some glamorous name. We could tell some tall tale that it and it alone could finally pierce the evil magic that earned Ruthless all his abominable fortitude. It wouldn't seem like murder. It'd be ascendency. That'd be victory enough. At least it would be a victory.

I feel the air coming in and out of my nose, hot like a dragon. I feel positively malignant. No. This is my victory. None have suffered at Ruthless's hands as I have, and I alone should have the honour of routing him. I will best him. I will pull myself from this mire and rise above him in some high and virtuous fashion. I will blaze a path for my people. My Darling.

My Darling. I freeze. I'm in the stairway. Alone. I rush back the way I came, past my Allegia. I should fly, but I don't think to. My feet carry me as fast as they can. I don't even know their limits, but I'll find them. That air going in and out my lungs felt so potent a moment ago. It burns me now. Where is she? Until now, I've always known. Where is she?

I return to Ruthless's cell, my Allegia at my heels. Anger courses through me, an ocean pounding a dam.

I find her there, sitting on his knee. I see the fresh young face I love so much. She plays with him. He holds her mask in two fingers. The fourth mask he's held. He dodges her bumbling swipes at it easily. She giggles, takes the hand on her back for the safety and devotion she's known all her life. She has no idea. How could she? She's so happy. I love her so much for it. Even if it brought her here.

Ruthless looks up at me. Without the smile he's giving her moving at all, it changes completely.

I approach as slowly and calmly as I can muster, try to keep my fear from my daughter.

"Darling," I say, I hope assertive but pleasant. "To me, please."

She starts towards me, but his hand slides around her shoulder just firmly enough to keep her.

"Darling. Well named," Ruthless says without menace. He turns back to her, whimsy in his voice. "You like it?"

She shrugs. I love her perfect face so much. Why do I ever cover it up? I don't look at it enough.

"She's very sweet," he says, handing her back her mask so she may occupy herself. "Most kids don't like me."

"It's been a good life," I say. "Nothing to fear."

"So far," he teases.

I swallow, try to summon some saliva to my mouth. I tap my leg to pry away Darling's concentration.

"It's time to go, my love," I say.

Ruthless adjusts his knee, drawing her closer.

"You know, I think you're right," he sighs, turning her face away from him, positioning himself behind her. "Long day. Very long day. How about we all go home? Darling goes with you."

He lifts his chin to his kin behind me. I don't look at them.

"They go with me," he says, tossing Darling's hair. "Every last one of them. Two happy families complete again. Seems fair, right? All things considered. More than fair."

I won't be intimidated. I can't be. My Allegia draw their swords. Ruthless doesn't budge.

"I prefer we all stay together," I tell him, straightening my back, pushing down my ire with steady breath.

He pulls Darling closer and drapes an arm over her. Finally, she senses the unease in the air. Our first failure. She looks up at Ruthless, but he won't take his eyes off me, waiting for something I won't dare give him.

"You don't want to be where I've been," he warns, looking, deep, deep into me. "You don't want to go where I'm going."

I can't be made a fool of. If the Royal Family is going to be worth anything, I can't give him a single thing. If he wins here, we're all dead, dead of a thousand little deaths sure to come. Only the impetuous can't see past the one to see the many. He thinks because I am kind, because I love, I don't know hard things. I've bore loss. I've shed tears. I will again. I will not shrink.

My Allegia turn their swords on themselves, rest the points right on their chests. Ruthless stays very still, but he's not so practiced as I am. He surrenders nothing, but I see it all. Frailty. Cowardice. He stares a hole through me, turns my Darling away from me. He presses her head into his chest with his giant, dirty hand. It engulfs her face, blinding her with its mildness.

He accuses me with his eyes. He cautions me. He doubts me. He mocks me. I can't abide it. I lower my head to evade his gaze.

"My family..." I can barely mutter, quaking. I am resolute.

One of my men plunges their sword into their chest. Ruthless winces, covering Darling's eyes. He wraps both his arms around her, holds her closer, and I'm sick. He protects her. He protects her from me. My man collapses to the floor, emptied.

"All I've ever loved or ever will," I say vehemently, more vehemently than ever. I feel something awakening in me, and Darling is somewhere far from my heart and mind. "You've taken what can never be returned. And you dare to threaten the dearest of it?"

My second man follows suit, makes a wet pile of himself. I save the old woman, Ruthless's favourite, for last.

Ruthless trembles, gnashing his teeth, eyes wet with rage. He's squeezing Darling so close to him. I hear her worried panting. I see his fist bunching the fabric of her dress, and I'm so purely, rapturously happy. Finally, truly, I've hurt him.

"Nothing comes before the family," I say with certainty

I've never felt. "Long may we reign."

Ruthless searches the old woman's eyes, a pleading child. Her sword plunges into her all the way to the handle. After all this time, and far too late, he accepts she's gone. He shuts his eyes and bows his head, his very being withering. All those hard, jutting places in his body recede.

He lets Darling go. She runs to me. I don't even think of her as she hugs my leg. She takes in the bloody floor curiously. I don't care. There is glory here to savour. I can't waste a scrap of it. The Great Ruthless weeps, defeated. Profoundly defeated. Like no man I've ever seen.

I commit every bit of his misery I can to memory. Finally, his shields are lowered. So much he's kept hidden pours out of him, and he's as pathetic and pained as all the petty tyrants come before him. He retreats into the wall, retreats into himself, retreats from everything. I see him flee. He runs to his place, that one beautiful place he's always kept.

She's there again. Finally, like an infant, his need overwhelms his senses. He lets himself see her. He soothes himself with her shining face...

No.

CHAPTER 29: MENDALA

Small

I love Elizabeth so much. And she loves me. She does. Differently. It delights and dismays me. She does not see me as I see her. She does not need me.

I want to touch her. I want to feel her skin, her hair, her lips. I want to hold her in my arms and be held back. I want to be everything to her as she is everything to me. When she grazes my hand or touches my back, I feel my blood rush through me. She is oblivious. I go to my bed and wait up all night, listening for something of her through the walls. I think of going to her until I fall asleep, and then I dream of her coming to me.

I try not to be greedy. I don't want to be a rich man who hates his palace because he lusts after loftier splendour. I laugh every day. I am comfortable. When a dour mood descends upon me, Elizabeth quickly shakes me from it. When I catch her in her thoughts, looking at nothing in some forlorn manner, I try to return the favour. Sometimes, I succeed. Not always. I shouldn't expect perfection, I tell myself. I should treasure what I have.

We struggled for a long time choosing a name for when I was among people. I didn't feel right picking. Neither did she. I forced her hand. Anything I chose for myself would feel too much like a lie. Whatever Elizabeth decided, that's who I would be.

She settled on Mendala. At first, I thought she was teasing

me. Then, I saw she meant something earnest and pure with it. I was mended, and now I mended others. I still haven't taken to it. I'm slow to answer when I hear it called. Maybe I'll grow into it. In the meantime, Elizabeth is considerate enough to call me sister as much as she can.

We're in town now. My hair has grown long enough for desperate mothers to peddle their sons to me. I decline. Though the women pester and ply her, Elizabeth always defends my verdict. I appreciate that more than I ought to. I like to believe she's afraid to part with me. In my fantasies, she hoards and covets me.

Today, I am bothered less than usual. People are otherwise occupied with something. We follow scurrying feet and whispering villagers to the town square. At the chapel, a man with ostentatious robes in colours so bright they're impossible to miss stands on a platform. Behind him, hanging off the chapel walls, are two banners blazing the Royal Sigil.

"The Blight!" the colourful man bellows to a rapt audience, loud enough so that all may hear. "The wayward and wicked Ruthless defeated and humbled at the feet of our sublime protector, Prince Mathius! A sick man healed! A heretic believes! A rebel serves! The miracle of miracles in our time!"

"Ruthless lived?" someone asks, bewildered.

"Ruthless lives!" says the colourful man, hurling his arms out wide.

"He is captured?!" an old woman demands, anxiously clutching her shawl.

"He came to finish his evil work!" continues the colourful man, his face red and feverish with ecstasy. "He challenged our resplendent Prince at Hospice and hurled his evil spear! But our gods are invincible! Mathius the Mighty! He seized Penance, faced the Blight, and struck him down!"

The assembled gasp and harumph. I finally look to Elizabeth. Her face is a mask, cool and skeptical. She only waits.

"But!" the colourful man yelps, raising a pointed finger. "Power is not only a weapon but a tool! The gods recognize our courage and our suffering. Even in the wretched! Mathius the Merciful! Ruthless witnessed the awesome vigour and magnanimity of our Prince and begged forgiveness! And he was reborn!"

The assembled murmur and tut to each other, incredulous.

"He is converted!" screeches the colourful man, pumping triumphant fists. "Loyal and true as you or I! Such is the Prince's valour! Such is the Prince's righteousness! Ruthless serves in our courts! He fights for our armies! He worships our gods!"

"Where?" Elizabeth interjects.

"He is embraced!" The colourful man wraps himself in his arms. "He is drawn near! He knows hallowed ground and the innermost circle. The Summer Palace! The place only gods and the chosen know!"

The colourful man blathers on, but Elizabeth has already turned her back, returning the way we came.

"Ruthless the Believer! Ruthless the Redeemed!" I hear him say, his voice fading into the distance. "Love your gods, brother and sisters! Love your gods and know all things are possible! If he may be saved, you may be saved!"

We don't say a word to each other all the way home. Elizabeth does not hurry. She looks straight ahead as though she does not even see me. I try to keep as calm as she is. My heart's in my throat.

I'm in a panic by the time we reach our yard. I want her to look at me. I want her to wipe her brow, to caress Bandit, to do anything that strays her for even a second from her path. She doesn't. She goes to her room and begins gathering her things.

"Don't," I finally squeak, tears in my eyes.

She pauses, looking at the contents of a drawer she emptied over her bed. This is so important. I am frenzied, overwhelmed by the task before me.

"Don't go," I plead. "Stay. It isn't true. How could it be? How could he be taken alive? That's why they said he's at the Summer Palace. Because no one could prove otherwise!"

"I could," she says. She recommences stuffing her things into a sack.

"Then they have him," I blurt out urgently, stumbling over my words. "Then he gave you up. They knew you would come because only you know the palace. It's a trap. Those are the only two possibilities! He betrayed you, or he's *dead*!"

The bite I put on the final word startles me, but it doesn't deter Elizabeth in the slightest.

"If he betrayed me, they'd be beating down my door as we speak," she counters, not even raising her head from her things.

"No! No, don't you see?" I say, my mouth ahead of my mind. "You could run! You could get away! This is how they fight! They'll have you this way! On their terms! On their field! They caught us all like this!"

"What if this is him calling to me?" she asks, her breath picking up, my furor finally stirring something in her. I've reached her. Moved her. "What if Rufus gave in so that I might hear? What if he needs me? What if I didn't answer? He'd do anything for me."

I grab her arm, try to pull her from her things.

"If he would do anything for you, he'd have stayed!" I yell, tugging on her. "He didn't! I could have gone! All those Nameless are my brothers and sisters too! I'm stronger than I've ever been! I stayed! I put you ahead of them all!"

She jerks her arm free. She finally turns to me, sticks a bitter finger in my face.

"You did this!" she screams. "You sent him away! You blamed him! You made him do your work, and now you're trying to take his life! You can't have it! I won't let you! I love him! Not you!"

I see her lurch a little bit at the malice of her words. Regret flashes in her eyes. She knows how I feel. She always has. She finds herself. She hardens.

"If he loved you, he wouldn't call. He wouldn't pull you down with him," I utter, burrowing myself into somewhere coarse and callous. "He's a coward. Or a betrayer. Or dead."

She lilts. Maybe at confronting the truth. Maybe at the thought of hurting me more.

"Go away," she hisses quietly, certainly, hoisting up venom from deep inside her. "I don't want you. You were useful. A pair of hands. That's all."

I steel myself against her.

"You were in a pit," I tell her. "Everything you did dug it deeper. I pulled you out."

She does not blink. She does not wince. She sets her jaw, grabs my collar, and forces me backwards all the way out of her room. She slams the door shut in my face.

* * *

I listen to Elizabeth from my bed, my back turned to my door and all the world. I hear her stomp frantically about, muttering, assembling herself for her long journey. I lay very still, trying to blacken my heart to her. I can not.

Finally, a lull. A pause long enough for me to believe she might be finished, long enough for me to believe she hesitates. I lay and wait, hoping she stays where she is forever. Before long, I hear steps, slow and steady. A chasm in my stomach grows wide enough to swallow me whole.

I hear my door creak open. I do not look. I hear feet approach me. I smell her. I know her scent so well.

She lowers herself into my bed. She presses herself against my back. Her arms clutch me to her. I feel her head lean against mine. She does it without desire. There is no apology, no pledge. She needs nothing from me. It is mercy. It is forgiveness. It is love.

I weep. I am loved.

* * *

She is gone.

CHAPTER 30: THE FAR-REACHING HEART

Elizabeth

It was wrong of me to let you go, Rufus. Wronger still to hate you for leaving. I don't hate you anymore, or what led you away from me. It brought me Small.

She'll forgive me in time. I hope. I lashed out at her. It wasn't fair. I saw an obstacle in her, a wall between you and me, so I climbed over her. I forgot the friend I had in her, the love she had for me. I hope I see her again and have another chance to draw her near after all this is finished.

I shouldn't have waited for you. I should have chased you down from the moment I knew you were gone. Why didn't I? Why didn't I keep you from this fate I dreaded? Maybe I could have turned you back. Maybe, with time, you could have forgiven yourself for leaving your brothers and sisters.

No, of course you couldn't. That'd have weighed on you all your life. Should I have joined you? Taken up arms with you? Were your goals so twisted, so evil? Even now, I don't doubt your good intent. Did I believe in you so much? Did I really think you could do something so impossible as defeat Mathius and break open Hospice, and all I'd have to do was forgive you? How could I dare expect that of you?

I didn't want to face my brother. I still don't. I suppose it's why you didn't ask me to. You tried to protect me. You loved me too much to ever set me against Mathius. I had to come to that myself. I've drawn the line in the sand, Rufus. I rejected the kingdom, and now I reject my brother if it means winning you back.

I wanted not to need you. I wanted to stand on my own and prove my strength. People define strength too much by independence. We're afraid to need each other, to owe each other, to trust each other, because nothing can hurt us like we hurt one another. Yet the whole lesson of civilization is that we are stronger together. We carry one another, stand on each other's shoulders in a million invisible ways. That's the trick of life. You have to lower your guard to be known, you have to risk pain to experience joy. There is no love without vulnerability. Sometimes, there's nothing braver than being open.

I've forgiven myself now for wanting you, Rufus. I am better for you, and you are better for me. I will save you. And you will save me. And I will save you. On and on. We will dance in that circle so long as we both shall live. An unbreakable loop.

✳ ✳ ✳

It's a grey day when I finally reach the Summer Palace. The water is choppy and dark where it hits the shore. The walls of the castle are tall, cool, and uninviting. I can only just barely see the top of the keep jutting over them, the angular pagoda attacking the sky.

I never loved this place. I look back on it without affection. Even so, it's so different I don't recognize it. I remember colour. Yellow sand. Green trees and bright banners. I can still feel the breeze that came off the sea to rescue me from hot days. It makes me cold now. This whole place makes me cold.

It's quiet. So quiet. All I can hear is the tide crashing hard against jagged rocks. Shouldn't there be voices? The pacing of busy feet, the humming and rattling of important work? A palace is a little city, after all. Its servants are taught to be silent, I suppose, to not disturb their masters. But this is a tomb.

I survey the outer walls, looking for some point of entry. They are smooth, almost polished, with nowhere to dig in my hands or feet. I'm no Nameless. I don't know how to go where I'm not wanted. Small would have thought of something. Some pick or axe that'd dig an ugly hole in these pristine walls to serve her purpose.

I'm looking for some drainway or sewer grate when suddenly I hear heavy grinding. I scurry to a bush for some meagre cover, and I see the immense front gate opening. Inch by inch, its two doors twist and part wide. I wait, but nothing emerges. I look down the road and see no one coming.

I understand. These doors are for me. I am expected, after all.

Who spotted me? It doesn't matter. They likely still see me now. I raise my chin and rise out from my hiding spot with all the confidence I can muster. When I round one of the grand doors, I'm greeted by a solemn welcoming party in the courtyard. They carry flags rigidly and wear their blood-red uniforms crisply and cleanly. They do not move. I wonder if they even see me from behind their masks. They are like a painting, the very picture of discipline.

I look over my shoulder when I hear the doors closing behind me. I see packs of bald heads in ragged clothing huddle around large gears, forcing them round by hand and pulling the gate shut. They are Nameless, but there is no humiliation or subjugation in their eyes. They do their labour with disaffected, oblivious faces. Something awful has happened.

The welcoming party all pirouette the moment the doors lock back in place. They march in perfect, frightening synchronicity deeper into the palace, waving their flags in rhythm too precise to be at all musical. I follow. I know where they are taking me.

The parade brings me to the training grounds before splitting into two symmetrical lines and bordering the walls. I see the little awning beneath which Father sat and evaluated me so many times. I notice a flag on a big sturdy post atop the pagoda. No, not a post. A spear. Penance. Our family crest flaps on a banner hanging off the famed stone insignia.

I walk towards the center square of the grounds, feeling at once like a hundred eyes are on me. The red men remove their helmets, and suddenly the walls are lined with bald heads in proud, loyal garb. They look at me but do not see. I droop my head to better gaze beneath the awning's tarp, and there he is, sitting in Father's chair. Mathius.

He wears what must be his best robes. They are heavy, so heavy they're almost armour, but intricately sewn and patterned with rich, deep colours. His mask is golden and ominous, his horns as sharp as any sword. He looks so sinister. He must expect a war.

Darling sits beside him, distracting herself with a carved, wooden dragon. I've never seen my niece. She is deeply, blissfully engaged with whatever thrilling adventure goes on in her head. She mutters pressing, sensational dialogue to herself, pitching her voice up and down for her invisible cast of characters. I bite my tongue to keep myself from saying hello.

Mathius leans forward in his chair, entwining his fingers so he doesn't fidget. He regards me, gives me every chance to say something to him. I have nothing for him. No excuses. No regrets.

"We're alone," he says, tilting his head a little at his servants. "Or may as well be."

I look around at the men and women that were once Nameless. They stand like statues, their flags in front of them, their grips unwavering.

"Do you like them?" he asks, knowing I couldn't possibly. "I've been working at it since you left. I had to. Couldn't trust people anymore. I started with loyals. People who were eager to better serve the kingdom. Then, I moved to prisoners. People who only defied us for lack or want. Then, the Nameless. Now, they all serve without a thought to themselves. That's where all evil really stems from, I think. Selfishness."

He says the last word pointedly.

"Sometimes, even the best of us put their needs ahead of the greater good," he continues. "We stop fighting. We run. Not these people. Not any more. I trust them as much as I trust my own hands. I won't settle for less. Not after Reznick. Not after you."

He lets the silence hang heavy, foreboding. Tentatively, he reaches his thumbs beneath his mask and peels it back. In so many ways, he's as I recall him. He's still handsome, delicate. Yet he does not shine with hope and kindness. He is jaded, wisened, weary with pain and heartache.

"I've missed you," he says, fragile as glass. "I've always missed you. Even when you were in my life. When Father sent you away and I came to you up in your tower…"

He pauses, quivering.

"It wasn't for you," he says with a little shake of his head. "No one wanted me to do it. Father, the advisors, they'd have all been happier if I pretended you didn't exist. But I couldn't part with you."

He looks away from me, grappling with a memory so real and vivid it may as well be happening now.

"And then you were gone," he begins anew. "Lost. And I was alone. I had to be so strong. For Reznick, for Father, for the kingdom. So many depended on me. Yet every night when I laid my head down to sleep, I wished I might dream of you. That you might visit me as I visited you."

He looks upon me with pleading eyes. He smiles faintly, faltering.

"Now…" he hushes, a hint of exaltation in his voice. "You're here. And all my dreams are true. Except…" He sours before my eyes. A dark bitterness surfaces. "I wonder… with all your gifts, with all the grace of your far-reaching heart… how could I have meant so little?"

His face turns to steel, a mask as stern and dire as was ever fashioned. He looks at me with accusation, with vengeance. There's danger in the air. He looms, a judge awaiting a desperate defence.

"Mathius..." I begin, compassion in my voice. It offends him.

"I know the way," he interrupts, scowling. "Love for all. Kindness and charity. But there is order in the world. There must be. It's why we're here!"

His voice rises. I've never heard him angry. I feel like all the world is trembling, cowering.

"It's what we're for!" he barks, spittle flying. "To make sense of it all! To make life mean something! We are gods! We come first! We show the path, share the light! And when the kingdom needed you most, when I needed you most, you abandoned us! I know your life wasn't what you wanted. It could have been. It would have been. You should have believed in me. Trusted me. I would have protected you. Made a place for you. But you threw it away! For what?! The Blight! A low THING, a wretched thing! A sullyer! A defiler!"

"You don't know him!" I proclaim, rising to meet his fury and startling us both.

He's quiet for a moment. He frowns, nodding his head, coming to some understanding.

"I know him very well," he says, narrowing his eyes. "As I know you. You always loved the weak, the little, the ugly. The birds with wounded wings, the rodents with broken feet. Was that what he was for you? Another pet? Was he sweet to you? Did he reward your affection? It must have been gratifying, seeing him grow. Seeing him change."

He says the last word with such ice it sends a chill up my spine.

"I have him," he says curtly. "Your pet. Would you like to see him?"

Mathius snaps his fingers. A pair of servants pull open an ornate door then clear the way for a grim procession. Four strapping bodies strut out, chains in their hands. They surround on all sides some gloomy, dirty, terrible creature. It does not fight them. It shuffles at a pace that matches their proud trots. It is docile, biteless.

They undo the chains and step aside to present me with a better view. The creature is hunched but still titanic, all but naked save for rags around its waist and legs. It's a man, or it was a man. Now, it's more like a tangle of mud, hair, and muscle.

I stoop my head, praying I might look and find something to dispute what I know. He doesn't raise his eyes to meet me. Through his long beard and ratty knots, I see him. For a single vanishing second, I am elated. It's my Rufus. But it isn't. He isn't mine.

He's harder and more formidable than I've ever known him, more fearsome and primal than even the creature that in my nightmares killed Darnett. His cheeks are sunken. His lips are cracked and dry. His eyes. His beautiful eyes. They are grey. They see nothing. Not even me. He's here. Right here in front of me. But he's gone. Further than he's ever been.

He sways just a little, his long arms dangling almost to the ground. I swear I hear his yellow nails scratch the stone beneath our feet.

"You won't reach him," I hear Mathius say.

I wonder if he's been talking this whole time, and I'm only just now hearing him.

"He's mine," he says. "He's an animal, you see. It's all he's ever been. He serves his master, is only so good as his master. Whatever you saw in him, it was only there because you put it there. He can not be changed. Only mitigated. What do you see now, hmm? What is his true nature?

"Blight!" Mathius exclaims, jolting me alert.

Rufus lifts his heavy head and stares at me with indifferent eyes.

"Hurt her," Mathius says bluntly.

For a tantalizing second, Rufus does not move. Then he pounces, his hands pulling and pushing him across the floor in concert with his feet like some gruesome ancestor between man and monster. He's on me so suddenly. He swipes at me, just missing. I feel the wind of his colossal paw slice past my ducking head. It could have split me in two.

He's fast. Faster than I am. He's too big and long to get away from. He could reach out and snatch me if I tried to run. I step sideways around him, keep him turning in tight little circles with me. It's hard for him to get proper angles this way, but it only stalls him.

In a blink, he twists the opposite direction I'm taking him. It affords him the momentum he needs to cut me off, and it sends me stepping backwards. That could be all. That could be my life. He closes on me.

An arrow cuts through the air and sinks into his reaching hand. Rufus retracts his fist, little more than inconvenienced. I see Mathius search the walls for its source, annoyed.

Before either has a chance to find her, Small leaps out from nowhere at Rufus, knife drawn. The sneak. She got the drop on all of us. She's come so far. I'm proud of her until I realize what she's about to do. The knife. Rufus has no idea. He's busy prying the arrow out of his hand.

I pull him away. It takes me flinging myself to the ground to do it. The arrow tumbles out from his grip and he totters enough for Small to miss. That was her best shot. Mathius sees her now, and that means Rufus does too.

She tries to fight him. The fool. She cuts and kicks at him. He dodges the knife and blasts his way through the kick, slamming her into the floor. Her knife clatters across the stone, rushing out of her hand as quickly as the breath from her lungs.

I dive at Rufus before he can do any damage. I cling to his neck and push him sideways. I'm lucky I eat. I'm lucky Rufus fed me. If I were as light as when I first met him, I might have bounced off him. Small has a chance to escape.

She rolls to her feet and draws her bow with expert speed. That's not what I wanted. Get away, Small. Run.

Rufus thrashes as I wrap my arms around his neck and squeeze my thighs above his hips. I choke with all my might, but I'm not sure he really notices. I feel childish as he whips me about. Small hesitates, unsure of her shot. She doesn't want to hit me. Good. That'll keep her from hitting Rufus.

Rufus hurls me over his shoulder like a missile at Small, taking us both out. Oh no. When I open my eyes, Rufus is already on Small, pinning her. He postures up. He rips the quiver and its arrows off her back and hurls it all into the distance. She fights and wriggles helplessly in his grip. He pulls back his fist. I hurl my whole body around his arm, but he throws me aside halfway across the grounds.

Small moves her head just in time to miss a fist that shatters stone tile. Rufus grabs her by the throat, steadies her. He will not miss again. I can't get to her. He demolishes her with a slicing elbow. It cuts her open. She's bleeding. Badly.

I sprint at them as fast I can. I can hear Small gasping. Good. She's alive. She's tough. She might survive the one more blow he'll get in before I reach him. If I'm lucky. She has no chance if there's a third. No one would.

I pick up a shard of rock as big as my fist from the tile Rufus shattered. I smash him across the head with it. I don't even think about it.

Rufus rolls off of Small. Blood trickles down his crown and over his eyes, but he's not even dazed. Just irritated. He bares his teeth at me, straightens his back, shows me all his immensity. I place myself between him and Small, but he has no interest in her anymore. She is vanquished.

He waits for me. Challenges me. I think about how I'd feel if he struck me. Would I even get a chance to feel it? Or would he take my life too quickly? No, Mathius wouldn't want that. Hurt her, he said. I'll feel every bit of it. Unless I win.

With a roar, I rush Rufus. He punches and kicks at me, but I'm quick. I slip by his strikes. I clock him across the head with my rock, hoping it doesn't explode into a million pieces. It holds, but so does Rufus. He reaches for me, but I pummel him again. And again. And again. And again.

Finally, he slows. Finally, I bring him to his knees. I grab my rock in both hands and raise it high over my head. But I can't bring it down. He looks at me from behind blood and hair, and

I see my husband. I see the pain I recognize so well, the pain we fought against.

I hesitate. He grabs me, rips the rock from my hand. He's on top of me so fast. He's so heavy. No way I can get out from under him. I feel both his hands close around my throat. I feel his nails digging into my neck, piercing. My eyes start to blur.

I don't want to look at Rufus. I don't want to see him like this. So I turn away. I see Small, barely conscious, barely alive at all, yet still drawing her bow from flat on her back. She lets loose an arrow. It's already wet with the blood from Rufus's hand. It must have been closer than her quiver.

It stops in the air halfway to us. Mathius floats down from his throne. With a flick of his wrist, he sends Small careening across the training grounds. Her head cracks across a wall. She tried. She really did.

"Maybe the kindness I treated you with doomed me," Mathius posits, striding across the grounds towards me. "Maybe somewhere deep in you, in that secret, dark place people keep hidden from themselves, some part of you pulled you towards that brutality in Ruthless. Maybe you loved him because you feared him. Because you knew that if ever you were wrong, if ever goodness failed you, if ever the world proved its corruption to you beyond every doubt, you had a weapon to set upon your enemies. You would finally have power."

Mathius bends down into my view. I can barely hear him.

"You didn't need him," he utters meekly. "You had me. I loved you." He bristles at the inadequacy of the phrase. "I love you. Don't fight me. We belong together. Be mine again. Ask me to stop."

I'd die before I ask Mathius for anything ever again. I might. The world is going dark. I look up at the mindless beast Mathius has sicked on me. I pretend it's my husband. I make-believe Rufus is somewhere in there. He's so angry. In such pain.

I want to tell him it's all right. I want to assure him I know it's not his fault. I shut my hands over his wrists, fondly. It's okay. I love you anyway.

A glimmer of something flickers across his face. Light. My ring caught the light. He winces a little.

I see my brother over Rufus's shoulder. Mathius is afraid, reluctant. He's never been near something so horrid. Do it, I tell him. Finish your work. I dare you.

A flash. Suddenly, my gasps find the air that eluded them. My hands rush to my throat, and I clutch my neck. It's damp with little droplets of my blood. I hear a sharp, childish scream. Darling.

As my eyes focus, I see Mathius staggering backwards, confused. My neck is nothing to his. His is gushing, opened wide by huge, gnarly gashes. He trips over his own feet, falling to the floor. Rufus closes on him, his yellow nails dripping red. Mathius looks up at him, aghast, gulping for breath, his mouth full of blood.

Rufus climbs down on top of my brother. He pounds at him with remorseless, hammering fists. They're harder and more barbarous with each swing, even after Mathius' skull caves in. Rufus doesn't stop until exhaustion overwhelms him. A howl rips out from somewhere deep in his gut, filling the palace with fury, agony, and everything but relief.

All around us, Nameless fall in heaps where they stand, marionettes cut from their strings. Their vacant faces look vaguely surprised yet all the more lifeless.

Mathius is a smear now, a heinous stain defiling these distinguished grounds. Rufus stays there in the slop a while, heaving. I watch his back rise and fall. He trembles as he catches his breath. There are lash marks, burns, scars like canyons all about him.

Finally, he hears something that stirs him from his trance: Darling, snivelling. He scans his surroundings quickly, not recognizing them. He spots her hiding behind the throne. He leans tenderly towards her. He reaches out a reassuring hand that's doused in her father. She screeches and shrinks into herself, rightly petrified. Rufus flinches and timidly draws back his hand.

"Rufus?" I barely manage to squeak out between coughs. My voice is hoarse, my throat still nearly crushed closed.

He freezes. He knows my voice even now, even different. He hasn't seen me yet. He's not ready. He looks down at what's left of Mathius beneath him, at the hundred dead Nameless that lay in piles all around him. I don't know if he remembers, but he understands.

"Rufus?" I call, failing to put sweetness in my voice. I'm so faint, so frail. Barely louder than a murmur.

I know he hears it. I see his whole body sag. He listens to me calling and Darling sobbing.

"My love?" I say, dragging myself nearer to him.

He climbs to his feet. I try to rise to mine, but I stagger back down to the floor, sluggish, dizzy. He's drifting away from me. He can not face me. He's so ashamed. Please. My love. Look at me.

I call and call, try to be loud and unrelenting. He's so fast. Or I'm so slow. I can't get to my feet. I try, but I can't. Try. Once more. I almost make it, but I trip over some Nameless husk. My eyes go black. When the world comes back to me, Rufus is gone again.

I lay there on the floor a minute, wheezing. I want to scream, but I'm too tired. I just ball my fists. Contemplate the sky.

Before I have time to feel angry, or vengeful, or even mournful, I hear Darling crying again. She hasn't stopped. I wonder how it ever left my mind.

I'm strong again. Recovered. At least a little. I make it to my feet, shamble towards the throne. I find her cowering, thighs pulled to her chest, head buried in her knees. She looks up at me.

"Hello," I say as soothingly as I can. The softness of my voice serves me. "It's okay. It's over."

She raises her head a little, scrutinizing me. I approach. She doesn't move. Good.

"You don't know me," I continue. "But we're family. Can you see? I look like your father a bit, right? Maybe even like you?"

She takes me in, squinting her eyes. She nods her head. I smile wide at her. I reach out for her mask, slowly, carefully. She lets me lift it off her head.

Her cheeks are flush. Strands of hair stick to a face slick with tears. She's so young. So lovely. I've just met her, but she seems so familiar.

"Good," I say.

For a moment, I feel a warmth in my heart so bright it wets my eyes. Then the grief comes. Darling and I share a loss, and it falls to me to steer her through it.

"Something bad happened," I begin haltingly, as simply as I can. "Really bad. I'm sorry. But things are going to be better now. I promise. All right?"

She considers me suspiciously. She nods her head again and reaches out her arms for me. I lift her to me. I hold her close.

"I've got you," I tell her. "I've got you."

Small

I've been following Rufus for hours. I can't guess where he's going. I'm not sure he knows. Away. He's going away. That's what's important. He hasn't reached the ends of the earth yet, so on he shuffles.

We're deep in the woods now. He doesn't see me. No one sees me. Not anymore. Mathius didn't. The Nameless didn't. Elizabeth didn't. Even after I rescued her, I was invisible again in an instant. Once Mathius cast me aside, I was the furthest thing from her mind. She didn't see me go. Didn't even think to look. I wonder how long until she noticed I was gone. If she noticed.

I saved her. For a year, I saved her. Or tried to. She didn't see me. Didn't even think of me. After all the time we shared, she put Rufus first. When he left, it was the child. There's no room for me. There never was.

All that strife, all these miles, and he left her. She would have taken him back. She would have forgiven him. If he could have faced her. If he could have asked. He cast it aside. What I've been chasing, what I've been fighting for just a scrap of, what's been just out of reach no matter how far I strain. He left it in the dust.

What's he looking for? There's nothing out here. No town or soul for hours. Maybe he doesn't have enough mind left to know what he wants. Maybe he's as simple as some unthinking creature passing time until the next opportunity to eat. If I asked him, could he answer? Can he speak? Could he tell me what happened to him, to the Nameless? Could he explain how he failed them so spectacularly?

I doubt it. All I see before me is a wounded, diseased animal, wiling away its waning moments. Painlessness. That's what he wants. Some cliff to jump from. Some sea to drown in. You don't need either, Rufus. You have me.

I shoot an arrow in his back, catch him just beneath the shoulder. He stays on his path, undeterred. He doesn't even look back for an attacker. I shoot again, lower, deeper into the meat of him. He stumbles a step but still trudges on. Another. Another.

Finally, he slows to a stop. He lurches, falls to his knees, braces himself with a hand. I circle around to show myself to him. He looks up at me, unafraid. I draw another arrow.

"Is Elizabeth all right?" he asks, startling me. His tongue is heavy, inarticulate from lack of practice. "Is she happy?"

I set my jaw, beat back a grimace. I place the arrow into my bow and pull back the string. He does not balk.

"Are you?" he asks, hoping earnestly.

"If I told you she was," I begin, holding the string tight. "If I told you we were… would it be enough? Could you stay away?"

The question takes the air out from him. His head sways a little at the thought, but he gathers himself. I see him scour for words, his mind reeling to explain something.

"I don't want to hurt anymore," he says. "It's all I do. All I see when I close my eyes."

He shuts his eyes and inhales so deeply it cranes his neck skywards. I pity him. I truly do. I feel benevolent, secure in the rightness of what I do. I see your suffering, Rufus. I am here for you. I am your sweet salvation.

"Hurt faces," he continues weakly. "Everywhere I look. Couldn't add her to them. I can't look at any more hurt faces…"

Understanding overtakes me. I've been so wrong. The hate, the disdain washes away from me. I see the toll his life has taken on him. I see all the violence he's inflicted returned and doubled back inside him, and I am horrified.

He's been a stranger to me before now. He mourns so much. Loves so much. Everyone. His enemies and victims maybe most of all. And I love him for it. How can I hurt what I love when I see here before me where it leads? How can I do harm for good? How can good come from anything but love?

The tension of my drawn string reasserts itself at the front of my mind. I feel the burn of it in my arms. It begs for release.

EPILOGUE

Elizabeth

I always wanted to be a mother. Funny how you want most whatever is denied you. From as soon as I was old enough to understand, I was told it was impossible, abominable. My father, his father, and all the fathers for generations forbade it. Naturally, it was a cornerstone of the freedom for which I longed.

When I loved Rufus, I thought a child was a matter of time. It never happened. He blamed himself as he did for all things, all the way up to harsh winds and hard rains. He yearned to give me what I wanted, but I'm not sure he trusted himself to be a parent. That was ridiculous, of course. Raising a child is love first, patience second, and everything else pales so much in comparison they hardly merit mentioning. He'd have been as fine a father as he was a husband. I know it.

It's amazing how happy you can be without getting what you want. I was resigned to never having a son or daughter to call my own. I had closed my heart to the possibility. I was content to drop in and out of the families of friends. With Rufus by my side, I had plenty. I was satisfied.

Now, he's gone. When he left, there was nothing I wanted more than to see him back. I fought it, denied it, but there was no escaping it. It's still true. I try not to think of him. He comes to me often. I'm surrounded by memories of him. Whenever I labour with some unpleasant task, I reminisce over all the times he spared me the misery. When I lie awake in the night, I long for the rise and fall of his chest beneath my head. I try to cast him from my mind, but even when I sleep, he finds me in my dreams.

Yet I am happy. I appreciate what I have. I find new roads to joy with Evelyn every day. That's what I call Darling these days. She's a funny, curious child. Whether it's climbing trees or digging in the yard, she likes anything that makes her dirty. She's giddy now, helping me garden. I toss the potatoes I pull in high arcs, and she giggles ecstatically as she tracks them through the air and snares them in a sack. She has a good eye. I discover new talents in her everywhere I look. I can't help but wonder about her future. I look forward to the great woman she'll become. She is so full of possibilities.

A dread overcomes me. She might not always be so bright, so merry. She knows pain already, and she will know it again. I can't keep her from it. I don't know if she thinks of Mathius. She doesn't ask about him anymore. She's so young. I wonder if she even understands what happened to him. I search my mind for memories of my world when I was her age and come up empty. Maybe she won't remember. Maybe I can fill that hole Mathius left in her. Maybe I can flood her childhood with such happy times that he will fade from her thoughts like a passing stranger. Maybe I can spare her that aching gnaw that tormented Rufus.

I ponder what I'll tell her when her powers emerge. Will she be as mighty as Mathius was? What if she grows so strong she sees nothing of herself in me? She will ask about her father, even if she can't recall him. Maybe especially if she can't recall him. So it always is. We want what we lack, and she will lack a father. How much of the truth will she need? How deeply will the betrayal run?

What's Bandit barking at? I thought he was too old to be so angry. He never gets this worked up anymore.

Someone's at the gate.

THE END

Manufactured by Amazon.ca
Bolton, ON